ONE HUNDRED ACRES

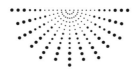

CIN MEDLEY

MED'S PUB
PUBLISHING

ONE
Hundred
ACRES

CIN MEDLEY

The characters in this book are not real people. They have been made up. They are by no means related to or pertain to real people.

This material is copyrighted. Any use of any portion of this book is prohibited without written permission from the publisher.

Published by: Med's Pub Publishing
Copyright © 2016 C. J. Medley
All Rights Reserved
ISBN-13: 978-0-9974021-6-2
ISBN-10: 0997402164
Editing and Proffed by: Kendra's editing and book services-Kendra Gaither
Cover Designed by: Amanda Walker PA and Design
Formatting by: Med's Pub Publishing

I just want to take a minute to thank everyone involved in my life for encouraging me to write and for loving the words on the pages.

My husband and daughter, thank you so much for putting up with my singing while I have the headphones on as the stories flow. I love you both to the moon and back.

And I want to say thank you to Veronica for supporting me and for reading my pages. You made me write the naughty. I adore you.

CHAPTER ONE

DUKE REYNOLDS

"Listen, man, I feel like shit. I'm going to head back to the house." Duke looked toward his brother.

Laughing, Derek said, "You should probably quit drinking. I don't know why you're so upset about Julie and Teddy. She was cheating on you for over a year. Bitch ain't worth it, man."

Duke chuckled. "Yeah, I know, but the heart wants what the heart wants. The chick was fantastic in bed, and I really think I might love her."

Shaking his head, Derek turned to him with sincerity. "No, man, you didn't love her. You just loved the great sex. That chick has nothing going on. You just liked the piece of ass. Man, get over her already. She's been out of your life for six months, and she ain't coming back."

"I'm working on it. Just isn't as easy as you would think. I'll be up at Dad's. There are some things I need to talk to him about before I head out."

"You going to Boot's tonight?"

Duke laughed. "No, I think I'm going to take your advice and keep to myself for a while. I'm not going to get over her if I keep showing up where she is. Besides, I have to head up to Bozeman for a few days to pick up that motor. I'll see you when I get back. Try not to burn the place down while I'm gone."

Derek nodded at his brother as he rode off. Duke hit it hard through the field. Riding up to the barn, he noticed a horse standing outside of the house. He took his horse into the stable and brushed her down. As he walked to the big house, he saw the horse was gone. Taking the steps two at a time, he opened the door to the kitchen and called out, "Hey, Dad, you in here?"

"Yeah, I'm back here."

Duke walked through the kitchen into the dining room. His father was a big man, with broad shoulders. He was sitting at the table with papers spread out all over the place. He looked tired. "Whatcha doing here?" Duke asked as he pulled out a chair to sit at the table.

"Just going through some things. Why are you here and not out helping your brother with the fence?"

"Joe and Alex are out there with him. I'm not feeling too good, so I thought I would head home and crash before I head up to Bozeman."

His father chuckled. "You really should quit drinking so much."

"Yeah, I'm working on it." He picked up a paper that looked like a bill of sale. Across the top it said *Land Agreement between Richard Reynolds and Loren Mitchell.* "What's this?"

His father looked up and took the paper out of his hand. "It's really none of your business."

"Dad, this ranch is my business. What's going on? Are you selling it? Because if you are, then I want to buy it."

His father chuckled. "I am not selling the ranch. When I'm gone, it's yours."

Duke sat there looking at his father. Never in his life would he have ever thought his father would part with any of his land. Hell, it'd been in their family for over a hundred years. It was one of the biggest privately-owned ranches in the state. Covering sixty-five thousand acres, it even had its own river.

"Dad," Duke began, but his father interrupted him.

"Listen, son, it's a hundred acres. It's not a problem."

"Do you need money? I have a great deal saved."

He laughed. "No, son, I don't need any money."

"Are you going to tell me why you sold it then?"

"Well, first of all, it really is none of your business, and second, I never said I sold it."

Duke sat there looking at him. "Don't tell me you gave away a hundred acres?"

His father set down his pen and looked his son in the eyes. "Duke, you are my oldest son, and when your mother passed, God rest her soul, you were here for me. But she has been gone for ten years now. I don't want to sound ungrateful or rude, because I love you, but it really isn't any of your damn business what I do with my land. If I want to sell it, I will. If I want to give it away, I will. If I want to lease it, I will. It's mine to do with what I want. I appreciate you being concerned, and if there was anything that was important enough to tell you I would, but this is none of your business. Now, what did you need to talk to me about? I've got all this to go over." He swiped his hand across the table.

A million scenarios blew through Duke's mind as he watched his father, flabbergasted. "Whose horse was out in the yard earlier?"

"I didn't see a horse."

Duke shook his head. "Stubborn as always. Listen, I'm going to take a few days off. I need to head up to Bozeman."

"That's fine, the boys can finish the fence. How long you gonna be gone?"

"Three, maybe four, days."

"Hey, while you are up there, stop in and see if that part for the tractor is in yet. It would save me some time if you brought it back with you."

"Not a problem," Duke said as he stood. "I'll see you in a few days."

His father nodded and went back to his paperwork. Duke walked out the front door and stood on the porch, feeling something wasn't right. Shaking his head, he headed to his Jeep and made his way home to crash for a few hours.

Walking into his bedroom, he peeled off his clothes and headed to the shower. He stood there letting the hot water run over his body. He really needed to get Julie out of his fucking head. Derek was right; she wasn't worth it. The only thing she had going on for her was that fantastic body—those fuckable tits and that fantastic ass. "Shit," he moaned as he grew harder and harder thinking about her. *Could it be just great sex?* he asked himself.

As he washed himself, he found his hand wrapped around his erection. Looking down, he couldn't help but wonder if he was enough for her. *What could I have done differently?* Shaking his head and closing his eyes, he thought about how her tits would bounce as he thrust into her. He knew he was big enough, and he felt her when she came, so what was it? His hand moving a bit faster, he felt his stomach muscles tightening. He pictured her big nipples taut and wanton of his lips. "Aww, fuck," he yelled as he pulsed with his release. Wave after wave, he leaned against the shower wall. He let it all go, his hand on the wall holding himself up as his legs shook. He stood there with his hands on the wall and his head hung until the water ran cold. Even then, he stood there, punishing himself for wanting her.

Julie Front destroyed him. She took everything he had and then threw it all in his face. She was a beautiful, sexy, enticing vixen who took what she wanted without caring a bit how her actions affected those around her. Duke actually thought she was the one. Having to deal with her and his childhood friend was something he was having a hard time doing. Drinking seemed to be the only way to cloud his mind.

Shaking his head, Duke reached for the knob to turn off the water then grabbed a towel. He didn't even bother drying off. Walking into his bedroom, he collapsed on the bed.

CHAPTER TWO

LOREN MITCHELL

COMING HERE WAS *the right choice.* She sat on her horse looking out at the great expanse in front of her.

Richard Reynolds was her father's friend and her godfather, although she had no idea until about three months ago. They served in the Vietnam war together. When he came to Texas for his funeral, he left her a letter.

Loren didn't get to say goodbye to her father because she was in a drug-induced coma for five months. It took her a year to recover from the brutal attack that nearly ended her life. Even after spending nearly a year in rehab and therapy, the fear was still present in her mind. Not being able to go back to work, the memories being too much for her, she spent her time never leaving her house. The doctor told her it was Agoraphobia, the fear of going outside alone. Now, here she sat on her horse looking out at thousands of acres of land alone. At least there weren't any people around. She was doing what she needed to do to survive.

Her mother gave her the letter from Richard after she'd recovered and returned home from rehab. She had set it on her table and left it there for months. When she finally decided that she needed to leave Austin, she discovered the letter as she packed her things. Her father had left her a sizable trust fund, and with it she purchased a tiny house to pull behind her truck, deciding she was going to just travel around and be alone. There was no trust in her bones anymore. No one was safe; no one was truly trustworthy. When she discovered the letter, she opened it and read what Richard had written to her. The contents of that letter made this her destination.

Dear Loren,

My name is Richard Reynolds. Your father and I served in the Vietnam war, where he saved my life on more than one occasion. I am so sorry for your loss, especially the circumstances in which he left us.

Over the many years since the war, we have done our best to stay in touch. I know you probably aren't aware of this, but I am your godfather. Your godmother was my wife, Alison, but unfortunately, she passed away many years ago from cancer.

I know that you are a brilliant neurosurgeon, and I am sorry for what happened to you. That man was not a man. Men don't do those things to women. When you recover, and when you are ready, come and see me. I can help you with the aftermath of all that has happened. Your father and I went through some pretty mind-altering shit, and well, let's just say it's not anything I want to relive or discuss. But we helped each other through the bad times, and together, we worked our way through it on my father's ranch.

Your mother filled me in, but I won't pretend to understand or to know what that monster did to you. I am sure that anything I have to say isn't going to help you, but I am here to listen and to help in any way that I can. Please come whenever you want. I have been in the same place for the last sixty years, at the Double R Ranch about a hundred miles northeast of Boze-man, Montana. Look for a small town called Buffalo, then go into the post office and ask them where we are.

It is with the deepest sorrow that I write this letter. Loren, I hope you take me up on my offer of help.

Sincerely,

Richard Reynolds

Loren reached up and wiped the tear off her cheek. It took over a year before the nightmares stopped. She trailed her fingers down the scar that ran just along her jaw and up onto her cheek. As time progressed, it got lighter and lighter. The ugly, jagged, deep red line was from the knife that was meant to slit her throat. In the beginning, Loren couldn't even look at herself in the mirror. Shaking her head, she turned her horse toward the makeshift barn she had built. After she got her horse Cupcake settled for the night, a gift from Richard, Loren made her way to the house and took a hot shower. As she dried herself off, she stood in front of the mirror looking at her marred body. Eleven stab wounds healed, the memories dealt with and put away. The only thing left were the fading scars.

No man would ever see her the same again. No matter how long and beautiful her hair was, no matter how curvy her body, no man would ever touch her. Her fingers traveled across her stomach, up her chest, touching each of the scars. She remembered each time he slammed his knife into her, each scream she let loose as he pulled it out and did it again. She could hear his words in her ear as he had her pinned with his arm around her neck. *'Fucking whore, you killed my brother. Now you are going to die.'*

These thoughts used to scare her. They used to rule her, binding her with nothing but fear. Not anymore, not since she took back control of her life. Turning her back to the mirror, she looked over her shoulder at the jagged scar where he cut her as she tried to drag herself across the parking lot to the hospital doors. He inflicted one last kick to her ribs, knocking her unconscious, leaving her to die. Then, like the coward he was, he ran.

When her father and mother received the call that she had been in an accident, they rushed to the hospital. When her father heard what had happened to her, he had a massive heart attack and died in the hospital emergency room on the floor next to her bed. That was one year, ten months, three weeks, six days, and eighteen hours ago.

Loren had been here in Montana on the Double R Ranch for close to eleven weeks now. No one knew she was here. She hadn't seen a living soul, except for when she went into one of the small towns surrounding this ranch, and the few times she happened upon two male lovers in the fields. She secretly watched them and the love they shared with each other. Loren knew she would never know that bond.

She visited Richard two, maybe three, times a week. When she sought him out, they immediately hit it off. Loren hadn't laughed in a long time, but when Richard shared stories of her father with her, she couldn't do anything but laugh.

He had offered her the land to park her tiny house on, no strings attached, explaining to her how this land healed him and her father. Together, they worked the ranch while Richard's father owned it. Loren accepted his offer and had been here since.

CHAPTER THREE

DUKE REYNOLDS

WAKING up early was programmed into his DNA. Working a ranch was from dawn 'til dusk and sometimes longer. When he looked at the clock, he couldn't believe he'd slept the night away. Pulling on his jeans, Duke made his way out to the kitchen to make some coffee. Picking up his phone off the charger, he saw a few text messages from his brother Derek.

Hey, man, where are you? At Boot's, some hot chicks here.

Duke laughed. "No thanks, baby brother," he said to his phone.

Next message: *Showed your pic to this chick. She says come on down she'll take care of you.*

Duke opened the pic his brother sent him. "Not bad. Nice tits." Duke liked a woman with big tits, but he was more of an ass man. Most women who had big tits usually shared them with everyone. Shaking his head, Duke laughed. He was done with meaningless sex.

The last text read: *Sorry, brother, took them both home. Your loss.*

Duke laid his phone down, laughing and grabbed his coffee, then walked to the window. His apartment was small and on top of the local pharmacy. He could move back to the ranch; it would probably be the best thing for him. But he liked having his own space. The sun was just coming up. Usually, he would be heading off to work, but today he was heading off to Bozeman. He needed to get away for a few days. Normally, it would just be a day to pick up the part he needed, but he wanted to clear his head. Spend some time alone.

He walked out into the new morning sun, threw his bag in the back of his Jeep, and headed out of town. As he drove, he couldn't help but think about that land agreement he saw at the ranch. Something to look into when he got back to town. *Who is Loren Mitchell? Is that a woman or a man? Why did my father not tell anyone about giving up a hundred acres of land? Who does that?* He didn't really want to think about it; he had more shit in his brain than he needed. Mainly Julie Front.

For two years, they were together, and for the last eight months she was fucking his oldest friend. Honestly, Duke was pissed, but he couldn't be pissed at Teddy. Julie was a major babe. But Duke actually thought they were going to get married. He'd even gone to Bozeman to check out rings for her. Good thing he didn't buy one. His cock still ached to be buried deep inside her. She had the perfect ass, and he could still feel how tight she was when he pulled her up on her knees and took her from behind, which was her preferred position. As he drove thinking about all the times they had sex, never once could he remember making love to her. Never once could he remember holding her afterwards. She always rolled away and slept with her back to him. When he would try to snuggle up behind her to hold her, she would tell him she was hot.

Rubbing his jaw, he felt like an idiot. Why hadn't he seen it? Was Derek right that he'd been blinded by the sex. Julie was a wild cat in bed; he was never unsatisfied. Looking back, they never really went out anywhere, except to the bar, where she would make it known to every woman in there that he belonged to her. He remembered one time when two girls were talking about him. She walked up to them and said, "Look all you want, ladies, but he belongs to me." *Who does that?*

He never meant anything to her, except for sex. Trying to get her out of his head, he reached for the radio and turned it on. Song after song that played reminded him of her. Laughing, he turned it off.

Maybe if he went out and had sex with a few random women while he was up in Bozeman, it would help him forget her. He wasn't a bad looking guy, he admitted, looking at himself in the rearview mirror. His eyes were green—his mother's eyes, his father used to tell him. They weren't an ordinary green, but the green you'd see in the tall deep grass of a lush meadow. His jaw was strong and a bit square. He kept his facial hair trimmed, but it'd been years since he shaved it off. He kept it long to hide a nasty scar from where a horse kicked him and split his jaw open. His hair could use a trim, he realized. Since Julie left him, he hadn't bothered to cut it. Sitting up taller, he could see that it sat just on his shoulders. He was buff, ripped with muscles, but that was just from years of working on the ranch. He didn't work out, and he didn't run. He worked.

He knew his cock was bigger than most, but it fit his six-foot-two height. His hands were rough from years of abuse, his skin tan and a bit tough from working in the sun, and the Montana winters were difficult at best. His teeth were straight and white; his mother made sure of that. Years of braces, all the boys had them.

Why couldn't he just pick up a few women while he was out of town? It'd been months since he felt the soft skin of a woman, the feel of decent nipples in his mouth. The taste of their essence on his tongue. God, he was getting hard just thinking about a woman's mouth on his cock. The burn of his release. Yeah, he was getting laid while he was in Bozeman.

Pulling into town, he went to his favorite hotel and got himself a room with a view of the mountains. After dropping off his bag, he headed out to the restaurant across the street. He knew a woman there from his frequent visits. She always flirted with him, so today he was making it his mission to smile more and maybe make some plans. He needed to get laid and he needed to forget Julie. Walking in, he scanned the room to see if she was working. Nope, no sight of her. Duke sat down and ordered breakfast. As he sat there eating, he couldn't help but notice a young woman across the room. She had long blonde hair nearly to her waist. From the side, she was stunning. He couldn't help but stare at her. When she turned her head toward him, they locked eyes. Hers were trance inducing. He felt his breath catch in his chest when she gave him a tight smile. She slid out of her booth and picked up her ticket. Turning, she headed toward the cashier. Duke couldn't help but take in the perfect ass in her perfect fitting jeans. She had on red cowboy boots and a blue button-down shirt. She paid her bill and walked out the door. Duke turned his head to follow her as he watched her get into a pickup truck and pull away.

"Fuck me," he whispered to himself. *Who the hell was that?* He wanted to get up and chase after her, but he knew better. A woman who looked like that most always had a man to go home to. He smiled, shaking his head as the waitress walked up.

"Can I get you anything else, darling?" she asked.

"No, I'm good. Just the check." He smiled at her.

"You're not from around here, are you?" she inquired.

"No, just in town for a day or two."

"Well, I hope to see you again." She was flirting with him.

Duke smiled at her, then picked up the bill before paying and leaving. He stood outside and looked down the street in the direction the pickup went in. He couldn't get her out of his head. *She was stunning.*

Duke jumped in his Jeep and went to pick up his part, then he headed over to pick up the motor for his dad. On his way back to the hotel, his phone rang. He fished it out of his pocket as he pulled over. Looking down, he saw it was his brother Derek.

"Yeah," he said.

"Hey, man, why didn't you come down to Boot's last night? That chick was fucking hot, and let me tell you, man, did she taste fantastic," Derek said.

Duke laughed. "Well, I'm glad you had yourself a bit of fun, little brother. But I'm not playing around with little girls anymore. You keep her for yourself."

"Man, let me tell you, she and her friend were fucking wild. I got to watch some chick on chick action last night. Have you ever watched a chick eat another chick out? It's fucking fantastic. I swear I was hard all night long."

"Maybe for you, little brother, but I think I am beyond that shit. I'm too old to care. Why are you calling me?"

"I wanted to know where the hell you were. Why aren't you here?"

"I'm up in Bozeman. If you would keep your dick in your pants and pay attention, you would know. I told you yesterday that I was coming up here. I'll be back on Friday."

"No, man, you need to get back here today. We have the back forty to do. We've already lost three head. A fucking huge tree came down and took out the fence. Dad told me to call you and everyone else. We need to find those cattle and get the tree up and the fence taken care of. I've already called in reinforcements, so get your ass back here."

Fuck! "Yeah, I'll see you in a few hours. I just need to pick up my shit from the hotel."

"All right, I'll let Dad know. He's on his way out here now."

He hung up and headed back to the hotel. No way was he going to be able to lurk about and see if he could find the mysterious woman with the mysterious eyes. It was a little over two hours back to the ranch. As he pulled into the drive, he saw all the trucks. Damn, he did call in reinforcements. Today was a four-wheeler day.

Duke pulled up to the big garage. Jumping out, he opened the big doors and walked in. He started putting chainsaws, chains, extra gas, gloves, and a few axes in the basket on the back of his four-wheeler. Ten minutes later, he was headed out of the garage.

CHAPTER FOUR

LOREN MITCHELL

DRIVING BACK FROM BOZEMAN, Loren couldn't help but think about the man in the restaurant. God, he had beautiful eyes, but the way he stared at her made her very nervous. The last time a man looked at her like that, she ended up in a coma and had nearly lost her life.

She remembered how sweet he was; how wonderful he was. They had been on a few dates, but never alone. Loren was new to the dating game. She had goals and never had the time to have a boyfriend. She was busy flying through high school, graduating at the tender age of fourteen. Then she worked through two years of graduate school and three years of medical school before she started her internship. She managed a sixteen-year process in only eleven years. She was the youngest neurosurgeon in the country. So, dating was not something she did. But he was so sweet to her and treated her very respectfully, so much so that she thought she might actually lose her virginity to him, until that night when she walked out of the hospital after a six-hour surgery. It was two in the morning. She had just reached her car when he walked up behind her. She thought for sure he was going to rape her, but he didn't. That was not his plan.

To have a stranger look at her like that now, well, it made her skin crawl. Instead of staying the day to do some shopping, she left

Bozeman and headed home. She didn't need anything important; she just felt like being a girl and buying something pretty. Not that anyone would see it, but still, it felt good to spoil herself.

Loren had been in Montana for three months now and this was her first trip to the big city, and from the way she felt, it would be her last. There was no way she was putting herself in that position again. Her father was the only man in her life, and when he died, her godfather became her strength. Although she didn't know Richard very well, he had been nothing but kind to her. He gave her the land she was living on and told her she could do anything she wanted.

So far, she had planted a garden and built a greenhouse so she could grow her vegetables in the winter. She built herself a chicken coop so she had eggs, and a make-shift barn for her horse. Her supplies should be in soon to start a real barn, and she had her dog—a rescue her mother got her when she came home from the hospital. Jaz was a mix of German Sheppard and Labrador. She was a good friend, trusted, and usually went with her everywhere. She was very protective of Loren.

Time flew by as she drove engrossed in her own thoughts. She pulled into town and stopped at the feed store to see about her lumber and tools, hoping they would be in. They weren't expected for a few more days, but she needed a few groceries for the next few days.

As she walked in, Mr. Jordan greeted her. "Good Morning, Miss Mitchell."

"Good morning, Mr. Jordan. I was wondering if any of my supplies came in. I was in town and thought I would check."

"Well, all of your tools are here. I'll have one of the guys load them up in your truck."

"Thank you, any word on the lumber?"

He smiled. "Nope, but I do have a truck coming in tomorrow. I can have the guys deliver it for you if it comes in."

Mr. Jordan had no idea where she lived, and she wasn't about to have a bunch of men know where her home was. Smiling, she said, "That's all right, I'll just come back in a few days. I'm in no hurry."

She pulled out her wallet and handed him her credit card to pay for the tools and supplies. Mr. Jordan had the guys load her truck, and then she walked across the street to the grocery store to pick up what she needed. She wanted to make a casserole for Richard. She'd made a pie last night for him. He had mentioned to her that he didn't get much in the way of home cooked meals since Alison passed away.

She headed home and made the casserole for him. She and Jaz climbed in the truck and headed over to his place. When she arrived, she saw all the trucks and started to panic. Pickup trucks meant men, and men meant trouble. Pausing before she got out of the truck to contain the fear rushing through her body, she took a deep breath and got out. Jaz wouldn't let anything happen to her. Jaz took off running through the yard as she headed up the steps to the front door. She knocked a few times but no one answered. Opening the door, she yelled in. "Richard, it's Loren." There was no response, so she headed into the kitchen, where she put the pie and the casserole on the counter. She found a piece of paper and wrote a note.

Thought you might like a home cooked meal and some pie. Just warm it up in the oven for twenty minutes and you should be good. Talk soon.

L.

When she walked out the front door and onto the porch, she could hear an engine running. Looking around, she spotted a four-wheeler at the edge of the property toward the huge garage. Jaz was wagging her tail at whoever was on it. She couldn't see who it was, but her heart started racing. As she headed down the stairs toward her truck, Jaz saw her and came running toward her. After she opened the door, Jaz jumped in and Loren got in after her. Quickly, she pulled out and started down the driveway. Turning her head, she saw the man on the four-wheeler and realized he was the guy from the diner. *Who is he? Why is he here at Richard's house?* Snapping her head back, she continued down the driveway.

Duke

16

Duke sat there on his four-wheeler in shock. "What the hell?" he said as he watched the truck fly down the driveway. It was her, the woman from the restaurant in Bozeman. *What is she doing here?* She'd come out of the house. He headed over to it and walked in, looking around to see if anything had been stolen. When he entered the kitchen, he saw the food on the counter and the note. Reading it, he smiled. "L? Who are you and why are you in my father's house?" Just then, he remembered the paper he saw yesterday. Walking back into the dining room, he found the paper and began to read.

Turns out, his father did give the land to her. "A hundred acres to a Loren Mitchell. But why? Why would he just give it away? Is she his girlfriend? No way, she's way younger than him." Duke stood there in shock. But he knew he needed to get out there and help the rest of the men with the fence, so he put the paper back and headed out to help the guys.

"Well, it's about time you got here," his father said to him.

"Yeah, well, I was in Bozeman. You knew that," Duke said to his father.

"Derek said he called you nearly three hours ago."

"I was up at the house. Apparently, you had a visitor." Duke's father stopped and looked at his son. Duke just stood there staring at his father. "Anything you want to talk about?"

He could see his father growing agitated. "Keep your nose out of my business," he snapped.

Duke put his hands up. "No need to get pissy about it. Just wanted to let you know you had some company."

Derek walked up. "What? Dad's got a girlfriend? Who is it?" He turned to look at their father.

"What I do is none of your fucking business. Now get to work." He grumbled and walked away.

"What was that about?" Derek asked Duke.

"I have no fucking idea, but I will tell you this. I have every intention on finding out. Come on, little brother, let's get this done."

It took most of the day to cut the tree down and to repair the fence. The younger brothers, Alex and Joe, hunted down the three missing cattle. The day was long and the sun about to set by the time everyone got back to the house. Duke had forgotten about the woman who visited his father. Everyone climbed in their trucks and headed out for a beer. Duke headed home. It was already close to nine at night and he was exhausted. Not even bothering to take a shower, he dropped on the couch and crashed.

Richard made sure everyone was gone before he went in the house. He found the note on the counter and smiled. He appreciated the meal, especially after the long day they had all had.

Loren

LOREN SAT IN HER CHAIR WATCHING THE SUN SET. SHE COULDN'T GET that man out of her mind. *Why was he at Richard's? Who is* he? Maybe, she thought, *I was seeing things.* She had in the past, when getting freaked out, seen people who weren't who she thought they were. Maybe her mind was playing tricks on her. The guy freaked her out in Bozeman, but maybe this guy wasn't him. She got up and went into the house. Reaching into the cabinet, she pulled out her gun and made sure it was loaded. Then she pulled the shotgun off the wall and loaded it before hanging it back above the door.

"This is ridiculous; no one even knows I'm here. Get a grip, girl," she said to herself and laughed. It was early still when she looked at the clock. "Maybe I should just go to bed and read." Nodding her head, she went to the bathroom and changed into her shorts and t-shirt. Grabbing one of her new romance novels, she headed up to her loft.

She must have fallen asleep while reading, because when Jaz started barking, she nearly threw herself off the loft. It was light out, so it had to be morning. Wow, she must've been tired. A truck was pulling up as she looked out the window. Smiling, she went to the bathroom to change into her clothes. Just as he knocked on the door, she opened it.

"Good morning, Richard. What brings you all the way out here?" she said with a smile.

He chuckled. "I came to thank you for the meal and the pie. It was just what I needed. We had a tree go down and take out our fence, and a few of the cattle got away."

"Well, that would explain all the trucks out there yesterday. Did you get it fixed?"

"We did."

"Come on in, I'll make us some coffee. Have you eaten yet? I can make you some eggs or some pancakes."

"Oh, no, coffee will do. Already ate this morning," he said as he came in. "You know, from the outside, this place looks so tiny, but in here, it's pretty big."

She laughed. "It's big enough for me and Jaz, and it's mobile."

"Listen," he said as he sat down on the stool that was by her table. "I want to let you know that you are welcome anytime. Even if I'm not there, you are more than welcome to stay until I get back. I'm usually there. I'm getting a bit old to do any real work out there in the fields. The boys mostly run things. I just do the paper work and work on the equipment. So, next time you come, and you see the truck there and I don't answer, just come in and look for me."

"Thanks. I know this is new for us, and I would never want to be a bother or to make you feel as if you need to drop everything just because I come to see you. I know you worry about me, but I am doing really good. I am used to the solitude out here. I've got Jaz and my horse, so I pretty much keep to myself." She handed him his coffee. "Come on, we can sit outside. I love this time of the morning."

Richard followed her outside and they walked around to the other side of the house and sat in the chairs. "I remember when we got back from the war. Your dad and I used to do this every morning before we headed out into the fields, and every night we would sit and have a beer or two."

"Yeah, he and my mom would sit out on the back porch at the ranch every night."

A nice silence fell over them. Richard said in a very kind voice, "He was so proud of you. I remember when you were baptized. It was the first time I saw you. When I looked into your eyes, I knew you were special. I was so proud that he asked me to be your godfather. He was my oldest son's godfather as well. But you, with those eyes, I have never before and have not since seen eyes that color. I remember when we came home, Ali went to the library and looked it up. I can't remember what she called it, but having eyes that color is a rare genetic mutation, a sort of phenomena. You are a rare human being. I am so happy you survived."

Loren reached up and wiped a tear from her cheek. "I'm just glad that he was here for all of my accomplishments."

"Yes, but he missed the greatest one. The one where you survived."

She nodded her head. "I miss him, Richard. Every day."

"I know. I miss him as well. Did you know we talked once a week? He would tell me all about your life, as I would with mine. He was a great friend. The best."

She reached over and squeezed his hand. "I'm glad he had such a wonderful friend. I think he made the best choice when he chose you to look out for me."

Richard chuckled. "Have you talked to your mother?"

Loren laughed. "Yes, I called her yesterday. I think she wants to sell the ranch. Too many reminders. She and my Aunt Liz are thinking about going to Hawaii. Maybe spend their lives traveling the world. Mom never left the ranch. They got married and had me, so they spent all their time taking care of it. I think it would be good for her."

"Don't you want it?"

"No, Dad made sure I had enough money to last a lifetime. You gave me this incredible piece of land, and well, I know I will never be able to operate again."

"I'm sorry he took that from you."

"I know. I tried to go back, but I couldn't make it into the parking lot. I needed to get out of there. Parking lots and me are not compatible anymore."

"What about here? We have a sort of hospital. I know Doc is going to retire in a few years. I mean, you're a brilliant neurosurgeon, and well, we don't exactly need one around here, but you are a physician, so why not."

Loren laughed. "No, I think my doctor days are over. This is my life now. Here, being me. I feel safe for the first time in nearly two years. Even going up to Bozeman freaks me out. I just find that talking to people is not something I have gotten used to. I just don't trust people."

"Yeah, I don't blame ya there. I guess we do what we need to do to survive. When Ali passed, I spent six months in the house. I refused to leave it. But then one day I went to sit on the porch and then into the barn. We all work at our own pace. At least you went to Bozeman, that's a start."

"I guess you're right."

They sat there drinking their coffee not saying anything. When Richard finished, he stood up. "Well, I guess I should get back. They'll be wondering where I got to."

She laughed. "I'm glad you came by." Hugging him, she took his cup and walked him over to his truck.

"Remember what I said. You come by whenever you want. My door is always open."

"Thank you, Richard. Maybe I will stop by tomorrow. I need to go and pick up some lumber from Mr. Jordan. I'm going to start my barn."

He laughed. "You do realize I have four boys? I could send them over and they would have it done in a few days."

Smiling, she said, "I kind of want to do it myself. But if I have a problem, I will definitely ask for some help."

Richard climbed into his truck and started it up. Loren backed up and watched him drive away, waving just as he drove down the hill out of sight.

"Hey, girl, you want to go for a ride?" she asked her dog. Jaz jumped up and ran to the barn. Loren laughed, going inside to grab her boots and put the cups in the sink. Fifteen minutes later, she was flying across the field on her horse with Jaz following close behind her.

21

It was undeniably the most beautiful feeling. Miles and miles with no fences. Every day for months, this is how she spent her days. Riding free, nothing to keep her down. No strings, no commitments, no people. Richard was a good man, a good choice her father made.

Today, Loren decided to have her lunch by the river. As she sat in the tall grass eating her sandwich, watching Jaz play in the water, she reflected on the life she could have had, on the life she did have. It was what she had always wanted, to map the human brain. According to her peers, she was the best in the country. So many lives she saved. With only one loss in the three and a half years she'd practiced, she was the best. That one loss nearly cost her, her own life. Now, because of the fear, the scars, she would never hold a scalpel in her hand again. Looking down at her hands, she realized she was shaking. Just thinking about cutting into someone made her afraid.

Lying back in the grass, looking up at the sky, she cried. There was no reasoning for it; well, that's not true. Her life was over. She would spend her days here on this ranch, hidden from life, hidden from society. A ghost of her past self. She wondered if this was what people felt like when they decided to commit suicide. Although death was not an option, because her father would be so disappointed in her, and she never wanted that.

Jaz started barking, so she wiped her tears and sat up. There was a rider off in the distance. Loren got up and got on her horse. "Come on, Jaz," she yelled at her. They took off in the opposite direction, heading toward Richard's house. There was no way she was leading this rider to her home. Looking over her shoulder to see if the rider was following her, she saw Jaz trying to keep up. "Come on, girl, you can do it," she yelled.

It didn't take long to reach Richard's. As she flew into the yard with Jaz behind her, Richard was walking out of the barn. He looked up and smiled as she came to a stop.

"Twice in one day," he said as she climbed down.

Laughing, Loren said, "Well I thought I would come over and share a piece of that pie with you." She wasn't sure she should tell him about the rider at the river.

"Now you're talking. Come on in, I just made a pot of coffee." They climbed the stairs and went inside. Loren sat at the table in the kitchen as Richard poured them each a cup and then cut some pie for them. "Were you out for a ride?"

She laughed. "Something like that. I ride every morning, and today we were down at the river. So, I thought I would come by and have some pie. When my lumber gets in, I'm going to be pretty busy, so I figured we could spend some time together."

"You just make sure you come by and see me once in a while," he said with a chuckle.

Richard enjoyed having her company. She was like a fresh breeze. Sometimes he wished he'd had a daughter. He shared more stories with her about her father. They spent most of their time laughing, eating pie, and drinking coffee. Like two old souls.

~

Duke

DUKE RODE UP ON HIS HORSE AND SAW HER HORSE OUT FRONT. HE walked into the house hearing her laughter. *What the hell is going on?* He just stood there as he listened.

"Well, Richard, I should be heading out. It's a long ride back."

Duke heard the chairs scrape across the floor in the kitchen. His feet started to move when he heard his father say.

"You come back soon."

"I will, I am going to make Mom's lasagna tomorrow. I'll make extra and bring it by."

The voices were getting closer to Duke. "Can you bring more pie?" his father asked. Duke was two steps from the door when it swung open.

She laughed, still looking at Richard, and said, "Of course. What kind would you like? Oh, I know. Strawberry."

His father chuckled. Duke froze in his spot when she lifted her head and was face to face with him. Loren backed up and moved behind his father. Richard reached behind him to wrap his arm around her. He could feel her whole-body trembling. She buried her face in his back, grabbing his shirt.

"What are you doing here?" Richard nearly shouted at Duke.

He didn't know what to say; he was shocked. Her eyes, he had never seen eyes that color before. *She is beautiful. Who is she? What is she doing here with my father? How does he know her?*

"Well?" Richard said.

"I... um... I was out riding and saw someone down by the river. When I started toward them, they took off. I followed them here. The horse outside, who's is it?" Duke tried to look around his father, but he was a big man, and that woman was so tiny.

"You need to leave now," Richard said.

Duke stood there shocked. His father had just thrown him out. "But."

"Just go. Get on your horse or in your Jeep and get out of here."

"But, Dad," Duke stuttered. He was in shock.

Richard took a step backwards into the kitchen, closing the door behind him. Spinning around, he wrapped his arms around Loren. She was hyperventilating. He reached for the bag on the counter and handed it to her. Putting it over her mouth, she started breathing in and out. "It's all right. That is my son Duke. You're all right. Breathe." Loren nodded her head and continued to breathe into the bag.

Duke stood in the dining room in shock. *What the fuck is going on?* He heard his father's voice talking softly to her. "That's it, breathe. You all right?"

He watched as the door pushed open and his father came out. "I told you to go, now please do as I asked. This doesn't concern you."

"Who is that?"

"None of your business. Now please, Duke, just go," he pleaded.

Shaking his head, Duke turned and walked out of the house. Richard followed him, watching as he mounted his horse and headed toward the barn. Turning, he went back to the kitchen. Loren was sitting at the table with her head in her hands. "I am so sorry," she whispered. "I don't know what happened."

"No need to apologize. Are you all right?" he asked as he sat across from her.

Laughing, she said, "I'm fine. I should get going. It'll be dark soon."

"Why don't you leave Cupcake here and I'll drive you home? I'll come and get you tomorrow and you can ride her home."

Loren nodded. "Thank you."

Duke was walking out of the barn as Richard closed the passenger door of his truck. She was sitting in the seat, and what he guessed was her dog was in the truck bed. He stood there looking at her; he had never seen anyone more beautiful. She turned her head as his father backed out and looked him in the eye then just turned her head as they drove away. Duke had no idea how long he stood there after they left. It was Derek who snapped him out of the trance he was in.

"Hey, we're going to Boot's. You want to come?"

Duke looked at him. "No, I need to go home. I'll see you in the morning."

"Your loss, man. More chicks for me." Derek slapped him on the back as he walked by. Duke snapped his head up, looking at his brother.

What the fuck is wrong with me? Jesus! Duke headed to his Jeep. As he pulled out he saw her horse. He couldn't leave it there. He stopped and got out, taking the horse to the barn. He brushed it down and fed it. This way his father didn't have to do it. He wanted to know who she was. He couldn't get her out of his head. He had never in all his life imagined a woman could be so beautiful. He made his way home and jumped in the shower. He didn't bother eating, just plopped on his bed naked.

When he closed his eyes, all he could see were her eyes, her face. "Who are you, beautiful?" It took a long time for Duke to fall asleep, and he did not sleep well.

~

Loren

LOREN COULDN'T STOP SHAKING. RICHARD WAS TALKING TO HER. "I AM so sorry about that. The boys are never at the house during the day. I didn't realize how upset you would get."

"It's fine, it was just a shock. I guess I haven't gotten completely over my fear," she said softly.

"Well, it won't happen again," he said sternly.

"Richard, they are your children. There is no reason for them to be banned from your house. I will just be careful. It's fine, really. It just shocked me is all." She wasn't sure who she was trying to convince, him or herself.

"I would suggest you meet them all, that way it would be easier for you to visit. But Derek is a horn dog and would say inappropriate things to you, and I won't have that. He hasn't learned any manners. He was still young when Ali passed."

"I should meet them. You're right, Richard. I don't want to cause friction between you and your sons."

"If you want to meet them, perhaps we should do this one at a time. There are four of them." He chuckled. "Bring Jaz with you. I know how much she protects you. Why don't we try this tomorrow? You can meet Alex, my youngest. Very quiet that one is."

Loren chuckled. "We should have done this months ago. I'm so sorry for causing a rift between you and your children."

"Don't worry about it. Duke will get over it. He's very protective of me and a very feeling guy. He gets that from his mother."

"Oh, I don't know. He might get that from you."

They pulled off the main road and headed toward her house. As they pulled up, Richard said, "I will see you in the morning. You gonna be all right tonight?"

Loren looked at him and smiled. "I am fine, really. It was just a shock, that's all. I feel rather foolish."

Richard turned and looked at her. "Sweetheart, I felt your body shake. You can try all you want to convince me, but I know what I felt. No woman should feel that fear. I'm thinking that maybe if you met my sons, you might feel a bit more relaxed, knowing there are at least five men who would do anything for you and would never hurt you."

She reached out and touched his arm. "Thank you, Richard. I will see you in the morning."

Loren climbed out of the truck and let Jaz out of the back. Together, they watched Richard leave and then went in the house. As she got Jaz her food, she smiled. "Did you see him? He was beautiful. Those eyes. Who has eyes that green?" Jaz sat there and looked at her like she had three heads. Loren just laughed and got herself something to eat and then showered and went to bed.

The night was long, and she struggled to sleep. Fear overwhelmed her, though it was something she thought she had a grip on. Going back to therapy wasn't an option for her out here. Sleep finally won over, but it wasn't restful.

~

Duke

THE BOYS FILED IN AS USUAL TO SAY GOOD MORNING. DUKE DIDN'T SAY much. He just stood in the kitchen watching his father.

"I need you all to have a seat. I have something I need to tell you," Richard said.

Duke thought, *It's about fucking time.* He stayed standing. He wasn't sure he was ready to listen to his father tell them he had a girlfriend.

Richard started. "You all know I was in the war. But what you don't know—"

Duke jumped to a conclusion and said rather meanly, "She's our sister?"

Richard looked up at him. "You really need to shut your mouth. This isn't any of your business until I make it your business. Can I finish?" Richard snapped. None of the boys had ever seen their father so firm with anyone. Duke nodded and walked to the other side of the room.

Derek watched him. "What the hell is going on?"

"Dad here has a girlfriend," Duke spat.

Richard stood up and walked over to his son. "You really need to shut your mouth right now and let me talk. Otherwise, this isn't going to work. Now shut the hell up. I have somewhere I need to be."

Duke backed up from his father. Never had he felt such rage from him. He shut up and let his father talk.

"Now, I was in the war and I had a buddy. He saved my life many times. When we got out, we came here to heal. We worked this ranch with my father and your uncle. I met your mom and then he moved to Texas. My father gave him the money to buy the ranch his wife still lives on today. We kept in contact our whole lives. A few years ago, remember when I was gone for that week? Well, I went to Texas. He passed away suddenly."

There were condolences all around the table.

Richard didn't know how to tell the next part, so he paused for a few minutes trying to gain his composure. "The circumstances surrounding his death are difficult at best. But the young woman that was here yesterday, Duke, is his daughter. She is, in fact, my God daughter. I gave her that land because she needs it to survive. What happened to her was horrific, which is what caused her father to have a heart attack. It's not my story to tell you, and I'm pretty sure she doesn't want me to tell. But she has been here for over three months now, and it would seem that Duke keeps running into her." They all looked at Duke, who was just standing there in shock. He had misjudged his father, and for that he felt shame. "Last night, we talked. She is eventually going to run into to each of you, and if last night was a prelude to what will happen when she does, we figured it was best if she met you all."

"What happened last night?" Derek asked, looking at Duke.

But Richard answered. "Duke saw her out by the river and spooked her. She came here and then ran smack into him on her way out. Let's just say she was a little more than uncomfortable." Richard turned and looked at Duke. "I'm going to pick her up and bring her back here to meet you. She left her horse here, and she rides every morning. Thank you, Duke, for putting Cupcake up for the night. I appreciate it." Duke nodded. Turning back to the boys, Richard said, "I need for you all to be on your best behavior. Don't move fast toward her and try not be assholes."

"Dad," Derek began. "What happened to her that she is hiding out? Is she like a criminal or something? Are you hiding a fugitive?"

"Don't be an asshole, Derek. No, she is not a criminal. As I said, it is not my story to tell. I don't think Loren would approve if I told you anything more about her. She just wants to be left alone. But, as I said, she comes here at least three times a week, and she rides the ranch every day. This is just so she can feel more comfortable and not have to worry about any of you scaring the shit out of her. I also want to add, if you happen across her little house out there, my suggestion is to stay away or you might get yourself shot, and she doesn't need any more guilt on her shoulders. It's bad enough her life has been destroyed once; she doesn't need it again. Now, I am going to pick her up. You all stay here and wait for me. I will come and get you one at a time so she isn't so overwhelmed. I'll be back in a little while."

Richard stood and looked at Duke as he walked out the kitchen door. The brothers sat there not saying anything to each other. Derek looked at Duke. "Care to elaborate?"

Duke didn't say a word. He didn't have any words to say. When Derek saw her, he was going to go insane. There had been no other woman who could or would match her beauty.

RICHARD CHUCKLED AS HE WALKED OUT THE DOOR. HE KNEW THAT look in his son's eyes. He knew that Duke was taken by Loren. He almost felt sorry for him, with what Julie did to him and now Loren. She wasn't going to give him the time of day. Richard couldn't help but feel the rift forming between him and his oldest son. He would take Loren's side over Duke's, and he wasn't sure Duke would understand.

Pulling up to Loren's house, Richard saw her and Jaz standing on the porch. She smiled and waved to him as he put it in park. She headed toward the truck as Richard got out.

"Good Morning, Richard. Did you sleep well?" She smiled at him, giving him a quick hug.

He chuckled as he led her over to the passenger side. "I slept very well. How about you?"

Opening the door, she climbed in. "Not so well."

Richard walked around to open the tailgate to let Jaz in and then around to his. Climbing in, he smiled at her and said, "We don't have to do this today."

"Yes, we do. It's time. I don't want to feel like I did yesterday. I am a part of your life now, and I still can't believe none of us have run into each other before this." She paused. "Richard, are all your sons as big as Duke?"

He laughed. "Pretty much. Is that going to be a problem?"

"No, just preparing myself."

CHAPTER FIVE

THE BOYS SAT at the table without saying anything while they waited for their father to return with this mystery woman. A half an hour later they heard the truck hit the long drive. They all looked at each other. Then the door opened, and they heard their father laughing. "Come on, Jaz, let's sit in here. I'll be right back."

Walking into the kitchen, he said, "Now, I think it is best to do this one at a time."

But the door opened, and Loren walked in. "Actually, this is kind of silly." She lifted her head and they all gasped. She smiled. "Hi, I'm Loren. I know the eyes are a bit spooky."

None of them moved. Derek was even stunned. He was first up. "I'm Derek, second oldest. It's very nice to meet you." He put out his hand, but she just looked at it. Then Joe and Alex introduced themselves.

She turned to look Duke straight in the face. He couldn't help but notice as she squared her shoulders. Richard walked up to Loren, and she turned her head to look at him. Duke noticed the long scar that ran along her face. "This is Duke, my oldest," Richard said. Duke nodded. He didn't think his mouth would work.

Loren turned and looked at him, smiling. "I'm sorry about yesterday."

Duke nodded, totally mesmerized by her eyes. "I'm the one who should apologize. It was rude of me to act the way I did. I had no idea who you were. I have seen you around, but my father refused to acknowledge who you were. I guess I was a bit frustrated with him. So, please, accept my apology."

Derek sat there watching his brother.

Loren smiled at him. "Thank you. I'm a bit skittish when it comes to people, but I appreciate your kindness."

"Great, now that everyone has met, get to work. This ranch isn't going to run itself. Come on, Loren, I'll take you to Cupcake."

She turned and looked at each of them, memorizing their faces. "It was nice to finally meet you all." Duke stood there watching them walk out, as were all the brothers.

No one moved or said a word. Derek was the first. "I think I'm in love. Did you see those eyes? That ass? Jesus!"

Duke shook his head. "Little brother, that woman is so far out of your league, you aren't even in the game." Alex and Joe laughed.

"Oh, and you think she is in your league?" Derek snapped.

Duke laughed. "Not even close. But the difference between me and you is that I know it. Dad said she had something horrific happen to her."

Alex spoke. "I wonder if that's the reason for the scar on her face."

"What scar? I didn't see a scar," Derek said.

"That's because all you saw, all you ever see, is sex," Joe said and stood to leave. "I'm going to work." He walked out the kitchen door. Alex followed him, leaving Derek and Duke alone in the kitchen.

Derek looked at Duke. "Well, brother, if you have an interest in that beautiful woman, say something now, because if not, I am going after her."

Duke chuckled. "Derek, do yourself and everyone around you a favor. Grow up. That woman is not someone you can play with and discard. Dad has kept her safe for a long time. There is a reason she is here. That is his God daughter. She is off limits. Don't cross that line."

Derek stood. "Don't tell me what I can and can't do. You are not my father."

Just then, Richard walked in the door. "No, but I am. She is off limits, Derek. You don't know what her story is. The only reason you met her today was because of her reaction to Duke. She needed to know who you all were to feel safe. Do not cross this line, son. You will not like the consequences. Think of her as the sister you never had. Kid gloves. That is your only warning."

Derek laughed. "What? Dad, are you choosing her over your own children? Or is it you want her for yourself?"

The fist came out of nowhere. Duke watched as his father punched his brother in the jaw. Derek went flying across the kitchen, slamming into the wall across the room. "You arrogant piece of shit. Just because you look the way you do doesn't give you the right to use women the way you do. I didn't raise you to be this man. You have been told, do not approach her in any way, shape, or form. Don't even look at her. If I hear or see you anywhere near her, you'll get another one of those." Richard turned and walked out of the house.

Duke stood there in shock. In all his twenty-eight years, he had never seen his father strike anyone. His reaction told him that the scar on Loren's face meant more than anyone has said. Turning, he looked at his brother, who was getting up off the floor with what looked like shame on his face. He rubbed his jaw and looked at Duke. "I guess she is off limits."

"Don't cross him, brother. He is our father and deserves our respect."

"I know. What he said about me is the truth. I do use women."

Duke nodded. "You do, indeed. You are twenty-six. Shouldn't you be looking for the one who will be your wife?"

Derek chuckled. "I could say the same to you, brother."

"Yeah, I thought I had found her, but I guess I was wrong."

"Come on, we have work to do," Derek said as he made his way to the door.

Duke followed him. As they were headed to the barn, he looked up to see Loren talking to his father. Duke nodded his head to her and she cut him a small smile. He heard her say goodbye and that she would drop off dinner later in the day. His father smiled at her and patted her leg as she took off on her horse with her dog following behind.

Richard turned to see his sons walking toward the barn. "Derek," he called out. Derek stopped and turned to his father with his head hung. "I'm not going to apologize for hitting you. You were out of line, and I meant what I said."

"I understand. If it means anything to you, I am sorry for what I said."

"Thank you," Richard said and headed to the house.

Loren

LOREN HEADED BACK HOME. THE RIDE WAS, AS ALWAYS, BEAUTIFUL. It was coming up on the end of June, so soon it would be the fourth of July. She knew that they had a festival in town; she'd seen the flyers posted around. But she would spend it at her house. When she got home, she took Cupcake and got her settled and then went in and took a quick shower. She cooked and baked most of the morning. When everything was ready, she loaded up her truck and went in to change, then headed to Richard's.

It would be easier now that she had met his boys. At least she wouldn't shoot one of them. All morning, her mind kept wandering to Duke. His eyes were the most captivating. He was very quiet at the house, and his eyes followed every move she made. It was uncomfortable, while in the same sense, it was comforting. Almost as if he wanted to protect her. She was pretty sure she was wrong, as she was usually wrong when it came to people.

As she pulled into the long drive up to the house, she began to grow a bit nervous. *Will I see him?* Probably not, it was still early in the day, so hopefully they would all still be out working. Derek bothered her more than Duke. The vibe she got off of him was not a nice one.

He seemed very arrogant, and arrogant men were always a handful. She knew this from med school. Well, she had decided they weren't going to stop her from having a relationship with Richard. He stepped into the fatherly role in her life when she needed one the most.

As she pulled up in front of the house, she made a mental note to remember each truck that was parked there, just in case they happened upon her little house. She parked and got out, letting Jaz out. She took off immediately, heading for the barn.

"Jaz, come on," she called after her, but the dog kept running.

Inside the barn, she was greeted by Duke. "Well, hello there," he said as he patted her head. "What are you doing here?" Then he heard her voice.

"Jaz! Come on, girl."

The dog's ears perked up and she turned to run back to Loren, who had her body stuck inside the passenger side of the truck. Jaz ran up and leaned against Loren's legs. Duke had followed the dog out of the barn. As he was walking up, he heard Loren laugh and say, "You silly girl, you are going to make me fall. Come on, I need to get all this stuff in the house."

Duke cleared his throat, so she would know he was there. He watched as her body stiffen. He saw her hand tremble. "Do you need some help?" He asked gently.

She turned her head and looked at him. Duke saw the fear in her eyes; she tried to hide it but he saw it. She smiled a little smile. "Sure, if you wouldn't mind. I think I made too much. I thought you guys would want to have a meal with your father tonight. I know this must be a shock to you all." She turned and handed him a pie. "Careful, I'm afraid it's still a bit warm." Turning back into the truck, she handed him another pie.

"All this for us?" Duke smiled.

"When I get... well, I like to cook. It makes me happy." She picked up a huge pan of food. "I made my mom's lasagna. I hope you all like it."

"So, you've been cooking like this for my dad this whole time?" Duke asked her.

He watched as her face blushed and her head tilted down a bit. "Yeah, he has been very kind to me. I know your mom passed away, and I'm pretty sure he doesn't know how to cook all that well."

Duke laughed. Loren felt a bit more at ease. They made their way to the porch. Loren reached to open the door. "Richard," she called out as she pushed the door open.

He walked in from the dining room. "What have you got here?" he asked as he took the pan from her. His face was a bit concerned when he saw Duke walk in behind her with a pie in each hand.

Loren turned and took one of the pies. "I made dinner for you and your sons. I thought after the shock of this morning that you all would like to have a meal together." Smiling, she said as she leaned into him, "And I made strawberry pie with strawberries from my garden."

Duke watched as his father chuckled. "You didn't need to do this. I told you before that I can fend for myself."

She laughed as she walked past him and into the kitchen. "I didn't need a hundred acres of land either, but you were kind enough to give it to me. The way I figure, you are due home cooked meals until you leave us, so deal with it."

Duke just stood in the doorway and watched the scene play out before him. *Who is this woman?* She was so relaxed around his father, but so intense around everyone else.

His father looked at him. "Well are you going to stand there all day or are you going to bring that pie in the kitchen?"

Duke moved forward into this twilight zone that had become his life. When he made it into the kitchen, Loren was bent down putting the large pan into the oven. Duke nearly dropped the pie when he saw her. *Fucking perfect.* The pie pan hit the counter hard, making Loren jump and move to the counter. Duke couldn't help but see the terror in her eyes.

"Sorry," Duke said gently.

Richard saw the whole thing happen. "Loren, why don't you join us for dinner?"

Her eyes darted from Duke to Richard. He watched her visibly relax and smile at him. "Don't be silly, this is for you all. Maybe next time. I have some things I need to take care of anyway. I have to go see Mr. Jordan about my lumber. Just set the oven to three fifty for about fifteen minutes and you should be good. I'll come back in a few days to pick up the pans and to drop something else off." She walked over to Richard and gave him a quick hug. Duke noticed a mark on her shoulder as her arms went around his father. It seemed to continue down under her shirt. Turning to Duke, who was still in awe of her, she smiled and said, "Thank you for your help. I hope you enjoy dinner."

He just stood there and watched her walk out of the kitchen. Richard watched his son. When he heard her truck start, Richard said, "Sit down, son. You and I need to have a talk." Duke looked at his father and sat down. Richard began to talk. "What is going on in your head?"

"I'm not sure. For the first time in my life, Dad, I haven't a clue."

His father chuckled. "If I do this, if I tell you about her, you must keep it to yourself."

Duke thought about it for a minute. Did he want to know about her, or did he want to keep it a mystery? "Dad, you don't need to betray her confidence."

"She didn't tell me anything in confidence. In fact, she didn't tell me anything."

Duke crinkled his eyebrows. "What do you mean?"

"She is not some poor, helpless little girl, son. She is tough as nails. She's been out there all on her own for over three months. She has built a small barn, a green house, a chicken coop, and is building a bigger barn for the winter. She has a garden that puts your mothers to shame. She just had a horrific thing happen to her, and in the process, she lost her father and herself. But don't think for one minute that she needs saving."

"I wouldn't be arrogant enough to think that, Dad. You have to know me better than that. But I would like to know something. Are her eyes really that color?"

"Yeah, it's a very rare genetic mutation. One in like a billion chance of it happening. There's more to those eyes than the color."

"They're incredible. I thought they were contacts."

"Most people do, but I can guarantee they are not. I was there when she was baptized, and the priest was afraid of her." He chuckled. "I think he thought she was some kind of demon. You know, she never cried when she was a baby. She never got hurt. She was always just so beautiful."

Duke smiled at his father. "I think that is putting it mildly. I've never seen a woman more beautiful. She is flawless."

His father's face contorted. "She doesn't think that anymore. Well, she never thought that way to begin with, but now, she is a shell of the woman she was two years ago."

"Dad, you don't need to do this. If she wants any of us to know, she will tell us on her own."

His father nodded. Duke noticed he reached up and wiped his eyes, then he stood up and walked to the door. "You boys should stay for dinner. She made all this food for us. I think it would be nice." And he walked out into the dining room and then out the front door.

Duke sat there looking at his hands. Whatever happened to her was horrific enough to bring his father to tears. He couldn't even imagine. But it would have to keep. Today was not the day for telling stories.

The boys came in and everyone sat around and ate dinner together. Each of them had a slice of the pie. Derek didn't say much. In fact, he said nothing until he got up to leave. "I'm heading home. Thanks, Dad, for dinner. I didn't know you knew how to cook."

Richard chuckled. "I didn't make it. Loren did."

Derek nodded and left. Duke couldn't help but wonder if his brother was going out to get drunk again, which prompted him to get up and clear the table. When he finished, he said, "Dad, I'm going to head out. I'll see you in the morning."

His father nodded, and then Alex and Joe headed home. Duke drove by Derek's place on his way home, and sure enough, his truck was parked in his driveway. He couldn't help but wonder if what his father had said to him made a difference. Pulling up to the curb, he got out and walked up to the door and knocked.

Derek opened the door. "What are you doing here?"

"Just checking up on you. Everything all right? You didn't say much at dinner."

"Yeah, I'm fine, just going to crash. Been living hard these past couple of months. Just thought I'd take a break."

Duke nodded. "Good to hear. I'll see you tomorrow." He turned and walked back to his truck with a smile on his face.

LOREN SAT IN HER BACK YARD FINISHING HER LASAGNA. SHE NEEDED TO feed the chickens and then clean up her kitchen. But she couldn't stop thinking about Duke. He didn't say much, only watched her, which both made her nervous and excited. He was strikingly beautiful in a manly sort of way. She imagined what his chest looked like under that shirt. "Bet it's rippled with muscles," she whispered to herself. Laughing, she got up and walked to the makeshift barn and grabbed a bucket of chicken feed before heading toward the chickens.

She was daydreaming as she fed them. Something she hadn't done in years, something she hadn't allowed herself. But thoughts of Duke Reynolds and his deep green eyes haunted her.

When she finished with the chickens, who probably got more feed than they normally would have, she went back to make sure Cupcake had food and water, then back to her house to clean up. Sleep was not an easy thing to come by this night.

Duke

DUKE WOKE EARLIER THAN HE NORMALLY WOULD HAVE. HE NEEDED TO get to Mr. Jordan's to get a supply of nails and some lumber to fix the roof on the barn. Another good rain and they might have a problem. He made his coffee and jumped in the shower.

Mr. Jordan was just opening up when Duke walked in. "Hey, Duke, what can I do for you."

"I need a box of nails and about fifty two-by-fours. We've got a sagging roof. I'm worried that with one more good rain we will have a problem."

"No problem. Give me a few minutes. You got your truck or the Jeep?"

"Jeep."

"All right, if you want to pull around to the back, I will help you load them."

Duke pulled the ranch credit card out of his pocket and handed it to Jordan. He rang him up and headed to the back. Duke walked out as Loren was pulling up. She didn't see him until she was about two steps from him. Looking up, she took a step back. Duke noticed her shudder.

"Good morning," he said gently.

She smiled her shy smile. "Good morning. Is everything all right?"

Duke tilted his head. "Yes, why? Do I look like something is wrong?"

She smiled. "No. I mean, I guess I wasn't expecting to see you here."

Duke smiled at her, looking into her incredible eyes. "No, we have a sagging roof on the barn, so I stopped by to pick up some lumber to fix it today. What are you doing out so early?"

She smiled, and Duke felt himself inhale a deep breath. It was the first time she'd actually smiled fully. "I'm here to pick up a load of lumber myself. I'm starting my barn today."

Duke was shocked to say the least. "Alone?" He didn't mean it to sound demeaning.

Her reaction shocked him. She actually laughed. "Yes, by myself." Leaning into him, she said, "I'm not a defenseless little woman, you know."

Duke laughed. "I never said you were. It's just a big job. Being a gentleman, I must offer my services, if you need them."

Loren smiled. As she moved away from him, she turned her head and smiled, saying, "If I need them. Have a good day."

Duke stood there with a stupid grin on his face as she walked into the store. Shaking his head and chuckling to himself, he climbed into his Jeep and headed to the back of the store. Ten minutes later, Loren pulled up with her truck.

"Fancy meeting you here." She chuckled as she got out.

"I think you are following me." Duke smiled at her.

She stunned him when she busted out laughing. Her smile was full on, reaching to her eyes, which crinkled along with her nose. *Stupid.* He stood there looking stupid. She breezed by him and started loading two-by-fours into the back of her truck. Duke had just loaded the last of his, and without asking, he started to help Loren. With him and Jordan helping, it didn't take long to fill the back of her truck.

Jordan came out with a giant box of nails and put it on the front seat of her truck. "Well, thank you, gentlemen, for your help." She turned to Duke. "Let your dad know that I will be by in a few days. Oh, did you all enjoy dinner?"

Duke smiled at her. "Yes, ma'am, it was mighty delicious. Especially the pie." *What the hell was that? I sound like an idiot.*

Loren smiled at him. He thought he saw her blush a little, and she nodded to him and walked to her truck. Duke stood there as she drove away. Jordan startled him when he said, "Beautiful woman. Too bad she has that scar running down her face."

Duke turned and looked at him. "Well, that was rude."

"No, I didn't mean it like that. I meant, something terrible must have happened to scar her beautiful face. Maybe a car accident or something. She is a lovely woman."

Duke chuckled. "Yes, she is. You have a good day." He got in his truck and headed out to the ranch.

~

Loren

AS LOREN DROVE OUT OF TOWN, SHE GIGGLED, SAYING TO HERSELF, "OH my God. Who am I? What was that?" *Was I flirting with him? No, I was just being nice. He is, after all, Richard's son. He wouldn't hurt me. Would he? He is someone who could hurt me.*

She pushed all of that aside in her mind. There was no use thinking those thoughts. She knew she would never, could never let anything happen. No way could she let anyone see her scars. It was bad enough she had the one on her face. Looking in the rearview mirror, she ran her hand down her jaw. *I wonder what he thinks. I wonder if Richard told them what happened to me.* Panic started to rise in her. "He wouldn't have done that," she said out loud.

Before she knew it, she was pulling up behind her house and parking her truck. For the better part of her day, she unloaded the wood from her truck, dug the holes for the footings to her new barn, and set the posts.

When she finished, she went in and took a shower and slipped on a sun dress. There was no one around to see her scars. Grabbing a cold glass of lemonade, she went to sit in her yard and look at the work she had accomplished over the last several hours.

Loren smiled as she sat looking at the posts she'd set all by herself. Laughing, she couldn't help but remember when she and her father built their barn. He taught her a lot of things. Especially how to be independent. Looking around, she smiled at the chicken coop she built, the green house, the makeshift barn for Cupcake. When she finished her drink, she got up to feed the chickens and Cupcake. Jaz followed on her heels. She liked to chase the chickens around. But, tonight, Loren wasn't going to give her the chance.

"Not tonight, Jaz. I'm tired. It's been a long day, and I have to get up early and go get another load of wood. That barn isn't going to build itself." Just as she finished her sentence, Jaz's ears perked up. "What's the matter, girl?" Loren set her bucket down and turned toward the house just as Jaz took off running. A bit of fear welled up in her. It was around seven at night, still light out. There shouldn't be anyone or anything around. She headed toward the house. As she rounded the corner, she heard a truck. Pausing before she headed inside to get her gun, she spotted Jaz running toward her. The truck was right behind her. It was Richard. Letting out the breath she hadn't realized she was holding; she breathed a sigh of relief. He pulled up and continued to the back, and she noticed the back of his truck filled with lumber. "Crazy old man." She chuckled and headed toward the truck as he backed it up to her already hefty pile. As he opened the door, she said, "What are you doing here?"

"Well, I thought I would give you a hand. I was in town and picked up a load for you. My way of thanking you for dinner," Richard said. She laughed, but when Duke walked around the truck, she froze. "I brought some help. I hope you don't mind."

"Let me go change and I'll help," she said and turned to go back in the house.

Duke stopped in his tracks when she turned around. He could see the huge jagged scar on her back. It didn't stop on her shoulder like he thought, and from the looks of it, it continued past her dress. When she rounded the corner, Richard turned and looked at Duke.

"Dad, what the hell?" he whispered.

"Forget you saw it. Just keep it to yourself," Richard whispered. "Come on, let's get this wood unloaded so we can leave her in peace."

Duke felt as if his stomach was going to turn over. He swallowed the bile rising in his throat. Turning to his father, he nodded, and they began to unload the wood. Loren came out a few minutes later and the three of them emptied the truck. It took about a half an hour. When they finished, Loren said, "Why don't you two take a load off and I'll get us some homemade lemonade."

"Who am I to refuse a pretty girl," Richard said. She laughed and they followed her up to the house.

A few minutes later, she came out with a tray. On it was a pitcher of lemonade, three glasses, and some cookies. "I made these yesterday. Help yourself. They're oatmeal raisin." She poured them drinks and then sat on the grass. "I appreciate you bringing the wood. It will save me a trip."

"If you want, I can meet you in town in the morning and fill it back up again," Duke said softly.

She looked at him and then at Richard. Richard gave her a gentle smile. Loren hesitated. If he did that, it meant they would be alone here. "Well..."

Duke interrupted her. "I don't have to. I just thought you could use the help. It's not a problem. I have a barn to repair anyway."

Richard interjected, "I can have Derek work on it until you get there. Loren, are you all right with that?"

She didn't want to be rude or sound ungrateful. But she wasn't sure it was a good idea. "I'm pretty sure I can handle it. But thank you anyway," she said to Duke.

He nodded at her and smiled. "Not a problem, and you are welcome."

"Well, we should be heading back. Thank you for the drink and the cookies," Richard said. When he stood, Loren hugged him.

"Thank you," she said softly.

Duke nodded to her and she watched them walk back to the truck, then waved as they pulled away. Loren went in the house and locked her door.

Duke

DUKE DIDN'T SAY ANYTHING FOR A WHILE AS HIS FATHER DROVE DOWN the makeshift driveway. Hell, if you didn't know where to turn, you would never see it. Finally, he found his voice. "Dad, what happened to her?"

"Son, if I tell you, it will change your perception of her. I see the look in your eyes. I'm not a blind old man, you know. And I also see the look in her eyes. Let it happen naturally, Duke. When and if she feels ready, she will tell you. If I tell you, it will change the way you see her and possibly the way you are starting to feel about her."

Duke chuckled. "What exactly do you see?"

Richard just laughed. They didn't say anything else the rest of the way to the ranch. When Duke got out of the truck, he said, "I'll see you in the morning."

"Duke, why don't you call it an early day tomorrow? We can take two trucks up to Jordan's."

Duke smiled. "Not a problem, Dad. I'll see you tomorrow."

As he drove home, he couldn't get that scar on her back out of his mind. Who was he kidding? From the moment he saw it, he wanted to hold her. To make her feel safe. Shaking his head, he couldn't even imagine what happened to her. Whatever it was, he wanted to know. He drove past Derek's place. His truck was parked in the driveway; maybe he did learn something about himself. Duke smiled and went home.

As he lay in bed, he couldn't get that scar out of his mind. *What the hell happened to her?* That wasn't from a car accident. Someone hurt her. He tried to sleep, but it was a fitful one.

CHAPTER SIX

LOREN WOKE EARLY, just as the sun was rising. She laid in bed and watched it rise out her window. This was a beautiful place, and she felt safe here. Smiling, she got up and had her breakfast. Today, she took Jaz with her to pick up her load.

Mr. Jordan and one of his workers helped her, so it didn't take long. By the time she got back, she decided to forgo the unloading and chose to cook instead. Today, she made a pot of spaghetti sauce. By the time she finished and the sauce was on a low simmer, she made lunch and then went out to unload the truck. Just as she laid the last boards down, two pickup trucks pulled up, Duke and Richard. Both trucks were loaded down with wood.

Shaking her head and smiling she walked up to them. "I think I am going to have to pay you for all your help. You really don't need to do this."

"Nonsense," Richard said. "No need to pay us."

She laughed, looking at Duke and said, "Shrugging your work off on your brother?"

"Nope, just left it. It'll still be there tomorrow." He smiled at her.

"As will all this wood. I have another twenty-four hours before I can start building. The posts need to set."

He smiled at her. "Can I ask you a question?"

"That was a question." She giggled.

To Duke, it was music to his ears. "Who taught you how to do this?"

When her smile faded, he wanted to take it back.

"My father and I built our barn back in Texas, the summer before I went to college."

Duke nodded to her and began hauling wood. The three of them worked for about an hour unloading the trucks. Richard said to her, "Listen, we are going to run back to Jordan's and get another load for you. Why don't you come with us? We have a lot of daylight left."

"Well, I wish I could, but I have sauce simmering on the stove."

"Sauce?" Duke said.

She smiled. "Spaghetti sauce. I was going to jar some up and bring it up after I took a shower later. But if you are going to be working for me, I suppose I could feed you both. Would you like to stay for dinner?" She was looking at Richard.

He chuckled. "I never pass up a home cooked meal. We'll be back soon with another load."

She watched as they climbed in their trucks. Her eyes shifted from Richard to Duke, who was watching her again. He nodded and smiled at her. She smiled back and turned to head to the house. She figured she had enough time to make some bread for garlic bread, so she got busy. By the time they returned with the wood, she had it rising in the warm kitchen. Heading out to unload the trucks, she found herself a bit excited to see Duke again. Watching him lift the wood made his muscles flex, and he had some muscles. Hell, she wasn't dead.

Laughing as she walked up caused Duke to ask her, "Do I look that funny?"

She laughed again. "No, I was just thinking to myself. You know, you have to enjoy your own company living out here by yourself. I'm actually kind of funny."

Duke laughed. "I bet you are."

They worked for another hour, and when they finished, Loren looked at the pile of wood. "I'm going to need more wood."

Richard laughed. "Well, I have nothing to do all week."

She turned and looked at him. "Thank you, but you don't need to do anymore. Come on, I've got a few beers if you want one."

"Beer sounds good to me," Duke said as she headed to the house. "So, Loren, don't tell me you built this little house as well."

She laughed. "No, but I did design it to fit me and Jaz."

"Where did you get Jaz. She's a good-looking dog. Is she a Sheppard?"

"My mom gave her to me after the..." She paused. "She is a Sheppard, Lab mix. My best friend."

Duke wondered what the after was. He almost asked her but decided not to. She was talking to him freely so he just let it go. They walked up to the house, and Loren went in to get some beers. While she was in there, she put the bread in the oven and started the timer. Walking out, she handed them each a beer and sat down in the grass. "The bread will be done in twenty minutes, so dinner will be in about thirty. Is that all right?"

Richard smiled at her. "Better than all right. But you don't have to feed us."

"Don't be silly, Richard. You just loaded and unloaded four pickup trucks worth of lumber. Personally, I think I'm getting the better end of the deal. Besides, I was just going to bring the sauce over to you."

They laughed and sat without talking, enjoying their beers. Duke broke the silence. "This is a nice piece of land. I'm glad my dad gave it to you."

"Me too," Loren said as she looked out at the land.

"Did you build that chicken coop?" Duke asked, already knowing the answer.

"Sure did. The greenhouse, too. That was hard. It took me almost a month. I broke a few of the glass panes on the top, but I managed. I ordered all the pots and seeds. Mr. Jordan should have those in pretty soon."

"How do you have electricity out here?" he asked.

"I have solar panels on the roof and a tank to catch the rain. Although, we haven't had much, so I had to have someone come out and fill my tank twice already. But I have another one on order, so when it rains, I'll be all set." Duke sat there with a secret smile on his face. She had it all together. Self-sustainable. "I'm trying to leave the least amount of a carbon footprint as I can. That and I don't want to destroy this land."

Richard looked at her. "Would it be acceptable to use your restroom?"

She chuckled. "You know where it is. Help yourself."

Richard got up and left the two of them there. Duke looked at her, as he always did. Loren smiled at him. "Why do you always look at me?" she asked quietly.

Duke was caught off guard. "I'm not sure. Does it bother you?"

"Sometimes, yes, it does."

"I'm sorry, I don't mean to make you uncomfortable," he said.

"It's just… Well, I don't know, maybe it's because I'm not used to someone looking at me all the time. Mostly, people are looking at my scar, but you don't seem to be. You seem to be looking at my eyes."

He smiled. "They are incredible eyes. I've never seen eyes that color before."

"Do they make you nervous?"

"No, not at all."

She laughed. "Most people think they are contacts."

"I would imagine they do. Can I ask you a question?"

"Sure."

"What did you do before you came here? You had mentioned you went to college."

She looked at him and swallowed. She knew one day someone would ask her this question. "I was a neurosurgeon. But not anymore," she said softly, turning her head away.

Duke didn't know what to say. *A neurosurgeon? Fuck, what happened to her that she isn't anymore?* "I'm sorry, it's none of my business. I don't mean to pry."

"No, it's all right. It's who I was, what I did. Now, I am me and do this."

"This is good."

She chuckled. "Yes, this is very good. Will you excuse me? I think the bread is done. Do you want garlic bread or just bread and butter?" She stood up as Richard walked up.

"If I was choosing, I would say garlic," Duke said.

"Make that two," Richard said.

"Garlic bread it is then. I'll be back in a few minutes. Do you guys want another beer?"

"I'll come and get them so you don't have to come back out, and if you don't mind, I'd like to use your facilities to wash up," Duke said as he stood. He really wanted to see the inside of this tiny house. Loren nodded and he followed her in. He was a man, after all, and of course, he had to look at her ass. What a fine, fine ass it was.

"The bathroom is there." Loren pointed to a door to his right.

Duke looked around. The kitchen was to his left. It was rather large, with a full-size stove and oven and a full-size refrigerator. There was a set of stairs that ran along the back wall. Looking up, he saw the ceiling was dotted with skylights. The loft where he would imagine was her bedroom was rather large. It covered the entire kitchen. As Duke turned to go to the bathroom, he saw a nice size sofa, and along the back wall was a bookcase. He walked into the bathroom, closing the door behind him. It was rather spacious, with a toilet, sink, and a reasonable shower with what looked to be a small tub.

When he came out of the bathroom, a dining table had mysteriously appeared, partially covering the bottom two steps. It was set with three place settings. Duke stood by the door totally in awe of the space. It was decorated simply, a few touches here and there which he imagined were Loren. There were fresh flowers on the counter in the kitchen. On the counter, he noticed clean dishes sitting next to a full-size sink.

Loren smiled at him as she opened the fridge grabbing two beers. "This place is great," he said. "It's tiny, but not."

She laughed. "I'm a tiny girl. It's perfect for me." And perfect she was. She handed Duke the beers. "Would you give that to your dad? I need to stay here; otherwise, the garlic bread will burn. Five minutes?"

"Sure thing," he said, reaching for the beers. His fingers brushed hers as he took the bottles.

The sensation he felt, they both felt, caused Duke to pause. He heard Loren's intake of air as their eyes met. For Duke, it was as if time froze. Looking into her eyes felt like magic. The whole thing lasted a few seconds, but to Duke, it felt like a lifetime. Loren pulled away first and went back to the kitchen, leaving Duke just standing there, watching her.

Loren peeked up at him, their eyes connecting again. "Do you need any help," he asked softly, nearly a whisper.

Shaking her head, she said just as softly, "No, I've got this." Then she nodded.

Duke turned and opened the door, walking out to hand his father a beer. He sat down stunned. *Who is that woman?*

"Something happen in there?" Richard asked him.

Chuckling, Duke said, "Not sure."

"Just take it slow, son."

"Yeah."

Nothing else was said, and the quiet felt good for Duke. He so enjoyed the ranch, especially at this hour, when the work was done, the day was coming to a close. When the sun set, the sky was darker than dark. The stars shined the brightest out here. He knew he could never live in a big city. He was a country boy.

"Dinner's ready," Loren called out the door.

Both Richard and Duke got up and went inside. Duke was amazed at how comfortable the three of them were in her tiny house, that wasn't tiny at all. They ate and talked. Richard told stories and they laughed. Duke felt a special bond with his father this night, something he had forgotten as he grew up and moved out on his own. When they finished, Loren had pie, of course. All in all, it was an evening well spent, with good company, good food and good times.

"Well, I'm going to head back. I will see you in the morning," Richard said to Loren.

She smiled and hugged him. "Thank you for your help today."

He nodded and left. When Loren shut the door and turned, Duke was standing, collecting the dishes to carry to the kitchen.

"Here, let me get those," she said as she reached for the plates, taking them from Duke.

"I'll help you clean up." He took the glasses off the table.

Loren put the plates on the counter, then turned to open the fridge. "Nonsense, why don't we just leave this and go out and have another beer and watch the sun set. It's one of my favorite times of the day."

Duke set the glasses on the counter and took the beer she offered him. Together, they went out and sat in the chairs. The moment couldn't have been more perfect, he thought. The quiet, the sky and all of its magnificent colors, a cold beer after a fantastic meal, and the company of probably the most beautiful woman he had ever seen.

"Thank you for dinner. It was delicious," he said, looking at her.

She smiled. "Thank you."

Looking at her posts, he said, "You sure you can build that barn by yourself? Not that I am doubting your mad skills. I mean, look at that wonderful chicken coop."

Loren was taking a drink from her beer and started laughing, spitting it out on the ground. Duke started laughing with her.

"I'm sure. Well, at least, I hope I'm sure. When I did it with my dad, there were two of us. Raising the roof may prove to be the hardest, but I'm up for the challenge, and I have a few months before the cold starts."

"How about you let me help you?" he asked her sweetly.

She sat there thinking then turned her head to look at him. His eyes were so green. "Why aren't you married?" she asked, "Oh, God, I'm sorry. That was so rude." She shook her head. "I shouldn't have had these beers."

He chuckled. "No, it's fine. I had a girl. We were together for two years. I thought she was the one. I even went looking for rings up in Bozeman for her. But one day a few months back, I had the flu and went home. When I got there, she was in bed with one of my oldest friends. We kind of broke up after that."

"Oh my God. I'm so sorry. That had to be horrible."

"Well, it was and it wasn't. We didn't really have all that much in common. I mean, I thought I loved her, but now that we aren't together, I'm not sure that's what it was. I think it was just great sex."

He noticed Loren blush. "That's so sad."

Nodding, Duke agreed, "Yeah, it is. How about you? Why aren't you married."

Loren didn't say anything. Duke watched as her whole body tensed up. She got up and started walking toward the new barn. Duke sat there watching her. He watched as her hand came up to her face, his heart racing. She was crying. He got up and headed toward her. "Hey, are you all right?" he asked her softly, trying with all he had not to reach out and touch her.

"Yes," she whispered.

He couldn't stand it anymore. He watched as his shaking hand reached up. He gently curled his fingers around her tiny shoulder. "Loren," he said, turning her slowly. "I'm so sorry. I didn't mean to upset you." His hand was tingling at the touch of her skin. He fought to keep his thumb from gently caressing her.

"I'm not upset," she whispered as she wiped her face again. "It's just that I can never get married."

"Why would you say that?"

"Because no man would ever want me," she answered matter of fact as she walked away, heading toward the field beyond the barn.

Confused and scared by the words she said, he followed her as she chugged her beer. She stopped walking about two hundred feet from the barn. The last bit of the sun was hanging on. It was more than halfway beneath the horizon. He stood next to her, not saying anything. She reached over and took his beer from him and chugged it. "Sorry, I'll get you another."

When she turned to walk away, Duke reached out, putting his hand on her stomach to stop her. It covered her entire stomach, nearly hip to hip. "Loren, don't. I don't want another beer."

She laughed; well, it was a half-laugh, half-cry. "Well, I think I might."

"You are beautiful," he whispered, stepping closer to her.

She turned her head toward him, "No, I'm not," she whispered so quietly he barely heard her.

His other hand came up and he cupped her face, tilting it up so he could look at her. "Yes, you are," he whispered as his head slowly moved toward hers.

Looking into his eyes, Loren licked her lips. Duke brushed his lips across hers. To Loren they felt like feathers. "Duke," she said breathlessly, just as he full on kissed her. The bottles dropped to the ground, and her hands found their way to his chest. He was totally prepared for her to push him away, to slap him. But she didn't. She let him kiss her. Bringing his other hand up to cradle her face, he deepened the kiss. He could taste salt as their tongues touched. He pulled back to look at her, seeing tears streaming down her cheeks.

"I'm sorry," he whispered as he touched her forehead with his.

Licking her lips, she said, "I'm the one who is sorry."

He chuckled. "Why are you sorry? I kissed you."

She took a step back from him, his hands falling away from her face. "I know you see the scar on my face, and I know because I feel you watch me, that you saw the scar on my back. What I don't know is what your father has told you."

Duke shook his head. "I've asked, but he said it wasn't his story to tell."

She smiled a little smile. "No, I suppose it isn't."

"If I ask you, will you tell me?"

"I've never had to tell it before. I'm not sure I can," she whispered.

Duke stood there looking at her. All he wanted to do was scoop her up in his arms and hold her. "Then don't. It's not necessary. I'm sorry if I overstepped. But I'm not going anywhere. I would like to continue to grow this friendship. Can we do that? Forget the kiss?"

She smiled. "I would like that, to continue to grow this friendship, but I can't forget the kiss. It was the single most perfect thing about me. Thank you."

Stunned, Duke stood there looking at her. *How can she say that?* She was perfect. He was sure that he was falling for her. "Good, now can I walk you home? I have to get up early to haul some wood for this slave driving woman I met a week ago. I mean, she thinks she is the boss of me or something."

Loren laughed. "I would like that very much. And if this woman is so mean to you, then why are you working for her?"

Duke chuckled. "She has the most incredible eyes, and she bewitches me with them." He was looking at her when he said it, and he saw her blush. At the door, he reached up, wrapping his fingers around her head, rubbing his thumb across her cheek. "Good night, Loren. Sleep well."

"Good night, Duke, and thank you for the kiss."

He dropped his hand, laughing. "Anytime, beautiful." He turned and walked back to the truck. She watched him drive down the makeshift drive that was actually a field. When the tail lights disappeared over the ridge, she went in, closed the door, and leaned against it. Her fingers traced to her lips. "He kissed me," she whispered to the room. Smiling, she pushed off the door and cleaned up the kitchen, putting the leftover spaghetti sauce in containers to take to Richard. When the house was clean, she took a shower and went to bed, thinking about Duke and that kiss.

Duke

DUKE DROVE HOME WITH THE TASTE OF HER ON HIS LIPS. IT WAS THE single most excellent kiss he'd ever shared with a woman. She was shaking in his arms. Her words hung in his mind and his heart. *Why would she think no man would ever want her? What the hell happened to her?*

As he lay in bed, the questions rolled in his mind. That kiss stayed with him. He needed to be careful. She was starting to trust him, and according to his father, that is something she didn't do. The way she shook when someone got close to her or moved too fast around her was bothersome.

Duke sat up straight in bed. "Someone attacked her. Those scars are knife scars," he said to the empty room. He got up and went out into the living room and grabbed his phone. He looked up her name.

Article after article popped up on his phone. He scanned through them, reading about her achievements. She was the best neurosurgeon in the country. Revered by her peers. Graduated from high school at age fourteen, Harvard Medical School in three years, top of her class. Honor after honor.

Then he came to the article that stopped his heart and brought tears to his eyes. Words floated together. *Left for dead, stabbed eleven times, face slashed, back opened from shoulder to waist, coma for five months, rehabilitation for over a year, father had a heart attack and died in her room.* Duke dropped his phone and his heart ached at what he read. He couldn't imagine anyone hurting someone like that. Not her, not Loren. She was so kind, so sweet. Why would anyone want to hurt her like that? Duke sat on his knees in his living room, hurting for her. Gut wrenching pain seared through him as he tried to stop the words from flying through his brain.

He laid on the floor and let the tears fall for the pain she'd endured as he drifted off to a restless sleep. When his phone rang, it startled him awake. Picking it up, he answered. "Yeah," he barked.

"You all right?" Derek said.

"Yeah, why wouldn't I be?"

"Well, it's ten in the morning and Dad's wondering where you are."

"Shit. Fuck! Tell him I'm on my way to Jordan's and I will see him there."

"Hey, Duke, you sure you're all right? Something happen with Julie?"

"What? Fuck no, I just slept late. See ya later." Duke hung up, dragged himself off the floor, and got dressed. He didn't make coffee, he didn't eat, he just wanted, no needed to see her. Loading the one-by-fours into his truck was quick. He was a maniac.

On his drive out to her place, he couldn't stop thinking about how scared she must have been. How strong she was to have survived. He found himself feeling proud of her. Impressed even more, in awe of the woman.

When he pulled up, Derek, his dad, Alex, and Joe were all unloading trucks of wood. "What the fuck," he said to himself. He didn't want anyone there with her.

Climbing out of the truck, Jaz ran up to him. "Hey, girl," he said as he squatted down to pet her.

Loren walked up. "So, am I going to have to regulate your beer intake?" She giggled. "Hungover?"

Chuckling, he looked up at her. "Not at all. I had some things on my mind and couldn't sleep."

"Oh yeah, and what would that be?"

He stood up to his full height, reaching up to run his thumb along her jaw. Leaning in, he whispered in her ear, "A certain kiss."

He felt her swallow. "Yes, that kept me up last night as well."

Without them knowing, Richard stood across the way watching the interaction between them with a smile on his face. He knew that Duke was falling for her, and from the look on Loren's face, he believed she was falling for Duke. His heart was full. Richard knew Duke would take care of her, that he was a good man and he would protect her, even if it was from herself. Nodding his head, he went back to work.

"Good to know," Duke whispered to her. Smiling, he dropped his hand and looked around. "It looks like the whole crew is here."

"Yeah, Richard thought it would be better if they just got all the wood and then I wouldn't have an excuse to run around. I could just get busy."

Duke laughed. "Sounds like Dad. Well, I should get to work. According to Jordan, there is another truck load coming in today."

She laughed, following him to the back of the truck. Together, they unloaded it, along with the four others. When they finished, Loren pushed the hair off her face and took a deep breath. Laughing, she said, "Well, I think I have some work to do."

No one said a word. The boys just stood there looking at her.

"What?" she asked.

Derek spoke. "You are going to do this by yourself?"

"I am indeed," she said, squaring her shoulders.

"Well, boys, let's get back to the ranch. We have a barn to repair. Weatherman says rain is coming in the next few days. I figure, if you all work on it together, we should get it done by the end of tomorrow."

"Thank you all for doing this," Loren said as they scattered to their trucks. They all waved to her. She stood and watched as they drove away, one by one. Duke was the last to leave. He smiled at her and tipped his hat at her. She felt her heart jump and a smile came to her face. She tipped her hat to him as he drove away. Turning around ready for work, she said to Jaz, "Well, girl, you ready to get started?" Jaz barked at her and she laughed.

Loren spent most of the day framing out the barn, losing complete track of time. When she nailed the last board on for the day, she smiled, satisfied with her accomplishment. Next was to make the framework for the top of the barn. She needed to go into town in the morning and pick up the hardware to connect the joists.

She hauled all her tools back to her makeshift barn then fed Cupcake and the chickens. When she went in the house, she made herself a sandwich. Sitting on her little porch steps, thoughts of Duke and that kiss invaded her mind. His eyes that morning, how they looked into her soul and touched her heart. He was thinking about their kiss all night, too. She couldn't help but smile. "Come on, girl," she said to Jaz. "I need a shower and then some sleep."

Duke

DUKE WAITED UNTIL HIS BROTHERS LEFT FOR THE DAY BEFORE HE headed home. As he came out of the barn, he saw his father sitting on the porch watching him. Smiling, Duke walked over to him and sat in the chair next to him.

"I saw what took place this morning," Richard said to him.

"Just having a conversation." Duke chuckled.

"Last I remember, conversations didn't require touching like that. Something you want to talk about?" He chuckled.

Duke didn't say anything for a long time. "We were just talking."

"Okay," his father said.

"Dad," Duke paused and swallowed hard. "How did she survive it?"

His father didn't say anything for a long time. "She was in a medically induced coma for five months." His voice was shaky. "Be careful, son."

Duke nodded, and they didn't say anymore for a long time. They just sat there. "Well, I'm going to go. I didn't sleep well last night."

"You aren't drinking again, are you?" his father asked gently.

Duke chuckled. "No, Dad, I think those days are behind me."

"Good to know, son. Try and be here early. I want to get that roof finished before the rain comes," Richard said as he walked off the porch.

Duke drove home thinking about how her skin felt under his fingers. She was so beautiful, and brave, and strong. Never would he underestimate her. Pulling up to his apartment, he got out. As he walked up to the door, he heard someone call his name. Turning, he saw Julie walking up. Shaking his head, he said, "What do you want?"

"Well, I haven't seen you around for a while. I miss you," she whined.

"Julie, go home. I'm not interested. I have to be up early," he said as he reached for the door.

Julie put her hand on his. He stood there looking at it, but he felt nothing. Pulling his hand away, he looked at her. She had lust in her eyes. There was no way he felt anything for her. It didn't matter to him that she was beautiful, or that she was fantastic in bed. He wasn't taking this ride again.

"Duke, we're so good together," she purred.

He stepped away from her. "Listen, you fucked my oldest friend for a year while we were together. I can't forget that. I don't want you, Julie. Not anymore. Now, please, just go." He put the key in the door and went inside, leaving her standing on the street.

Duke ran up the stairs to his apartment and locked the door. There was no way he was getting involved with her again. Not after that kiss. He took off his clothes and jumped in the shower. He needed to be up early.

While he lay in bed, his mind wandered to her eyes, her incredible haunting eyes. What color was that? He sighed, smiled, and closed his eyes to sleep.

CHAPTER SEVEN

LOREN

LOREN WOKE JUST as the sky was changing from black to a simply beautiful array of pink. As she looked out her window, she could see part of the sky still dark with the night and the other part bringing a new day. A good day.

Stretching, she crawled out of bed, grabbed her clothes, and made her way down into the kitchen to make some coffee and eggs for herself. When she finished, she took the giant roast out of her fridge, seasoned it up, and put it in the oven. She was going to slow cook it all day while she worked, and then take it over to Richard's for them to eat.

After she fed Cupcake and the chickens, she jumped in her truck and headed into town. Mr. Jordan's place should be open by the time she got there. She loaded her basket full of everything she needed, paid, and was walking out of the store when Duke pulled up. She hadn't noticed him, and when he said good morning to her, it kind of scared her and she dropped her box on the sidewalk.

"Shit," she said as she bent down to pick everything up.

"I'm sorry, I didn't mean to startle you." Duke squatted down to help her.

"No, it's fine. I just had my mind somewhere else." She smiled at him.

"Probably the same place mine has been."

Loren looked up at him, their eyes locking. They stared at each other for a minute or two. "Maybe," she whispered then turned away. As she put the last bracket into the box, she lifted it, standing.

Duke stood up and smiled at her. "Good Morning, Loren."

The smile on her face touched her eyes. "Good Morning, Duke. Have a good day." She turned and headed for her truck, leaving Duke standing on the sidewalk looking like a love-struck teenager.

Loren looked at him as she backed out of her spot and just smiled. He watched as she drove out of town. Walking into Jordan's, he picked up the supplies they needed to finish the roof today and headed out to the ranch.

Loren spent all day making the beams for the roof. When she finished, she stood proud at her accomplishment. After putting her tools away, she headed to the house to add all the vegetables to the roast to cook, then she showered and changed.

She made her gravy and packed everything into her truck before heading over to Richard's, smiling as she drove the twenty minutes to the house. Pulling up, she opened the door and Jaz jumped out, taking off to the barn. Loren just laughed and shook her head.

Grabbing the huge roasting pan off the floor of her truck, she headed into the house. Opening the door, she called out, "Richard." But no one answered. She went to the kitchen, put the roast in the oven, and turned it on.

She found a piece of paper in the dining room and wrote a quick note.

Richard,

I made dinner for everyone, my thanks for the help yesterday. It's four-thirty now, so it should be done by five-thirty or six. Just warm up the gravy and you are good to go.

Thanks Again.

L.

Leaving the note on the counter, she headed out to get the gravy and the pie she made the other day. Taking them into the house, she put the gravy in a pot with a lid and put it on the stove top. Smiling to herself, she headed outside, but just as she opened the door, a Jeep pulled up outside the barn. She stopped when she saw a very leggy brunette with some pretty short shorts on climb out.

"Duke," the leggy woman yelled out. "Duke, where are you?"

A minute or two later, Jaz came running out of the barn and stopped to look at the woman. "Well, who are you?" she said as she bent to pet her. Jaz backed away from her. Loren couldn't help but smile. "Stupid dog," she said loudly.

Then Loren saw Duke walk out. "Hey, she's a smart dog, aren't you girl?" Loren smiled. But it was a short-lived smile. The leggy woman threw her arms around Duke's shoulders and kissed him right on the mouth.

Loren's heart stuttered in her chest. She stepped off the porch and headed to her truck. Jaz took off toward her as Duke pushed the woman away from him. He stood there frozen as his eyes locked with Loren's, as she stood with the door open waiting for Jaz.

When Jaz jumped in, so did Loren. She pulled out of her spot and took off toward home, shaking her head. What did she expect? He was a gorgeous man. To him, she was probably just another notch in his belt. Why did she think she was any different?

Duke

"FUCK!" DUKE YELLED. "WHAT THE HELL ARE YOU DOING HERE? I TOLD you last night I was done. I gotta go?" He turned, walking to his Jeep, yelling to his dad. "Dad, I gotta run. Check the kitchen."

"Wait, Duke. Where are you going? I came to see if you wanted to go to the fourth of July festival with me," Julia said.

Duke turned to her. "Julie, I wouldn't go to hell with you. Leave me alone." Climbing into his Jeep he took off after Loren. There was no way he was going to let her think there was anything between him and Julie. But when he pulled up to her house, she wasn't there. "Fuck!" he yelled as he hit the steering wheel.

Climbing out of the truck, he walked up to the back of her house and sat down in the chair. Not knowing how long he sat there with his head in his hands, he finally heard her truck. As Loren walked up to him, he lifted his head. He could see that she had been crying. He stood up.

Loren put her hand up. "You don't owe me anything. I get it. She is very beautiful, and I'm pretty sure she doesn't have any marks on her. It's fine."

"Loren," he said.

"Listen, Duke, we don't know each other. We are hardly friends. I basically told you the other night what my life is going to be, so I get it."

"What exactly do you get?" he asked. His heart was slamming in his chest. He knew now she had feelings for him.

Shaking her head, she reached into the bag she was carrying, which he hadn't noticed, and pulled out a beer. She twisted off the top and chugged it down. He stood there watching her empty it. "I get that," she belched, "I get that this," she waved her hand up and down her body, "looks nothing like that. I'm not stupid." Reaching into the bag, she pulled out another beer and did the same thing. "Hell, I spent over a year in therapy before I could even get up the nerve to look in the mirror again, so I get it. I really do. And I'm okay with it."

"You don't look okay." He smiled at her.

"Don't be turning on that instant charm thing you do, with those green eyes of yours. I'm not stupid. I'm just something new to play with." She giggled, "Too bad I'm a horror freak show you don't want to see." Her voice wavered and cracked. Reaching into the bag, she produced another beer. Twisting off the cap, she chugged it down, emptying it.

Duke was impressed. She was from Texas, so he had no doubt she could drink him under the table. "Loren, can I explain what you saw?" he asked.

"No need to explain. I don't care. We shared one kiss because we were in a moment. A stupid moment where I forgot all about this." She waved her hand up and down her body again. "I won't do that again. Don't worry about it. Go home, go back to your father's. I made dinner for you all to thank you for delivering the wood. Go eat your rewards." She started walking toward the house.

"Loren," he said.

She spun around. "What do you want, Duke? What? You want to see the freak show?" She dropped the bag on the ground and pulled her shirt over her head, dropping it on top of the bag. Then she undid her jeans and pulled them to her knees. Her arms spread out on either side of her. "See? Do you see, Duke? No man is ever going to want this when they can have that." She turned slowly for him, showing him every stab mark on her body.

Duke stood there looking at her. He counted the scars, eleven in all. They were all over her chest, stomach, and he could see one that went under her panties. God, they matched her eyes. He could feel the tears in his eyes as they flowed over the edges. Who would do that to someone? As she turned, putting her back to him, he saw the scar down her back. *My God, someone sliced her open.* His heart broke for her. When she turned to face him again, she saw he was crying.

"See? I'm so ugly, you cry." She bent and pulled up her pants. Picking up her shirt and beer, she turned and walked away from him.

Duke couldn't breathe. "No!" he yelled. Loren jumped and froze. He moved around to the front of her. "Look at me," he whispered. She shook her head. "Look at me."

Her head rose, and he saw the pain in her eyes. He saw the hurt he caused.

"You are beautiful," he whispered. He reached up and wiped the tears from her cheeks.

"Please just go back to the leggy woman. Just please go, Duke."

"I can't," he whispered. "I can't."

"You don't want this. I don't want this. I have nothing to give you. I can't even give myself to you. Just…"

Duke put his hands on her face and kissed her. Sealing his mouth over hers, stopping her words. She tasted like beer and heaven to him.

She kissed him back. God help him, she kissed him back. She pulled back and shoved him away from her. "No, I'm nothing, I have nothing to give you."

Duke stood there stunned as she moved around him and ran into her house.

Loren leaned against the door and cried, her hand coming to her lips. She left the beer sitting on the counter and stripped off her clothes and got in the shower. No amount of scrubbing would remove the scars. No amount of tears would wash the pain away. Even when the water turned cold, she still scrubbed at them. Her skin became raw, the washcloth leaving burning marks across her skin as she scrubbed them.

Finally, she ended her torture. She hated what he did to her. Grabbing a towel, she wrapped her raw body in it and opened the door. Making her way to her loft, she dug out some clean clothes, her sleep shorts and a t-shirt. Laying on her bed, she looked out the window toward the makeshift barn. The little light on the outside cast a shadow on Duke's truck. He didn't leave. Loren lay there thinking about what happened. She survived. That was her punishment for letting that man die. She survived.

The tears just came. They didn't stop. Closing her eyes, she finally fell asleep. Sometime in the night, she got up to use the restroom. She was wide awake. Looking out the window, she saw Duke's truck still parked out there. "Why is he still here?" She opened the door and Jaz ran out before her. "

"Hey, girl," she heard Duke say.

Loren walked to the back of the house and sat down. "Why are you still here? You should be home in bed with the brunette, having a life."

"The leggy brunette is my ex. She was at my place last night when I got home. She wants me back. I told her no. In fact, I shut her down and went in the house. Today was her trying again. And again, I told her I didn't want her. I want nothing to do with her."

Loren chuckled. "Well, it didn't look that way to me. But it doesn't matter. You will always be connected to her. She will always come back to you. Duke, truly, I am not an option for you."

"Loren, when I kissed you, I meant it."

She laughed. "I'm just new. You said it yourself, it's the eyes. If I could stand to have contacts in, I would wear them. I don't know how many times men have told me how beautiful I am. How incredible my eyes are. I am, or was, some kind of novelty. They just wanted to be with me because of my eyes. None of them were worth my time. Duke, I feel comfortable around you and your brothers. But that is just because of Richard. Trust me, if we had met on the street, I wouldn't have looked twice at you." She wanted to hurt him, make him go away. She couldn't do this. She would never be able to do this, not with him, not with anyone. No one would have her.

He chuckled. "Nice try. You didn't know me in that restaurant, and you shared a look with me."

"So, I never said you looked like a troll."

He laughed. "So you like the way I look?" She didn't say anything. "Loren, I was on the receiving end of those kisses. I am not imagining what we felt. This isn't one sided. I saw you. I saw each mark, each scar, and I'm not afraid. My heart exploded because I couldn't imagine the fear you felt, the fight you fought to survive. And you did. You survived it, and now you are here. For whatever reasons, you are here." He watched as she wiped the tear from her cheek. "Loren," he whispered, reaching for her hand. She let him hold it. "I'm not going to hurt you. The only way you are going to believe me is by my actions. I'm not going anywhere. You will see." He leaned in and whispered, "I so totally enjoyed kissing you, and I am going to do it again. You can bet on that."

She squeezed his hand. He got off his chair and kneeled in front of her. "You are so beautiful. Believe that. I don't lie."

She smiled. "You are such a bad liar," she whispered.

Duke smiled at her. Reaching up with his other hand, he cupped her face, pulling her toward him. "No, I don't lie," he whispered as his lips brushed hers. "I'm not going anywhere. I'll wait for you." His mouth covered hers gently. Pulling back, he looked into her eyes. "I'm going to go home now. I just waited to tell you that. Sleep well."

She nodded, because she was unable to talk. Watching him walk away, she felt the loss of him. Without thinking about it, she jumped up, calling out to him. "Duke." He turned and jogged up to her. "It's late, you don't have to drive home. You can stay here."

He smiled at her. "I've seen your couch. I am six-two. No way am I going to fit on it. It's fine, I can go home."

She smiled. "You have at least a forty-five-minute drive to town. You said I can trust you?" He nodded. "I can share my bed with you."

"Loren, no. It wouldn't be right." He was being noble, although he had no clue why. Anything, he would give anything to sleep with her in his arms.

She giggled. "Jaz can sleep between us. I have a very big bed."

He looked at her tiny house and laughed. But who was he to argue? It's what he wanted. He could be a gentleman. It was the middle of the night and he was beat. "All right, as long as Jaz is there. I don't want you to take advantage of me."

Loren laughed, turning toward the house. "No chance of that happening. I'm saving myself for marriage."

Duke about had a heart attack. *Did she say what I think she did? Holy shit, no fucking way is she still a virgin. Look at her. Fuck.* He followed her into the house.

"You know where the bathroom is. When you get done, just climb the stairs. Watch your head."

He nodded and went to the bathroom. When he came out, it was dark except for a soft light coming from her loft. As he started up the stairs and the loft came into view, his eyes couldn't comprehend what he was looking at. She had a king-size bed up here with room to move around on either side. There was a nightstand on either side, one drawer each and very little. There was a dresser just to the left of the stairs, which served as a short wall. She was sitting up on what he believed to be the side she slept on. There was a dog bed at the foot of her side, and Jaz was curled up in it. Her tail wagged when she saw him.

"Wow, not what I expected," he said gently.

She just giggled. "Jaz doesn't want to sleep by you. She thinks you snore. Is that all right with you? I mean, I don't want you thinking I am going to seduce you."

He laughed as he crawled over to his side, pulling his shirt over his head. He laid back and undid his jeans. Loren laid down with her back to him so he didn't feel uncomfortable. She felt him get under the covers. "You in?" she whispered.

"I'm in. Thanks for this. Good night, Loren," he whispered.

She turned off the light. "Good night, Duke."

He laid there with his arm behind his head, smiling. Her bed smelled like her, like vanilla and strawberries. He closed his eyes and sleep came easy for him, as well as for Loren. During the night, she had rolled over and put her head in the crook of his arm. Unknowingly, he wrapped his arm around her, then turning on his side, he draped his other arm over her waist. She was tucked into him when he woke. He didn't want to move; she felt so good in his arms, like she belonged there. In his heart, he knew she did. He waited for her to wake on her own. It wasn't until the sky started to light up.

As Loren began to wake, she realized that she was wrapped in Duke's arms. She felt so safe. Smiling, she tilted her head up and was met with his incredible green eyes. He slowly removed his arm from her waist.

"Good morning, Duke," she whispered.

He couldn't stop himself. She was so damn beautiful. His hand came up to touch her face. His mouth had a mind of its own, brushing across her lips with his. Loren responded, she wanted to kiss him. He made her feel beautiful, something she hadn't felt in a long time. Duke opened his mouth to her, and a beautiful dance began between them. He felt himself pull her closer to him. He wanted to feel her body on his. Loren's hands slid up his chest, setting Duke on fire. She moved them to his face and then his hair, pulling him closer. He deepened the kiss. How could he not? She tasted like heaven. Such a slow and beautiful kiss, nothing hurried.

He knew he had to stop, though he wanted more. Hell, who wouldn't want more? But not like this. Not coming off last night. Hell, he still believed she was a virgin. Slowing down the kiss, he gently pulled back, their eyes connecting. "So beautiful," he whispered, gently brushing his lips across hers.

Loren smiled at him. "Sorry about that," she whispered.

His thumb traced along her bottom lip. "Nothing to be sorry about. Loren, please don't forget this. Don't think it means nothing."

"I won't forget," she whispered, leaning toward him to kiss him again. This time, she initiated it, and it was full of fire.

They lay in each other's arms enjoying the euphoric feeling of something new between them. There was no touching, no feeling each other's bodies. It was a simple blissful mating of the mouths, their tongues getting to know one another, becoming comfortable with this incredible dance.

Loren pulled away. "The sun is up now. I'm sure your father is wondering where you are."

He chuckled. "I'm sure he'll be fine. But I should get going, because I'm pretty sure if I stay in this bed any longer, I know I'm not going to want to get out."

He watched as she blushed. "I know, I don't want to. But you are right. I'll get up first so not to embarrass you."

Now, it was Duke's turn to blush. He was fully hard, and in his boxers, there was no hiding it. He chuckled. "How very gallant of you."

As she rolled over and scooted to the dresser, he caught a glimpse of her perfect ass in her tiny sleep shorts. He couldn't hide the moan that escaped him. Loren turned to smile at him. "Is there a problem?" she said playfully.

Rolling over onto his stomach, he moaned. He felt the bed dip, and when he turned over, Loren was close to his face. She covered his mouth with hers. "Thank you, for everything you said to me last night. It meant a lot."

He reached up and took her face in his hands. "I meant every word of it, beautiful. Every fucking word of it." Pulling her down on top of him, he kissed her with every ounce of passion in him. When he wrapped his arms around her like this, he realized just how tiny she was. He could lay his hands flat on his own sides with her wrapped in his arms.

Loren pulled back a little. "I should go and get dressed so you can take care of things." She had a wicked smile on her face as he let her go and she crawled down his body. Again, he was treated to her incredible ass as she stood to go downstairs.

Duke laid in the bed for a few minutes after she went down, trying to get himself under control. In all his adult life, he had never felt like this. His urge was always to release his desire, but not today. Today, he hurt, yes, but not like he had in the past. In the past, it was all about raging hormones; now, it was something new, something different. He heard Loren come out of the bathroom. "Do you want some coffee?" she asked him.

"Coffee sounds great." He smiled as he grabbed his jeans and pulled them up. Sitting up, he pulled his t-shirt over his head then turned and started making her bed.

Loren opened the door and let Jaz out. As Duke came down the stairs, he saw her dropping bacon in the pan. There were eggs on the counter. He went toward the bathroom, closing the door behind him, and spotted a new toothbrush on the sink. Smiling, he did his business and then brushed his teeth. When he came out, Loren was flipping the bacon. "How do you like your eggs?" she asked, handing him a cup of coffee.

"Over easy, but you don't need to feed me," he said softly.

Laughing, she said, "Don't be silly. I can't send you out there to work in this heat all day without the proper nutrition, and besides, I know you didn't eat dinner last night. So, how many? Three?"

He chuckled. "No, I didn't eat last night, but I was where I wanted to be, and food was not on my mind. Yes, three is fine."

She turned, looking at him as he sat on her loveseat. "What was on your mind?"

She drew him in with her eyes, with her sweet sultry look, that he was pretty sure she had no clue she was giving him. Bringing his cup up to his lips, he said, "You," as he took a drink. "Good coffee." He smiled at her.

Loren felt her heart flutter. "Three eggs coming up." He watched her as she cracked egg after egg into her pan. She could feel his eyes on her, making her feel excited about what was happening between them. But as always, the dark monster that lurked just below her finely tuned exterior kept her from really letting anything come to the surface. She walked over to the table and set the plates down. Duke got up and sat down. "Breakfast is served," she said playfully.

He sat down. "Thank you," he said as he began to eat.

Loren sat and ate her food. About halfway through her eggs, she said, "Why do you watch me?"

Duke chuckled. "To me, you are like a beautiful sunset. A different color every second as it sets. Each time I look at one, it's different. More beautiful, if that's possible."

Loren felt her body blush from her toes to her head. She lifted her eyes to look at him. "I'm not that. I'll never be that."

"You are to me." He reached to touch her hand. "I told you last night. I'm not going anywhere, except to work." He stood and put his plate on the counter. "Thank you again."

Loren stood to follow him outside. They walked together to his truck. Duke turned to her, reaching up to cup her face with one hand. Bending to reach her mouth, he kissed her deeply. When he pulled away, he whispered, "To last me until I can do it again." He kissed her again. Just as quickly, he let her go and climbed in his truck.

Loren stepped back and watched him drive away. She went about her morning business of feeding Cupcake and then the chickens. She collected the eggs and headed back to the house. Her eggs were cold, so she gave them to Jaz then cleaned up. "Time to get to work," she said to Jaz. Together, they headed out back.

With the help of some rope and Cupcake she managed to get one of the roof braces in place. It took her all day, but she got it up and secured it. She cheered herself when she released the rope and it stayed in place. She hit the joist with her shoulder, and it didn't waver. Smiling, she climbed down and put Cupcake out in the little pasture she had fenced off for her.

She was cleaning up when Jaz took off out to the front of her house. As she was walking out of the barn, she heard a truck. Grabbing the rest of her tools, she went back in the barn. When she came out, Richard was climbing out of his truck.

"Wow, you did that all by yourself?" He smiled at her, looking at her first roof joist.

"I did. Well, me and Cupcake. Took me all day, and a lot of figuring, but I got it up there, and it's sturdy. I did my father's shoulder test."

Richard laughed. "I remember he tried that test on the barn out in the back, the one with the four wheelers in it. He went flying when the joist gave way, thought he broke his neck."

Loren busted out laughing. "Yeah, he told me about that. But, in his version, you didn't secure the brace properly."

Richard laughed. "I didn't. But he doesn't need to know that."

They laughed. "Can I get you a beer, or some coffee?"

"That would be nice. I brought your pans back." He opened the truck and pulled out her pans. "Thank you for dinner. It was delicious."

Loren took the pans from him and they headed up to her house. "So, what's your poison? A beer or some coffee?"

"Coffee would be nice, thank you," Richard said as she opened the door.

He followed her in and she made some coffee. They sat at the table not saying anything. "Is something on your mind, Richard?"

He chuckled. "I suppose there is. I heard from Joe what happened out at my place yesterday."

She crinkled her eyebrows. "What happened?" She was genuinely concerned.

Richard gave her a strange look, like she was crazy. "Between you, Duke, and Julie."

Loren laughed. "Nothing happened. I dropped the dinner off and saw him in an intimate embrace with her, so I left. There was no drama." *At least, not there*, she thought to herself.

"Well, perhaps I was misinformed. I was under the impression that something happened. Duke took off after you, and he didn't return until this morning, and he was wearing the same clothes he had on yesterday. I don't mean to pry into your personal life. But he is my son, and you are my God daughter. I promised your father I would protect you and take care of you."

Loren felt herself blush, and she smiled at him. "I'm glad that you are worried about me. It's part of why I am here. I am comfortable and not afraid so much as I would be, as I have been in a city. Duke wasn't at dinner because he was here with me. He had the same clothes on because he spent the night."

Richard slammed his hand on the table. "That son-of-a…" Loren put her hand on his to stop him.

"Richard, it wasn't what you think. I was upset, yes, when I saw her wrapped around him. I didn't even know why. Maybe because I think I like him. If I'm being honest here, he kissed me a few days ago. It wasn't what you think. It just happened. I thought deep down inside that it meant more to me than to him yesterday. You know what happened to me, and you know how I feel about myself. Well, when I saw her gorgeous body wrapped around him, I got upset." She laughed. "I went into town and bought some beer, and by the time I got home, he was here sitting out back. I think I was wallowing in my own self-pity. I chugged a few beers while we had it out. I told him to leave. I told him I was not an option for him. That I could never be what he deserved. That he should go and mend it with her. That she was everything I could never be."

Richard held her hand. "Loren, that is not true. You are ten times the woman she could ever be."

Squeezing his hand, she continued. "I got a bit over dramatic, brave I suppose, and I stripped down to my bra and panties and showed him why he should choose her."

Richard looked at her. "What did he say?"

Swallowing the lump in her throat, she whispered, "He cried and told me I was beautiful."

Richard smiled. He knew his son was an honorable man. "So, why is he still wearing the same clothes?"

"Well, after my fit of drama, I went into the house and went to bed. Because of the beer, I got up in the middle of the night to use the bathroom and saw his truck was still here. He was sleeping in the chair out back. I went out, we talked, and he was going to leave. It was the middle of the night, and I couldn't let him drive all that way."

"He spent the night here? With you?" His body tensed. He really didn't want to have to kill his son.

Loren giggled. "Yes Richard, he even slept in my bed. But he was a complete gentleman. Nothing happened. Nothing at all. This morning, I made him breakfast and he went to work."

"So, nothing happened?" Richard said.

She giggled. "I appreciate you worrying about me, Richard, but you raised Duke. Is he not a good man? Should I be worried about him?"

He laughed. "I did raise him, and yes, he is a good man. But I raised Derek as well, and I'm afraid he would've tried his hardest."

"Good thing then that it was Duke. Richard, Duke and I had a moment in Bozeman in a restaurant, long before we knew each other. I don't know what is happening between us, but he promised me that he was going to prove to me that he is worthy of me. Whatever that means. We don't know each other, but I think I would like to get to know him better."

"That is a good idea. Take it slow."

Loren busted out laughing. "Thank you, Richard, for caring enough to be here and for being totally uncomfortable with this discussion. I appreciate it."

"Just making sure one of my sons doesn't do something he will regret."

"I'm sure what is or isn't happening between us is something we have to figure out. I can guarantee you that no lines will be crossed. I mean, I was drunk last night when I stripped in front of him, and I was being a bitch. He never touched me, never attempted to touch me. I'm not even sure he could bring himself to touch me. I know I can't let him get that close. I have nothing to offer him. You know what happened to me. I know you haven't seen the scars, but I do. Every day. It took me nearly a year to even look in a mirror." Her voice got quieter, sadder. "That leggy brunette is and always will be far more than I can ever be. He loved her once, perhaps he still does on some level. I'm not stupid. She is far more beautiful than I could ever be. I'm pretty sure she is flawless. Me, well, I have thirteen marks on my body that say otherwise." She took a deep breath. "I told Duke all of this. I'm not in over my head. I am a woman, and he is so handsome. He kissed me and I enjoyed it. But that's all it was. Friends is all we can ever be."

"Aww, Loren. That is so not true. Everything that you just said is not true. I don't know what is in his head, but I do know that he is interested in you as a woman."

She shook her head. "It's just because I'm new. Because of these eyes. He said so himself, that they bewitch him. The novelty will wear off eventually. I'm not in over my head, and I like to think that on some level I still have the ability to think rationally." She chuckled. "Says the girl who left the world and is hiding out on a ranch in the middle of nowhere."

He patted her hand. "Well, I'll get out of your hair. I just wanted to make sure you were all right." He stood and opened the door.

Loren followed behind him out into the evening. They walked silently to his truck. She hugged him and watched him drive off. Reaching up to touch her lips, she smiled as she remembered the way Duke's lips felt on hers. "Jaz, what am I doing?" The dog looked up at her. "This can't happen." She nodded and went to the barn to saddle Cupcake. She hadn't ridden in a few days. "Hey, girl, feel like stretching your legs?" She patted the horse on the neck.

They trotted out to the field, and Loren kicked her in the sides and they were off. There was no specific direction they ran. She just needed to clear her head. As the sun was setting, Loren started back home, reaching it well after dark. As they trotted up to the barn, she saw a truck parked next to her barn. She rode up on her horse to find Duke lying in the back with his legs hanging off the tail gate.

"What are you doing here?" she asked as she climbed off her horse.

"I'm not really sure," he said sitting up.

Loren smiled at him. "I had a visit from Richard today. He's a bit concerned with your chivalry."

Duke busted out laughing. "Seriously?"

"Yeah, pretty much. And you're welcome." She teased him, walking toward the barn. She went in and started taking off Cupcake's saddle.

Duke followed her and was leaning against the door. "Why?"

"Why what?"

"Why am I welcome?"

Loren put the saddle away and grabbed the brush and started brushing Cupcake. "For saving your life, of course."

"And exactly how did you save my life?"

Loren tossed the brush in a bucket and fed Cupcake, then grabbed the bucket and filled it with food for the chickens. As she walked out, she stopped in front of him, putting her hand on his chest. She felt his intake of air. She patted him and looked up into his eyes. "Because your father was going to kill you for sleeping with me. He thought you deflowered me." With a wicked gleam, she smiled and continued out to feed the chickens.

Duke stood frozen to his spot. A warmth like he'd never experienced moved through his body. *Deflowered? Fuck! She is a virgin.* He finally got the feeling back in his legs and pushed off the door, walking toward her. "So, you're telling me that my father came over here to discuss whether or not I was a gentleman?"

She laughed, and it was music to his ears. "He sure did."

"And what did you tell him?"

With her wicked look, she said, "The truth." When she saw his face, she laughed. "Relax, big guy. I didn't tell him that you held me while we slept or that you kissed me stupid. I just told him what happened and why. Your brother Joe told him that something happened between you, me, and the leggy brunette."

Duke smiled. "So I kissed you stupid, did I?"

Rolling her eyes, she walked past him back into the barn. "Out of all that, the only thing you heard was that you kissed me stupid?"

"Well, a man likes to know these things." He puffed out his chest.

She walked past him to her house. "Easy, boy, pretty soon that ego is going to be bigger than you."

He stood there and watched her silhouette disappear around her house. The light in the bathroom turned on. He knew she was in the shower, so he walked up and sat down in one of the chairs. He wanted to kiss her again, to hold her in his arms. He wanted her to know he was serious about this. He wanted to get to know her, to know her. All day today, he couldn't get her out of his mind. Even when Julie showed up again, begging for him to take her back. Wanting him to escort her to the fourth of July festival. Duke told her no, again and again. He knew where he was going to be on the fourth, and that was right here in this chair. It was Friday night, and he didn't want to be anywhere but here. He saw that Loren had a makeshift fire pit, so he took it upon himself to build a small fire for them.

Twenty minutes after she went in the house, she came out in a little sun dress. "You're still here?" She sounded shocked.

"Yes, is that a problem?"

"Depends." She sat in a chair.

"On what?"

"On what you plan to gain from all of this. Because it can't be me."

He stood up. "Hey I brought some beers. You want one?" She watched as he walked to his truck and pulled out a small cooler and walked back.

As she looked at him, she couldn't deny the fire stirring in her gut. He was gorgeous. He was ripped with muscles and had perfectly straight, white teeth. He could use a haircut, but she wouldn't change a damn thing about him. She knew in her heart that he belonged with someone who could and would give herself to him completely.

DUKE WATCHED HER FACE IN THE LIGHT FROM THE FIRE. IT WOULD tense then relax. They sat for a long time, sipping on their beers but not saying anything. He didn't care, he just wanted to spend time with her.

"Duke," she said.

"Yes."

"Why me?"

"I don't understand your question."

"Why are you here? What could I possibly give you? I have nothing."

He didn't say anything for a long time. He just stared into the flames. Then he set his beer down and got up, moving to kneel on the ground in front of her. "There isn't a reason why, but a feeling deep in the pit of my gut that tells me I can't walk away. I don't know how to explain what is happening to me, but when I saw you in that restaurant in Bozeman, something in here changed for me." He tapped his chest right over his heart. "I followed you out but you were gone already. Then I saw you at my father's. Do you remember that day? I was on the four-wheeler." She nodded. "When I saw you standing on that porch, I literally lost my breath. I thought it had to be fate, because there you were. When you looked at me, my heart stopped. It wasn't the color of your eyes, because I couldn't see the color. It was you." He took a big breath. "Then that day in the dining room of my father's house, when you looked up into my eyes, I felt you. I felt everything about you. I was filled with a sense of, I don't know. Completion. I am drawn to you, Loren. I couldn't stay away if I tried, and believe me, I have tried. But every time we crossed paths, or shared glances, I felt it stronger and stronger, this pull."

She sat there with tears falling from her eyes with no knowledge she was crying. No man had ever said anything close to that to her. He reached up to wipe them away. "Don't cry, beautiful. I told you, I'm not going anywhere."

"What do you want from me, Duke? I have nothing to give you," she whispered.

"You, beautiful. I want you," he whispered as he moved closer to her.

"I'm nothing," she whispered as his mouth covered hers.

She opened to him, felt his passion, his desire for her. "You are so wrong," he said into her mouth. "So wrong." He kissed her again. Slowly, he pulled back. "How about we just stop worrying about it and let it be whatever it's going to be?" She nodded. Duke saw the fear in her eyes. "Come here, beautiful." He pulled her off her chair onto his lap. He wrapped his arms around her. "Whatever will be, will be."

She giggled. "That's from the old Doris Day movie."

"Do you feel better?" She shook her head. He chuckled.

"Am I hurting you?" she whispered.

"Not at all." He breathed in her scent, vanilla and strawberries.

They sat, with her on his lap, watching the fire for some time. Time had no meaning where Duke was concerned. He could've sat like that all day or all night. She fit in his arms. The fire slowly burned away.

"Come on, you need to get some sleep," he whispered to her.

"I don't want to. I feel..." She stopped.

He chuckled. "Yeah, I know what you are saying."

"Duke?"

"Yeah?"

"Will you..." She stopped and looked up at him.

God, she was breathtaking. "Yes," he whispered as he kissed her. They sat kissing until the embers faded away in their fire.

Pulling back, Loren said, "You have to get up early."

He chuckled. "I do. It seems my father has sentenced me to help this crazy woman build a barn. He said she raised the first joist alone with her horse. Said she was slamming her shoulder against it to see if it would hold."

She giggled. "He is so funny. I don't need your help."

"That may be so, but can I help you? It would give us more time to get to know one another." He kissed her again.

"Well, since you asked me so nicely, I think it would be all right. But, it's late, and by the time you get home, you won't get much sleep. I'm a slave driver and would want you back here at the crack of dawn. If you haven't gotten enough sleep, you could be more of a hindrance than you are actual help. And I need to pay attention to the dangerous job ahead of me, not worry about my workers."

He kissed her tenderly. "What do you propose we do about that? I could come after I've had my required amount of sleep."

"I guess I might be able to compromise. With the understanding that it would be in my best interest."

"Of course, your best interests are always most important."

Turning her head, Loren leaned in and floored him with her kiss. He felt his hands move around her, pressing firmly on her back, pulling her into his chest. When her chest touched his, he couldn't stop the moan that came from deep inside of him. God, she felt like heaven.

Pulling back a little, but not away from him, she swallowed and said, "You could stay here again."

He knew how much it took for her to say that to him. He wanted nothing more. "Would that be a good idea?"

"Probably not. Duke, I've never been with a man. I think you know that. Your father promised me that you were an honorable man. I am not afraid when I am alone with you. It's just the opposite." She swallowed. "I feel safe," she whispered. Duke didn't say anything, he just felt more of what he had been feeling. "I haven't felt safe in a long time. I don't think I can give you what you want right now. But..."

Duke stopped her with a kiss. "No, don't say anything more. I would love to stay with you. But that, what you said right there, makes me say no to your invitation, for now. I want you to feel safe. So, I am going to walk you to your door and kiss you goodnight. Then I am going to drive myself home and come back in the morning."

She smiled at him. "See? Noble."

He laughed, helped her stand, and then got up. "Far from noble. Trust me, I want to go in this house and climb into to bed with you and kiss you and hold you all night long. But there will be time for that. I want this with you, and I am more than willing to work on it and do my best not to let you believe or think you are just some notch on my belt."

She laughed, turning to him. "Thank you." He wrapped his arms around her and kissed her goodnight.

Loren went in and locked the door, making her way up to bed. She heard Duke's truck start and pull away. Laying in her bed, she thought about the kisses they shared, about the words he said to her. *Could he be real?* Closing her eyes, sleep came easily to her.

❧

DUKE DROVE HOME WITH A SMILE ON HIS FACE. HE KNEW HE WAS falling fast for Loren. She was a woman of unique ambivalence. Pulling up to his apartment, he couldn't help but notice it was just after one in the morning. He chuckled to himself as he climbed out of his truck.

He walked into his apartment, slipped off his clothes, and jumped in the shower. With flashes of Loren in his mind, he felt himself getting hard. His hand slid across his stomach, washing the day's grime off of him. His fingers touching his cock sent shudders through him. Shaking his head, he thought, *No way, not today*. That belonged to her. He would suffer the fate of blue balls.

He turned off the water, grabbed a towel, and dried himself off. Then he walked into his bedroom and dropped down onto the bed. He didn't turn on any lights. What was the point? He was there to sleep and change clothes. Hell, he didn't even want to be there. Lying on his back with his arm behind his head, he closed his eyes, and the memory of Loren in his arms was there to comfort him. He felt his cock getting harder as he remembered her body against his. His hand moved down and he grabbed himself, giving a few pumps to his cock then grabbing his balls. Jesus, he was hurting and in need of a release.

"Do you need some help with that?" A voice came out of the darkness.

Duke knew the voice. Reaching over, he pulled the sheet over his body. "What are you doing here, Julie? I told you today, I want nothing to do with you."

"Apparently, you are thinking about me. You're hard as a rock." He felt the bed dip with her weight as she leaned into him. Her hand came to rest on his stomach just above the head of his cock.

Duke hmphed and moved her hand. "Trust me, this has nothing to do with you."

"Well, sure it does. You haven't been seen with a woman since me, so it has to be me."

"Julie, I've been nice about this," he said as he got up and grabbed some clean clothes, getting dressed. "And now I am going to tell you one last time, maybe in a way you can understand me. I don't fucking want you. You cheated on me for a year. I am so over you. Just the thought of touching you or even fucking you makes me want to vomit. Stay here if you fucking want. I'm leaving. And stay the fuck away from me, or I am going to get Charlie involved. I'm done, Julie."

He walked out of his own house at one-thirty in the morning and headed to Loren's. He would sleep in the truck by the barn.

～

JAZ, HEARD THE TRUCK PULL UP AND CRAWLED UP NEXT TO LOREN, sticking her nose in her face. "Mmm, what's wrong, girl?" Jaz nudged her. Loren rolled over and looked out the window. "What's he doing here?" she whispered. She got up and made her way out to his truck and knocked on the window. Duke sat up. "What are you doing here?" she asked him.

"You wouldn't believe me if I told you. Go back to bed. I'm fine out here."

She laughed. "Get out of the truck, Duke." She opened the door.

"I'm fine, Loren, really."

"Come on." She reached for his hand and pulled him out. "I can't sleep knowing you are out here. It's fine. You can tell me what happened, but if I'm guessing, it has something to do with the leggy brunette."

"I'm embarrassed to tell you what happened, but yes, it's the leggy brunette," he said.

Loren laughed as she pulled him into her house. "Lock the door. I'm going back to bed."

He followed her up the stairs, getting a perfect view of her perfect ass. "At least you took a shower," she said as she turned away from him while he got undressed.

"How do you know I took a shower?"

"You smell clean." She giggled.

He got under the sheet and laid on his back. Loren rolled over to look at him. "Tell me what happened."

"She was at my place, sitting in the chair in the bedroom. I didn't turn on any lights when I got home. I just dropped my clothes and got in the shower. This is the embarrassing part. While I was washing myself... well, I... I um..."

She giggled. "I am a doctor, you know. I do know what happens."

"Oh, God, I'm dying here." She giggled. "Anyway, I didn't do anything about... you know, and I got out and went to bed. I was laying like this, and well, I was thinking about you and our kisses and... you know. She thought I was thinking about her and offered to relieve me of my... um... you know." Loren busted out laughing. "This is not funny," he said.

"Oh, but it is! Go on."

"I told her I didn't want her, said a few not-so-nice things to her. She wouldn't leave so I got up, got dressed, and came here. I told her that if I found her in my house again, or if she harassed me again, I was going to the police. And now, I am here, beet red in the face, sleeping in bed with you, after leaving my ex half-naked in mine."

"She was naked in your bed with you?" Loren wasn't sure she like that thought.

"Yes, but I didn't stay there. I came here, totally prepared to sleep in my truck."

"Why didn't you go to your father's?"

He rolled onto his side, reaching up to move the hair from her face. "You smell better."

Loren laughed so loud Jaz picked her head up and looked at her.

"I am so glad I can bring humor to your life at my expense." He pouted.

"Oh, you poor baby. Having to leave your bed because there is a stunningly beautiful, leggy woman with perfect tits in your bed. I feel so bad for you."

"Yes, you should feel bad for me. I am tired and in need of sleep."

"Goodnight, Duke," she said, giggling as she turned her back to him. Reaching up, she turned off the light.

"Good-night Loren," he whispered. He didn't roll over but stayed on his side. As his eyes adjusted to the dark, he could see part of the scar on her back. This close, it looked huge.

He couldn't help himself; his hand just moved on its own. His fingers gently started at the top of her shoulder and moved slowly down. He felt her body stiffen. "It's all right, beautiful."

"Please, Duke. Don't," she whimpered.

He pulled his fingers away. "Loren," he whispered.

She shook her head, but she didn't move. He put his hand up again. His finger trailed down her scar, then up. He spread his fingers out to touch the rest of her skin.

Loren turned to face him. "Why are you doing this?"

"Because, I can't not do it. I want to touch you, beautiful," he whispered into her mouth just before he kissed her.

Loren kissed him back, her heart slamming in her chest. He wanted to touch her. She felt herself move closer to him. Pulling back, she whispered into his mouth as her hands cupped his face, "Why?"

"I don't know. I just know that I have to. May I?"

She looked at him for a long time and then rolled over so he could touch her back. His fingers started at her shoulder and worked their way slowly down until they met back of her shirt. After a slight pause, he continued over her shirt to her waist, then slowly and carefully he lifted her shirt. He trailed his fingers along her scar, feeling her body tremble with each touch.

"You are so soft," he whispered. Moving closer to her, he brought his mouth down gently on her scar. He felt her intake of air. "Relax, beautiful."

She couldn't. He was the only man who had ever touched her. His mouth continued down her back, over her shirt to her waist. Loren held her breath as she slowly turned onto her back. His mouth was now level with her stomach. Closing her eyes, she lifted her shirt completely off her body, exposing the majority of her scars.

When she looked at Duke, his eyes were closed, and fear welled up inside of her. She knew she was too horrible to look at. She went to roll back over, but Duke put his hand on her stomach to stop her.

"Loren, what are you doing?" His voice sounded strained.

"I don't know. I thought…" She stopped.

"What, beautiful? Tell me what you thought," he begged her.

Shaking her head, she lifted her arms to cover her breasts. "No." She sounded so full of pain.

Duke moved up her body so he was lying next to her. Slowly, he removed her arms and wrapped his around her, pulling her against his chest. "Ahhh," he moaned when their skin made contact. "Tell me," he groaned.

"I thought you might want to touch me," she whispered.

"Do you want me to touch you?" He searched out her mouth, kissing her deeply. His leg slid between hers as he rolled her on her back, his lips never leaving hers. Her nipples were hard as pebbles pressing into his chest. He was so hard, he swore he would internally combust.

"I think I do, yes. Duke, I feel safe with you. I need you to see what he did to me, what happened to me."

"Let me turn on the light, beautiful, so I can see." He moaned in her mouth, kissing her again, deeply. With her hands in his hair and his wrapped around her, he pulled her beautiful body against his. He couldn't get enough of her. She was heaven to him, a place he never wanted to leave. He felt her hand leave his head, and then the soft glow from her light filled the loft. He didn't want stop kissing her, but she needed him to see her. Pulling slowly back, he moved his hand to her face and looked into her beautiful eyes. "You don't have to do this if you're not ready. I am happy to just lay here and hold you, kiss you some more."

Smiling her sweet smile, she nodded her head. He kissed her gently and pushed up onto his side, his eyes closed. She reached up and touched his face. "Open your eyes, Duke. It took me nearly a year to be able to look at myself," she whispered, her voice full of emotion. He took her hand in his and kissed it. Moving it above her head, he kissed her again.

Pulling back from her, he opened his and looked into her perfect eyes. Her pupils were dilated, making the lavender color appear nearly purple in color. "So beautiful," he whispered to her.

His eyes moved down her face to her mouth as she drew her bottom lip between her teeth. He continued to her neck, to the first scar that was on the top of her right breast. His fingers gently touched it. He leaned in and kissed it. The second was near her sternum on the left breast. After kissing it, he moved on. Her breasts we ample, and he was sure they would fit in his hand easily, but that wasn't what this was about. Her nipples were big and hard and dark pink. He wanted to feel one in his mouth, but he didn't. She was trusting him to look at her scars. He touched and kissed each one. When he reached the waistband of her shorts, he got up on his knees and gently pulled them down. So far, he had kissed nine, but there were two left. One was just below the waist of her shorts on the left hip. He touched it and then kissed it. Moving her shorts down just a bit more, he found the eleventh one just on her hairline. When he touched it, her back arched off the bed. He looked up at her, noticing her stomach muscles had tensed. Bending down, he planted his lips on the scar as she cried out. Her whole body trembled.

Duke pulled her shorts back into place and crawled up her body. As he wrapped his arms around her, pulling her into him, he could feel her shaking. He whispered, "Thank you," as he covered her mouth with his. Reaching up, he turned off the light, still holding her close. When the kiss ended, no words were spoken. He held her, and together they slept.

CHAPTER EIGHT

DUKE WOKE BEFORE LOREN. The sky was light but the sun had not come up yet. She was still in his arms, their bare chests touching. Last night was so beautiful. She'd let him in. She'd let down her walls and let him in. The joy that filled him was beyond his comprehension. Never had he felt like this. He was pretty sure he was in love with her; hell, he was pretty sure he was in love with her from that first sight in Bozeman.

His hand started moving along her side, her skin so soft, so creamy. She smelled like heaven to him, her vanilla and strawberry scent. Closing his eyes, he relived every moment of the night before. How scared she was when she bared herself to him. How gentle he had been with her. She was delicate yet strong.

Her hand moved up his chest, her fingers pressing into his pecs. He chuckled as she tilted her head up. Her beautiful violet eyes stared into his. He would never want another. When she pushed herself up his body, her nipples trailing along his chest made him instantly hard, so hard that he felt pain in his cock.

"Good morning, Duke," she whispered as she kissed him. He wrapped his arms around her and pulled her on top of him.

"Good morning, beautiful," he whispered, deepening the kiss.

They laid together for a long time, enjoying each other. "Thank you for letting me in," he whispered against her lips.

Her soft smile melted him, turned him to mush. "Thank you for wanting in."

He kissed her again then flipped her onto her back. "May I look at you in the light again?" he asked. She nodded and he lifted himself off of her. His eyes gazed at her body, stopping at her chest, her nipples puckered hard like pebbles. "You are so beautiful," he said, looking into her eyes.

"Duke," she whispered.

"Yeah," he whispered back.

He watched her swallow hard. "Will you touch me?" Her face blushed pink.

His eyes never leaving hers, he moved is hand slowly up her body from her waist, stopping just below her breast. His thumb barely grazed the underside. Loren closed her eyes and licked her lips. He waited for her to open them again. Slowly, they fluttered open, and he gently moved his hand up to cup her breast. "Prefect," he moaned. It fit perfectly, filling his hand. He brushed his thumb across her nipple, watching as her mouth opened and a quiet moan escaped. He gently squeezed it and rolled her nipple between his fingers. He could feel her hips gently start to push into his thigh. He moved on to the other one, doing the same thing, listening to her quiet mews of pleasure. He wanted to feel one in his mouth. He wanted to taste it, to experience perfection.

He lowered his head tentatively. Her eyes opened and locked with his. He wasn't sure if he saw fear or lust in them. He hesitated just above her nipple. If he did this, he could never go back. He would have to have all of her. Slowly, he opened his mouth.

Loren could feel the heat of his breath on her nipple. *Oh, God*, she thought. The warmth of his tongue as he touched her caused her to shudder. His lips, his perfect lips closed around her nipple, and she felt her whole-body fill with electric warmth. Her hands reached for his hair, then she felt his teeth as he sweetly and gently nipped her. Fire blew through her body, right to the core of her being. "Ahh," she moaned as she burned from the inside. Again and again, he did it, each time sending electricity pulsing through her.

Somehow, he sensed her body was calming, and he lifted his head and covered her mouth with his. They kissed while she shook in his arms, until her body had calmed completely. Pulling away from him, breathless, she looked into his eyes and whispered, "What just happened to me?"

Duke smiled at her. "Aww, beautiful, you just came apart in my arms. It was wonderful to feel."

"Duke?"

"Yeah?"

"I'm scared."

"Me too, beautiful. Me too."

"Well, that's not very encouraging. You're the one with all the experience here."

He laughed. "I'm sorry, sweetheart, but what just happened is something I have never known before. I'm just as scared as you are." He looked at her, and gently, he said, "But we are in this together. This is new for both of us. I'm not going anywhere. I already told you that."

"No?" She ran her fingers through his hair.

"No." He kissed her.

Nodding, she sat up and grabbed her shirt, pulling it over her head. He watched as she crawled to her dresser. He could see the wet spot on her shorts, and his cock was ready to explode. "Oh, God," he moaned.

"Something the matter?" She smiled at him. She knew he had an erection; she could feel it, and she knew he needed to release it. But she didn't know what to do, or even if she could do anything to help. She smiled, and in a tiny voice, she said, "You need to relieve yourself, don't you?"

He chuckled, feeling his face getting warm from the blush. "I'm sorry, but I do. God, this is so embarrassing."

"I don't know what to do, how to help you. This is so new. I'm not sure I could do it."

He sat up. "Hey." He scooted to the end of the bed and wrapped his hand around her neck. "I never asked you to do anything. Don't worry about this. It's my problem. No pressure here. I told you, I am happy just to hold you and kiss you. This is my problem."

She looked at him with the sexiest fucking look he ever saw, and said, "Would a cold shower help?" She was serious.

He smiled. "No, baby, it won't. I've had this since I met you."

"Oh," she said in a tiny voice. "I should go get dressed. Would that help?"

"I'm sorry, I don't mean to make you feel uncomfortable. I try to keep it contained."

She giggled. "Duke, I am a doctor. I do know what is happening to you. I know the anatomy of what's happening between us. If you want to relieve yourself, you can use my shower. Or I can go outside."

She watched as his face turned bright red and he fell back on the bed. "God, this is so embarrassing." And it was; he was actually a bit humiliated. He had a fucking rock-hard erection, which is a totally normal thing, and he was embarrassed about it. He laid there with his arm over his eyes, trying to think of a way to end this conversation, when he felt her hand on him through the sheet.

His hand automatically reached for hers to stop her. Gently, he pulled her hand away and sat up. "No, Loren. You don't need to do anything. This is my problem. There is no pressure at all."

She looked at him, pulling her lip in her mouth. "It's so hard," she whispered, trailing her eyes down his chest. He swallowed hard as they came to his cock. He watched as she licked her lips. She slipped her hand from his. He didn't want to let it go; he didn't want her to feel that she had to do this. He watched her as her fingertips slowly pulled the sheet away. "Uh," she whispered. He swallowed hard.

Her eyes looked up into his. He didn't see fear in them, he saw wonder. She looked back down at him and moved her hand so her fingers gently touched him through the fabric of his boxers. She touched the visible wet spot at the head of his cock. Loren wrapped her fingers around his shaft and he closed his eyes. It felt so good, her warm tiny hand grabbing him.

He felt her fingers move to the waistband of his boxers, then she looked at him for permission. He swallowed hard. "Loren, you don't..." She shushed him as she pulled them back. He watched her face as her eyes looked upon him.

"Duke," she whispered. "Look at you. So beautiful." Slipping her hand in, she wrapped it around him.

"Oh, God," he moaned. "Loren, I can't..."

"Yes, you can." Her hand moved along his cock.

"Ahh," he moaned. He slowly laid back. "You don't need to do this."

"Do you want me to stop?" Her hand moved slowly up and down his erection.

Duke bit his lip. She felt so good. He was going to lose his shit. Two strokes and he was coming undone. "Ahh, shit." He groaned as he spilled it all over his stomach. Pulse after pulse, he came harder than he ever had before. When he finished, she was still holding him, looking at his stomach and then at him. He picked his head up he saw the wonder in her eyes. "I am so sorry about this." He had never apologized for an orgasm in his life.

She smiled at him. "Well, that was a first for me."

Shaking his head, he took the t-shirt she handed him to clean himself off. "I am so embarrassed."

"Why?" she said softly. "It was beautiful. Didn't you like it?"

He sat up, grabbing her face, and seared his lips against hers. Kissing her hard and deep, he told her, "I loved it. Thank you."

She smiled at him. "You know I've never done that before. So, for my first time, it was good?"

Duke took in the wicked grin on her face. "Oh, God, sweetheart, it was better than good."

She giggled. "I'm going to go get dressed. The hamper is right over here on this side of the dresser." She pointed to a bin against the wall. He watched as she climbed down out of the loft.

Lying back on the bed, Duke took a deep breath. He was so fucking in love with her, yet he had no idea how the hell it happened. Still shaking from that earth-shattering orgasm, he reached for his jeans and pulled them on. Grabbing his t-shirt, and the one she gave him to wipe himself off, he tossed one in the hamper and took the other one, along with his socks, with him down the stairs.

Loren was just coming out of the bathroom, and she looked up at him and smiled. There was nothing awkward about it. He walked by her, touching her face as he went. She went in the kitchen to make coffee and to scramble some eggs.

"Do you mind if I put some cheese in these eggs?" she called out.

"Not at all," he said through the door.

They ate, smiling at each other, then they headed out to get to work. Loren fed Cupcake and the chickens while Duke hauled all the tools out of the barn.

For hours, they worked raising beam after beam, laughing, talking, and joking around. By the time lunch came around, they had gotten up three beams. "Not bad," Duke said, admiring their work.

"Yep, and just five more to go. Come on, I'll make us some sandwiches. I have some leftover spaghetti sauce I was going to take over to your dad. Did you want to stay for dinner?"

He smiled at her. "I would love to, but I am going home tonight."

She giggled. "I don't have a problem with that."

He grabbed her around the waist and pulled her in for a kiss. "You are a cold-hearted woman."

She busted out laughing and pulled away from him, heading toward the house. As she started up the stairs, she heard a truck pull off the main road. She waited for it to come into view. It was Richard, and he had someone with him. Loren went in to make sandwiches for her and Duke.

When she came out with the plates, Richard and Duke were in a heated discussion, and Joe was sitting in the chair. "What's going on?" she asked.

"Dad's heard some not so nice things about Duke. Apparently, he is back with Julie, and Dad's not happy about it."

"What do you mean?" She felt her heart start racing.

"I guess they spent the night together last night and he got a little rough with her. She showed up at the house this morning covered in bruises.

She turned and looked at Duke, then at Richard. Her stomach tightened. She needed to be anywhere but here. *Did he hurt her? Is that why he came back here?* Setting the plates down in the chair, she headed toward Cupcake. She still had her saddle on. Loren climbed on her and took off, with Jaz right behind her.

DUKE WATCHED HER GO. THERE WAS NOTHING HE COULD DO. SPINNING around, he looked his father right in the face.

"Dad, do you think I am capable of hurting a woman? Any woman?"

"Not the man I raised."

"I will tell you exactly what happened. I came out here last night to talk to Loren. We had a few beers, then I went home. It was about one when I got there. I took a shower and went to bed. Julie was in my room sitting in a chair in the corner. She made several passes at me, but I told her get the fuck out of my house. I got dressed and I left. I came back out here, with every intention on sleeping in my truck. I was going to come to your house, but I figured I was working here this morning so I just came here. Loren woke up and came and got me, and I slept in her house. Before you get upset with me, nothing happened. I told her what happened with Julie, and she made fun of me then we went to sleep." He was lying, but his father didn't need to know what happened. "Dad, I didn't have sex with Julie. I didn't get rough with her, and I certainly didn't hit her. She is a manipulative bitch and she wants me back."

"Does she know about Loren?"

"Nobody knows about Loren. Hell, I don't even know about Loren. We are just getting to know each other, and now this bitch is going to pull this shit. You saw her face when she rode out of here."

Duke walked away from him and headed out into the field to see if he could see her. "Shit," he said.

"Duke, I think you need to come back to the ranch with me. We need to get this settled. Julie is there with Derek and Alex."

"Fuck!" he yelled. "Fine, whatever. Obviously, I'm not going to be able to talk to Loren, so let's go." He took off his work belt and dropped it on the pile of wood. He got in his Jeep and followed his dad back to the ranch.

~

LOREN RODE HER ASS OFF. SHE DIDN'T KNOW IF SHE SHOULD BELIEVE him or not. She trusted him to look at her. She trusted him... She pulled on the reins. Sitting there on her horse, she smiled. **She trusted him.** She closed her eyes and thought about everything he'd said to her, the way he held her, the way he kissed her. The way he touched her, gently, tenderly. He wasn't this man Julie said he was. She trusted him.

Turning Cupcake toward Richard's, she took off across the field. That leggy brunette was there, and she was going to find out exactly what went on. Riding up to the back of the house, she got down and went into the kitchen where she could hear raised voices.

She walked into the dining room and stopped when she heard the woman say, "He came on to me, dragged me up to his apartment. He tore my clothes and had his way with me. Every time I tried to stop him, he slapped me and told me to shut up, that I was his and he was taking what he wanted from me." Loren had to cover her mouth to stop from laughing.

"You are such a fucking liar, Julie!" Duke yelled.

"Duke, there is no need to speak that way," Richard said.

"What time did this happen, Julie?" Loren couldn't tell who asked that question.

"It started around eleven, and he left me beaten and naked in his bed around six this morning," Julie sobbed.

"That is complete bullshit," Duke said.

"Well, if it's complete bullshit, Duke, then where were you?" the mystery man asked.

"I... I was sleeping in my truck," Duke stuttered.

Loren stood there amazed; he didn't want anyone to know where he was. He didn't want to drag her into this.

"I want him back and he knows it. He knows I love him, and I made a mistake when I cheated on him. I feel so used. He told me he loved me, then he did this to me. How am I supposed to go to the festival looking like this?" Julie was crying.

Loren had had enough. She stepped into the living room, walking right up to Duke, and slipped her hand in his, giving it a squeeze. Loren knew she was lying.

Duke looked at her in shock. She smiled at him. "Hi," she whispered.

Richard looked at her and smiled. He knew right there that Julie was lying and he owed his son an apology.

"Get your hands off of him," Julie yelled and stood up.

Loren smiled at her. "He wasn't with you last night."

"Who the hell are you? Yes, he was with me."

"My name is Loren." She looked at a cop sitting next to Julie, who she guessed owned the voice she'd heard. "Duke was with me."

"I'm sorry, miss, but who are you?"

"My name is Loren Mitchell."

Derek, Joe, and Alex all smiled. Derek was happy for his brother.

"She is lying," Julie said. "She isn't even from around here. He was with me." She looked at their hands. "Don't touch him!" she yelled. Loren smiled at her.

"Would you be willing to testify in court?" the cop asked.

Loren laughed. "There won't be a need for this to go to court. I'm from a small town, too. You know everyone in this room. I'm pretty sure you and one of these boys went to school together. You've probably known Duke your whole life. Is he the type of man who would hit a woman? Is he the type of man who would take sex when he wanted it? I know for a fact that he isn't. He is a good, kind man." She turned to look at Julie. "We don't know each other, and honestly, you aren't the type of woman I would want to know. You had a good man and you threw it away by sleeping with his friend. Now, that man doesn't want you anymore, and you have been trying to get this one back. Well, Julie, he isn't coming back to you. You know why?"

Julie looked at her. "He loves me, and I love him."

"No, he doesn't love you. I'm pretty sure he loves me." Loren turned and looked at Duke. He had a huge smile on his face.

Reaching up, he cupped her face. "Who are you?" he whispered, running his thumb along her jaw.

Loren looked at the cop. "I have things to do. If you need a statement from me, let Richard know. He knows how to get in touch with me." She turned to Duke and stood directly in front of him. "I hope this all works out for you, but I'm going to go. I'm sorry that I doubted you. I won't make that mistake again." She smiled and let go of his hand. Walking past Richard, she reached out and squeezed his arm then left.

Duke and his brothers all stood there watching her walk out the door in awe. Smiling, Duke turned to look at Julie. She stood there with her mouth hanging open.

"You love me," she sobbed. "I know you do. I'm sorry I cheated. I won't do it again."

Shaking his head, Duke said, "I told you time and time again, we are done. I don't want you. I don't love you."

"How can you love her? She has that horrible scar on her face. She is deformed. Look at me. This is what you love." She cried.

Duke shook his head. "I really don't know what I ever saw in you." He looked at the cop. "Charlie, either arrest me or get her out of my father's house. I have work to do."

"Come on, Julie." Charlie stood and looked at her.

"But what about him assaulting me."

"I don't believe Duke hit you. Come on before I get you for filing false reports."

Julie stood and looked Duke right in the face. "This isn't over. I know you love me."

"Yes, Julie, it is over."

Charlie escorted Julie out of the house. Derek walked up to Duke and slapped him on the back. "I guess congratulations are in order. I'm happy for you, man."

Duke laughed. "No congratulations. We are just friends, getting to know one another."

Derek smiled at him, and the boys left the house, leaving Richard and Duke alone.

"I suppose I owe you an apology," Richard said.

"No, Dad, you don't. Loren did something she shouldn't have done."

"What? Was she lying?" Richard questioned him.

"No, she wasn't, but she shouldn't have defended me like that. She only exposed herself to Julie. That girl is trouble with a capital T. Loren doesn't need the shit storm Julie is going to deliver."

Richard chuckled. "You will see how wrong you are about that. I'm glad you two are getting to know one another. She is a good strong woman, an equal for you."

Duke laughed. "We are by far equals. That woman is beyond me in every way. If you compare us, I am a but a cherry pit to her watermelon."

Richard laughed. "Go find her."

He didn't have to tell Duke twice. He hugged his father and went to his Jeep. He needed to find Loren to make sure she was all right.

Loren felt good when she walked out of the house. She knew Duke was honest. She knew how she was starting to feel about him. She rode Cupcake hard back to her house. She had the pulley set up and was working on getting another beam up when Duke pulled up.

"What are you doing?" he shouted to her.

"Working. I've got a barn to build." She smiled at him.

He laughed, grabbing his tool belt, and headed over to help her. They got two more beams set in place by the end of the day.

"Do you want a beer?" Loren asked him when they finished.

"Sure, but I would like something else as well." Duke smiled at her.

"And what would that be?" She walked up to him, putting her hand on his chest.

"This," he whispered as he kissed her. Loren leaned into his chest and wrapped her arms around his neck. Duke picked her up and she wrapped her legs around him.

She started to giggle, pulling out of the kiss. "I've seen this in movies, and I always wondered what it was like. Am I heavy?"

Duke laughed. "No, beautiful, you're not. So, what do you think about this?" He squeezed her thighs.

She laughed. "I like it." She kissed him again, and he set her down.

"I'll put all this away," he said as he started to haul the tools into the garage.

Loren went in and grabbed a pot, filled it with water, and put it on the stove. Then she grabbed a jar of spaghetti sauce out of the fridge and put that on to warm. Looking around, she saw the leftover bread on the counter. She got it ready to make garlic bread then grabbed two beers out of the fridge. When she opened the door, Duke was getting ready to knock. He wrapped his arms around her waist and kissed her.

Laughing, they went to sit in the chairs. "I'm sorry about all that shit today," Duke said.

"I'm not. It made me realize that I trust you. When I left, I know I hurt you by thinking you could do something like that. I had to come to Richard's. I needed you to know that I was sorry I doubted you."

He just sat there. He had never known this kind of trust before. "You can trust me. I'm a bit worried though."

"Oh, why?" She felt a bit uncomfortable.

"Loren, I know Julie. This might have been some sick attempt to get me to notice her, but you made yourself known now. She can be vicious."

"It doesn't matter. The truth had to be told." She turned her head to look at him. "Thank you for trying to protect me back there."

Duke reached over and took her hand. "This is new between us. I didn't want to make any assumptions about what is happening between us."

She smiled, squeezing my hand. "Duke?"

"Yeah?"

"I'm afraid that I was the one who made the assumption. I was the one who declared our relationship without even considering how you felt."

He chuckled. "You were right. I don't know when it happened, probably the minute I saw you, or the second I had a real conversation with you. But you were right."

"I know."

Neither of them said it out loud, but Duke knew how he was feeling and so did Loren.

"You hungry? I have leftover spaghetti if you're interested."

"I'm interested."

Loren let go of his hand and went into the house. She put the spaghetti on and cut the bread to make garlic bread. She was nervous about what she'd said at Richard's about Duke loving her. *Did I say the right thing?* Watching him touch her scars, kissing each one, she saw the look in his eyes, how careful he was not to touch her in that way. Then, when she touched him, he came almost instantly. *What am I feeling in all of this? Is this love?*

While eating dinner, they talked and laughed. When they finished, they took their beers and went to sit outside. The sun was setting when Duke said softly to her, "I'm going to move back into my dad's."

"Why?"

"Well, Julie has a key to my place, and it's a forty-five-minute drive from here anyway, and Dad's is only twenty. I'm not going to play this game with her, and she isn't going to quit."

"Well, it will be nice to have you closer." She almost wanted him to stay with her, but that was crazy. They'd only know each other for two weeks.

"It will. That means I can stay here a bit later before I have to go home tomorrow." Loren nodded. "Speaking of home, I'm going to get going. I'll be here early so we can get those other three beams up." He stood, pulling Loren up with him. "Thank you for today, especially this morning. Let me walk you back to the house." Smiling, she led the way. Duke reached for her hand as they reached the stairs, pulling her to him. "I am honored for what you gave me last night," he whispered.

Loren felt her face flush as she nodded. For some reason, she felt tears welling up. Duke saw her eyes glass over in the soft glow of the light. He reached up with his thumbs and wiped her tears as they fell, pulling her in for a sweet kiss.

"Good night, Loren. I will see you in the morning."

He went to step back, and she wrapped her fingers around his shirt, pulling him back to her. "Thank you," she whispered.

Duke smiled. "I do you know," he whispered.

"I think I do, too."

He kissed her again and then walked away. Loren went in the house, leaned against the door, and let the tears fall. They weren't tears of sorrow; they were tears of happiness. Had she found him, the man who would or could love her marred body?

CHAPTER NINE

As Duke drove to his father's house, he couldn't get the smile off his face. He did love her, and she loved him. *How is any of this possible?* He chuckled to himself. His father would be shocked to see him.

Pulling up to the ranch, he parked and climbed the stairs. When he walked in, his father was sitting at the table doing paperwork.

"What brings you by this time of night? I thought you would be with Loren."

Duke sat down. "Dad, I think I'm in love with her."

Richard laughed. "I knew that the day you officially met her. So, what are you going to do about it?"

Duke chuckled. "Well, I wanted to know if I could move back home."

"You are always welcome here, son. But can I ask why?"

"Julie has a key to my place, and it is forty-five minutes from Loren's. I'd like to be closer. I don't want the hassle that Julie is going to bring. If it wasn't for Loren today, things might have turned out differently."

"Yeah, Julie Front is going to be a problem for you, son. Loren was right; she is going to try to be a part of your life now that you have moved on. To be honest, I never knew what you saw in her. She is a bit shallow."

Duke laughed. "That she is, but to be honest with you, Dad, I was thinking like Derek. She has a body that just doesn't quit."

Richard chuckled. "In life, son, it's not about the body. Sure, it's a bonus when the woman you choose has a fantastic one, but when you love someone, it's about what's in here," he tapped his head, "and here." He touched his heart.

Duke sat looking at his father. "You know, Dad, my whole life I listened to your words. When I was old enough to figure life out, I left home thinking I had all the answers. I've made mistakes." He chuckled. "Apparently, bigger ones than I thought. But here I am, twenty-eight years old, and I'm asking you if I can live at home again. I didn't know shit about life. I didn't know shit about love. But now..." He paused. "Now, I think I am finally growing up."

"To be honest with you, son, I was praying Julie would never be my daughter in law. I was praying she wasn't going to be the mother of my grandchildren."

Duke chuckled. "Yeah, I almost made that mistake. Listen, I'm going to head up. I need to be up early to get over to Loren's. Oh, and thanks, Dad. I appreciate the reprieve from work here to help her."

Richard chuckled. "I have an ulterior motive."

"I'm sure you do. Good night, Dad."

"Good night, son."

Richard watched his oldest son climb the stairs to his old room under his roof. He was glad that he and Loren had found each other. Loren deserved to be happy, and Duke deserved to have a woman like her. He couldn't have been prouder of his son.

LOREN LAID IN BED RUBBING HER FINGERS OVER HER LIPS, REMEMBERING how it felt to kiss him. She loved the feeling of falling in love with him. Trust is an issue she had worked on since her attack. *Does he know what happened to me?* She was pretty confident that he did. He was careful and loving when he touched her. Giggling, she couldn't believe she let him touch her boobs. "Oh my God." It felt incredible, the way his tongue suckled her nipple. She wanted him with her now.

Closing her eyes, she tried to sleep, but it wasn't going to happen. An hour passed, then two. Looking at her clock, she realized it was just after eleven. "Oh, God, Jaz. I can't sleep. Come on, let's go sit outside."

Loren climbed down her stairs, grabbed a beer from the fridge, and went to sit outside. How strange life was. Two weeks ago, she was sleeping, coming to terms with how her life had turned into. Then, right out of left field, she gazed across a restaurant and her whole life changed. *Who falls in love in two weeks?* Laughing, she looked at Jaz. "I think I'm crazy." Jaz wagged her tail, laying her head on Loren's foot.

A few minutes later, Jaz picked her head up and looked toward the road. "What is it, girl?" She jumped to her feet, her tail wagging. Loren smiled. She hoped it was Duke. When Jaz took off running toward the front of her house, Loren followed her. The Jeep pulled up ten feet from her and Duke got out. Before Loren could say a word, his mouth covered hers.

Picking her up, he walked up the stairs, opening the door. He walked her into the house, waiting for Jaz to come in, then kicked the door shut and locked it. "I do, you know," he whispered between kisses. He managed to get his boots off and carried her up the stairs, sitting her on the top one. "I can't sleep," he said into her mouth. "You, you're all I can think about. Loren," he rasped out of his mouth.

She backed up, moving to the bed, while he knelt on the stairs watching her. She smiled at him, pulling the covers back. With his whole body shaking, he crawled up her bed, up her legs, kissing her.

Loren was trembling. She wanted him here with her. She wanted to be in his arms. She wanted this. Duke wrapped his arm around her waist, sliding her down the bed, her t-shirt riding up her body and gathering under her breasts. Her hands moved down his body, pulling his shirt up and over his head. Looking into her deep purple eyes, he said, "May I?"

Loren shuddered. Her stomach tightened and she felt her nipples get hard. She nodded her head. Duke was moving slowly. He kissed her stomach as he moved up her body. His thumbs moved her t-shirt and he took in her luscious nipples, so hard and wanton of his mouth. "Loren," he whispered as his mouth surrounded one, drawing it in, licking and sucking it. Her body arched into his.

"Ahh," she called out, her hand going into his hair. "Duke," she moaned as he moved to the next one. "Oh, God, what is happening to me?"

"Come here," he whispered, pulling her to him. Closing his eyes, he held her. It was no time at all and they were both sleeping, exhausted. Neither of them moved until the sun burst through the early morning sky.

Duke woke to a soft giggle. When he opened his eyes, he was greeted with the lovely scent of vanilla and strawberries, and her beautiful eyes gazing at him. "Mmm," he moaned, pulling her on top of his chest. "What's so funny?" He wrapped her in his arms.

"You. Last night, you were so…"

He chuckled. "Yeah, I was. I just needed to be here with you."

"Duke, what are we doing here?"

"Aww, beautiful, I wish I knew. I can't seem to stay away from you."

Loren looked up at him. "This is all happening so fast. Maybe the leggy brunette was right?"

"Hey." He rolled her over so he could look at her. "First of all, the leggy brunette is never right about anything. Second, yes, it is happening fast. I just know how I feel, and I'm going with it. I've never felt so connected to someone like I do you. I'm not going anywhere. If you want to slow this down and not end up like this," he looked down at her bare chest, "then I'm all right with that."

She shook her head. "I like ending up like this. I'm just not sure what other people will say."

He chuckled. "Other people? My father, you mean."

"Duke, he means the world to me. I don't want to hurt him or the relationship you have with him."

"Then we should talk to him, let him know how we feel. But I think he already knows. I do talk to my father, you know. Come on, let's get up and have some coffee. If you want, we can go over and talk to him together. I don't want you to feel bad or confused about how you feel, or how I feel about you."

Loren nodded. They got up and she got dressed and made some coffee. As they were getting ready to head over to Richard's house, his truck pulled up. He didn't look happy to see Duke there.

"Let me handle this," Loren whispered as Richard got out of the truck.

"We were just coming to see you," she said, smiling at him.

"Well then, I saved you the trip." He smiled at her but scowled at Duke.

"Good morning, son. Seems you weren't at breakfast."

Duke chuckled. "Subtle, Dad."

"Richard, we need to talk to you about what seems to be happening between us."

His eyes softened when he looked at Loren. "Would seem a great deal is happening."

She laughed. "No, Richard, not really. At least, not in the sense that you are implying. Duke has been a complete gentleman."

Duke watched his father relax a bit. "Oh?"

"Dad, I know you think this is moving fast. Hell, we think the same thing. But it's like we have no control over it. I respect Loren, and I am not about to do something that is going to make her feel anything less than that respect. We think we might be falling in love. Hell, all I can think about is seeing her, talking to her, laughing with her. Last night, I laid in bed thinking about her out here with thoughts of Julie in her head, and I needed her to know that she isn't in mine. I want this with Loren. I want to get to know her. I want to spend time with her."

"What does Loren want?" Richard said.

Loren smiled. "The same thing. Richard, if you have a problem with this, please let us know. I have grown to love you dearly and hurting you or making you angry is not an option for me, for either of us. I suppose, we are seeking your approval to move forward, to allow what we are beginning to feel for one another to grow, or not. We just want to find out where all this is going."

Richard stood there for a few minutes, not saying anything. Then he cleared his throat. "Loren, I trust you and I trust my son. I made a promise to your mother and to myself that I would do everything in my power to help you move on with your life, to help you feel safe. Duke is a good man, one of the best. I suppose I have his mother to thank for that. You have become like a daughter to me, and I guess I am reacting like any father would. I don't want your reputation soiled by any of this."

She giggled. "Richard, no one knows me here, and I'm not worried about it. I'm twenty-six. It's not like I'm sixteen and the sexy, older man is after me."

Duke smiled. "You think I'm sexy?"

Loren looked at him. "Not now," she whispered.

Richard laughed. "I guess I'm just an old man with old values."

"No, you're not. I hold those same values, Dad," Duke said.

"In my day, the behavior of you boys would be unacceptable."

"Dad, I am not Derek."

"No, but your relationship with Julie is the perfect example. When I met your mother, we waited until we were married."

Loren laughed. "Richard, with all due respect, Duke and I have not had sex. I'm still a virgin. It's not like that." Duke swallowed hard and closed his eyes. *Fuck, I was right. This just makes her all that more special.* "But I might add, it's not because I was trying to save myself. I just didn't have the time. I wanted the life I had, and it took everything in me to achieve it in the time frame in which I did. But now, after what happened to me, I know it probably isn't going to happen for me."

Duke looked at her. She couldn't have been more beautiful, more desirable to him, than she was right now. He reached up and touched her face, looking deep into her eyes. "You deserve nothing less than to be loved for the rest of your life, and I am going to prove that to you." He touched his forehead to hers and whispered, "If you let me, I will love you until I die."

She smiled at him. "You don't know that. What if you figure out I'm not the one for you?"

Duke laughed as she turned her head to Richard. "We don't want to hurt you. If Duke staying here with me upsets you, then it won't happen again. There are enough hours in the day for us to get to know each other."

Richard smiled at her. He knew what he saw, what he heard. They were falling in love. Duke would be the one to give her the life she deserved.

"Richard, I feel safe with him. Please, trust us to do what is best for us."

"Come here," he said, pulling her into a hug. His eyes locked with his son's over her shoulder. "Be careful with her, son. She is a good soul, and she deserves nothing but the utmost respect."

Duke smiled at his father. "You and Mom raised me right, Dad. I'm not going to hurt her or take a chance of not being able to hold her."

Richard let Loren go and hugged Duke.

"Do you want some coffee, Richard?"

"No, I need to go supervise those boys. Not sure they have a clue what they are doing."

"Dad, I can come and help. We should have the last two beams up by lunch."

"That would be great. When are you going to pack up your place?" Richard asked.

"Well, I have no desire to run into Julie, so I was going to ask the boys if they would do it for me."

"Might be a good idea," Richard said. "You two have a good morning." He nodded and walked back to his truck.

Duke and Loren stood there watching Richard drive away. Turning to him, Loren smiled. "I don't think I want to work today. I've let my garden go unattended, and I haven't ridden Cupcake in a few days. Not to mention, I feel like cooking. So, why don't you go and finish your father's barn, then recruit your brothers to help you move out of your apartment. I think you need to spend some time with your father."

He wrapped his arms around her waist, pulling her to him. "What if I don't want to go?" He pouted.

She laughed, pushing up on her toes to kiss him. "Too bad. Now go. There is no need to neglect your work. I'll be here. In fact, I think I'll make a few pies and bring them over. Go on."

"You sure?"

"Yes, go get your work done. If those storms are coming, that barn needs to be fixed. Mine will wait. I have all summer to finish it."

Duke kissed her. "All right, but I'm going on the record here saying I don't want to go."

Loren laughed. "Duly noted."

He smacked her on the ass as he walked away. "I will see you later."

"Damn right you will," she called after him.

DUKE LAUGHED AS HE DROVE AWAY. HE DIDN'T WANT TO LEAVE HER; HE never wanted to leave her, but she was right. That barn needed to be fixed, and he needed to empty his apartment and move back in with his father.

He pulled up in front of the barn and climbed out. "Hey, I thought you were helping Loren this morning," Richard said to him.

"Yeah, well, she told me to come home and finish my work. She is going to do other things today, and we need to get this barn fixed. When we are done here, I was hoping everyone would help me move back home."

Richard laughed, slapping Duke on the back. "She is good for you."

Duke laughed with him. "Yeah, Dad, she is."

They got to work. It took the rest of the morning to finish the barn. They all had sandwiches and then took the five pickups into to town to pack Duke up.

"So, you're moving back home?" Derek asked.

"Yeah, after what that bitch did, I'm not about to put Loren through her crazy crap. This way, she can't say I raped her."

"You and Loren are serious?"

"We're new. We are getting to know each other, and so far, I like her."

Derek laughed. "She said she thinks you love her."

Duke smiled. "Yeah, I think I do. She is a remarkable woman."

"Is she good in bed?"

Duke turned and looked at his brother. "Are you serious right now? Why would I ever tell you that?"

Derek laughed. "So then, no."

"Is sex all you ever think about? Come on, there is so much more to a woman that just her body."

"Well, that's easy for you to say. Loren is smoking hot."

Duke shook his head. It didn't take long to empty his apartment. By the time they got back to the ranch, Loren was there waiting on the porch. She smiled when they all pulled up. She got up and walked up to Richard, giving him a hug. "I guess your boy is coming home."

Richard laughed, pulling her close so he could whisper in her ear. "He's just coming home to be closer to you."

Loren blushed. "Perhaps."

They both laughed. Duke walked up. "To what do I owe this pleasure?"

"I just brought your dad some pie and some strawberry jam that I made."

He put his hand on his heart. "I'm crushed."

She laughed. "So, what's all this?"

"I told you I was moving back. I don't want the headache of Julie Front in my life."

"Hmm, good to know." She turned to Richard. "Enjoy the pie. I'm going to get going. I want to make some barn doors this afternoon."

"Thank you again. See you soon." Richard smiled at her.

She turned and headed to her truck. Duke just stood there smiling, watching her walk across the front drive with Jaz following behind her. She opened the door and Jaz jumped in. His heart jumped when she climbed up, watching her perfect ass in those perfect jeans.

"You're drooling," Derek said, laughing.

"Shut the fuck up." Duke chuckled.

Loren and Duke locked eyes as she started the truck. She smiled at him, and her hand on the steering wheel gave him a secret wave. He couldn't stand it any longer. He trotted over as she put the truck in reverse. He pulled open her door, threw the truck in park, and pulled her out. "Leaving without say goodbye?"

She was laughing. "I thought we were supposed to be secret."

Duke busted out laughing. "Not here, darlin', not anymore. You declared me as yours, so now, public displays of affection are fair game."

She wrapped her arms around his neck. "Oh yeah?" She tilted her head down, her hair falling around their heads as she kissed him. "You have work to do."

"And what are you going to do?" he whispered back, kissing her again.

"Any damn thing I want."

He laughed, sitting her back in the truck. Stepping between her legs, he kissed her properly. "I will see you later."

She laughed, and before she could say anything, a red Jeep pulled up. The leggy brunette jumped out and headed toward Derek. "Where's your brother? His neighbor said he moved out."

"I'm going to go. Seems you have some shit to deal with." Loren turned in her seat.

"Loren?" Duke looked at her.

"I'm good. Goodbye, Duke." She smiled at him.

He squeezed her leg before he moved back and shut her truck door. Julie turned, looking right at her, saying to Derek loud enough for everyone to hear her, "What's that little bitch doing here? Who does she think she is?"

Duke chuckled and jumped up on the running board of Loren's truck and leveled her with a kiss. She busted out laughing. "So much trouble you are in right now."

"Goodbye, Loren. I'll see you in a little bit, as soon as we get this all in the house."

Loren looked over his shoulder to see Julie marching across the drive. "Just don't bring the leggy brunette with you." She nodded toward Julie. Putting her truck in reverse, she pulled out as Duke jumped down.

He stood there looking at her as she drove down the drive. "What the hell are you doing, Duke?"

He laughed. "What do you want, Julie? I'm busy." He walked around her, not even looking at her, and headed back to the trucks.

"Duke! Duke, I thought we could talk."

He ignored her and started hauling his belongings into the house. Joe took his couch, Alex took his table and chairs home, and Derek took the rest. Duke piled his clothes and personal belongings into his old room, and then they switched out the beds. He was a big boy and wanted his big bed. When they finished, Duke grabbed a beer and sat on the porch. Julie had sat on her Jeep, waiting for them to finish. She hopped down and headed his way.

"Why won't you talk to me?" she said sweetly to him, sitting in the chair next to his.

"I've got nothing to say to you." He took a swig of his beer.

"Who is that girl, Duke? Why were you kissing her?"

"It's none of your business, Julie. We've been over for a long time."

"But you love me. You told me so."

"Yeah, I was wrong. I didn't love you. You had nothing to give me except your body, and well, you seem to give it to everyone else as well."

"So, what does this girl give you that I can't?"

He laughed and leaned forward. "I am not discussing her with you. I've told you repeatedly that I am not coming back to you. We are done."

"But you wanted to marry me," she whispered. "I'm ready to get married."

He smirked. "I was wrong for even considering it. We are not an item anymore. We are not compatible, Julie. We have absolutely nothing in common."

"And what could you possibly have in common with that girl?"

"Go home, Julie."

"My home is with you."

"Not anymore, it hasn't been for a long time. Just go home and leave me alone."

"Why did you come back here? To be with this girl?"

"No, Julie, I moved back here to get away from you. Now, leave and do yourself a favor; don't come back or I will have Charlie arrest you for trespassing." He stood and walked past her. She put her hand on his thigh, but he pulled it away. "Don't touch me. I'm not yours to touch." He continued into the house, shutting the door behind him.

His father was sitting in the dining room. "That girl is going to be a problem."

"Yeah, I know. Listen I'm going to take a shower and head over to Loren's. I'm going to ride a four-wheeler over. I don't need Julie following me out there."

"Probably a good idea. You coming home tonight?" Richard asked.

Duke chuckled. "Anything's possible."

Richard laughed. Duke ran upstairs and showered then put on clean clothes. He grabbed a six pack out of the fridge and the little cooler off the porch. It took him about half an hour to reach Loren's. He pulled up and parked behind the makeshift barn.

When he came around the corner, Loren was sitting in one of the chairs. "What took you so long?" She had a huge smile on her face.

He set the cooler down, walked up to her, grabbed her under her arms, and lifted her out of her chair into his arms. He leveled her with a deep, tongue-thrusting kiss. "Did you miss me?"

She busted out laughing. "God, did I ever." She wrapped her legs around him, pulling herself up his body so her head was higher than his, her hair falling around them. He inhaled her fantastic scent of vanilla and strawberries. He instantly got hard. Her mouth teased his as she sweetly and sensually kissed him. "You're so lucky I'm not a jealous woman."

He laughed, smacking her on the ass. "That's such a shame because I am a very jealous man."

Her words came out in that fucking sexy ass voice of hers. "You have nothing to worry about with me. I know what I have with you."

"Fucking right. You want a beer?"

She shook her head. "No," she whispered.

"What to build a fire?" He kissed her again.

She shook her head. "No," she answered, deepening the kiss.

"Loren." His voice cracked a bit.

"Duke," her sexy voice said.

His feet were moving, their mouths closed over each other's. Before he realized it, he was sitting Loren on the top stair to the loft. She pulled back, drawing her bottom lip into her mouth. She knew what she wanted; she'd known since that first night. Never had she met a man who made her feel this way—safe, beautiful, desired, and wanted. Looking into his beautiful green eyes, she reached down and pulled off her shirt. She heard his intake of air. Her hands were shaking as she reached behind her back to unclasp her bra.

Sliding it off her arms, she dropped it on the floor next to her shirt. She scooted back, slipping off her shoes, and undid her jeans, pulling them off. Turning, she crawled over to her bed.

Duke knelt on the stairs in shock. He wasn't sure he could do this. She turned to look at him, her hair falling down her chest covering her beautiful breasts. *Fuck!* "Fucking beautiful," he whispered. His hands were moving on their own. His shirt hit the floor next to hers. His shoes fell down the stairs. His jeans, he left on the stairs. Slowly, he moved toward her. He was fully hard. *God, she is fucking prefect.* He started at her feet, his mouth touching every part of her leg. When he reached her panties, he inhaled then started on the next one.

When he finished, her chest was heaving and her mews were driving him insane. He needed to hear more. Leaning forward, he kissed her stomach. Her hands moved down to play with his hair. His hands resting on her hips, his fingers pressed into her beautiful ass. He gently turned her over; he needed to see it, to touch it.

"Fuck," he whispered. She was wearing lace panties that barely covered her ass. "You are fucking gorgeous. Beautiful," he whispered as he leaned forward and kissed her cheek. His hands needed to touch her, so he did. Her mews and moans drove him to hear more. He licked, kissed, sucked, and bit her ass. He could feel her body shaking, but it wasn't fear. Orgasm after orgasm rippled through her body. He was so hard.

Slowly, he turned her over and crawled up her body to kiss her. She devoured his mouth. "Duke," she whispered. "Oh, God, Duke." He just kissed her deeper. Pulling back, he looked into her eyes. He had to taste her. He needed it. Slowly, he moved down her body. When he reached her panties, he stopped. He just couldn't bring himself to do it. Not yet.

"Duke," she whimpered.

He could feel her body shaking. Knowing how scared she was, he moved back up her body, wrapping his arms around her and pulling her to his chest, kissing her.

He felt her leg come up over his hip, the head of his cock inches from her center. She pulled him close. She shook in his arms, her hips rocking against him. "Loren," he cried out as he exploded, spilling himself in his boxers.

When they finally calmed down, she pulled back and looked at his face. "Why are you crying?" Duke shook his head, unable to speak. "Please, Duke, what's wrong?"

He could see her starting to panic. "You. Are. So. Beautiful," he managed to get out, pulling her to him. She nestled into his neck, holding him. They didn't say anything for some time. "Loren?"

"Duke, you are so beautiful," she whispered as she pulled back and kissed him sweetly.

"I nearly," he began, but she silenced him, kissing him again.

"I wanted you to."

He shook his head. "It would have been wrong. I want nothing more, but not because of drama in our lives. Not because either of us are scared, not because we can't control ourselves. When I make love to you, beautiful, it will be because it's the right time."

"I know, but can I say that I want to. I've never felt like this."

"You've also said that you've never allowed yourself the time to be with anyone. If I am your first serious relationship, then you need to be sure. I know how I feel, beautiful. I don't know how it happened because it's been just two weeks. We can't do this yet. I know, once we do, I will never be able to get enough of you. You need to make sure it's what you want as well." She nodded her head as he wiped her tears. "Don't cry, beautiful. I'm not going anywhere."

Tilting her head down to his chest, Duke pulled her in and held her. He thought she had fallen asleep. "Were those orgasms I had?"

"Oh, God, yes. And they were magnificent." He smiled, running his fingers down her back.

"I wanted you so desperately," she whispered, giggling.

He rolled them over. "And I came like a fifteen-year-old." He laughed.

She giggled. "You did, and you're a sticky mess."

"I'm not embarrassed about it. I was so turned on."

"Yeah?"

"Oh yeah. Let me get myself cleaned up. I don't have anything clean to put on."

She laughed. "I suppose my bed's not a virgin anymore."

Duke laughed, "I suppose it's not. Where would I find a washcloth?"

"In the cabinet in the bathroom. I have an old pair of sweats that might fit you." He watched her go to the dresser, grab the sweats, and hand them to him.

Duke kissed her and scooted down the bed. Taking the pants from her, he headed down the stairs. When Loren chuckled, Duke turned to look at her. She had her lip between her teeth. "You are so beautiful," she said. Duke felt himself blush.

When he came back, she had put her t-shirt back on and was sitting up. He crawled up the bed and kissed her stomach. "I want to taste you," he whispered to her, his head on her stomach as she played with his hair. "I want to do so much with you." He could smell her release. His cock was getting harder and harder. He moved his head down, his fingers trailing along her thigh. He felt her slide her leg open a bit, inviting him to move further. He smiled as his fingers touched her center.

"Mmm," she moaned.

Lifting his head, he turned it to see her face as his fingers slipped into her panties. Her back arched. She was so wet; he needed to be careful.

"Ahh, Duke."

"There is so much more," he whispered as he gently slipped his finger inside of her. His thumb caressing her bud, he gently stroked her. Her back arched as she cried out. He felt her orgasm blow through her whole body. Wrapping his arm around her, he felt every shudder.

Loren lay on her back in a state of euphoric bliss. She had never known touching could be this good. She was glad she waited for him. He was the only man who could love her this way. He saw her scars once, committed her body to his memory. Now, he didn't even see them; he saw her and only her. As he moved up her body, she grabbed his face, sitting up to meet him, closing her mouth over his. He felt her hands moving down his chest, to his cock. God, he wanted to come. He needed to come again. When her hands wrapped around him, he pulled back, crying out. Loren started to move her hand, stroking him again. She pushed the sweats down so she could see all of him, so she could watch him.

"Ahh, God. No," he groaned, reaching for her hand to stop her.

"No, let me," she said as she looked into his eyes.

"You don't have to do this." He moaned as she stroked him.

"Will you let me?" She looked hurt.

"Oh, God, beautiful." He reached for her, pulling her to him, kissing her. "I want it all with you, but I am willing to take our time. This is a big step what we are doing."

"Would it make a difference if I told you I want to do this?"

"It makes a world of difference, but let's just take our time. There is no hurry." God, he was so hard, but he just kissed her hard and deep. Loren continued to stroke him with such tenderness. No woman had ever taken this much care with him. "Oh, God, beautiful."

Loren sat up to look at him. "Duke," she whispered, her eyes traveling up and down his body, her hand running from his chest to his cock. "Will you come for me?"

He nodded and swallowed. He didn't think he could manage to

speak. He watched as she slowly moved her hand along his cock. He knew it was going to happen fast. "Ahh, God." Her hand gripped him so tight, and the friction made him feel so warm. There was no time to warn her; it startled him as he pulsed. Again and again, he pulsed. He couldn't move. He had no control over his body, but she kept going. His head back, his mouth opened as Loren milked him.

His hands moved to her ass, pulling her closer to him. He managed to maneuver them without breaking their kiss to lay back on the bed, wrapped in each other's arms, and they fell asleep.

CHAPTER TEN

DUKE WAS AWAKENED by Loren's body twitching in his arms. She was dreaming. He felt her fingernails press into his chest. He pulled her closer to him, but she jerked away, pushing on his chest. He released her immediately. "Loren," he whispered.

Jaz was up and in the bed. She got between them and laid next to her. Duke sat up and turned on the light. Jaz was touching Loren's face with her nose. Then Jaz pushed on her chin. Her body stopped twitching, and she wrapped her arm around Jaz. "It's all right, girl, just a dream," she whispered.

Realization flowed through him. He didn't even realize he was moving until he was out of bed. He flipped off the light and made his way down the stairs, where he picked up his clothes and got dressed in the bathroom. Quietly, he opened the door, walking out into the night. He didn't know what to do. She was dreaming about what happened to her. Jaz was a service dog. It hit Duke like a bulldozer. "She suffers from PTSD."

It all made sense to him. It wasn't just her scars. She was out there because she suffered from PTSD. "Fuck," he whispered, looking at the house. Closing his eyes, he sank to his knees and covered his mouth as

119

he cried. His beautiful girl, she believed herself unworthy of anything. Not love, not caring, not anything. His heart hurt for her.

He needed to talk to his father. He gathered himself up and went to the barn, where he saddled up Cupcake and headed home. There was a full moon so it was easy to find his way. The light in the living room was on. His father was still up.

Duke took the stairs two at a time and walked into the house. His father took one look at him and was on his feet, moving toward him. "What's the matter?" Richard said.

Duke grabbed his father. Hugging him, he cried into his neck. Richard held his son while he let it all out. "Duke, did something happen to Loren?" Duke shook his head. His father physically relaxed and held him.

When Duke got it all out, he pulled away from his father and went to the bathroom to blow his nose. When he came out, his father was sitting in his chair. Duke sat on the couch.

"Jaz is a service dog, isn't she?" Duke asked very softly.

Richard shut off the television. "What do you mean?"

"She suffers from PTSD, from what that bastard did to her." He just stared off into space. "It's why she doesn't feel worthy of love. It's why she is here. She is terrified all the time, isn't she?"

"Duke, what happened?"

"We were lying in bed talking and she fell asleep. Hell, I fell asleep, then she started to twitch and her nails dug into my chest. The next thing I know, Jaz is between us, touching her face with her nose. Then she pushed on her, and Loren wrapped her arm around Jaz and said, 'It's all right, girl, just a dream.' I sat there looking at her and it hit me."

Richard hung his head. He didn't know what to say, how to say it, so he just did. "Duke, I know this is none of my business, but have you two slept together?"

"No, Dad, we haven't."

"Duke, she came here to heal. She was doing so good. This is why I was so worried about the two of you. I am worried about Julie. If Loren snaps, it isn't going to be pretty. If you don't think you can handle this, you need to walk away now."

"What are you talking about?" I seriously think I am in love with her."

"Duke, please don't take this the wrong way, but you've only known her for a few weeks. What happened to her was worse than surviving a tour is the Middle East. That man's intent was to end her life. No one should have survived what happened to her."

"I read the article," Duke admitted.

"That article doesn't tell the whole story. Only Loren can tell you what happened. She has never spoken about it. She keeps that demon locked away inside of her. Even her psychiatrist couldn't get her to talk about it. I have spoken to her mother at length about this. Loren has never faced what happened to her. She is very fragile; you saw her reaction to you that first day. Do you know she has guns strategically placed all over that house, barn, chicken coop, and even in the damn green house?"

"Dad, what can I do to help her?"

"You say you are in love with her. Is she with you?"

"I'm pretty sure she is."

"I have talked to her mother about this. This place helped her father overcome his PTSD, but she needs to talk about it. I think you should try to get her to talk about it. Does she trust you?"

"She says she does."

"Do you believe her?"

"Yes."

"Then go pack a bag. We can get along here without you for a few days. Go stay with her, see if you can get her to talk to you. I'll come around in a day or two to see how things are going. Use finishing the barn as your reason for staying."

Duke chuckled. "Three days ago, you were over there wanting to kill me for sleeping there."

"Yeah, that's because I know what is going on with her, and I didn't want you to take advantage of her."

Duke laughed. "Thanks, Dad, but I'm not a pig, you know."

"I know, and I apologized for it. Now, go pack a bag and get back. How did you get here? I didn't hear the four-wheeler?"

"I rode Cupcake. I didn't want to wake her up."

Richard laughed. "Well, I can guarantee you she is up now."

"Yeah, you're probably right." He got up and ran upstairs and packed a bag for a few days. Coming back down, he said, "Thanks, Dad."

"No thanks needed. I'll see you in a few days."

Duke went out and climbed on Cupcake and headed back to Loren's. When he walked up to the door, it opened and she was standing there fully dressed with her keys in her hand. She smiled at him. "Into stealing horses now?"

Duke chuckled. "No, I wanted to go get some clothes, but you were sound asleep. It was still early so I just took Cupcake so I wouldn't wake you."

She laughed. "Nice try." Setting the keys on the counter, she opened the fridge and pulled out two of the beers he had brought with him. "Come on." She moved past him and out the door.

Duke followed her with a stupid grin on his face. She sat in the chair and he sat next to her. "I was worried that you bailed on me," she said staring off toward the barn.

"Why would I do that?"

"Because of the dream. What did I say?"

"What do you mean? You didn't say anything." Now she had his attention.

"When I woke up, Jaz was in my arms instead of you. Jaz only gets in bed with me when I have those dreams," she said quietly.

"Loren," Duke began.

She shook her head. "I haven't had them in a long time; well, since I've been here actually. Your father was right. This place is magic. It heals the soul."

Duke just sat quietly. He couldn't push her. She would tell him in her own time. He saw her reach up and wipe her tears. His heart slamming in his chest, he turned to look at her.

"I've never talked about it. I'm not sure I can."

"Why do you think the dreams came back? Was it because of what we shared?"

"I don't know, but for the past two years, I haven't allowed myself to get comfortable. I'm comfortable with you. I feel safe with you. Maybe it's my subconscious telling me it's time to let it go. I don't know, but I'm not sure I can do this, Duke." She was crying now.

Duke got up and pulled her off her chair into his lap. "You don't need to do anything you don't want to." His heart hurt for her. She was shaking in his arms. "I told you before, and I will tell you until the day you die, that I am not going anywhere. I love you, Loren, more than I did yesterday, and I am sure that tomorrow I will love you more than today."

She nodded. "But it isn't fair for you not to know what is inside of me, what makes me do the things I do, act the way I act. I'm so scared all the time, except for when I am here like this in your arms. I never thought I would ever know this feeling. Not after what happened." She chuckled. "I have nine guns strategically placed around this property. There isn't a place that I go that I don't have access to one."

Duke laughed. "Well, thank you for warning me not to sneak up on you."

She tilted her head up, putting her hand on his face. "I would never hurt you."

Duke kissed her lightly. "Same goes for me. When you are ready to talk to me, to share it with me, you will. I'm in no hurry. We have the rest of our lives."

She smiled. "Yes, perhaps, but I am fearful that you will run for the hills after you get to know me better. I cook to calm myself down, and you've seen how much I cook."

"My mom has been gone for ten years. I could use some good cooking. Besides, if tonight was any indication, we are going to need our strength."

"Why won't you make love to me?" she whispered. He watched as her face blushed.

"Because we aren't there yet. I'm not about to take that part of you until you are ready. Hell, until I am ready. Baby, you are still a virgin, and if you haven't noticed, I am a gentleman. Do I want you?" He laughed and pressed his crotch into her. "Yes, I want you. It hurts I want you so bad. Will I take you in uncontrolled passion and desire? No, baby, I won't. I'm not that man. I want this with you always, I'm sure of it."

She snuggled into his chest. "So, why did you go get some clothes?"

Duke laughed. "Trust me, there is no way I am going to sleep alone after tonight. We have a barn to build and I need my sleep. If I wasn't here, I would just lay awake thinking about being here. So, I figured, if it's all right with you, I'll stay with you for a few days." He leaned in and whispered, "Besides, I seem to always be hard and my boxers get wet and that's just gross. I needed clean underwear."

Loren busted out laughing. She loved how he always made her feel safe. "I love you, Duke Reynolds."

"That's a good thing, because I love you, Loren Mitchell."

He kissed her and she climbed off his lap and back into her chair. Duke grabbed his beer and sat on the ground between her legs. They didn't say anything; they just enjoyed the night while Loren played with his hair.

"What did Richard say?" she asked softly.

"He's the one who told me to stay here with you."

"Hmm, it's funny, he was here a few days ago ready to kill you, thinking you took advantage of me."

"That's what I said to him. But he convinced me that he was only looking out for you."

"He's become my savior in all of this mess that was my life. He gave me this land. He talks to me almost every day. I think he understands what I am going through. He tells me stories of him and my father and the things they overcame to get where they could be normal again." Her voice was softer somehow. Duke noticed a calm had come over her.

"I don't know those stories; he's always just been my dad."

"The same for me. Sometimes, I can see the pain in his eyes. But I think, if it wasn't for him, I'd still be locked away in my house in Austin. I didn't leave it for over six months. I couldn't bring myself to walk out the door."

"What made you decide to do it?"

She laughed. "Jaz. One day, the mailman knocked on the door and Jaz went nuts. She wouldn't let me open it, so he had to leave the package on the step. It hit me that day, she didn't feel comfortable with him, so she was protecting me. I knew then that she wouldn't let anyone hurt me. When the dreams were bad, even as a puppy, she would get in bed with me, touch my face with her nose, and if I didn't wake up and talk to her, she would nudge me until I did. It's the only time she gets in the bed."

Duke reached up and squeezed her leg. He knew she was starting to open up to him. Even though he was terrified to hear what she had to say, he knew it would only bring them closer. Closer to the day when she was completely healed, the day they would make love.

"Speaking of bed, should we go back to it?"

Loren chuckled. "Why, Mr. Reynolds, would that be an invitation to get naked with you?"

Duke laughed, getting up on his knees and wrapping his arms around her waist. "Only if you want to," he whispered as he kissed her.

"Oh, I want to. I love the way you feel against me. I never knew a man rippled with muscles could be so comfortable."

"You think I am rippled with muscles?"

She giggled. "Don't be coy, Mr. Reynolds."

Picking her up in his arms, he carried her into the house. Jaz was right behind them. Sitting her down, he locked the door. "May I?" he asked.

She nodded and watched him take off his boots, then he bent to take hers off. Smiling at her, he pulled his shirt over his head, then wrapped his arms around her, kissing her. When he pulled back, his hands slid up her sides, taking her shirt with them. He pulled it up and over her head, only to discover she wasn't wearing a bra. "Hmmm, this is new," he whispered as his hands cupped her breasts.

"I thought I would entice you to come back home with me." She closed her eyes as he squeezed her breasts.

"You were on your way to get me?" He kissed her.

"Yes," she cried out as he rolled her nipples between his fingers.

Slowly, his hands moved down her body, his fingers slipping into her shorts, unbuttoning them then pulling the zipper down. His hands slid around to cup her ass. "You have an incredible ass, Miss Mitchell." He pulled her to him, her arms wrapping around his neck.

"You have incredible hands, Mr. Reynolds." She moaned as he hooked his thumbs in her shorts, pulling them down to her thighs. They fell the rest of the way down her legs and she stepped out of them. Her hands slid down his chest to his stomach. Undoing his jeans, she did the same, only she continued down to her knees.

Before he could stop her, she covered the head of his cock with her mouth. Duke nearly collapsed from the sheer pleasure she brought him.

"Ahh, fuck, Loren." He moaned as her hands slid up his thighs. He stepped out of his jeans and stepped back, kneeling, shaking his head. "Beautiful, please don't take this the wrong way, but no."

She smiled. "But I want to." Her hands moved to wrap around him.

Duke closed his eyes and swallowed. "Not yet. We... I..." He was enjoying her stroking him. Her hand reached under, cupping his balls. "Ahh, beautiful, what are you doing to me?" She was so gentle.

"I've never wanted to do this, Duke, but I want to now." She kissed him.

His hands flew to her face, holding her head as he deepened the kiss. "Please, baby. I just can't. It's not right."

She drew her lip into her mouth and slowly released him. Their eyes never looked away. "I like the way you feel in my hands... in my mouth. It's very soft on my tongue."

Duke swallowed. "I love the way you feel on me, you beautiful, incredible woman," he whispered to her. She smiled at him, kissing him.

He managed to lay her back on the floor, covering her body with his. He rested on his elbows, his hands in her hair, kissing her. Shifting, he slid his leg between hers. She lifted her leg over his hip. Duke's hand trailed down her side to her ass, and he pulled her onto her side then onto his chest. Her hair fell around them.

"Let me take you to bed."

She smiled at him and nodded. When she climbed off him, he got up on shaky legs and grabbed his boxers out of his bag, slipping them on. Then together, holding hands, they climbed the stairs to her loft. Jaz was already in her bed sleeping. As Loren crawled onto the bed, Duke couldn't help it. His hands reached for her hips, stopping her from lying down.

His mouth opened as he planted a very wet kiss on her ass. As he closed his mouth, he bit her gently. How he wanted to be buried deep inside her. Gently, he pressed on her back so she would lie down, then he turned her over, kissing her through her panties. "Duke," she whispered as he moved to her breasts, to her perfect hard nipples. Loren cried out as she began to come undone. Duke felt her body respond to him. Goosebumps appeared all over her. Moving down her body, he laid his head on her stomach and wrapped his arms around her. *One day. One day, this is where my child will be.* He knew she was the one for him. He was going to marry this woman. Loren's hands moved to his hair. "You all right?" she whispered.

"Yes, just thinking about how lucky I am to have you to love, to have you love me in return."

"I do, you know?"

"I know." He picked his head up and smiled at her, his fingers gently touching her through her panties. He watched as her eyes closed to the feeling. Duke slipped his fingers under the waistband and through her wetness. "God, beautiful, you are so wet." Her back came off the bed as he kissed her lovingly. Taking his time, he simply made love to her with his fingers and his mouth.

"Oh, Duke, it's happening again," she moaned as she came undone. Her whole body tightened.

He paused while she came. "That's it, beautiful," he moaned, then he covered her mouth with his, pulling her into his arms and holding her. Loving her, wanting nothing more than what he had in his arms. Duke thought she'd fallen asleep; he lay holding her as he started to drift off.

"It was the middle of the night," she whispered. Duke's eyes opened. "I was just leaving after a major surgery, a car accident. A little girl wasn't wearing her seat belt, and she went through the windshield. I remember I was so pissed. I couldn't understand why her parents didn't have her in a car seat. I was checking my text messages, hoping there was one from him. I was really starting to like him. He was funny, charming, and very attentive. We had gone out a few times. Never did I feel uncomfortable with him. No warning bells went off in my head.

"I was halfway to my car when he grabbed me from behind and slammed his knife into my gut." He felt her hand move to the scar on her stomach. "I remember everything, every one of them. He pulled the knife out, and I leaned forward as he slammed it into me again." Her hand went to her hip. "He hit my bone. It hurt so bad. I tried to scream, but he was choking me. I managed to get his arm in my mouth when he was moving his knife up to my neck. His arm was in the way, so I bit down, and he dragged it along my face. By that time, my endorphins kicked in and I couldn't feel the pain anymore. But I could feel the knife each time he slammed it into me. The things he said to me haunt me."

Duke pulled her to him, tears flowing from his eyes. His heart broke for her.

"In all the years I have been a surgeon, as many times as I performed that operation, I lost only one patient. His underlying injuries wouldn't allow him to survive, but it was his brother. His only brother. I didn't know. Every time he stabbed me, he told me I was to blame for his death. He believed an eye for an eye. A death for a death. A life for a life. When my resistance failed, he just dropped me to the ground and stood over me. I tried to get away, tried to crawl away. He sliced my back open, nearly severing my spine, and then kicked me in the ribs. My body finally gave up and I blacked out.

"I don't know who found me or what happened, or that my father died next to my bed when he saw me. I was in a coma for five months. I didn't talk for eight months after that. The dreams, the recall of it all in my mind, nearly drove me to suicide."

He felt her body shake as she drew a breath. Duke couldn't talk. He just held on to her. No other words were said. They both cried themselves to sleep holding on.

~

Loren woke before Duke. She slipped out of bed, wanting to let him sleep. She grabbed some clothes and made her way to the shower. She couldn't believe she'd told him. It was easier than she thought it would be.

When she walked out of the bathroom, he was sitting on the stairs in his jeans. Loren walked up to him, stepping between his legs. "You all right?"

"Baby, I am better than all right. How about you?" His hand came up to touch her face.

She leaned in and kissed him. "I'm better now," she whispered. "Thank you."

He smiled, knowing what she meant. "Anytime, gorgeous. Anytime. Mind if I use your shower?"

She giggled. "You should have joined me."

"You're killing me. You know that, right?" He chuckled.

"I'll make us something to eat. Three eggs?" She turned to move but he grabbed her by the hips, pulling her so her back was against his chest. He kissed her neck, breathing in her vanilla and strawberry scent. His hand slowly moved up her body, coming to rest just beneath her breasts. Loren reached up and put her arms around his neck, stretching back, pushing her breasts outward. She turned her head to kiss Duke as his hands came up and cupped her breasts. He gently squeezed them, making her nipples taut. "Duke," she whispered.

Smiling, he slid one hand down beneath her jeans and into her panties. His finger slipped through her folds. "Mmm," he moaned in her mouth. He pulled his finger out and let her go. With a wicked smile on her face, she turned and flung herself into his arms, kissing him hard. She nearly knocked him into the wall. Duke grabbed her ass, pulling her up his body. Loren straddled him.

"You are so naughty," she whispered, smiling at him.

He was pretty sure she had no clue what she did to him when she spoke in that fucking sexy ass voice of hers. It made his heart beat faster every time he heard it. They felt different today, closer. Calmer, if he was putting a name to it.

Duke slowly pulled out of the kiss. "If we don't stop, Loren, we aren't getting out of this house anytime soon."

She giggled as she moved off of him. He watched as she walked to the kitchen. He needed a minute to get his bearings. She made him feel like putty. Smiling, he licked his lips and got off the stairs. Loren was getting bacon on and making coffee, when he walked up behind her and pressed his cock into her ass. "See what you do to me?"

She leaned back against him. "You do the same to me."

He chuckled, kissing her neck. "I know. I felt it."

He went to the bathroom to take a shower. She had all kinds of bottles in there. She opened the door. "I got this for you." She handed him a bottle of shampoo and some soap. "I didn't think you wanted to smell like a girl all day."

He laughed. "I like the way you smell. Vanilla and Strawberries."

She felt herself blush as she walked out. Smiling, she finished the bacon and cracked the eggs in the pan. As she was putting the plates on the table, Duke walked out of the bathroom with just his jeans on. Loren felt her heart flutter as she looked at him. They hung low on his hip. She could see the V that sculpted his lower body. "Fuck, Duke," she whispered.

He smiled and chuckled. "What?" He bent down to kiss her.

"You're fucking gorgeous." She felt herself blush.

"Thank you. You're not so bad yourself."

They ate while smiling at one another. When they finished, they went out and started on the last three beams, talking, laughing, and sharing everything about themselves. She listened to Duke tell her stories of all the trouble he and Derek would get into as children. Then Joe and Alex were born and they were worse still.

They made sandwiches together and ate outside for lunch, still laughing and sharing shy smiles. When they finished, they put into place all the support beams and called it a day. "I'm going to head into town and pick up some supplies. Do you want to come?" she asked him.

He smiled at her. "I would love to come. Our first shopping trip together."

Loren busted out laughing. "Oh, how romantic."

Duke grabbed her around the waist and kissed her. "Hey, I know how to show a girl a good time." Laughing, Loren grabbed the keys to her truck and tossed them to Duke. "I get to drive? But you asked me on this date."

She grabbed the keys out of his hand and took off running toward the truck laughing. He caught her about halfway there, lifting her up and carrying her the rest of the way. He opened the passenger side, letting Jaz jump in first, then he sat her down. "But..." she said and he kissed her.

"No buts. I'm driving." He reached for the keys, but she wouldn't let them go. His other hand came up to her neck and he leaned in for another kiss. This one took her breath away. She let go of the keys to bury her hands in his hair.

"Drive then," she whispered as she turned to put her seat belt on.

Duke laughed and shut her door. He watched her as he walked around the front of the truck. She gave him a quirky little smile, making him laugh.

They laughed and talked all the way to town. Together, they shopped at the grocery store, laughing and making fun of each other. When it came time to pay, Loren pulled out her credit card, but Duke covered her hand and slid in front of her with his back to the clerk, handing her his credit card. He put his hands on her hips. "There is no way you are paying for this. Don't argue with me."

"Next time, it's mine." She smiled at him, putting her card in her pocket.

"It will never be your time," he whispered, kissing her on the forehead. He turned around to sign the machine, thanking the cashier who was smiling like a smitten teenager at him.

Loren pushed the cart out to the truck and started to load everything in the back next to Jaz. When Duke walked out, he was graced with her perfect ass leaning into the truck. He was instantly hard. Shaking his head, he couldn't for the life of him imagine life without her. He walked over and leaned against her, whispering in her ear, "You are so beautiful."

Giggling, she pushed up and he moved off her. "Right back at you, babe." She grabbed two more bags and put them in. Duke loaded the rest and pushed the cart back toward the store as Loren got in. She was petting Jaz and didn't see Julie walk up to Duke. It wasn't until Jaz growled that Loren turned to see Julie with her hands on his chest. Duke was trying to get away from her, but she had a hold of his shirt. "Stay here," she said to Jaz as she got out of the truck.

"Julie, I told you not to touch me," Duke said with his hands on her wrists.

"Duke, you love me. You wanted to marry me," she whined and pleaded with him.

Loren walked up and tapped her on the shoulder. Julie let go of Duke and turned around. "Would you mind not putting your hands on him? Now he's going to smell like that horrible perfume you wear." Looking at Duke who was smiling, she said, "You done? I'm ready to go." She turned to walk away and Julie grabbed her arm.

"Who exactly do you think you are talking to?" Julie said to her.

Loren could hear Jaz going crazy in the truck. Duke was looking at the dog. Jaz managed to get the door open and was running toward them. Loren simply said, "Sit." Jaz stopped and sat right next to her, leaning on her legs. "Take your hand off of me."

"Or what?" Julie barked at her.

"Or my dog is going to remove it for you."

Julie looked at Jaz, who had her teeth bared and was growling. She let go of Loren. "He doesn't belong to you," she said.

Loren laughed. "It's not your decision or mine. He chooses, not you. He doesn't want you. Look at you. You can have any man you want. He doesn't want you, Julie."

She laughed. "And you think he wants you? Look at you."

Loren smiled at her. "His choice." When she turned to walk away, Julie reached for her to grab her arm again, but Jaz stepped between them and barked at her.

"Jaz," Loren said, and just as quickly, Jaz was next to her. Duke followed behind her, opening her door and letting Jaz in first and then helping Loren in. He shut the door, never taking his eyes off of her as he walked around to the driver's side. Climbing in, he looked at her then at Jaz, who sat between them looking at Julie with her teeth bared.

He chuckled as he started the truck and put on his seatbelt. He went to put the truck in reverse, when Loren's hand touched his leg. She squeezed it. He put his hand on hers, slipping his fingers under it. "Get us out of here," she whispered.

Duke put the truck in reverse and pulled out. He drove down the road a ways and then pulled over. Loren had her seatbelt off and was in his lap before he knew what was happening. She was shaking as she wrapped her arms around his neck, pulling herself close to his chest.

"I've got you," he whispered. "I've got you." She buried her face in his neck and cried. Duke held her close. Jaz pushed her way into their hug, leaning on Loren. Duke didn't understand what was happening, but he caught on when Jaz put her face on Loren's. She wrapped her arm around Jaz and Duke held them both. As Loren calmed down, Jaz moved back to her spot.

"Thank you," she whispered to Duke.

"Anytime, anywhere, always," he whispered back, kissing her head. "I love you."

Loren pulled back to look at him. His hands moved up to her face to wipe her tears away. "Some shopping date, huh?"

Loren giggled. "The best one I've ever had."

Duke smiled. "Come on, let's go home."

Loren climbed off Duke's lap sitting next to him, putting the middle seatbelt on. He kept his arm wrapped around her, keeping her tucked into his side. They drove for a little while when Loren spoke.

"I'm sorry about that back there."

"Don't be ridiculous," Duke said softly.

"I don't mean the crying; well, I do, but I meant what happened with Julie. I had no business getting out of the truck."

"You have every right. I'm with you. We are together. No one has the right to touch me, just as no one has the right to touch you. Not with the intent Julie has." He squeezed her shoulder. "Loren, I don't want to be with her."

"I know. I just don't know what came over me. I swear I'm not jealous," she whispered.

"Aww, baby, you don't need to worry about her." He pulled her closer.

Loren giggled. "I'm not worried about her. Well, maybe just a little because she is gorgeous. I just didn't like that she was touching you the way I touch you."

Duke pulled over to the side of the road, putting the truck in park. Loren sat up as he turned to her. "No one touches me the way you do." He chuckled. "Trust me, no one has ever touched me the way you do."

She smiled at him. "And how do I touch you that makes it so different?" She was serious.

"Don't you know?" Loren shook her head. "You touch me with love, with tenderness, with desire. The look in your eyes, the feel of your hands, your mouth, these lips." He reached up and ran his thumb along them. "I've never known that feeling. I wouldn't ever do something to stop that, or to give you cause to stop touching me like that."

"Yeah?" she whispered, drawing her bottom lip between her teeth.

"Oh, yeah." Duke leaned in to kiss her. "Can I take you home now? I would really like to kiss you some more." He smiled at her.

She laughed. "Oh, Mr. Reynolds, I think you want to do more to me than kiss me."

"Miss Mitchell, you are so right," he said as she grabbed his face and kissed him.

"Then take me home," she whispered in his mouth before she pulled away.

Duke put the truck in drive and they headed back to her tiny house. When they arrived, he brought all the groceries in while Loren put everything away. "I need to get something on for dinner. How about a stir fry? It's quick and easy."

Duke picked her up and carried her up the stairs, sitting her on the loft floor. "I'm hungry for something else," he whispered.

Loren felt herself blush. "But…" He stopped her from talking when he covered her mouth with his.

"I want to taste you."

Loren looked at him. She knew he would want to do this, and she was so ready. Smiling, she giggled and crawled over to the bed. Duke followed her, pushing her back on the bed while he kissed her. "What are you hungry for?" she whispered between kisses.

His hand cupped her breast. "These," he rasped out.

She closed her eyes, enjoying the feel of his hands on her. "Mmm, what else?"

His hand moving down her body, he undid her jeans and slipped his hand in them. "This," he whispered. "So very much this."

Loren's body lifted off the bed. "Ahh," she cried out. "Duke." She shuddered.

"That's it, baby. So beautiful," he whispered to her as he watched her come. When she came down, he got up and pulled her jeans off. Loren closed her legs at the knees, biting her lip. Duke knew she was scared. "We don't have to do this."

"I want to, I'm just a bit scared. I've never done this."

He moved so fast, pulling her to him. "Hey, never will I force you."

She kissed him. "I want to. I so really want to." She pulled away from him, laying on her back. Her eyes never leaving his, she nodded to him.

Slowly, he moved to kneel on the bed at her feet. She was beautiful, her chest heaving up and down in anticipation. Her were nipples so hard, and gooseflesh crawled along her skin. Gently, he reached for her feet, slowly pulling them down one at a time and placing one on either side of his. His eyes never left hers. He needed to know she was all right. This was such a big step for her. He watched her eyes dilate and turn deep purple. "You are so beautiful," he whispered.

Slowly, he moved his eyes down her body, drinking her in. Perfection was the best word to describe her. As he came to her plush mound, he realized she was a true blonde. Closing his eyes, he swallowed. His mouth watered. He caressed his hands up her legs, gently pushing them apart. She glistened as she opened for him. He moved his hands to either side of her hips, inhaling her scent. Getting comfortable—well, as comfortable on his stomach as his erection would allow—his fingers moved into her hair. "God, beautiful. Look at you."

He moved his mouth to her and slowly made love to her with his tongue. She blew through two orgasms before he ever got to her swollen bud. "So good," he moaned as he drew her into his mouth, gently suckling her.

Loren cried out as she went over the edge. Her whole body convulsed as a full-blown orgasm ripped through her. Duke couldn't get enough of her, loving the way she responded to the gentlest touch. She gave him everything. When he finished taking all she had to give him, he crawled back up her body, kissing her. Pulling her into his arms, he held her.

They lay wrapped around each other. She drew little circles around his nipple. "I don't know what happened to me today."

"Loren, can I ask you something?" He was gentle with his words.

"Yes," she whispered, swallowing.

"Since we met, the occasions that were uncomfortable, did you fall apart like you did today?" She nodded her head. Closing his eyes, he said, "How many times baby?"

"A few."

"Do you know why this happens to you?" His hand rubbed up and down her back. He didn't even see her scars anymore, nor did he feel them. They were very much a part of her beauty.

"Not always."

"Do confrontations upset you? Do they make you afraid?"

"Duke, everything makes me afraid. People do. I have mapped the human brain. It took a long time to do. I know what every blood vessel does, how every little electrical charge sparks a reaction. But I don't know human nature. I don't know why people do what they do. That man was someone I trusted, someone I felt comfortable with, and he did this to me. He couldn't understand that his brother's underlying injuries were the reason he died. But yet he blamed me."

"I don't know why people do the things they do. I couldn't tell you why Julie thinks she has any claim on me. But do you think it was your fault, what he did to you?"

"I used to. I suppose, on some level deep inside, I still do. On any other night, I would have stayed at the hospital. But that night, for some reason… Well, not just some reason. I was hoping to see him. I left to go home. I always stayed with my patients through the night. But not that night. I was being selfish. So, in a sense, it was my fault."

"No, Loren, it was not your fault. Don't you realize that he would have waited for another night. A night you two were truly alone. A night where no one would have found you. A night that would have taken you away from me forever."

He felt her smile against his chest. "You didn't know me."

"No, but if all of this didn't happen to you, I wouldn't know you now. I wouldn't get to look into your incredible violet eyes. I wouldn't get to touch you like this. I wouldn't get to kiss you or hear your laugh. I wouldn't get to make love to you."

She tilted her head up. "But you haven't made love to me," she whispered in her sexy fucking voice that turned him on.

He rolled them over and kissed her. "No, I haven't. But I am going to. And in case you are wondering, I plan on being the only man who ever does." He kissed her again.

"You are so sure of yourself." She giggled.

"I am, beautiful, as you should be. I'm not going anywhere. Loren, maybe thinking that what happened, when it happened, brought you to me. Brought you to us, to this life we have now. To the life we are going to have for always."

"Duke," she whispered. "How can anything be guaranteed?"

"Nothing in this life is, beautiful. All we have is here and now. But there is nothing wrong with wanting. Do you want a life with me?"

She laughed. "Considering the position I am in right now and knowing that no man has done to me the things you do to me, I am in this life with you. I want tomorrow, and the day after, and the day after that. I want you always."

His hand cupped her breast as he kissed her. "Then you shall have it. Because I want nothing more than you."

"As good as this feels, we need to eat, and I have to feed Cupcake and the chickens."

He pouted. "But I want this," he said as his mouth wrapped around her nipple.

"Ahh, God, Duke," She moaned.

Pulling back, he smiled at her and plopped back on the bed. Giggling, Loren got up and grabbed a little sun dress, slipping it over her head, and then made her way down the stairs.

Duke followed her. "I'll go take care of Cupcake and the chickens."

"Thank you." She kissed him.

While Duke was tending to the animals, Loren managed to cut up everything for the stir fry, then grabbed her basket and headed out to the garden. Duke was coming out of the barn as she crossed the lawn. He watched her as the sun shone through her little dress. His cock hardened at the sight of her.

She picked strawberries and some tomatoes along with some other fruit. Duke made his way to the chair to watch her. She was beautiful, and innocent, and scared, and broken. He wanted to mend her heart and make her feel safe. Not to mention, if she bent down again he was going to have a hard time not making love to her. She wasn't wearing anything under that dress. He knew this because he watched her get dressed.

Loren finished and headed back to him. She could see the lust in his eyes, and she could also see the erection in his jeans. Walking up to him, she set the basket on the ground and straddled him. "Seems you have a problem."

He chuckled. "And what would that be?" he asked, knowing damn well what she was talking about. But the fact that she was spread wide sitting on his thighs only made him harder.

Bending her head to kiss him, her beautiful blonde hair tumbled around their faces. "You're so fucking hard. I could see you across the lawn."

"Mmm, yes, you are correct."

"Come inside with me. I'm wanton of you," she whispered in his mouth as she seductively kissed him.

"I can't do that?"

She pouted. "Why?"

"Because you shouldn't be doing that to me."

"Why not? You did it to me."

"That's different."

She giggled. "Why is it different?"

"Because, you are the woman and I am the man. It should be about your pleasure, not mine."

"But it would give me great pleasure to give you pleasure."

He chuckled. "Nice try, but I'm all right."

She rubbed her hand along his cock. "If you say so." She smiled and climbed off him.

It took everything he had not to grab her. "I'll be inside in a minute."

Loren giggled and made her way into the house. She pulled some pie dough out of the fridge that she had made earlier in the week and proceeded to make two strawberry pies. As she was putting them in the oven, Duke walked in. "You ready to eat?"

He nodded and headed to the bathroom to clean up. It didn't take Loren long to make stir fry, and within fifteen minutes, they were eating. Duke didn't say anything during dinner, not even while they cleaned up. When Loren pulled the pies out of the oven, she made her way upstairs to change her clothes.

Duke was outside sitting in the chair drinking a beer, lost in his thoughts. Everything she had told him was bothering him. The way he had assumed it was acceptable to touch her the way he had. To let her touch him was wrong. She was suffering from PTSD and he needed to help her, not take advantage of her. His father was right about him, and what she said about human behavior. Why would he do that? Was it because he was a horny ass pig of a man, or was it because he was selfish and wanted to know what she felt like, what she tasted like? He was there to help her, to comfort her, not to ravish her body and take what he wanted. But that's what he was doing.

Loren put one of the pies in her pie carrier and put it in the truck. She didn't know why Duke denied her, or why he wasn't talking, but she needed to talk to Richard. Jaz jumped in the truck and Loren started it up and headed to Richard's without saying anything to Duke. He was so wrapped up in his own thoughts that he didn't even notice she was gone.

Pulling into the drive at the ranch, she saw Richard sitting on the porch with Derek. They were laughing as she got out of the truck. She smiled at Richard. "I bought pie over for you."

"Please tell me it's strawberry," he said.

"It is," Loren told him as she pulled it out of the truck.

"Well, Dad, I'm going to get going," Derek said.

"All right, I'll see you in the morning."

Derek smiled and walked down the stairs. "Good to see you again, Loren."

"Good to see you, too," she said as she made her way to the porch and took his seat. Setting the pie down on the table, she sat back in her chair.

"Where's Duke?" Richard asked.

"I'm not sure. Richard, I need to talk to you about some things. Do you have time?"

He laughed. "For you, I have all the time in the world. What's going on?"

"Well, last night I told Duke what happened to me, every detail that I could remember. I've never told anyone before, but I figured these feelings I have for him aren't going away. If anything, they are getting stronger."

"This is good, Loren. Your doctor said you needed to talk about it."

"I suppose, but it doesn't feel good. I feel like he has changed toward me a little."

"That's not true, honey. I know my son, and he is falling in love with you, if he hasn't already."

"We went shopping today in town and had a run in with Julie. After it was over, I think I had some kind of meltdown."

Richard looked at her. "What do you mean, you think?"

"Well, he was driving away, and I remember putting my hand on his thigh, asking him to pull over. I don't remember anything after that, until Jaz pressed her nose into my face a few times. Richard, I have no idea how long I was in his lap."

"Loren, how many times has this happened to you since you've been here?"

She smiled. "Duke asked me the same thing. Well, he didn't know about my loss of time, but he asked me how many times I reacted like that. I lied to him and told him a few, but honestly, Richard, it's been many. I didn't want to tell him. When we got home, he didn't talk. We snuggled for a bit, made dinner, and he didn't talk to me. He was sitting out back when I left. I don't think he knows I'm even gone." She wiped her tears. "Richard, I'm in love with him. I don't know how, but I know that when I saw Julie touch him, I felt it here." She touched her heart. "I'm terrified that who I am now isn't someone he would want. Yes, he tells me I'm beautiful and he makes me feel beautiful. But who I am now, in here, I'm terrified he won't or can't love her."

Richard leaned over and pulled her into a hug. "He loves you, sweetheart. He is a deep feeling man. Everything you told him, everything that happened would be more than most could handle. I'm sure he is just processing it all. You did right by coming here instead of just sitting there wondering. I'm sure he will talk to you."

Pulling away, she wiped her tears. "He told me that I should look at what happened to me, not in the negative, but in the positive, because it brought me here to him."

"That sounds like a man in love to me."

"I know this isn't something you are comfortable with, but you have become the father figure in my life, and as much as I love my mother, I was always closer to my father, so this conversation would be one I would have had with him. In fact, I sort of did, right before Bruce tried to kill me."

"Are we going to have the sex talk?" He was kidding.

Loren laughed. "Well, sort of. I want to make love with him, but he won't touch me."

Richard's heart smiled. "Loren, he is an honorable man."

"Perhaps, but he had sex with Julie."

"Yes, he did. Being a man, in our mind, it's different. Sex is just sex, but when we make love to the woman we love, it means so much more. He had sex with her. He didn't love her. He might have thought he did, and perhaps sex with her was great. But with you, he loves you. And I'm pretty sure I have something to do with why he won't."

"What do you mean?" She looked at him.

"I might have implied that you weren't that kind of girl."

She laughed. "I'm not. But I want to be with him. But he won't and I keep thinking, maybe because I'm so inexperienced is why he doesn't want to."

Richard laughed, and he laughed loud. "I'm a man, and believe me when I tell you, that is not it at all."

"See, now, why is that funny? I don't know. I'm so confused, and worried, and upset."

"Listen, sweetheart, just tell him the truth and trust him enough to hear you. He will talk to you. We process things differently than women do."

Loren nodded and picked up the pie. "Thank you, Richard. I'm going to put this in the kitchen." She walked in the house and put the pie on the counter. Opening the fridge, she pulled out two beers and went back to the porch.

Richard smiled. Taking the beer, he said, "Thank you."

They sat on the porch drinking their beers. "So, what are you going to do?" Richard asked.

She chuckled. "I'm going to drink this beer and then I'm going home to cook."

They sat there in the quiet for a bit while they drank their beers. Loren heard the four-wheeler in the distance. "Well, I'm going to go. Duke should be here in a few minutes. I'm sure he wants to talk to you, too. I'm sorry that you are in the middle of this. I've been thinking that maybe I should just go somewhere else. I have all that money my dad left me. I could buy some land somewhere. Maybe then Duke wouldn't be so conflicted. I feel like I've brought nothing but turmoil to you and yours. I'll talk to you tomorrow." She didn't give Richard time to respond; she just got in the truck with Jaz and headed home.

Richard watched as she drove away. His heart hurt for her. *Turmoil is right*, he thought, but it wasn't him and his, it was her. She was living in it. A few minutes after she pulled out onto the highway, Duke pulled up. It was obvious to Richard that he was disappointed, even worried that Loren wasn't there. Duke got off the four-wheeler and climbed the porch steps, sitting in the seat Loren had just vacated.

"She was here?" Duke asked.

"She was," Richard said. He was going let Duke talk.

"Dad, I'm lost." That's not what Richard wanted to hear.

"What can I do to help you, son?"

"Secretly give me the ability to read a woman's mind."

Richard's laughter rang out. Duke just sat there sulking. "Son, there isn't a man alive who hasn't wished for that. What's going on?"

"So much that I don't know where to begin. I think us being together is helping her a little, but I'm not sure half of the time. I'm so in love with her, and yet I feel like she isn't letting me in."

Richard chuckled. "She just said the same thing about you."

Duke closed his eyes. "Dad, I want to love her. I want to make love to her, and not because I am so horny my eyes are floating on backed-up semen, but because I want her to know how much I love her."

Richard nearly choked on his beer. "Duke, what are your intentions?"

"I want to spend the rest of my life loving her. I want it all."

Richard got up, "Stay here," he said as he walked into the house. He was gone for a little while, then the screen door opened, and he walked back out. Sitting in his chair, he set a box on the table.

Duke looked at the box and then at Richard. "What's that?"

"Duke, Loren is not the kind of woman that you have sex with. She is the kind of woman you make love to. I just explained this to her. She wants you the same way. I explained to her that Julie was the kind of girl you had sex with, because there weren't any feelings involved. But when a man makes love to a woman, it's because he loves her, cherishes her, respects her. If this is how you feel about Loren, then take that and do the right thing before you cross that line. Tell her how you feel, show her that you mean what you say. If you can't do that, then don't cross that line."

Duke swallowed hard. He had no idea what was in the box. With a shaking hand, he reached for the box. Holding it in his hand, he slowly opened it. He sat there with tears running down his face. "Dad, I can't."

"Yes, you can. Your mother wanted you to have it. She made me promise that, when you found the one that would love you like she loved me, I was to give that to you."

"But, Dad."

"No buts about it, Duke. That was given in love and received in love. If you love Loren like I loved your mother, then it will be given in love again, and if she loves you like I know she does, it will be received in love."

"We've only known each other for a few weeks."

Richard laughed. "Son, I knew your mother for three days when I bought that ring. It was one week when I asked her. I knew she was the one I wanted. Do you know that of Loren?"

Duke nodded. "Dad, if I was going to marry Julie, would you have given this to me?"

"No, that woman only loves herself."

Duke chuckled. "You're right. What am I going to do about her?"

"Leave that to me. She won't bother you again."

Duke looked at his father. "I'm going to take Roxy back to Loren's. She hasn't ridden in a few days, and I thought I would go with her."

"Take her. You're the only one she will let ride her anyway. Let me know how things turn out. Now go on, I've got some pie to eat." Richard got up and patted his son on the shoulder before walking into the house.

Duke put the four-wheeler away and saddled Roxy. It took him a while to get back to Loren's. When he walked out of the barn, she was sitting on one of the chairs. She was staring off into space as he walked up. He knelt in front of her, pulling her legs out from underneath her, and he laid his head on her lap. Her hand came up and she ran her fingers through his hair.

"Why did you leave?" he asked.

"Because, I'm scared. Confused," she whispered.

He picked his head up. "Talk to me."

"I lied to you earlier today. I suppose the guilt brought up a few other insecurities I might or might not be having."

"Tell me." He cupped her face with his hands.

"When you asked me if I have those moments, I told you a few. That's not true. I have them a great deal. I used to lose days of time while I was in my own head. Now, it's hours. Today, it was minutes." He wiped her tears. "I'm not sure how to tell you this, and I'm not even sure it's real. But I think I am so in love with you. I don't know how I can be, in such a short time, but I am."

Duke smiled, kissing her gently. "That's a good thing, baby, not a bad thing. I am so in love with you. Tonight, when you left, it was my fault for not sharing what was in my head and I am sorry for that. I know that you are still so fragile, and I don't want to treat you as if you are broken. But I was afraid, too. Everything you told me, and then watching you fall apart, shook me up a bit, because I feel so deeply for you. I want nothing more than to have you whole again."

"I know, but, Duke, I might not ever be. Can you live with that?"

"Yes, baby, I can."

She nodded. "Duke, I love you. I want this with you. Please be patient with me. I am getting better."

He shook his head. "I'm not going anywhere. I love you, Loren."

"Good," was all she said as she slid off the chair onto his lap. "I'm tired. Will you come to bed with me?"

"Yes." He stood up, taking her with him, kissing her. She put her feet on the ground and they walked into the house together.

CHAPTER ELEVEN

DUKE WAITED while Loren used the bathroom. When she finished, he went in. Loren made her way up to the loft and changed into her sleep shorts and t-shirt. When Duke came up, she couldn't help but smile. He had undressed in the bathroom. As he dropped his clothes on his side of the bed, Loren rolled over to face him.

"What do you sleep in at home?" she asked.

He smiled at her, kissing her. "Nothing."

"Oh." She smiled.

"Come here, beautiful." He reached out for her. Loren turned off the light and snuggled up next to him. "It's been a long day. Do you want to talk or just go to sleep?"

"Sleep, I suppose."

He chuckled. "You suppose? Is there something you want to talk about?"

"Why won't you make love to me, with me?"

Duke lifted her chin so he could see her face. "We will. I promise you, we will."

"Richard told me that when a man has sex with a woman, he doesn't really care about her. But when he makes love to a woman, she matters to him. Will we have sex or will we make love?"

Duke turned on his side, rolling Loren on her back. Looking her in the eyes, he said, "I will never have sex with you." He leveled her with his kiss. "To me, you are not a woman to have sex with. I will always make love to you." He smiled. "And on occasion, I will fuck you. But never will we have sex."

Loren's eyes went wide when he said he would fuck her. She couldn't imagine what that would be like. They lay kissing for a few minutes and then they snuggled up and went to sleep.

They woke together, had breakfast, and got to work on the barn. Together, they talked and laughed. Jaz chased the chickens around while they had lunch. "You want to take the horses out this afternoon?" Duke asked.

"That would be great. I haven't ridden Cupcake in about a week."

"I know, that's why I rode Roxy back. Dad said that you rode every day, but since I've been around, you haven't gone riding."

Loren reached out to run her fingers down his jaw. "It isn't because of you. I've been busy getting this barn up. But, yes, let's clean up and take a ride. I'll get the chickens if you get the tools? Or you can get the chickens."

He laughed. "I'll get the tools."

Duke watched Loren try and corral the chickens. Jaz wasn't helping any, but she managed to get them all before Duke was finished with the tools. Together, they saddled the horses, walking them up to the house. "I need to use the bathroom, and I'll pack us something to eat and drink, then we can go."

"Sounds good to me."

Fifteen minutes later, they were flying through the fields. Cupcake outran Roxy every time. They ended up at the river. Duke had grabbed a blanket and they spread it out. Jaz was exhausted and crashed immediately. They had their snack and laid on the blanket, talking.

Loren was on her stomach while Duke lay on his back. "I was thinking that maybe you would consider coming to the festival with me?" Duke asked.

Loren giggled. "Isn't that what the leggy brunette wanted?" She turned her head to look at him.

"I suppose it is, but it would be weird if I went with her."

Loren smiled. "But she did ask you first."

"Yes, she did. But I was already involved with you. So, I'm asking you if you want to go with me."

"Well, what exactly will we do at this festival?"

"We can ride some silly rides. We can play some even sillier games. We can eat food, drink a few beers. We can dance and then watch the fireworks."

"It sounds like there are a great many things to do at this festival." She giggled. "I would love to go with you. Would we be able to take Jaz?"

"If we can't then we won't go. We can just go sit up on the hill with her and watch the fireworks."

"You would miss the festival for Jaz?"

Duke rolled over onto his side. "Listen, I understand that Jaz is important, and I am all right with that. There is no way I would ever assume she wasn't welcome."

"You're very accommodating."

He laughed. "Darlin', haven't you figured it out yet?"

She pulled her lip between her teeth, shaking her head. "Figured what out?"

He rolled her over on her back and kissed her. "That I would do anything for you."

"Yeah?"

"Yeah."

They lay there kissing for a little bit then raced back to her house. Walking up from the barn, Jaz took off toward the road. "Someone's coming."

Duke laughed. "She's a good watch dog."

When they reached the front of the house, Richard's truck pulled up. Loren ran up and gave him a big hug. "What brings you by?"

"Well, your mother called, and we had a talk. I wanted to tell you I made her an offer on the ranch."

"Richard, you can't afford that. I know how big that ranch is."

"Yes, but I already own a third of it. So, I made her an offer and she accepted it. I wanted to be the one to tell you. Your mom is leaving everything in the house in case you ever want to move back there." He looked at Duke.

"I need to talk to my mom," Loren said, looking at Duke. "I'll be back in a little while. Richard, make yourself at home." She went in the house and grabbed her cell phone off the charger and her keys. Duke watched her drive away.

"Dad, what are you doing?"

"I'm making sure she has a future. Whether she is with you or not, she needs to have her family home. Besides, it's a good investment. It's a working ranch, and it will remain a working ranch. Cathy has an excellent manager who is going to remain on."

"Dad," Duke started, but Richard put his hand up to stop him.

"Duke, it was a good investment. She was going to sell it either way. I just bought it. If nothing comes of it, you can sell it when I'm dead."

"Do you want a beer?"

Richard nodded and they went to sit in the back of the house.

LOREN DROVE TO THE TOP OF THE HILL WHERE SHE ALWAYS WENT TO call her mom. It had the best reception. "Hi, Mom."

"Oh, hi, baby, how are you?"

"I'm good. I just talked to Richard. Are you sure you want to do this?"

"Sweetheart, I spent my life on this ranch. It was a wonderful life, but so much of it reminds me of your father. I would have done this a long time ago, but I wanted to stay with you. Now you are all the way up there, and there is no reason for me to stay here. Your Aunt Liz and I are going to travel. Maybe we'll come up there for a little bit. Richard said he had a big house and he welcomed us."

"I would love to see you."

"How are you, honey?"

"I'm good. I've been seeing Richard's son Duke."

"Oh, sweetheart, that's wonderful. Is he good looking?"

Loren laughed. "Oh, God, Mom is he ever. He is beautiful."

She laughed. "Of course he is. His father is quite handsome."

"Mom," Loren yelled.

"What? I'm not dead, darling." Cathy laughed.

"I know, but he is my godfather."

"Yes, and Duke is his son. Besides, I never said anything would happen, just that he was handsome."

"Okay, Mom, I just wanted to make sure you were all right with it all."

"Honey, I am glad he made me the offer. At least I know you will always have a place to live, no matter what happens in your life. And John is staying on to manage the ranch."

"Thanks, but I don't think I can ever come back there."

"I know, sweetheart, but it's an option for you. So, when we close, we are going to head north to visit you, and to meet your Duke. I love you, honey."

"I love you, too."

"So, did you two get everything worked out?" Richard asked.

"Not yet, but we are working on it. Dad…" Duke paused. "I'm a bit out of my league here. I don't think I know what I'm doing. I'm terrified I am going to get it all wrong."

Richard laughed. "Well, son, you wouldn't be a man if you got it right. You'll know what to do each time something comes up. Starting a relationship like this is like having your first child. You are terrified that you won't know how to hold it, or sooth it, or even take care of it. But the minute you hold it, all that disappears. Once you get your footing, you'll do fine. She is a good woman, Duke. She just had a horrible thing happen to her. Just be patient with her."

Duke laughed. "You have seen her, right? My patience is wearing thin."

His father laughed loudly. "Your mother made me feel the same way. She was so beautiful it physically hurt me to touch her. But the rewards will be tremendous."

"No offense, Dad, but you are talking about my mother."

"She was a woman first and foremost, and she was my wife."

Loren pulled up and walked around the house. "Everything all right?" Richard asked.

"I suppose. Thank you for offering to let her stay with you." She looked at Duke. "You get to meet my mom."

He chuckled. "If she is anything like her daughter, I'm sure it will be a pleasant meeting."

"Well, on that note, this old man is going home. You two have a lovely evening."

Loren hugged him goodbye and walked him to his truck. Duke followed. When Richard was out of sight, Duke turned to her. "If it would be all right, I think I'd like to take you to bed and hold you."

She smiled. "Please do. Under one condition though."

He chuckled as they made their way up the steps. "What would be your condition?"

"That you sleep the way you do at home. If you are going to be staying here with me, I want you to be comfortable."

Duke felt his face flush. He was glad it was dark out. He chuckled. "Come on, beautiful."

Loren cleaned up first, and while Duke did, Loren made her way to the loft. She decided to forgo the sleepwear and just got into bed naked. She was sitting on the bed when he climbed the stairs. Looking at her made him harder than he already was. Smiling at her, he whispered her name. God, he wanted her.

"Remember the other day when I had you by the front door?" she said softly. Duke noticed she was blushing. God, did he remember. "I want to do that again, please."

Duke swallowed hard. He would never forget that day. He couldn't find his voice, so he said nothing. Crawling up the bed, he kissed her sweetly. She pulled his shirt over his head, her fingers and hands touching him all over. "I love you, Duke. I want to give you the same pleasure you give me. Don't say no to me."

He couldn't say no to her. He didn't want to say no to her. She kissed him as her fingers undid his jeans, and she pushed them down his thighs. As she wrapped her hands around him, he growled deep in his throat. "Take them off," she whispered. Duke did as she asked. Looking at him, she licked her lips. "Duke," she whispered as she reached for him. He kneeled next to her as she got up on her knees, kissing him. He pulled her to him so their bodies touched.

"Loren, I want you. I want to make love to you."

"I want the same, but I want to do this to you first."

When she wrapped her sweet mouth around his head, he hissed in air between his teeth. "Fuck," he whispered. Loren pressed gently on his stomach, and Duke leaned back on his hands, pushing his erection in the air. He looked down at Loren, who sat looking at it with big eyes. Then she looked up at him.

"You are so beautiful sitting like this," she said to him.

He saw the love, the wonder in her eyes. He watched as she licked her lips and lowered her head. Duke closed his eyes as the warmth of her mouth engulfed him. If he didn't concentrate, he was going to blow. Slowly, she made love to him with her fantastic mouth. It was maddening for him. The feeling was beyond euphoric.

Loren pulled back and sat up on her legs, looking at him. Duke picked his head up and watched her looking at him. He was so hard. Duke smiled and nodded to her. He watched as her tiny silken hands touched his balls then cupped them. He groaned. "Does that feel good?" she whispered in amazement.

"Yes, baby. It feels incredible."

"Can I squeeze them? They are so soft."

"Yes," he moaned out in a raspy whisper.

She was so gentle. "Oh, God, Duke." She leaned forward and his mind went blank. All he could focus on was the feel of her as her mouth took him in again. She grabbed him with one of her hands and pulled him out of her mouth when he screamed out his release.

Loren sat back and watched him. She was amazed at how every muscle in his body was tight and the way his cum shot everywhere. When she was sure he was finished, she reached for the towel and slowly and carefully wiped him off. Then she sat back and looked at him.

As Duke gathered himself, he pushed up off of his hands. His body still shaking, he leaned in and kissed her. "You beautiful girl."

She smiled. "I liked that. You are so gorgeous," she whispered.

"Aww, beautiful, thank you. But you have it all wrong. Let me love you."

She drew her lip into her mouth. He took his time moving down her body, her mews making him harder. He wanted her. God, he fucking wanted her. By the time he got to her beautiful wet mound of fluff, he was rock hard again.

He licked her from bottom to top and slipped her bud into his mouth with his tongue. It was all it took and her back arched off the bed. "Oh, God, Duke," she cried out. Duke pulled away and crawled up her body, not touching her, and watched her as she came undone.

When she opened her eyes, they were deep purple. "You are so beautiful," he whispered as he kissed her tenderly. Her legs spread as he knelt between them. He sat back to look at her. She was covered in goose flesh, her nipples harder than pebbles. Her hips gently moved up and down on the bed. When he looked at her mound of fluff, he could see her essence slowly seeping out. His heart was full. There was nowhere else on earth he wanted to be. Leaning over, he grabbed his jeans, pulling out the box his father had given him. Setting it on the bed, he reached for her hands, pulling her up.

The words just came out of his mouth. "I never believed I would find you, the woman who could or would capture my heart. I didn't think this feeling really existed. But I am thankful and grateful for you in every way. Loren, I love you. I want you always. I promise to never waver in my love or my devotion to you. Do you trust me to love you 'til the end of our days?"

Tears fell from her eyes; she had always wanted a man to say these things to her. But she believed that after what happened to her, she would never hear them. That she would never find a man to love her like this. "Yes," she whispered.

Duke picked up the box, his eyes never leaving Loren's. He opened it, took the ring out, and said, "Loren Mitchell, will you give me the privilege of becoming your husband? Will you marry me and spend your life with me?" He took her hand in his.

"Yes," she whispered. As Duke slid the ring on her finger, she looked down. "Uh," she whispered.

When she looked up, Duke leveled her with a kiss. Loren wrapped her arms around his neck, and he picked her up and slid her onto his thighs, wrapping his arms around her. Pushing up to his knees, he gently laid them down. The head of his cock brushed through her. Pulling back a bit, he paused, looking at her. She put her hand on his face as he moved his hips, pressing into her. His tip slipped through her folds to find the spot he'd wanted since their first kiss.

They couldn't undo this; she was going to be his wife. He loved her, and she loved him. He moved his hips closer to her, and she opened as wide as she could. He watched as she drew her lip into her mouth. It made him crazy when she did that. Leaning in, he kissed her as he moved his hips even closer to her. His head was inside of her. Neither of them said a word. He knew he was going to hurt her. She was so tiny and so tight.

He moved again, letting her adjust to him. He wasn't even a third of the way in. Loren moved her hips, taking him a bit further. Duke watched her purple eyes as she watched his green ones. He pulled back and pushed in a few times. Duke took a deep breath. "I love you," he whispered.

"I love you," Loren whispered.

The minute she drew in a breath, Duke pushed forward. Loren cried out as he tore through her innocence. He pulled her to his chest as his tears fell. Her grip on him was choking him. He had never felt this; never had he known how this would feel to him. He was bonded to her forever. No woman would ever know this love he had for her. When she lessened her grip on him, he pulled back. She wiped his tears, kissing him.

Duke pushed the rest of the way inside of her, filling her. She nearly made him come undone. "I love you, beautiful," he whispered as he gently and slowly pulled back.

"Ahh, Duke." Her fingernails dug into his shoulders.

"You all right?" he asked, concerned.

She nodded and he pushed back inside her. She kissed him and, slowly, he made love to her. It went on for a long time. He kept biting the inside of his mouth to stop from coming. She felt like nothing he had ever known. "Oh, God, beautiful."

"Duke, what's happening to me? My body feels like it's on fire."

He smiled and moved his hand between them. One touch of his finger on her and she cried out, gripping his cock with her insides.

"Ahhh, Duke," she cried. He couldn't take it anymore. He let go to an earth-shattering orgasm.

They gripped each other, he bit her shoulder, and she clawed his back as they came undone together. Loren burst into tears, as did Duke, both of them shaking. The depth of love he felt for her was so overwhelming. Loren couldn't believe how wonderful she felt. Her soul was at peace in his arms. She felt whole. She felt complete.

As they calmed down, Duke picked his head up, resting his body on his elbows, kissing her deeply. He kissed the tears off her cheeks. "I love you, Loren. With all that I am, you will never know anything less."

Kissing deeply, she touched his face, whispering in his mouth, "I love you."

They kissed for a while longer. Duke leaned up and reached for the towel Loren had used to wipe him off. "I'm going to pull out then I'm going to use this to wipe you off."

She giggled. "I know there is going to be blood."

Duke felt himself blush a little. "I'm sorry about that." He slowly pulled out of her and put the towel on her. Loren moved her hand down on his and he pulled his away. Sitting back on his knees, he looked down at his cock. It was covered in blood. His heart swelled with love. She gave herself to him. He would love no other.

Loren cleaned herself off. "I should go to the bathroom."

"Hey," Duke said. "Are you all right?"

She smiled a smile that touched her eyes. "Why wouldn't I be? I'm in love. I'm going to marry the man I love, and I just made love for the first time. What could be wrong with me?"

Duke's heart fluttered. His hand reached up to touch her face. "Hurry back." He leaned in to kiss her.

He watched as she climbed down the stairs. Sitting there, he looked down at himself. He still had blood on him. He climbed down the stairs as Loren opened the bathroom door. "Do you want to take a bath with me?" she said shyly.

He smiled, wrapping his arms around her. "I would love to, but is your tub big enough for two?"

Loren laughed. "I designed this house. Come on." She grabbed his hand and pulled him into the bathroom. Duke looked around. "Watch." She grabbed a handle on the wall and pulled it up. The wall lifted to the ceiling. Under it, he saw half a bathtub. Giggling at his face, she pulled the two handles and the walls in the living room pulled and swung flush with the walls. Climbing in the tub, she lifted the love seat up, which slid off and over the side of the tub.

"Are you kidding me?" He was amazed.

Loren laughed. "You'd be surprised what is in this place."

Duke grabbed her, picking her up out of the tub and kissing her. Giggling, Loren kissed him back. He put her down and she turned on the water. As the tub filled, she got two towels out of the cabinet, setting them on the floor. She climbed in the tub, sliding forward, and Duke climbed in behind her, wrapping his arms around her waist and pulling her to him. They sat in the warm water relaxing. As she lay in Duke's arms with the warm water soothing her lower extremities, she looked at the ring he gave her for the first time.

Duke watched her admiring it. "It was my mother's. My dad gave it to me the other day. She told him before she died that she wanted me to have it when I found the woman who loved me the way she loved my father. I didn't know he had it."

"Duke, I can't accept this. Your father should keep it."

He chuckled. "I told him the same thing. He said, it was given in love and accepted in love, and it was mine to give to the woman I love because he knew it would be accepted in love."

"I do love you. I will cherish it always." She turned her head and kissed him.

They got out of the tub. "You want a beer?" she asked on her way up to the loft.

"Yeah, could you throw down my jeans? We can go sit outside."

Loren grabbed a little sun dress and tossed Duke's jeans down to him. He pulled them up as she started down the stairs.

"It's a shame, you know."

"What's that?"

"That you have to cover that marvelous body." She walked up to him and kissed him. Giggling, she headed out the door. "Come on, Jaz," she called out. Jaz came down the stairs and ran out the door.

Duke laughed and got two beers, following her out. They sat in the chairs holding hands and drinking their beers.

"Duke?"

"Yeah, beautiful?" He rubbed his thumb on her hand.

She set her beer down and got up, climbing on his lap and straddling him. Sitting high on his legs, he put his hands on her hips to hold her in place. "You really want to marry me?"

"Oh, God, yes, I do. I want to go to sleep with you in my arms and wake up to see your beautiful face for the rest of my life. Do you want to marry me?"

She nodded, her hands reaching to touch his chest. "I can understand now why Julie wants you."

He laughed. "And why is that?"

"Look at you. You're beautiful."

He laughed. "Well, thank you, but that's not why Julie wants me." She tilted her head and looked at him. He sat up and kissed her. "She wants my money."

Loren laughed. "I don't think that's it. I mean, we only did it once." Her hand slid down to his unbuttoned jeans, working the zipper down. She wrapped her hand around his already hard cock. "I think it's this and what you can do with it."

Duke chuckled and leaned back in the chair so she could get a better hold on him. "I don't think that's it. Mmm, baby."

Loren leaned down. "Do you like this?"

"Yes."

"Do you want me to stop?"

"No." He licked his lips. He lifted his ass off the chair and pulled his jeans down a bit.

"Duke," she whispered.

"Oh, God, Loren," he moaned as he pushed up into her hand.

She leaned in to kiss him again. His hands moved to her thighs, sliding up to her ass. He lifted her up, and she let go of him to get her balance. Duke smiled as he pulled her toward him, pressing her wet mound against his chest. Her head was down, with her hair surrounding them. He guided her down until the head of his cock was at her entrance.

She smiled. "Duke," she whispered as she covered his mouth with hers, pushing her body down. Duke guided her slowly onto him.

"Oh, God, baby," he moaned as she sheathed him.

She pushed the rest of the way down until she touched him. Loren knew the motions of this position, so she started to rock her hips back and forth against him. "Loren, God, you feel so good."

"Ahh, I'm going to do it again, Duke. I'm going to come. Ahhhhh! Oh, God."

Duke felt her contract around him. He grabbed her face and kissed her as he released everything he had. "Fuck," he whispered. They sat there kissing for a long time.

She laid her head on his shoulder. "I like the way you feel inside of me," she whispered, kissing his jaw. "You're so big. When I had you in my mouth, I wondered how you were going to fit. But you fit."

"I do. I was worried, too. But, see, it's what I said before about everything that happened. It brought you to me. So, it was destiny."

"You do fit, perfectly."

Duke kissed her. "That's because you're perfect."

She giggled and kissed him. It was a deep, passionate kiss. Duke felt himself getting hard inside of her. He ran his hands up her dress and cupped her breasts. Loren started rocking her hips. Duke started pushing up into her. Soon, they were moving in perfect unison, the rhythm driving them both crazy. Loren's fingers dug into his bare shoulders. Duke let go of her breasts and grabbed her ass as he thrust up harder.

"Ahhh, ahhh, Duke."

"Take me with you, baby," he grunted out.

She threw her head back as she let go. Duke sat up, grabbing her by the neck and covering her mouth with his while he released.

Loren started to giggle. "Yep, this is why she wants you."

Duke laughed. "She never had this with me, and she never will."

Loren smiled, putting her hands on his face. "I love you, Duke Reynolds."

"I'm not only honored, but privileged, to have that love. I will never do anything to give you cause to take it away from me." He kissed her. "You do know you are going to be a messy when you get up." She giggled. "Let me go in and get you a towel." She nodded. Duke knelt on the ground, gently laying her down as he pulled out of her. "Stay here." He kissed her.

Loren laughed. "How sexy is this? I am on the ground after making love because I'm full of sperm." She couldn't stop giggling.

Duke laughed, pulled up his jeans, and ran into the house to get her a towel. When he ran back out, he caught his foot on the chair and went flying to the ground, which sent Loren into another fit of giggles. He handed her the towel while he cried out from the pain. Cleaning herself off the best she could, she rolled over to kiss Duke. "I'm a surgeon. Where does it hurt?" She laughed. "Should I kiss your boo-boo?"

"It hurts right here." He pulled his foot up to show her. Loren bent to kiss his foot. "And here." He pointed to his knee. She kissed it.

"Does it hurt here?" She put her hand on his slight erection. He nodded with his pouty face. Loren opened his jeans and kissed his head.

"And here." He touched his stomach.

"Poor baby," she said in her fucking sexy ass voice that made him crazy.

"And here." He pointed to his nipple.

"Boy, that must be some serious injury if it hurts all the way up here." He nodded. She leisurely flicked his nipple then sucked it gently.

"And here." He pointed to his mouth.

Loren threw her leg over his waist and straddled him. "You poor thing. Everywhere hurts you." Leaning down, she pressed a sweet kiss to his lips. "Is that better?" she asked sweetly. Duke shook his head. She pressed another kiss, running her tongue along his lip. "Is that better?" He shook his head. Reaching up, he grabbed her around the neck and flipped her over. She squealed, laughing. Duke covered her mouth with his, kissing her deeply.

They were laughing and rolling around in the grass. Neither of them noticed the head lights or heard the truck pull up. Loren was squealing and they were laughing when she felt the vibration on the ground. Duke had her pinned with his body, her legs wrapped around him, when they heard someone say, "Jesus."

Duke turned his head to see his brothers, Derek and Joe, standing about five feet from them. Loren busted out laughing. She knew Duke had an erection and his pants were undone. He was barefoot and shirtless.

"Everything all right?" Derek asked, laughing.

"It's all good, brother. What can I do for you?" Duke said while Loren giggled. He turned to look at her with fear and panic on his face, which caused her to laugh even harder.

"Dad sent us over. He wants to talk to you both at the house," Derek said, moving closer.

Duke brought his leg over Loren's. She didn't have anything on under her little sun dress. She was still giggling. "Can you give us a minute?" Duke said.

Chuckling, Derek and Joe walked away.

Duke looked at Loren, who was still giggling. "Busted," she said.

"I am so sorry about that." He rolled off of her and did his jeans. She sat up, pulling her dress in place.

She climbed on him, kissing him. "You see, Mr. Reynolds, I have this ring here. It says that I can do these kinds of things with the man who will be my husband."

He grabbed her around the waist and sat up quick. She screamed and laughed. "Fucking right you do." He kissed her, just as Derek and Joe came running to the back yard. "Seriously, guys," Duke barked.

They laughed, and Derek said, "Hey, just making sure everything is all right, brother."

Loren laughed. "We are fine." She got up and gave Duke quite the view when she did. She heard him moan and giggled, helping him stand. She realized he still had an erection so she stood in front of him.

Derek stood there with a look of shock on his face. It was the first time he had seen the scar on her back. "Go on, little brother, we are fine. Tell Dad we'll be there shortly." He had his arm wrapped around Loren's waist.

"What..."

Duke cut him off. "Go on."

Derek swallowed and nodded. Turning, he walked back to the truck. When the headlights turned, he let go of Loren.

"He saw my scar," she whispered.

"It's all right. Come on, we need to change. I wonder what my dad wants."

She nodded. Hand in hand, they walked into the house with Jaz following them. Loren climbed to the loft to throw on a pair of shorts and a bra and t-shirt. Grabbing Duke's clothes, she was halfway down the stairs when he walked out of the bathroom.

"I wonder what's going on?"

"I don't have a clue," he said as he put his boots on. "You ready?" Loren nodded and the three of them left the house and headed to Richard's.

"What time is it?" Loren asked.

"Well, it was light when we out, so I would say around ten maybe.

Come to think of it, why would Derek and Joe still be at the ranch this late?" He pushed on the gas.

"Duke, please be careful," she said, a bit afraid.

He eased up on the gas. "Sorry, I guess I'm a bit anxious."

Loren reach out and put her hand on his leg, giving it a squeeze. "Everything's all right."

Duke nodded and put his hand on hers. It felt like it took forever to get there. When they pulled up, there were a lot of trucks parked in front of the house. Duke threw the truck in park and jumped out, turning to look at Loren.

"Go," she said.

Duke took off running, taking the stairs three at a time. He came busting through the front door looking for his father in the sea of faces. Finally, he found him, and his heart started beating again. He made his way to him and grabbed him, pulling him into his chest. "What the fuck, Dad? These two nearly gave me a heart attack."

"I'm fine. Where's Loren?" Richard said.

Looking around the living room, it hit Duke that the room was filled with men. If she came in the room, she would freak out. He made his way to the door. She was standing on the porch, visibly shaken. "Come here." He pulled her into his chest. "I'm sorry. I didn't know so many people would be here. You all right?" He could feel her calm down.

"I am now."

He pulled back, kissing her gently. "Come on, I won't let go of your hand."

She nodded, and they went into the house. Everyone was sitting, and those who didn't have a seat were standing against the wall.

"So, what's this all about, Dad?"

"Well, we have someone stealing cattle. Sixteen head from Larry, twenty-two from Hal. Total of about a hundred and fifty gone."

"What about ours?" Duke asked.

"We don't know. We need a head count tomorrow, so I'm going to need you all here at first light. Loren, can you ride with us? The more eyes the better."

"Of course, Richard." All heads turned to her. She stayed focused on Duke's hand and Richard's face. "Has anyone been hurt?"

"No, not so far, but we have a serious problem. The cattle all go to market in another eight weeks. Most of these men here need that money to survive the winters up here." She nodded.

"We'll be here in the morning. Sunrise guys." Duke looked at his brothers. "Dad, does Jake and his crew know?"

"Yeah, we got word to them. They'll all be here in the morning as well. We have a lot of ground to cover. You all get home and get some rest."

Duke and his brothers all nodded at their father and headed out. Loren stopped Duke on the stairs. "I need to speak to Richard. Would you please ask him to meet me in the kitchen?"

"You all right?" He pulled her to him to feel if she was shaking.

"Yes, I'm fine."

Duke nodded and they went back into the house. Loren went to the kitchen with Jaz, and Duke went to get his father. Loren was pacing the floor when they came in. "Loren," Richard said.

"About a week ago, I was out riding past the river to the north. I saw a pickup out there with a cattle trailer on the back. I didn't know any of the guy's trucks, so I just assumed it was one of them. It wasn't moving and there weren't any cows out there, but why would it be parked out in the middle of nowhere?"

"Have you seen anyone out by your place?" Richard asked, a bit concerned.

"No, nothing. Richard, if someone is stealing cattle, it could be a bit dangerous."

"It'll be fine. You don't have to go out. You can stay here and monitor things for me."

She shook her head and giggled. "No, I'll go. I'm going armed, but I'm going." She looked at Duke. "I'm not going to take a chance on something happening to you."

Duke laughed. "I do know how to shoot, you know."

"Doesn't matter. You aren't leaving me behind."

He nodded. Loren ran her hand through her hair and Richard saw the ring.

"One more thing," Duke said. "Dad, Loren and I are getting married."

His father smiled a smile that touched his eyes. "I see that." He pulled Loren in for a hug. "Welcome to the family."

She giggled. "Thank you."

When they pulled back, he took her hand to look at the ring. "It's where it belongs now. It looks good on you."

"Thank you, Richard." Looking past him to Duke, she said, "It was given in love and accepted in love."

"As I knew it would. Now, you two get going. Sunrise."

Duke nodded and they left. Once they were in the truck, Loren turned to Duke. "I think we should go back to my place, get the horses, a change of clothes, and then come back here."

"I was thinking the same thing." Duke smiled at her.

Once they were back at Loren's, Duke hitched the horse trailer to the truck and got the horses and saddles in it. Loren went in and grabbed a change of clothes, her boots, food for Jaz, her shot gun, and handgun. She loaded everything in the truck.

"Hold on, I need to get a few things." She smiled. Running to the barn and the green house, she came back with two more guns.

Duke raised his eyebrows at her. "Something I should know about?"

She giggled. "Long story. I need one more thing." He watched as she ran in the house and came out with a few boxes of ammunition.

"You know, you are freaking me out a bit." Duke smiled. He was really freaking out.

"What, not enough? Hold on." She went to the back of the house and grabbed one more gun. "Is this enough or should we get more?"

He looked at her. "You have more?"

She nodded. "Five more. Should I get them?" She was serious.

"Come here," Duke said and pulled her into his arms. "Loren, why do you have nine guns?"

"Because, Duke, I've lived in fear all this time," she whispered.

They stood there next to the truck, Loren in his arms. "I'm so sorry, baby. But not anymore. You've got me now. You don't need to be afraid."

"I know," she whispered.

He kissed her on top of the head. "Come on, let's go."

"Are these enough?" she asked as she climbed in the truck.

He chuckled. "Yes, more than enough."

"Maybe one more?" She was serious.

Duke chuckled. "We have enough."

Loren nodded and they made their way back to the ranch. They got the horses put in the stables, and then went up to the house. Richard was saying goodbye to the last rancher. "What are you two doing back here?" he asked as they walked up.

Loren smiled. "We didn't want you to be alone." Richard laughed.

"We thought it would be easier just to stay here tonight," Duke said.

"Well, your brothers thought the same thing, so come on in and let's get some sleep." He turned and they followed him in.

Loren, Duke, and Jaz headed up to Duke's room. Walking in, Loren laughed. "This bed is huge. It's bigger than mine, I think."

Wrapping his arms around her as he kicked the door shut, he whispered, "I'm a big boy." He kissed her.

She giggled as her hand ran the length of him. "Oh, I know."

They laughed and then Loren went to the bathroom to brush her teeth and change. When she opened the door, Derek was standing with his hand raised to knock. Loren stepped back and froze. He had on only his boxers. "Oh shit," he said, spinning around. "I am so sorry. I didn't know you were here."

Duke heard Derek talking and came out of his room. His heart started racing. He moved behind Derek to find Loren plastered against the wall, her clothes on the floor. He could see the tears building in her eyes.

"Hey, beautiful," he whispered, bending down so he was in her line of sight. But she didn't move. Jaz came into the bathroom, pushing him out of the way. She stuck her nose on Loren's leg a few times and then managed to get behind her, pushing her.

Loren's eyes darted to Duke's. He watched as she came back to him. "How long?" she whispered.

"Just a minute or two. Come on, let's go to bed." She nodded. Duke picked up her clothes and led her out of the bathroom.

"Sorry," Loren said to Derek who was standing with his back to her.

"No problem." He chuckled as the door shut to Duke's room.

Duke dropped her things and pulled her into him. "I got you, babe." He picked her up and put her on the bed. Climbing in behind her, he pulled her to his chest. "You want to talk?"

Shaking her head, she rolled over and buried herself in his embrace. Duke pulled the covers over them both and whispered, "I love you," to her, kissing her head.

"I love you," Loren whispered back, kissing his chest.

Duke smiled. Yep, this was the life he wanted. This was his woman, and he loved the way she felt in his arms. Sleep came easy for both of them. They had exhausted themselves.

CHAPTER TWELVE

LOREN WOKE in what felt like the middle of the night. Her leg was between Duke's. She smiled when she felt his slight erection. Her hand slowly moved down his body. Slipping her fingers under the waistband of his boxers, she found him semi-hard. She continued her quest, reaching his balls. They were huge and soft. "Mmm," she moaned as she cupped them in her hand, gently massaging them.

Duke moved his leg, opening himself up to her. She continued to massage him, feeling him growing harder along her arm. Duke pulled her closer. "What are you doing?" he whisper-moaned.

"Shhh," she said. He chuckled. Closing his eyes, he let this beautiful woman touch him. When he was fully hard, her hand moved up to grip him. Gently and slowly, she stroked him. "Duke," she whispered in her sexy ass voice that made him crazy.

He pulled off his boxers and rolled her over. He managed to get her naked then he laid down next to her. Kissing her, he rolled her onto her side so her back was against his chest. He cupped her breasts, rolling her nipples in his fingers. Loren turned her head to kiss him. Sliding his hand down her side to her hip and then her thigh, he lifted her leg onto his and slid between them. Gently, he rocked his hips, sliding through her, wetting himself. His mouth covered hers, muffling her moans.

When he was wet enough, he gently pushed inside of her. "Fuck," he whispered in her mouth. "God, baby, you feel so good."

"Oh, Duke," she whispered back to him.

She was full and he wasn't even all the way inside of her. With his hand resting on her hip, he pushed all the way inside of her. Slowly, he made love to her like this. It was intense to say the least. Slowly, in and out, they got a rhythm going, with her pushing back and him pushing forward and up. He made love to her, long and hard. He had never stayed this hard for so long. He built her up, kissing and touching her. She was basically immobile, under his control, and he like it. He loved bringing her pleasure. Duke felt her tighten around him and knew she was going to come. It would be her first orgasm from penetration. God, he loved this about her. Tighter and tighter, she got. He was doing everything he could think of to stop himself from coming.

He felt the groan bubbling in her chest. He knew she was going to explode. Then it happened, and he felt her contract around him, and he covered her mouth with his to muffle her cries. She pulled her mouth away, and Duke wrapped his arms completely around her while she took him to the edge of reason. Together, they came in a muffled silence. Duke pulled out of her and rolled her over, kissing her deeply. "I love you, beautiful," he whispered into her mouth.

Her hands on his face, she admitted, "I'm scared, Duke."

"Don't be, I'm right here. I'm not going anywhere."

She nodded and kissed him. He pulled her close and wrapped his body around the woman he loved, trying to make her feel safe. Together, they fell asleep. The light from the day woke Duke. It was bred in him to wake at this hour. With a smile on his face, and the woman he loved in his arms, he was a happy man. For the first time in his life, he knew what happiness felt like. His hand trailing along her spine, she began to stir.

"Mmm, good morning, fiancé," she whispered.

Duke rolled them over, covering her mouth with his, his hand wrapped around her head, his fingers in her beautiful hair. Pulling out of the kiss, Loren opened her eyes. Duke looked in them; they were deep purple. He chuckled. "I am beginning to know this look in your eyes."

She smiled. "I want to make love again."

He pressed his erection into her thigh, and her legs opened to him. Shifting his body, he slid deep inside of her. "You are so naughty," he whispered as he kissed her. Their bodies slowly brought the other to orgasm. "I love you," Duke whispered as he released.

Loren felt the warmth of his love fill her. They were a mess, and the bathroom was across the hall. "I need to take a shower. I'm a mess." She giggled.

"Come on. I'll stand guard." Duke chuckled, handing her his t-shirt from last night to clean herself up so she wasn't dripping. She wrapped herself in a sheet, and Duke pulled on his boxers. He cracked the door like they were in a spy movie. Loren couldn't contain her giggle. "Coast is clear," he whispered, stepping out into the hallway. She bolted across the hall and into the bathroom with her bag. Duke kissed her before she shut the door.

He smiled and sat down on the floor in front of the door. He listened to the shower turn on. He knew she was in there wet, and he knew what she looked like naked and wet. He closed his eyes, leaning his head against the door, and moaned silently. Joe came out of his room. "What are you doing?"

He startled Duke, who laughed. "Standing guard. Loren's in the shower and then I'm next."

Joe laughed. "Just like old times."

"Yep, and you should probably want to get that thing under control." Duke nodded toward his erection.

"Morning wood," Joe said as he rubbed his cock.

"Damn, boy, you're going to make some girl pretty happy."

Joe laughed, knowing damn well it wasn't a woman he wanted. He just didn't know how to tell his brothers or his father that he had a boyfriend. Joe went downstairs to use the bathroom.

Duke heard the water shut off. A few minutes later, Loren opened the door and Duke fell backwards into the bathroom. Loren giggled. "What are you doing?"

"Standing guard." He chuckled as he got up, pulling her into a kiss. "Be careful, there are four other men in this house sporting morning wood. I'll be out in a few."

"Duly noted, I'm going to get breakfast started. You boys have to eat."

Duke grabbed her. "I am no boy." He chuckled.

"Oh, I know." She smiled. After dropping her clothes off in his room, she headed downstairs. By the time Duke came down, Richard and Joe had already woken up and were having coffee.

"Well, the bacon is done. I need an egg count. I have muffins in the oven."

Duke smiled. "Three."

Richard. "Three."

"So, everyone wants three eggs? All the same, I suppose, over easy?"

"Yep," they all said in unison.

"Duke, wake up the other boys." Loren smiled at him.

He laughed, then getting up, he ran upstairs. Loren got back to cooking. She noticed the clock on the wall said five-thirty. They didn't sleep long, but she felt energized. As she was sliding eggs onto a plate for Richard, the others came down. Next, it was Duke, then Joe, then Alex, then Derek. She just had a muffin and some bacon.

"Boy, a guy could get used to this," Derek said.

"Yeah, well, don't," Duke said, smiling. "Oh, and while we are all here, I have something I would like to tell you. Loren has agreed to marry me."

"No shit! Well, that was fast," Alex said.

Loren laughed. "Yeah, I thought so, too. But who could resist him." She smiled at Duke.

There were congratulations all around. "Welcome to the family," Derek said and went to hug her, but she stepped back, looking at Duke.

"No offense, brother, but she doesn't like to be touched," Duke said, walking up to Loren, who just smiled as he wrapped his arm around her.

"I'll get the kitchen cleaned up," Loren said to Duke.

"I'll get the horses ready. Hey, where are all the walkie talkies?"

Richard answered. "They are on the dining room table. Make sure everyone has one."

They all filed out, and Loren got busy cleaning up. She made sandwiches for everyone, and grabbed some apples, then she put them on the dining room table with the radios and headed out to her truck. Duke walked up with Cupcake and Roxy as she was checking the guns.

She handed one to Duke with a side holster. "Just point and shoot. There are fifteen in the clip and one in the chamber. To release the clip, you push this down." She showed him and the clip fell out in her hands. "Then slide another clip in and you're good to go." She handed him three clips.

"Loren," he said. She turned to look at him. "We won't need these."

"Duke, please, just take it," she pleaded with him.

"If it makes you feel better, all right." He put the gun on his hip and the clips in his pocket.

Loren turned and made sure the rest of them were full. Walking up to Cupcake, she opened the saddle bag and deposited the other guns inside and then slid her shotgun in its holster. She clipped hers onto her jeans. "I made sandwiches for everyone. They are on the table. You want to grab ours when you get the radio?"

Duke reached up and touched her face. His fingers wrapping around her head, he pulled her in for a kiss. "It'll be all right."

She nodded. "I'm scared, that's all."

"I know, and I'm right here. Whatever you need, whenever you need it."

Loren wrapped her arms around him. "I need this."

Duke let go of the horses and held her for a few minutes. "I'll go get our food and radio."

She nodded and let him go. She turned to look at Jaz. Kneeling down, she said to her, "If I tell you to run, you run. If I tell you to hide, you hide. Understand?" Jaz barked at her. She hugged her dog. "I love you, girl." Jaz licked her face and Loren laughed.

When she stood up, Derek was standing there watching her. "You know, my brother is totally in love with you."

Loren laughed. "Well, that's a good thing, because I am totally in love with him."

"I'm glad you two found each other."

"Thanks," Loren said as she climbed up on Cupcake.

"Is that a gun?" Derek said in shock.

She smiled. "It is."

"Do you know how to use it?"

She laughed. "It wouldn't be near me if I didn't."

Duke walked up, putting their food in his saddle bag. Turning to Derek, he said, "We are headed out to the river where Loren spotted a truck a few days ago. Get those cattle in and keep in touch. We'll see you back here later. If you run into any trouble, give us a call."

Derek nodded, and Loren, Duke, and Jaz headed to the river. When they reached it, they crossed over and rode until they were where Loren saw the truck.

"Here." She pointed to the ground. "You can see the tire tracks, and look, a fire pit." She looked at Duke.

He pulled out the radio. "Hey, listen up, we are out by this river. These fuckers are camping on our land. We need some back up."

"On our way," Derek fired back.

"We should follow the imprints of the truck," Loren said.

"Which way was the truck facing?" Loren pointed west. "All right, come on."

"Jaz, stay close," she said.

They followed the truck imprints and found another campsite. "What the fuck? Loren, this is pretty close to your place."

She was looking around. "Duke, look." She could see smoke off to the north. "We need to wait for the guys."

"They are coming on four wheelers, too much noise. Come on." He pulled the radio off his belt.

"Hey, guys, listen, we found them. North of Loren's place. I need horseback only. Hurry, we'll wait."

Richard came across. "There are six of us on the way. We just hit the river."

"Come west, follow the tracks. About fifteen minutes."

"Gotcha, be there in a few," Richard said.

"Duke, these guys are in this for money. Please don't hesitate to use that gun."

"I won't, beautiful." He reached out and took her hand, giving it a squeeze.

Loren pulled her gun from her saddle bag and slipped it just under the saddle. Smiling at Duke, he chuckled and shook his head.

"What?" Loren smiled.

"Baby, they are just cattle rustlers. They won't have guns."

"We'll see."

Just then, they heard the horses. Richard rode up with five other men Loren didn't know. "Derek, Joe, and Alex are moving up the east side on the four wheelers. They'll come at them from the north and the east." He looked at Loren. "You ready?"

She smiled, pulling out her shotgun. "As I'll ever be."

Richard laughed. The other men just sat there looking at her.

They started moving forward when Derek came over the radio. "We are on our way down."

"Let's do this," Duke called out.

As they drew closer, Loren slowed. She waited for Jaz and got off her horse. The dog ran up to her. "Listen to me. You go there and you stay there." She pointed to the bushes. Jaz whined. "You go. Listen for me to whistle. Then come. You stay, Jaz. Now go."

Jaz sat there looking at her. She leaned against Loren's leg and then ran to the bushes. Loren got back up on her horse, looking at Duke, who walked over to her, grabbing her and kissing her. "You are fucking amazing."

She laughed. "You ain't seen nothing yet."

He chuckled, and they took off. As they approached, Loren cocked the shotgun. There were three men standing with guns pointed at

173

Richard. "Well, the way we see it, these here cattle were just roaming around."

"You are trespassing on private property," Richard said.

One of the men saw Loren. "Hey, look, there's that pretty little thing we saw last week. Why don't you come here, darlin'? You're all alone out there. We can show you a good time."

Duke moved in front of her. "Not gonna happen. Why don't you put your guns down and give us back our cattle and we won't press charges?"

The guy pointed his gun at Duke. "How about I shoot you and then take the little lady over there behind the truck and show her what a real man can do."

Loren giggled. Richard looked at her. She moved Cupcake out from behind Duke. "Why don't you do as the man asked?" she said.

The guy actually rubbed his cock. "Darlin' you are getting me hard sitting on that horse with those perky tits of yours."

She looked down at his hand. "Is that all you got? Not interested."

The guy pointed the gun at her. "Get your ass off that horse now, bitch."

She smiled at him. "No thanks." She lifted the shotgun and tilted her head. Duke's heart stopped.

Richard said, "Loren, don't do it."

"But, Richard, he called me a bitch. He has threatened to rape me. In Texas, I could kill him and it would be all right," she said as sweet as could be.

The guy looked at her. "GET OFF YOUR FUCKING HORSE!" he yelled.

"I don't think that is going to happen," Duke said as calmly as can be. Just then, Loren heard the four wheelers.

The guy with his gun on Richard turned just as Derek came flying at him, hitting him. He went sailing through the air as his gun went off. Loren fired the shotgun, hitting the guy who was screaming at her in the leg. Alex hit the other guy with the four-wheeler. The guy fired at him, hitting him in the arm. Loren was off her horse with a gun in her hand, running toward Alex.

"Loren, no!" Duke yelled.

The guy who she shot in the leg raised his gun, and she spun, shooting it out of his hand. Duke was right behind her. He ran over and grabbed the gun the guy dropped. Loren had torn off Alex's shirt. She wrapped it around his arm. "Hold still," she said to him as calmly as could be.

Duke stood there in shock, as was everyone else. No one moved as she worked on him. "Looks like it's just a flesh wound. You should get to the doctor just in case you need stitches."

Then she turned around and walked up to the guy who shot him, pulling her gun from her jeans and pointing it at him. "You shot my brother-in-law. In Texas, it's an eye for an eye, and we hang cattle rustlers there. So, consider yourself lucky." She shot the guy in the arm. "I don't like bullies or thieves." Then she just walked away. She walked past Duke, past Richard, past Cupcake. Duke heard her whistle, and she kept walking. They just stood there watching her.

She walked as far as her legs would carry her before she started shaking. Duke saw her drop her gun, and he took off after her. Before he could get to her, she went down to her knees. Then she fell on her stomach. Jaz made it to her before Duke did. She laid next to her, touching her face with her nose. Duke got on the ground next to her and waited. Jaz kept touching her face. It wasn't until Loren reached out for Jaz that Duke laid down next to her, wrapping his arm around her waist.

"I'm here, baby," he whispered.

She let go of Jaz and turned in his arms. She buried her face in his shirt and cried. Duke held her, not saying a word. He didn't know what to say, so he just held her. As she calmed down, she tilted her head up and kissed him. He didn't deny her; he would never deny her. He opened his mouth to her tongue and kissed her deeply.

When they separated, he whispered, "We are going to have our very first fight, but it can wait until later."

She smiled. "I know, but please kiss me again."

"Anytime, anywhere, beautiful." He covered her mouth with his.

He pulled back and whispered in her ear, "I want you so bad right now."

She giggled. "I know, I can feel you. Take me home, Duke. I want you. Then we can fight."

He laughed. "Come on, beautiful." They got up as Richard walked up.

"Charlie is on his way. Why don't you two take Alex's four-wheeler? He can ride Cupcake back. Loren, I'm sure Charlie is going to want to talk to you. Why don't you come by the house later? I'll have Derek grab some pizza from town."

They both nodded. Walking to the four-wheeler, she bent and picked up her gun, then Loren stopped at Cupcake and grabbed her saddle bag and her shotgun. She dropped it all in the basket at the back of the ATV. Duke climbed on, and she picked up Jaz and sat her behind Duke, and then got on, grabbing Duke's shirt. He nodded to his dad and they took off. They weren't too far from Loren's. When they arrived, Duke grabbed her saddle bag and the shotgun while she opened the door. Jaz ran up the stairs to get in her bed. Loren set the keys on the counter and opened the fridge, grabbing two beers. When she pushed the door closed, Duke grabbed her face, kissing her. She dropped the beers on the floor as he walked her back to the wall.

"Remember I told you I would never have sex with you?" Loren nodded. "What else did I say?" he asked as he pulled her shirt off her then moved to her jeans. She swallowed as he pulled them down, stopping to bury his face in her fluff. "What did I say, Loren?" He stood up, pulling his shirt over his head.

"You said, you would always make love to me, but sometimes you would fuck me," she whispered.

Duke kicked his jeans away, looking at her. "This is one of those times." He reached for her legs, lifting her off the floor and stepping forward. She hit the wall just as he covered her mouth.

There was no talking. He slid her down onto his cock, pushing up into her. "Ahh," she cried out as her head hit the wall. He wrapped his hands around the top of her thighs to control her body.

"You scared the shit out of me," he said as he gained momentum, pushing harder and harder into her.

"Duke," she cried out just as his mouth covered hers. It was a matter of moments before Loren was coming. She was tight around him and he blew. Jerking his hips, he pushed into her as hard and deep as he could, their kiss not ending. Duke slid her down the wall and came to rest on his heels.

He put his hands on her face, pulling her back. "You scared the fucking shit out of me."

"Are we going to fight now?"

Duke wiped her tears with his thumbs. "No, we're not going to fight. I don't want to fight. I want to make love to the woman who owns me."

"I like that idea better than fighting," she whispered as she kissed him. When they separated, Duke lifted Loren off him and helped her stand up, then he got up. He watched as she walked naked to the bathroom.

So fucking beautiful. He leaned against the counter, waiting for her to come out. A few minutes later, the door opened and she appeared. Her lips were a bit swollen from his kisses. He felt his cock getting hard looking at her. She was fucking perfect.

She saw his eyes filled with love. She licked her lips as she stepped forward. Duke took a step toward her. She scanned his body, his erection. He moved closer to her, his hand coming up to her neck, pulling her to his mouth. He pulled away and let go of her, stepping around her to use the bathroom. Loren continued up to the loft. "Jaz, go downstairs," she said as she petted her on the head. Jaz listened and Loren laid on her stomach.

A minute or two later, she felt Duke's mouth run up the back of her thigh. Then he was gone, then she felt him on the other one. "You are so beautiful." He kissed her ass. His hands coming to her hips, he pulled her up on her knees and proceeded to make love to her ass with his mouth.

Loren was in shock with the feeling of his tongue on her. With his fingers separating her cheeks, he tongued her hole, causing her to cry out. Moving down, he ran his tongue along her folds. "Heaven," he mumbled as he devoured her, bringing her the edge of orgasm, then he stopped and sat back on his heels.

He grabbed his cock and stroked himself then got back up and pressed into her slowly. "Ahhh, God, Duke."

"You feel incredible," he moaned as he slid all the way inside of her and pulled back slowly.

"Oh my God. Do it again," she pleaded.

He did as she asked, pushing in and then flicking his hips. In and out, he made love to her. She gripped him as she began to contract. Duke pulled out completely. "Come here, baby," he whispered as he wrapped his arm around her waist, pulling her up onto her knees, and then onto his thighs. His hands were all over her, grabbing her breasts, caressing them, tweaking her nipples.

"Duke," she whispered.

He stopped, knowing she was going to come. He wanted to heighten her orgasm. His hands slid under her ass, and he lifted her further onto his thighs. Reaching between her spread thighs, he touched and rubbed her clit. Loren wrapped her arms around his neck and arched her back as her orgasm built.

He was so fucking ready to feel her. He lifted her onto him. "Ahhh, fuck," he cried out as she slid down him. "Loren," he cried out as she based him. "Don't move," he growled. She held herself still. Duke kissed her neck. Moving her hair, he went straight for her pulse.

"Mmm, Duke," she moaned. "Duke."

"Push up on your knees," he whispered in her ear. The slide was maddening to him. "Now come back down. Slow, baby, or this will be over before we even get started."

"Oh, God, baby, you feel like heaven. Keep going, beautiful. Bring yourself around. Enjoy me, my love, as much as I am enjoying you," he whispered in her ear.

She moaned continuously as she moved slowly up and down. Duke felt her tighten. "That's it, beautiful. I feel you. Take your time." His hand moved lower on her stomach as she tightened around him.

"Aww, fuck, Loren." He was fighting his own orgasm. Tighter and tighter she got.

"Duke," she whispered as her head lolled back on his shoulder. He felt the first pulse of her orgasm. He slid his fingers through her fluff, right to her swollen bud. He gently pinched it between his fingers, feeling her body jerk as her orgasm ripped through her. He felt every sensation as she pulsed around him. Her cries filled the house.

Duke couldn't hold on any longer. His teeth sank into her shoulder, his lips surrounding the flesh as he sucked. They came together for a long time.

Loren became jelly in his arms. He gently lifted her off him and laid her on her stomach. He kissed her back, her scar, all the way down to her ass. Then he collapsed next to her on his stomach. He knew she would fall asleep. She was spent. Reaching up, he moved the hair off her face to see a small smile on her lips that tore at his heart. She could have gotten killed that day. It hit him like a ton of bricks. He had just found her, and he could have lost her. He cupped her face. "I love you, beautiful."

"Mmm, Duke. I love you."

"You sleep."

"But we have to go to Richard's."

"You sleep, beautiful."

She smiled and nodded.

Duke laid in bed waiting for her to fall fully to sleep. Then he got up and made his way downstairs. He got dressed, grabbed two beers, and went outside. Sitting on the steps, he cracked one open and sat there thinking.

How did she find the strength to do what she did? She fell apart after she made sure Alex was fine. He ran his hand through his hair. "Fuck," he whispered. He was so mad, so pissed off at what she did. *What was with her and those guns? It was like she knew to bring them.* There was so much he didn't know about her, so much he wanted to know. *God, she is magnificent. And her body. Fuck.* His mind raced. He finished his beer and opened the other one.

He was so involved with his thoughts that he didn't hear the door open. He didn't realize Loren was next to him until she touched him. He turned and looked at her. "You scare the fucking shit out of me," he whispered. He felt a tear fall from his eye onto his cheek. She reached up and wiped it away.

"I'm sorry," she whispered.

He leaned his forehead on hers, and they sat there like that not saying a word.

"I am so in love with you," Duke said. "I have never been so scared in my life. And as much as I don't want to admit this, I am so glad you brought those guns. How did you know?"

"I grew up in Texas. This shit happens all the time there."

He chuckled. "We should get going."

Loren nodded and got up to put her boots on. Duke followed her. With Jaz between them and her gun tucked into her jeans, they headed to the ranch on the four-wheeler.

As they pulled up to the front of the house, Duke nodded his head at the police car. Loren squeezed his side to let him know she saw it. He parked and Jaz jumped off. Duke got off first, turning to help Loren. He pulled her in for a kiss.

Smiling, they walked in hand in hand. Richard rushed up to her, grabbed her, and pulled her into a hug. "Don't you ever do something like that again. I nearly had a heart attack."

She giggled. "I'll try."

Richard hung on a bit longer. He turned to Duke when he released her. "We found all the missing cattle." Then he looked at Loren. "The guy you shot in the leg, well, he was confessing left and right. Derek told him he was going to send you to the hospital to finish him off if he didn't talk." Loren laughed.

Derek heard his name and came out of the living room. "So, you're a bad ass, huh?"

"Not really, I grew up in Texas." Everyone laughed.

They walked into the living room. Loren headed to Alex and knelt in front of him. "What did they say at the hospital?"

"Just a flesh wound like you said. Hey, how did you know what to do?" Alex asked her.

"I'm a doctor." She smiled at him.

He sat there looking at her. "Really?"

She giggled. "Really."

"Not just a doctor," Duke said as he knelt next to her, smiling at her. "She's a brilliant neurosurgeon."

"No shit?" Alex said and they laughed.

Loren stood and Duke followed her. "I'm hungry. I had quite the workout today. Can I get you something?"

Duke shook his head. "I'll come with you."

As they were heading into the kitchen, Charlie walked out with a plate of food. "Loren, right?"

"Right." She smiled.

"Listen, for the paperwork, I need a statement from you. Please tell me those guns are registered."

"They are, and I even have a conceal and carry."

"Good to know. We'll talk."

She nodded and they headed into the kitchen. Duke got Loren a plate, and they filled up on pizza and salads. Together they sat at the table, looking at each other and smiling. "I'm still mad at you," he told her.

"I know. Tomorrow, we can have a knock-down drag-out fight in the yard."

Duke nearly spit his beer out of his mouth. "You are so on."

Loren giggled. "It's good they got all the cattle back. When do they go to market?"

"The middle of September. Just as the cold starts to set in. I'm going to have to go out and find the fence that they cut to get on the ranch."

"That's fine, I need to cook anyway. Your dad is running out of food. I thought maybe I'd make him some stuff he can cook in the microwave."

"Sounds good to me."

"So, when are you going to move your things into my place?"

"Ahh... umm... I... umm."

Loren busted out laughing. "Oh my God, you should see your

face."

"What?" He felt himself blush. "I would never assume it would be acceptable."

"You stay with me every night. Why wouldn't it be? I like having you there, and you said so yourself that you just lay in bed awake thinking about me, as I do you."

"Loren, are you sure? Is that place even big enough for the two of us?"

Now, it was her turn to laugh. "Duke, you've been there nearly every night for a week. Is it big enough?"

He just smiled at her. "How about we try it out?"

She laughed again. "Whatever makes you happy."

Duke's face got very serious. "You. You make me happy."

Loren blushed as Charlie walked in. "Listen, I hate to intrude, but, Loren, can I get your statement?"

"Sure, have a seat." She looked at Duke, who stood and offered Charlie his chair, then went to sit next to Loren.

It took about fifteen minutes for her to tell him what happened.

"Charlie? Can I call you Charlie?"

"Of course."

"They had every intention of killing us and raping me. So, I believe I was justified in shooting them."

Charlie smiled. "I would have killed them."

She smiled back at him. "It was and never will be my intention to kill anyone. I'm a doctor and I swore to save lives, not take them."

"I know, Richard told me. Are you going to take Doc's place when he retires?"

She shook her head, squeezing Duke's hand. "No, I don't practice anymore."

He nodded to her and stood. "Thank you both. I have everything I need. Duke, I'll talk to you soon."

Duke nodded, and they both watched as Charlie walked out of the kitchen. Duke reached for Loren and pulled her onto his lap, wrapping his arms around her. "You all right?" he whispered in her ear.

She shook her head. "No," she whispered, kissing his neck.

"Duke..." Her sexy fucking voice made him instantly hard. She pulled back a little and he covered her mouth with his.

"Loren," he whispered. "Come on, let's go home."

"Home. I like the way that sounds."

He held her for a few more minutes then they got up. Loren looked down at his erection. Reaching for him, she stepped in, rubbing her hand the length of him. He chuckled. "Keep that up and we won't make it home."

She pulled away from him, her eyes purple. "Go pack some clothes."

He leaned in for a deep, sensual kiss.

Derek walked into the room. "Oh, excuse me," he said as he turned to walk out.

"No, it's fine," Duke said to him. Looking at Loren, he said, "I'll be back in a few minutes."

She smiled and nodded to him. Jaz stood and leaned against Loren's legs, looking up at Derek. Both Duke and Loren looked at her, then at Derek. Jaz started to growl. "What's going on, girl?" Loren asked. Jaz wasn't looking at Derek; she was looking at the door to the living room.

"Duke," she whispered. He grabbed her hand. "Something's wrong." She reached behind her, putting her hand on her gun. Duke watched her and then went to step away. "No, don't leave me," she whispered.

Derek looked at her. "What's going on?"

"Something is happening. She only does this when there is danger."

Derek turned and walked to the door, pushing it open. "Shit," he said loud enough for them to hear him. Turning his head, he whispered, "Julie is here."

Loren let out a breath and took her hand off her gun, pulling her shirt over it. Duke took her hand. "Come on, I'll go pack a bag. You come with me."

"No, I'm fine. Jaz is here. Hurry up."

He nodded and looked at Derek. "Make sure Julie doesn't touch her."

Derek nodded, looking at Loren. "You afraid of her?"

Loren laughed. "Nope. Afraid of what I would do to her."

Derek busted out laughing, which caused Julie to step back from the living room to look at him.

"Is Duke in there?" she asked.

"Nope," Derek said.

"Well, I know he is here. His Jeep is out there. I need to talk to him," she said.

Loren stepped into the room with Jaz next to her, growling. "Jaz, stay." Jaz sat down and Loren walked forward.

"Why are you here?" Julie asked.

"I should be asking you that."

"I need to talk to Duke. Not that it's any of your business," Julie spat at her.

Loren laughed. "Well, Julie, it is my business." She ran her hand through her hair, and Julie saw her ring.

"What the fuck is that?" She moved toward Loren. Jaz growled louder, and Julie stopped a few feet from her. She looked at Loren's hand and then at Loren. "He asked you to marry him?" She was so angry her face was beat red.

Loren didn't say anything at first. "None of this has anything to do with you. Why can't you understand that? He doesn't want you. He has told you that time and time again."

"Are you fucking kidding me right now? It has everything to do with me. He is mine!" she yelled.

Loren felt Jaz come up next to her and rub against Loren's leg. Shaking her head, Loren said as nicely as she could, "No, Julie, he is not. He doesn't want you."

Just then, Duke came down the stairs with a bag in his hand. "Julie, what the hell do you want?"

Her head snapped toward him. "Why, Duke? Why would you want to marry her? You love me. Is that my ring? Is that the ring you went to Bozeman to buy for me?" She had tears running down her face. Loren almost felt sorry for her.

Duke shook his head. "I never bought you a ring, Julie. I never wanted to marry you. You were the one who always talked about getting married, not me." She took a step toward him, but he backed up, shaking his head. "No, Julie. We are not ever getting back together."

"Yes, Duke. You love me, not her. How could you love her? Look at her. She has that horrible scar on her face. She's so ugly. Look at me. You've loved me for two years, Duke."

"No, Julie, I never loved you." He looked past her to Loren.

"I'll be in the truck," Loren said to him.

He could see the pain in her eyes. "No!" he shouted, moving past Julie to Loren. He wrapped his arm around her waist and pulled her to him. "No," he whispered. "No." Turning to Julie, he said in probably the most hateful voice he had, "Julie, get the fuck out of this house. Don't come back here ever again. I am not telling you again. There is nothing between us, and there never will be." Turning to Loren, he whispered, "Come on, beautiful, let's go home."

She smiled at him, and together, the three of them walked out of the house. Julie went to follow them and Richard stepped into her path. "You and I are going to have a little chat, and Charlie here is going to be a witness to it."

Julie looked at Charlie.

LOREN AND DUKE WALKED OUT OF THE HOUSE AND DOWN TO HER truck. Dropping his bag into the back of the truck, he pulled her into his arms, kissing her deeply. "You all right?"

She shook her head. "I want to go home, Duke. Take me home."

"You got it, beautiful." He reached behind her and opened the door. Jaz jumped in and then Loren. When she got in, she moved over to the middle of the truck. When Duke got in, she wrapped herself around him, kissing him.

"I'm sorry. I should have stayed in the kitchen," she whispered into his neck.

"Never apologize for standing up for us. I love you. Only you. There will never be anyone else. Just you. Well, and Jaz," he said softly.

Loren giggled. "She is a wonderful friend." Loren reached to pet her. "Aren't you, girl?"

"Come on, let's go home."

Loren nodded, pulling away from him. He kissed her once more then started up the truck.

RICHARD STOOD GLARING AT JULIE. "TELL ME, YOUNG WOMAN, WHAT your problem is."

"I love him." She sniveled.

"No, I don't think you do," Richard said sternly. Derek, Joe, and Alex stood behind her.

"You don't know what you are talking about, old man," she spat.

He chuckled. "I am going to say this just once, and you would be wise to listen. That man is taken. He loves her, not you. If you continue with this pursuit of yours, I am going to have Charlie arrest you. If I see you near my ranch again, or near my son again, you will be going to jail. If you go near Loren again, you will go to jail. If I hear of you even attempting to talk to Duke, you will go to jail. He is not yours; he was never yours. If you loved him the way you say you do, you would never have given yourself to his childhood friend. The only thing you want is his money, and perhaps his body, but it's not yours to have. Not anymore. His heart belongs to Loren. He is going to marry Loren, and he is going to have everything you could never give him. Is that understood?"

"You can't stop me!" she yelled at him.

Richard turned to Charlie. "Please arrest her for harassment, trespassing, and threatening my son."

Charlie smiled. "Julie Front, you are under arrest." He grabbed her arms, cuffing her hands. "You have the right to remain silent. Anything you say can and will be used against you in a court of law. You have the right to an attorney. If you cannot afford an attorney, one will be provided for you. Do you understand these rights?"

"Fuck you," she yelled. "You can't do this."

Richard chuckled. "I can and I did. Cross the line again and I will continue to have Charlie arrest you each and every time." Richard looked at Charlie. "Thank you, now get this bitch off my property."

Charlie dragged Julie out of the house, and she screamed all the way to the car. Derek looked at his father. "Good for you, Dad."

"Yeah, she doesn't want your brother. She just wants his money," Richard said.

Derek laughed. "What money? Duke doesn't have any money."

Richard just shook his head. "You boys should head home. We've got a long few days ahead. Make sure you bring an overnight bag; we have sixty-five thousand acres to ride."

They all said goodnight and headed home. Richard locked the doors and turned off the lights before taking himself to bed.

DUKE PULLED UP TO THE BARN WITH LOREN'S TRUCK. THEY DIDN'T TALK all the way back to her place. She slid out his door and Jaz followed her. Duke grabbed his bag out of the back of the truck, and they walked hand in hand to the house.

When they walked in, Loren put her gun in the drawer, took her shoes off, and headed to the bathroom. Duke took his things up to the loft and waited for her. He saw all the lights go off and then watched her climb the stairs. "The bathroom is free."

He smiled at her. Getting up, he pulled her to him. "Come here." She folded into his embrace. Neither of them said a word. Duke just held on to her. This wasn't a time for anything but closeness. She needed him, and he was not about to disappoint her. "I'm so sorry for that," he whispered to her.

Her hand slid up his chest. "There is nothing to be sorry for. You didn't do anything."

He chuckled. "I did. I was such a fool."

"The heart wants what the heart wants."

Duke laughed. "In this case, it's more like the cock wanted what the cock wanted. She was just a good ride, and I got sucked into the way she looks. Yeah, she may be beautiful, but she couldn't ever hold a candle to you." He lifted her face to his, kissing her. "You have me, heart, mind, body, and soul."

"I love you, Duke."

"I love you."

Duke rolled onto his side, turning Loren on her back. "Don't let what she said get to you. It is inconsequential. She is just pissed off because she can no longer play me, and she just wants my money. When we were together, I can't tell you how much money of mine she spent."

Loren giggled. "What she says doesn't bother me at all. I see the look in your eyes. I see how you look at me."

He leaned down and kissed her lightly. "How do I look at you?"

Her hand came up to touch his cheek. "Like you are right now, like you love me. Like you see only me."

"You're right. When I put this ring on your finger, hell, from the moment I saw you in the restaurant, I believe I would have moved heaven and earth to find you." He kissed her deeply. His hand moved from her waist up her body, pulling her shirt with it. Loren pulled away so he could lift it over her head. Duke couldn't help but look at her. She was wearing a little white lacy bra. He got harder knowing she had panties to match it. Licking his lips, his eyes moved up to hers. They were deep purple. "You are so beautiful."

She smiled at him, touching his face. "No, you are."

He moved his body so he was covering hers, putting all his weight on his forearms. They lay like this, just kissing. He needed to feel her nipples in his mouth. Hell, he needed to be buried deep inside of her.

Loren pulled away. "Duke," she whispered.

"Yeah, baby," he whispered back as he kissed her neck.

"Will you make love to me?"

Picking up his head, he smiled at her. "You sure? Because I really want to."

Smiling, she nodded. "Oh, I'm so sure."

Duke jumped up and ripped off his clothes, sending Loren into a fit of giggles. When he was completely naked, he slowly undressed her. As he pulled her shorts off, he heard himself moan. "Mmm, God, beautiful." He was right; she did have on a pair of tiny lacey panties. Gently, he rolled her over so he could see her ass in them. Starting at her shoulders, he touched her, kissing her all the way down her back. Gently, he trailed his tongue along her panty line, watching as his skin turned to goose flesh. Smiling, he slowly removed her panties, bringing them to his nose to inhale her scent. "You smell like heaven."

"Oh, God, Duke," she moaned.

Slowly, he pulled her up on her knees and then buried his face in her, taking her orgasms in his mouth. When he finished, he reached around and wrapped his arm around her waist, pulling her to his chest. Loren turned her head to kiss him and he devoured her. Her arms reached around his neck, pushing her perfect breasts outward for him to touch. Duke rolled her nipples in his fingers as she moaned and ground herself against his thigh. His hands reached down and gently spread her legs, then he pulled her up as his cock ran against her ass. He positioned her over his head. Loren shifted her hips and slid him inside her. Slowly, he lowered her onto him.

"Ahh," she moaned as he filled her.

"Oh, God, you feel so good, beautiful." When her ass touched his thighs, he nearly lost his mind. "Don't move," he whispered, trying to get control of himself. Wrapping his arms completely around her, neither of them moved.

Loren turned her head to kiss him. "Duke," she whispered in his mouth. He released her as their mouths made love to each other. Slowly, he helped her move up and down. Closing his eyes, he had to concentrate or he was going to blow.

"Loren," he growled. He moved his fingers to her bud and, gently flattening them, he moved in little circles. It took maybe two motions and she was gone.

She screamed out, "Oh, God, Duke. Oh, God." She constricted and pulled his orgasm from him like nothing he had ever known.

"Oh, fuck," he cried as he pulsed and pulsed. When he finished, he held on to her for a long time. He hadn't realized he was crying.

"You all right?" she asked, kissing his jaw.

He shook his head. "You make me feel things I've never felt. I fall deeper in love with you every moment of every day." He felt her smile. "I'm sorry that didn't last as long as I wanted, but I can't help myself."

She giggled softly. "It was beautiful, just like you. Don't stop falling in love with me. I never knew I needed you so deeply, in here." Her hand came up to touch her heart.

Duke lifted her off of him, turned her in his arms, and kissed her. Softly and sweetly, they made love with their mouths. "You are all I ever wanted in this life," he whispered to her as he laid her back on the bed, kissing her again. Pulling back, he grabbed his t-shirt and cleaned her up the best he could. Just looking at her, he felt himself get hard. When he finished, he lifted her leg into the crook of his elbow and slid deep inside of her. Loren's back arched, pressing her body into his.

Together, they made slow love to each other. "Oh, God, Duke. I love you," Loren cried out as her second orgasm from penetration blew through her body. Her fingernails dug into Duke's arms.

"That's it, beautiful. Let it go," Duke groaned out as his began. "Oh, God." His teeth clenched tightly. With each thrust, he came harder and harder. Loren held him close to her as he came.

"I've got you," she whispered as his body shook in her arms. "I love you."

Duke kissed her deeply. "What you make me feel, Loren, consumes me. Never have I ever known this. Never do I want to be without you. I love you." He rolled onto his back and pulled her with him. Together, they fell asleep, holding each other, with Loren lying on his chest.

CHAPTER THIRTEEN

Duke woke before the sky got light. Loren was still tucked in his arms on his chest. His smile was automatic. This was his life now and he couldn't be happier. Nothing would ever compare to this beautiful woman lying on top of him, holding him. He could feel his release all over him, and he fell deeper in love with her. He remembered Julie would always get up right away and take a shower.

His hands moved on their own, gently trailing along her spine to her perfect ass, cupping her cheeks. They fit perfectly in his hands. He feather-touched her, feeling her hips gently press into him.

"You are so beautiful," he whispered softly. "I love you." He wasn't sure if she was awake, but he didn't care. He needed her to know in that moment.

"I love you," she whispered back to him.

Duke gently rolled her over, grabbing her leg and lifting it over his hip. His lips brushed against hers. Loren gently ran her tongue along his lip. Instantly, he was hard, and he pushed so slowly into her. They made love for a long time, so slow, so beautiful. Gently kissing one another, touching each other's faces. The orgasm they shared was intense but relaxed. Nothing hurried, nothing rough, just slow loving.

"Mmm, how did I ever get so lucky?" Loren whispered.

He chuckled. "No, love, I am the lucky one. I will miss you while I am out there."

"I know, me too. But you do need to get moving. You take your shower first."

Duke shook his head. "When I pull out, you are going to be a mess. You go first. I insist."

Smiling, Loren reached for her shirt as Duke pulled out of her. She wiped herself clean and then headed to the shower. Closing her eyes as the water beat down on her chest, she was happy. Never believing she would ever feel like this, she knew not to get too relaxed. This is what happened before, and she ended up fighting for her life in a parking lot. Her eyes snapped open. Julie was the threat now. But, somehow, this was different. She knew about the threat. Loren finished washing and got out. "The shower is free," she called out.

A few minutes later, Duke opened the door. Smiling at her, he bent to kiss her, then got in the shower. She just stood and watched him. *Damn, he's gorgeous.* Smiling, she made her way back to the loft to get dressed. She gathered up all the laundry, Duke's included. She saw his bag and opened a few drawers, moving her things around so she could unpack him. Then she stripped the bed. Duke came up wrapped in a towel.

"I put your things in these drawers here." She opened the drawers. "The bottom one is empty as well, so when you bring more things, there is room. Also," she moved to his side of the bed, lifting the panels on the floor, "this is all yours as well. Mine is on the other side."

Duke sat on the bed. "You were right."

"What do you mean?"

"Well, you told me I would be surprised at what is in this place. That," he nodded to the storage beside the bed, "is a surprise. Thank you."

She shook her head. "There is no need to thank me. This is your home, too, if you want it." Her eyes lowered to the floor.

Duke lifted her chin as he leaned in. "I want it. More than you will ever know." He kissed her gently.

"I'm going to start the wash and make you something to eat. I have to go into town today and get some groceries. How about I drop you off at the ranch, then you can bring your Jeep back when you are done out there?"

"Sounds like a plan. I know this is stupid, but are you going to be all right while I'm out there?"

Loren laughed. "I've been fine for months out here alone before I met you. We will be fine. Besides, I want to work on the barn."

She moved to climb down and Duke grabbed her hips, pulling her back onto his lap. His hand trailed up the front of her shirt, cupping her breast. "I don't want you to be fine," he whispered as he rolled her nipples between his fingers. "I want you to need me and want me."

"Ahh," she moaned. "I do need you, and I always want you, Duke," she said in her sexy voice.

He pulled her around him, laying her on the bed. "I love you," he whispered in her mouth as he kissed her.

Loren flipped them over so she was straddling him. She moved herself down his body, undoing his towel. Her lips gently kissed each of his defined muscles along his washboard stomach. The head of his cock brushed along her chin. Duke's moans fueled her desire to hear him call out her name. Licking his swollen head with the tip of her tongue caused Duke to cry out, "Ahh." His hands moved down to move her hair.

Loren smiled and sat up. "Put your hands above your head." She smiled. Duke chuckled and reached for his head. "No touching, just enjoy me."

"Fuck," he groaned.

She slid him to the back of her throat and then out. Continuing a few times, dragging her teeth along him, he exploded in her mouth, screaming her name.

"Ahhh, Loren!"

Slowly, she suckled him, taking all that he had to give her. When she finished, she sat up on her heels and looked at the magnificent man lying sprawled across her bed. Her heart slammed in her chest knowing he loved her, that he was hers.

Duke slowly opened his eyes to look at her, with her sweet sexy fucking smile and her nearly purple eyes glowing at him, for him, because of him. Love wasn't the word to describe how he felt about her. Complete and total devotion. He never wanted to be apart from her. "I can't go," he whispered, knowing his heart wouldn't survive being apart from her. "I can't leave you."

Loren smiled and crawled up his body. "You have to go. Richard is counting on you."

Shaking his head, he said, "I won't leave you. I won't survive without you."

Loren giggled. "You will survive." She kissed him and rolled off him, heading to the stairs to go down.

Duke sat up and grabbed her by the hips, pulling her back on the bed. She was laughing as he laid on top of her. "I won't," he said in his sexy voice, kissing her deeply. Loren smacked him in the ass as he rolled off her. She got up and went down to make him breakfast.

They sat at the table eating together, not saying a word. When they finished, Loren went up to grab the laundry while Duke finished getting ready. "You have a washer in here?" he asked as she gathered the linens.

Wiggling her eyebrows at him, she laughed. "I do indeed."

He followed her downstairs to the back of the kitchen where she pushed on the wall. Two doors opened, and inside were a stackable washer and dryer.

"Holy shit," he said, amazed. "What else is in here?"

Loren laughed. "Sometime I'll show you. But we need to get going," she said as she started a load.

Duke smacked her on the ass. "I'm not going out there for two maybe three days, leaving you alone. I won't survive."

Loren busted out laughing. "You do realize how girlie that sounds? I was out here alone for months before we met. I am a big girl, you know."

He pulled her into his arms. "That may be so, but it doesn't mean I'm a big boy. I want to stay here with you. Come on, let's go see what Dad has to say about it." He kissed her. "Or maybe we could go back to bed."

She giggled. "Get the keys, big boy." Turning out of his arms, she yelled, "Come on, Jaz."

They walked out the door just as the sun was starting to rise. Duke opened the door, and Loren climbed in, and then Jaz jumped in next to her. Laughing, he walked around and climbed up in the truck.

When they pulled up in front of the house, Richard was sitting on the porch. Both of them climbed out of the driver's seat laughing, and Jaz jumped out and ran up on the porch to lie down next to Richard.

"Good morning, you two," he called out.

Loren ran up and hugged him. "Good morning to you. I'm going to go in and make you some breakfast."

"You don't need to do that." He smiled.

"I know, but I want to," she smart-mouthed him and went in the house.

Duke sat down next to his father.

"Well, you look pretty full of yourself." Richard chuckled.

"Dad, I'm in love. I'm getting married and I couldn't be happier."

Richard laughed. "I couldn't be more pleased with this turn of events. Loren is a wonderful woman."

"That she is. Listen, there is something I want to talk to you about." Duke leaned forward, resting his elbows on his knees.

"Don't worry about it, son. We'll be all right here."

Duke turned and looked at his father. "How did you know?"

Laughing, Richard tapped his temple. "I got the sense."

Duke laughed. "I suppose you do. It's just so new, and I just want to spend every second with her."

Richard smiled, clapping him on the back. "I know, Duke. You go, be happy. Think of it as a vacation. You deserve it. Hell, you've been on this ranch your whole life. We'll be fine without you for a while. Be happy, son. Loren's mom and her aunt will be here in a week. If I need you, I know where you'll be."

"Dad, it's not like I am abandoning you. I just want some time with her. I'm coming back to work, so I will look at it as a vacation like you said."

They both looked up as the boys drove up. Derek was the first one out of the truck. "Hey, you're here early." Laughing, he said, "What, did Loren kick you to the curb already?"

"You wish." Duke laughed.

"All right, boys, get it all loaded up. Duke is taking a vacation, so I need to get a hold of Jose`." Richard stood up and headed into the house.

Derek sat in his seat. "So, you're really going to marry her?"

"I am." Duke smiled. "I really am."

"Isn't it a little fast? I mean, you've known her for what, two, maybe three weeks?"

"I know it's crazy, but she is the one. I think I've waited for her for a long time."

"You're done with Julie then?"

Duke looked at him. "I was done with her a long time ago, why?"

"Well, she's pretty hot."

Duke shook his head. "If you do this, we are no longer brothers." He got up and went in the house.

Richard and Loren were sitting at the table talking when he walked in. "What's wrong?" Loren asked as she stood and walked over to him.

He smiled. "Nothing. You ready to go? I thought I'd drop my Jeep off at your place and then we can head into town."

"But aren't you going out with your dad?"

"Dad is giving me some well-deserved vacation time." Duke pulled her into his embrace.

"Is he now?" She giggled.

"Yep. Aren't you, Dad?"

Richard laughed. "Yeah. You two go on. I'll come by when we get back."

Loren pulled away from Duke and hugged Richard. "Thank you," she whispered.

He hugged her back. "He deserves it. The boy has never taken a day off. Now, go on and get. Thank you for breakfast."

Loren kissed him on the cheek. "Anytime. See you in a few days."

"I'm going to grab some more of my stuff. I'll be down in a few," Duke said as he kissed her temple.

Loren smiled at him and went to sit on the porch. Richard came out and sat with her. "You know, I'm happy that the two of you found your way to each other."

Loren chuckled. "You knew it all along, didn't you?"

He shook his head. "I don't know what you are talking about."

Loren reached over and patted his arm. "Yes, you do."

"I know my son, and I knew he would see past your walls. I know the heart that you have and the one he has. You two are where you are supposed to be, and I couldn't be happier. I am glad that you are finding happiness and the peace you deserve and have searched for."

Loren wiped her eyes. "I can't thank you enough for giving me all that you have, including your son."

Richard reached over and pulled her into a hug. "No need to thank me. Just be happy. That's all any of us wanted for you."

Loren nodded into his shoulder. "I've really grown to love you."

He smiled. "I've always loved you."

Loren pulled away, looking him in the eyes as tears fell down her cheeks. "I never thought I would know what love was after what happened to me. He is everything I could have ever dreamed of."

"As you are to me," Duke whispered. Loren turned to see Duke kneeling next to her. He brought his hand up to wipe her tears. "I love you, beautiful."

Loren nodded, throwing her arms around his neck. He pulled her off the chair and onto his lap, wrapping his arms around her. "I love you, too," she whispered into his neck.

Duke looked at his father as Richard wiped his tears. "Thank you," Duke, mouthed to him. His father smiled and nodded.

Derek was standing at the bottom of the stairs watching it all unfold. He felt his heart burst for his brother. "I hope one day I find what the two of you have," he said as he climbed the stairs.

Duke and Loren separated and stood. "I hope you do, too." Duke smiled at him. Turning to Loren and his dad, he said. "Thank you,

Dad. I'll see you soon." He took her hand, picked up his bag, and they headed to the vehicles.

"I'll meet you at the house," Loren said as he opened the door for her. Jaz jumped in before her.

"Hey," Duke whispered.

Loren turned, putting her hand on his chest. "Yeah?" she whispered.

Duke leveled her with a kiss. Smiling, she climbed into the truck and headed back to her place. Duke wasn't far behind her.

DEREK SAT ON THE PORCH IN THE CHAIR LOREN HAD BEEN IN, WATCHING as they left. "Dad, did you know this would happen between them?"

Richard chuckled. "I hoped. Your brother has been through hell with Julie. She nearly broke him. Loren was already broken, and I knew they could heal one another. I just didn't know how to make that happen."

"Dad, what happened to her? I saw a huge scar on her back last week."

"Someone she cared for hurt her. It's what killed her father. When he saw her, his heart gave out and he died right there next to her bed."

"Shit," Derek whispered. "Who could do such a thing to someone?"

"A very sick man. But he is no longer a worry for her."

"I hope he's in prison for the rest of his life. Did he rape her?"

"He's dead, and no, he just wanted to kill her." Richard got up and walked into the house. He bore a great deal of guilt but not enough to make he feel bad. That man knew the pain he caused Loren; Richard made sure of it.

Derek pulled out his phone and looked up Loren's story. He didn't feel bad invading her privacy; she was going to be his sister in law, and he wanted to know. When he finished reading the article, he realized he was crying. Looking up from his phone, he looked at the door to his father's house. His father made the right choice in bringing her here, bringing her to Duke. Nodding his head, he got up, putting his phone in his pocket. He wiped his face and headed out to the barn.

LOREN PULLED UP IN FRONT OF HER HOUSE AND GOT OUT OF THE TRUCK. She went in to go to the bathroom and to grab something to drink. Duke pulled in a few minutes later. Loren opened the door just as he walked up the stairs.

He didn't say a word to her when he wrapped his arm around her, covering her mouth with his. He kicked the door shut and dropped his bag on the floor. Turning, he leaned Loren against the door, pressing his erection into her stomach. "You are so beautiful. I love you," he moaned in her mouth.

Loren kissed him back. "You take my breath away, Duke."

They sat kissing for a while. His eyes filled with tears. There was no feeling in his life that ever compared to what he just felt with her. Love was not a big enough word to describe how he felt about her. Loren came out of the bathroom. Duke smiled at her and then reached up, wrapping his hand around her neck and pulling her to him. "Love isn't a big enough word to describe how I feel about you. You own me, beautiful." Kissing her, he whispered, "You fucking own me." Releasing her, he made his way to the bathroom, and when he came out, Loren was ready.

"You ready?" She had a smile on her face. Duke nodded and they headed out, taking his Jeep.

"So, what was that about?" she asked, smiling at him. "Not that I'm complaining or anything."

He laughed. "I wanted you to know how you make me feel."

"That good, huh?"

Laughing, he grabbed her hand and kissed it. "Better. You hungry?"

She giggled. "I am, actually. When we get home, I'll make us something."

"Home. I like the sound of that. But I was thinking maybe I could take you out, maybe have breakfast again at the diner. That way, when we get home, we could do that again."

Loren laughed. "You're on. But I'd like to try something."

Duke raised his eyebrows. "Is that so?"

Laughing, she said, "Uh huh."

Duke pulled up in front of the diner. As he climbed out of the Jeep, Loren told Jaz to stay. Duke opened her door, helping her out. They walked hand in hand into the diner. "Hey, Millie," Duke said to the waitress at the counter.

"Hi, Duke." She smiled at them.

"This is Loren," he said. "Loren, this is Millie. She's the owner."

"Nice to meet you," Loren said.

She smiled. "Nice to meet you. Go ahead and seat yourselves. I'll bring some coffee over."

They headed to a table by the window so Jaz could see them and sat across from each other in a booth. "The food is really good here," Duke said.

"I think I want some pancakes and some eggs with sausage." Loren smiled at him.

"All that?"

"I think I'm going to need my strength." She giggled.

"Damn right you are," he whispered to her.

Millie came over with their coffee and took their order. Ten minutes later, they were eating and talking, laughing and just being silly. It wasn't until Millie brought over the check that things got tense. "Duke," she whispered. When he looked up, she tilted her head out the window.

Loren turned first, then Duke. Julie had pulled up right next to his Jeep. Jaz was sitting in the driver's seat with her teeth showing, growling at her. "Excuse me," Loren said. Getting up, she headed toward the door.

"Fuck," Duke said under his breath. Standing, he dropped forty dollars on the table. "Thanks, Millie. Can you call Charlie for me please?" And he headed toward Loren.

"What the fuck? Do you follow him everywhere? Afraid he will come back to me or what?" Julie snarled at Loren.

Loren just smiled at her and got in the Jeep to calm down Jaz. "It's all right, girl. Sit." Jaz pressed her nose in Loren's face. "I'm all right," she reassured her. Jaz climbed in the back of the Jeep.

"What's the matter, you afraid of me?" Julie shouted.

Duke walked up to Loren's side of the Jeep. "You okay?"

She smiled. "I'm fine, I didn't want Jaz to bite her. Can we go?"

Duke opened her door. "Are you sure you are okay?" Reaching in, he pulled her close to him.

"I'm good. Honestly. I am not going to get down to her level." She reached up to touch his face. "I know where your heart is."

"Fucking right you do. You own me." He kissed her sweetly.

"Fucking right I do."

Duke laughed. While they were talking, Julie walked around to Loren's side of the Jeep. "What the fuck, Duke? You're not into public displays of affection." She looked at Loren. "You must give great fucking head for him to be with you. Look at you, with that fucking scar running down your face. I don't know why anyone would want anything to do with you."

Loren didn't look at her. Duke's eyes were locked on hers, telling her how much he loved her. He reached up to run his thumb along her bottom lip, and Julie reached up and grabbed his hand away. "Don't do this, Duke. She is nothing."

Jaz jumped at her. Loren put her hand up and Jaz froze. "Stay, girl, she isn't worth it." Jaz sat down and put her head on Loren's shoulder.

"Yeah, you're right to keep that fucking mutt away from me. Duke, we belong together. Come home with me." Loren put her hands on Duke's shoulders, her ring catching the sunlight. Julie grabbed her hand to take her ring off. Loren snatched her thumb between her fingers and snapped it, breaking it. "You fucking bitch! You broke my finger!"

Loren pressed on Duke's chest to move him out of the way. "Stay, Jaz," she said as she climbed out of the Jeep and got in Julie's face.

"Don't ever fucking touch me again. Stay away from me and stay away from Duke."

Julie was holding her hand, pulling back. Just as Charlie pulled up, she swung. Loren caught her hand mid-swing and threw her on the ground. Charlie jumped out of his car.

"Get her out of here, Charlie. I want to press charges against her. She assaulted Loren and threatened us." Duke was shouting, beyond pissed.

"Yeah, I saw her swing. Julie, you are under arrest for assault."

"She broke my finger. Look at my knees. That bitch hurt me and I'm under arrest?"

"Yep, come on." Charlie put the cuffs on her and put her in the back of his squad car. Turning to Loren and Duke, he said. "Listen, I'm sorry about this. Teddy bailed her out. I'm not so sure he will this time."

"Just keep her away from me," Loren said as she climbed in the Jeep.

Duke walked over to the squad car and said, "Julie, you are so beyond this. Just accept the fact that I don't love you. I don't want you. It's over."

"No!" she yelled. "You love me. I love you. We belong together."

Shaking his head, he said, "No, we don't." He walked back to the Jeep and they left. He headed out of town.

Loren put her hand on his leg. "Where are you going?"

"Away from here. Home."

She giggled. "We need to go grocery shopping. I am not about to let her disrupt our lives. Besides, she will be in jail, so we can shop without having to worry about running into her."

"You sure?" He smiled.

"I'm sure."

Duke chuckled at her and turned the Jeep around. They did their shopping, so much so that they filled Duke's Jeep. They laughed when they realized how much they bought. "I'm a big boy. I need a lot of food."

Loren laughed, wrapping her arms around his waist. "Oh, I know you're a big boy."

Duke grabbed her around the neck, tipping her back as he kissed her. "Fucking right you do. Come on, woman, let's get this home. I've got some plans for you."

Loren laughed. "I think that is the other way around, big boy."

They held hands all the way home. Duke carried in the groceries while Loren put everything away. He went to feed the horses and the chickens while Loren made some pie dough and dumplings. When she finished, she jumped in the shower then put on a sundress. She was taking some iced tea out to Duke as he came walking up from the barn so Loren sat down. As she watched him, she felt herself getting excited the closer he got.

"You are one mighty fine looking man," she said.

He smiled at her, kneeling in front of her, pushing her legs apart so he could get closer to her. "Trust me, I have nothing on you." He leveled her with a kiss. "Whatcha got there?"

"Iced tea." She handed him a glass.

He drank it down then licked his lips. "I'm going to take a shower."

Loren nodded and watched him walk away. Shaking her head, she smiled and got up to head to her garden. She pulled weeds, picked tomatoes and strawberries, and checked her peppers and carrots. When she turned to take her harvest to the house to wash it all up, Duke was sitting in the chair watching her. He was enjoying the view that the backdrop of the sun was giving him. He could see right through her little sun dress, and to him, it was the most glorious sight.

Loren smiled as she walked up to him. "I see you," she whispered as she knelt down in front of him, setting her basket on the ground. Her hands slowly travelled up his thighs to his bare stomach and chest.

Duke closed his eyes at the feel of her hands on him, so loving and gentle her touch. When her hands reached his shoulders, she dragged them back down to his unbuttoned jeans to rub him. "So hard," she whispered. Her fingers unzipped him. "So wanton," she moaned as she released him from his denim prison. "So beautiful."

Duke felt the heat of her breath on him, bringing a deep moan from his chest. Loren licked the bead from his tip. "Mmm, so good," she moaned in her sexy whisper voice. Duke opened his eyes just as she opened her mouth to draw in his swollen head. "So soft," she whispered. Again and again, she swirled her tongue around it. Duke closed his eyes and put his head back. She was making it very difficult to keep himself in check. He felt her hands gently tug on his jeans, so he lifted his ass off the chair a bit so she could pull his jeans all the way down. She slipped one leg out and then spread his legs. His balls hung off the edge of the chair. Loren slid her hands up his thighs and cupped them. "So big, so soft," she moaned.

Her tiny hands slowly moved up to wrap around him. Gently gripping him, she pumped his erection. Replacing one hand with her mouth, Loren slowly took him to the back of her throat. With each inward push, she worked him further and further down her throat. His head popped into her mouth with each pull back. For him, it was an internal battle not to come. He wanted to relish this gift she was giving him. Time and time again, she pushed him further down her throat.

"Oh, God. So good," Duke groaned. "So fucking good." On the next intake, Loren touched her nose to his stomach, holding him in her mouth and throat. Duke picked his head up, looking at her. "Fuck, you're beautiful." Her grip tightened on his balls as she withdrew, swallowing as he moved out of her. Duke couldn't hold it any longer. He had no control, shocking himself as he exploded, his head falling back. "Ahhhh, fuck." When she finished, Loren moved up his body, trailing her mouth from his stomach to his neck. She straddled him, taking his face in her hands, and kissed him slowly and sweetly.

"I love you," she whispered in his mouth.

His hands moved up her thighs, slipping under her little dress across her ass, pulling her dress with him up her back to her neck. Loren raised her hands as he slowly pulled it over her head. He dropped it on the ground then moved his hands around to cup her breasts. "So perfect," he managed to get out as he brushed her nipples with his thumbs. Loren lifted her head, leaning back so he could capture her nipples in his mouth.

Duke couldn't help but look at her. His hands gently caressed her perfect breasts, her nipples hardening with each pass of his thumbs. Duke gently pulled her forward, and his tongue burst into goosebumps as it wrapped around her. She was a magnificent creature and deserved every ounce of himself he could give her.

He took his time enjoying her nipples, bringing her to more than one orgasm. He knew she was dripping her sweet, sweet nectar, and his mouth watered knowing what was waiting for him. His hands moved from her breasts to her ass. He shook off his jeans and stood, taking Loren with him. Her mouth covered his as he made his way to the house. Once inside, he made his way up to the loft and gently laid her on her back.

His mouth took control, devouring her, slowly moving down her body. Loren felt his breath on her hairline and arched her back as he gently spread her legs. "Oh, God, beautiful. Look at you." Duke could see her creamy white release slowly moving out of her. Lowering his head, his tongue slid out of his mouth as he took her. His eyes rolled in his head as her flavor burst onto his taste buds.

Duke didn't stop. He continued his slow assault on her senses, bringing her to the edge of reason again. After one last lick of her heavenly essence, he wrapped his arms around her waist, slid his hand up her back, and lifted her onto his thighs.

Her mouth gently covering his, she kissed him, tasting herself on his tongue. With her hands on his face, he lifted her onto him, and she slowly slid down him, filling herself completely. When they were bone on bone, Loren pulled back. What she saw in Duke's eyes was more than she could ever want in this life. Love, devotion, desire, need, want and passion. Gently, she moved, Duke controlling everything. His gentle thrusts built her up internally. They gazed at one another and made slow, beautiful, intense love.

As they climaxed together, he held her tight, needing to feel her body shudder. This woman was everything he needed in his life. He had enough money to never work another day. Just knowing he could spend every second of every day with her was more than enough.

Duke gently laid Loren on her back, kissing her all the way down. Slowly, he pulled out of her, and she was spent. Her eyes closed, and her body went limp. Duke reached for a shirt from the hamper and gently cleaned her up. Her mews drove him mad as he wiped her clean. Tossing the shirt aside, he laid down on his back next to her, pulling her to him. He closed his eyes and was sleeping in a matter of minutes. Neither of them moved or woke for hours.

The sun rose and they stayed cuddled together. Hours past sunrise they slept. Jaz woke them. She needed to go out. Duke slipped out of bed and made his way downstairs to let her out. He followed her and grabbed his jeans, putting them on. Picking up Loren's dress, he couldn't help but smile at the way she made love to him with her mouth.

Turning to go in the house, he caught a flicker of light off in the distance. "What the hell is that?" He kept his eyes on it while he headed to the stairs. "Come on, Jaz," he said. Going in, he locked the door and then went to the bathroom before heading up to get a shirt. He found some paper and left a note for Loren.

Beautiful,
I'll be back in a bit. It's 9:30 now.
I love you
D

He put on his boots and headed out the door again. This time, he didn't look in the direction of the flicker. He saddled up Roxy and headed out toward the light. He was nearly to the top of the hill when he heard an engine start. Kicking Roxy in the sides, they took off. Just as Duke made it to top, he saw a red Jeep flying down the hill. "Fucking Julie," he said. Pulling his phone from his pocket, he dialed Charlie. "Hey, Charlie, it's Duke Reynolds. I just found Julie sitting on a hill just the other side of Loren's place, watching her house with a pair of binoculars. How the hell did she get out of jail?"

"Teddy bailed her out again. Listen, Duke, I will talk to her."

"Yeah, arrest that bitch for trespassing. She is on my father's ranch, and I am getting tired of this shit. I am going to have a chat with Teddy. This needs to stop."

"I know, man, but I can't not let her out."

"Well, get it in front of the fucking judge. Sooner rather than later."

"I'm working on it."

Duke was so pissed he hung up the phone and headed back to the house. When he walked out of the barn, Loren was walking toward him.

"Hey, where did you go?"

"You aren't going to believe me when I tell you," he said as he wrapped his arms around her, kissing her. "Good morning."

Loren giggled. "It's nearly afternoon. So, tell me."

"Well, I came out here when I got up to get my jeans and to let Jaz out, and when I was heading back in, I saw a flicker of light coming from the hill. So, I took a ride, and you will never guess who was up there."

"Julie?" Duke nodded. "How did she find out where my house was?"

"I haven't a fucking clue, but I want to take a ride. Come on, let's get your shoes on."

Loren nodded and they headed into the house. She threw on a pair of jeans and her boots. After grabbing two coffees in to go cups and some fruit for them, she reached in the drawer and took out her gun, clipping it to the back of her pants. Hand in hand, they walked out the door, Duke making sure it was locked. He opened the Jeep door for Loren and Jaz.

As they flew down the road toward town, Loren asked, "So where are we going?"

"To talk to my old friend Teddy. He's the one who keeps bailing her out. I am so fed up with this shit." Loren could see his jaw clench.

She reached over and put her hand on his leg. "Hey, she isn't going to come between us unless we let her."

"Loren, she is sitting on a hill with binoculars watching your house. Watching us."

"Yeah, that's a bit creepy."

They didn't say much the rest of the way. Duke pulled up to Teddy's house. "Well, look at that." He nodded to the driveway. "Julie's here. If I asked you to stay in the Jeep, would you?" He looked at her.

"Yes, I will stay in the Jeep, but please be careful, and try to be kind. And hurry up."

Duke reached for her, kissing her. "I love you."

"I love you, too."

Duke got out of the Jeep and headed for the house. Loren watched him while Jaz growled. She rolled down the window as he knocked on the door. Duke backed up as the door opened. She could hear him.

"Would you come out here and talk to me for a minute?" he asked his friend.

Teddy nodded and walked out into the yard, looking at Loren. "What's going on? I thought we weren't friends anymore?" Teddy said.

"Who told you we weren't friends? I know it wasn't me."

"Well, I just figured, seeing as how you walked in on me and Julie."

Duke chuckled. "Yeah, about that… Listen, man, I never loved the girl and she deserves someone who is going to make her happy."

Teddy smiled. Loren thought he was a rather good-looking man. He had a nice smile. "She seems to be happy with me."

"Is that why you keep bailing her out of jail?" Duke asked.

"Yeah, she said Charlie keeps saying she has unpaid tickets. I don't understand why me paying her bail wouldn't take care of that." Loren watched as Teddy scratched his head. She chuckled quietly.

"Did Charlie tell you that?"

"No, Julie did. Why?"

"Teddy, she hasn't been in jail for unpaid tickets. She has been harassing me and threatening me. Trespassing on my father's ranch. This afternoon, I saw her on a hill by Loren's house watching us with binoculars. She is stalking me. Yesterday, she attacked Loren and tried to rip her ring off her finger. Loren broke her thumb."

Loren watched as it all sunk in. "She told me she slammed her thumb in the car door."

"No, Teddy, she has been trying to get me to take her to the festival. Hell, she was in my bedroom a few nights ago, naked and trying to get me to fuck her. I had to move back home to the ranch. She is out of control."

"Are you fucking kidding me?"

Duke shook his head. "No, man, but I wish I was. She has gone bat shit crazy. You need to stop bailing her out."

Teddy looked past Duke at Loren, and she saw his face change to horror. Out of nowhere, Loren felt someone grab her hair and rip her out of the Jeep. Duke spun around when he heard Loren scream and Jaz barking.

Julie had grabbed her and thrown her on the ground, and she was kicking Loren in the back.

"Call Charlie," Duke yelled as he bolted across the lawn. Just as Julie pulled her leg back to kick Loren again, Jaz was on her, knocking her to the ground and grabbing her arm.

"Jaz, STOP!" Loren yelled. She let Julie go and stood next to Duke as he helped her up.

"Are you all right?" Duke was panicked, pulling her into his embrace.

"Yes," Loren said, turning around to look at Julie. She pulled out of Duke's embrace and dropped to her knees, grabbing Julie's arm. She checked it out, but Jaz hadn't broken the skin. Loren threw her arm down. "Touch me again and I will end you," she said to Julie.

"Your fucking dog bit me!" Julie screamed.

Teddy came running up. "What the fuck is wrong with you?" he yelled at Julie.

"He's fucking mine. She is wearing my ring he bought for me!" she cried.

Loren looked at her and laughed. "You stupid bitch, he didn't buy this ring for you or for me. It's his mother's. His father gave it to him to give to me. You need some serious help." She turned to Teddy. "If you bail her out again, you're the fool." Looking at Duke, she said, "I want to go home." She turned to Jaz. "Jaz, get in the Jeep." Jaz jumped back in the Jeep when she opened the door.

Julie screamed at her. "You are a lying bitch. That's my ring."

Loren shook her head. Stepping over to Julie, she put her foot on her wrist and bent down. "If I see you on my land again, I will shoot you for trespassing. Stay away from me." Loren stepped back into Duke's chest just as Charlie drove up.

"What the hell are you doing now, Julie?"

Teddy spoke. "Apparently, she was out at Loren's place spying on them. I had no idea what was going on. Julie told me you arrested her for parking tickets."

Charlie shook his head. "No, for the past two weeks, she has been harassing Duke and Loren. She even attacked Richard. What did she do now?"

"I watched her pull Loren out of the Jeep by her hair and then kick her in the back," Teddy said.

"Her fucking dog bit me," Julie cried.

"Funny, I don't see any blood," Charlie said. Looking at Loren, he asked, "May I see your back?"

Duke felt her go stiff in his arms. "I'm fine," she said.

"Well, it will help in court if I could get a picture of where she kicked you." Charlie smiled.

"Here, give me your phone and I will take the picture," Duke said. Charlie handed him his phone. Duke and Loren moved to the other side of the Jeep. Duke took a picture, making sure he didn't get her scar.

"Can we leave now?" Loren whispered to him. Duke nodded and opened his door for her to climb in while he went and gave Charlie his phone.

"I want her arrested for assault, trespassing, and stalking. I swear to God, Charlie, if you let that bitch out before she goes to court, I will have your job. I am so sick of this shit. She should get some serious mental help."

Duke walked around and got in the Jeep. Loren watched as Charlie helped Julie up and then handcuffed her. Teddy looked at Duke. "I won't bail her out again."

Duke nodded and they left. Loren didn't say anything all the way back to her house. When they pulled up, she went into the bathroom and took a shower. She let the hot water pound on her back, and she cried. *What the fuck? Am I ever going to have a normal life? Maybe I should leave.* She ran the hot water out and grabbed a towel. Drying herself off, she wrapped it around her and went up to the loft to put on some clothes. Instead, Loren laid on the bed and cried.

Life shouldn't be this hard. Is loving him worth this? I was so happy out here alone. She was so involved with her thoughts and with crying that she didn't hear Duke come up or feel him climb on the bed. When he touched her, she pulled away out of fear.

"Hey, beautiful," he whispered as he touched her arm.

Loren cowered away from his touch. "Please, just don't," she sobbed.

Duke sat there with tears of his own in his eyes. "Loren."

"No, Duke, please just go."

"I can't leave you like this."

She wanted to make him leave so she had to hurt him. "It's because of you that I'm like this. Please, just go. I can't do this."

Duke was crying. "I can't. Loren, I love you," he whispered through his tears.

"Please," she sobbed. "Please, just go." Then she shouted, "Leave!"

The force of her voice made Duke jump. Slowly, he moved off the bed, then to the stairs, never taking his eyes off of her. He got into his Jeep and drove away. He had to pull over because he couldn't see through his tears.

Loren cried herself to sleep with Jaz lying behind her nestled up against her back.

CHAPTER FOURTEEN

DUKE SAT on the side of the road for some time crying, sobbing. He didn't understand why she would push him away. Finally, he got himself under control and realized how pissed he was. Putting the Jeep in drive, he headed to town. It was time he and Julie had it out. It was time he made her understand what the fuck was in his head.

He pulled up in front of the police station. Taking a deep breath, he got out and went in. "Hey, Charlie, I need to see Julie."

He got up and Duke followed him to the jail. Once he opened the door, Duke walked in. "Thanks," he said.

"Just give a yell when you're ready."

Duke nodded and walked down to the cell Julie was in and sat on the floor with his back against the wall, looking at her. She was lying on the cot crying. "What the fuck is wrong with you?" he asked.

"I love you," she sobbed.

"No, Julie, you don't. If you did, you wouldn't have done what you did today."

"I hate her."

Duke chuckled. "You don't even know her."

"And you do?" She turned her head to look at him.

"I do. I am going to marry her."

"Why don't you want me anymore?" She looked him right in the eyes. He felt nothing for her.

"Julie, you slept with my oldest friend, in my bed, in my house. And you had been doing it for the better part of a year. How do you think that made me feel? You don't love me. Hell, I don't even think you like me. You just want me now because I stopped paying attention to you, because I stopped caring."

"Did you ever stop to think that maybe you weren't giving me enough of yourself that I had to go elsewhere for it?"

Duke smiled. "I've learned a great deal from Loren. If you felt that way, then that's on you. I gave all I had, and I would have given more, but you are the one who didn't accept it. We never made love. We never held each other. We never really had conversations or ate a meal with each other. What we had was alcohol and sex, and that is not love. It was just sex. Don't you see that? Julie, I want a family. I want the love. What I have with her is so real it scares me."

She was crying. "Why can't you have that with me?"

"I don't think you are capable of it. I don't love you. I don't think I ever did."

"But we were so good in bed."

Duke chuckled. "I won't deny that. I have never denied that. But it was just sex, Julie. Never did we make love, never were we tender. You didn't like that. You told me repeatedly that you just wanted to fuck."

"I thought that's what you wanted."

"You know that's not true. I tried many times to just be gentle. Hell, the only time you ever kissed me was in the bar, and that was because some other woman was looking at me. Julie, you want something I can no longer give you. I am in love with someone else."

"How can you love her? She is so scarred. She is so plain."

He laughed. "You don't know her. You know nothing about her."

"I do, too. I know she has the man I love."

Shaking his head, he said, "You just want my money, Julie. I know that now."

She sat up. "Fuck you, Duke."

"No, thanks. Please, just leave us alone. I don't want you. I don't even think I wanted you when we were together. The sex was great, but that's all it was."

"So, what you're saying to me is that I'm better in bed than she is?"

Duke laughed and stood up. "Julie, you are not better in bed. You will never be better in bed. You know why?" She shook her head. "Because you don't and can't love me in return. I love her, and she loves me. It makes a world of difference. Please, just leave us alone. I am not going to stop having you arrested. I am not yours. I am hers, and I am going to marry her."

"No, Duke, you can't," she whispered through her tears.

"Yes, Julie, I can and I will. Understand me, I don't love you. I don't want you. Even if Loren leaves me, I still won't want you. I'm done with this shit. Just stop, move on with your life. Teddy wants you. Hell, I think he even loves you. Be happy with him."

"But I want you."

Shaking his head, he said, "No, Julie, you just want my money. You always have. Hell, if you want it that bad, then take it. Just leave us the fuck alone. How much, Julie? A million? Two? Or would you want all of it? Tell me, so I can get the fuck out of here. I am done. I don't want you."

"You would give me all your money to leave you alone? To walk away?"

"Every fucking penny of it. That's how much I don't want you." Julie didn't say anything; she just stood there looking at him. She reached out to touch him and he backed away. "Don't fucking touch me. Let Charlie know what your decision is. I need to go." He turned and walked to the door, calling for Charlie. He didn't turn around when she whispered his name. Charlie opened the door and Duke walked away.

He made his way back to Loren's place, noticing her truck was still by the barn. He stood there looking at her house. The house he hoped to share with her as her husband. The house they would bring their first child home to. He couldn't help but smile. Walking up, Jaz ran up to meet him. "Hey, girl." He knelt down to pet her. "Where's our girl?"

"She's right here," Loren said softly.

Duke stood, looking at her. He could see her eyes were swollen from crying, but he didn't move. He wasn't sure where her head was.

"I'm sorry," Loren whispered. Tears were still falling onto her cheeks.

It took Duke three long strides to reach her. His hand came up to wrap around her head. He wiped her tears with his thumb as they fell. "You have nothing to be sorry for. It was all my fault. We should have never gone over there." Pulling Loren into his chest, he closed his eyes as her arms moved to encircle his waist. Her body shook as she cried. "Shh, it's all right, beautiful."

"I hurt you. I'm so... sorry."

"No, baby, you didn't hurt me. If anything, I am hurting you, us. I can't believe she is doing this shit. I went to see her. I wanted to know what was in her head. We had a long talk. I offered her all my money to stay away from us."

Loren pulled back. "I'll give her all mine, too."

He chuckled, bending his head to gently kiss her. "I have more money than I could ever spend in this lifetime. I thought it meant something to me, but it doesn't. You are the only thing that matters to me. I don't give a shit about the money. It's the only thing she wants from me, so I offered it to her."

"What did she say?"

"Not a damn word. I told her to let Charlie know how much she wanted."

"I know it's none of my business, but how much money are we talking about?"

Duke chuckled. "It is your business because you are going to be my wife. I'm not sure, but last time I checked, it was somewhere around eight million."

Loren pulled back and looked at him. "Where did you get eight million dollars from?"

He laughed. "I invested my pay from the ranch. I got lucky with some stocks I bought. I didn't need much to live off of, so instead of putting it in the bank, I invested."

"Does your father know this?"

Duke nodded. "He's the one who helped me. Can we not talk about this anymore? I would really like to take you in the house and hold you. Maybe make love to you." He pressed his erection against her stomach.

Loren turned out of his embrace. Taking his hand, they walked into the house. She left Duke to take off his shoes, and she made her way up to the loft. By the time Duke reached the top of the stairs, Loren was lying on her stomach completely naked. His heart nearly stopped when he saw the bruise on her back from Julie.

"Jesus," he whispered. "God, baby, does it hurt?" She shook her head. "Should we take you to see Doc, just to make sure?"

Slowly rolling over, her hand came up to touch his arm. "It's fine," she whispered in her fucking sexy voice that always made him instantly hard.

His eyes left hers to slowly admire her body as if it was a work of art. "God, you are so fucking beautiful," he moaned as he pulled his shirt over his head. Loren smiled and rolled back to her stomach as Duke took off his jeans. Slowly, he laid next to her, his fingers dying to touch her. Her head was turned so she could look at him. His hands embraced her head, his fingers in her hair. He gathered a fistful, pulling her mouth up to his lips. His actions were rough, but his lips were tender and gentle.

"Duke," she breathed.

"Yeah, baby," he whispered between kisses.

"Will you fuck me?" Her face felt like it would burn from embarrassment.

He smiled. "You sure? Because I really would like that."

She nodded and he let go of her hair. His hand moved on its own, down her back to her ass. Duke slowly got up on his knees, slipping one between her thighs. His hands never stopped touching her ass. "You have the most beautiful ass. God, baby, you are incredible." Loren just moaned as he massaged it. He pulled her cheeks apart and bent down to make love to her ass with his tongue.

"Ahhh, ohhh, God, Duke." She felt her orgasm building.

Duke slowly moved his finger, slipping it deep inside of her. Loren lifted her hips off the bed while he slid it in and out of her wet core. When it was slick with her juices, he slid it to her ass and pushed it slowly into her.

"Ahh, relax, baby," he moaned as it slipped past the tight ring.

"Oh, God, Duke. Yes, please... Ohhhh," she cried as he pushed further in her.

With his other hand, he reached under her and pulled her up and against his body, moving his other leg between hers. "So beautiful," he moaned as he pushed inside of her. "Oh, God, Loren." He closed his eyes to savor the feeling of this beautiful woman. He pushed his finger all the way in her ass. Slowly, he fingered her ass, in and out. Then he pushed another finger in her, stretching her virginal hole as he slowly fucked her.

"Duke," she cried as her orgasm ripped through her.

Duke had to stop moving or she would have taken him with her. With his head back and his fingers moving slowly in her ass, he enjoyed the glorious feeling of her coming on his cock. "Fucking fantastic," he moaned. When she finished pulsing, he pulled his fingers from her, grabbing his shirt to wipe them off, then gripped her hips. Pulling back, he slammed deep inside of her.

"Ahhh, God, yes!" she screamed.

A few more slow pulls back and quick and hard thrusts forward and Duke was ready to go. Biting his lip as he rode her hard, he realized what he was doing and stopped instantly. She wasn't Julie; this was how he fucked Julie. This was Loren, the woman he loved. Pulling out of her, he sat back on his heels and dropped his head into his hands. He couldn't stop the tears. He was using her for his own gratification, just like he used Julie, and Loren didn't deserve that.

Loren rolled over, sitting up. "Hey," she whispered as her hands went to his wrists. "Duke, what's the matter?"

He pulled away. Grabbing his pants, he left the loft. Loren didn't know what to do when she heard the door shut. Grabbing her shorts and t-shirt, she ran down the stairs and outside. Duke was walking toward the field, past the barn. She stood there watching him. He kept going, then he stopped and put his hands on his knees. She wanted to run to him, but she didn't. When Duke screamed, she jumped. Jaz stood up ready to run, but she didn't.

When Duke dropped to his knees, Loren took off running toward him. When she reached him, she fell to her knees. His head was hanging down and his shoulders were shaking. She didn't touch him, just waited. Not knowing what was wrong, she just knew not to touch him yet. As his shoulders started to calm down, Loren sat quietly on her knees, waiting for the sign she needed to touch him.

He raised his head and looked at her. "I... am... so... sorry," he sobbed.

Shaking her head, she said, "No. There is nothing to be sorry for." She reached up with her hand to touch his face.

Duke pulled away. "I don't deserve you."

Her hand fell to his leg. "Why?"

His eyes moved to her hand, and he gently removed it. "Because, I..." He started to cry again.

"Duke, talk to me. Tell me," she whispered.

"Because I don't know how to do this. I don't know how to separate it all," he blurted out.

"Separate what? How you feel about me? How you feel about Julie?" Duke nodded. "Oh, God, please don't tell me you want her?" Duke just looked at her, and she saw the truth in his eyes. Loren pushed up to her feet, turned, and ran into the field. She didn't stop running until her legs started to shake and she fell to the ground. She was running from his answer, from her fear. Loren didn't know how long she laid there. It was Jaz that brought her back. Looking at her, she knew what she had to do. She needed to get out of there. She needed to not be here anymore. She needed to leave here.

Standing, she turned around, but Duke was nowhere to be seen. Loren started back to her house, back to the place she finally felt safe but didn't any longer. As she cleared the yard, she could see his Jeep was gone. Running into the house, she made her way up to the loft and changed. Grabbing a bag from the storage next to her bed, she packed her things. Going downstairs, she grabbed her gun, wallet, phone, and keys. She made sure she grabbed Jaz's food, and then she wrote a note to Richard.

Dear Richard,

I am so sorry for leaving, for ruining everything within your family. I shouldn't have come here. I don't know where I'm going or what will become of me. Please sell this place. It holds too many memories for me. I love you. When I get where I am going, I will call.

Please accept this ring back. It may have been received in love, but I no longer believe it was given in love.

I won't be back.

Thank you for all that you have given me and for helping me along this journey of finding who I am. I know now that I am not the woman who should be with your son.

Loren

She took off her ring and set it on top of the note. Looking around, she said, "Come on, Jaz."

Together, they left her tiny house. She got Cupcake in her trailer with some hay and her saddle then left. She cried all the way to the state line. Home was the only place she could go, so she headed to Texas.

She drove all the way to Denver and had to crash. Finding an out of the way hotel off the highway, she and Jaz slept for a few hours. The next day, she drove all the way to Austin and pulled up to her parents' ranch just before midnight. All the lights were off, and she didn't see her mother's car anywhere. Which meant she was either at her Aunt Liz's or on her way to Montana. Loren got Cupcake set up in the stables and then went into the house. Her mother's room was empty. She checked the dresser and closet, but everything was gone. She was alone. The tears just came. Making her way to her old room, she collapsed on the bed and cried herself to sleep with Jaz laying behind her.

≈

WHEN DUKE LEFT, HE WENT TO HIS FATHER'S HOUSE. HE KNEW NO ONE would be home and he could be by himself to figure out what the fuck he was doing. *How could I hurt her like that? How could I feel as if I'm using the woman I love?*

He made his way to his room and fell on the bed crying. Julie really fucked him up. He believed he knew how to love; he believed he wanted to love Loren. But why was Julie still so deep in him. *Do I love her?*

His mind wouldn't shut up. Getting up, he rummaged through some boxes and found his Jack Daniels. He didn't even bother with a glass, unscrewing the cap and drinking right from the bottle. "What the fuck is wrong with me?" Duke drank until he passed out. It was the only peace he could get from himself.

He had to have been exhausted, because he didn't hear Richard when he came in his room and saw the empty bottle lying on the floor. Shaking his head, Richard went to Loren's. She wasn't there, and the horse trailer was gone. He tried her door and it opened. When he walked inside, he saw the note and the ring on the counter.

"Son of a bitch," he said to himself. He picked up the note and ring. As he read it, his heart broke. What did Duke do to hurt her like this? Richard took the note and ring, locking the door, and left and headed back to the ranch.

He wanted to go up and drag Duke out of his sleep and ask him what happened. Instead, he sat at the table and waited. He sat there for hours waiting. Then he heard Duke coming down the stairs. He waited for him to do whatever it was he was doing in the kitchen. Finally, he came into the dining room.

"Dad, what are you doing here?"

"I live here. What are you doing here?"

"I needed to think about some things, so I came here. That's all right, right?"

Richard reached into his pocket and pulled out the ring. "Depends on this." He laid the ring on the table.

Duke stood there, frozen in fear. It was Loren's ring. *How did he get it?* "Where did you get that?" he whispered, his mind spinning out of control. *Did something happen to Loren? Why does my father have her ring?*

"When I got home, I found you passed out. I thought you quit drinking?"

"I told you I have some things to think about. Dad, how did you get Loren's ring? Where is she? Is she all right?" Duke was panicking.

"You can't think about anything drunk, son."

"I know, Dad. Where is Loren?"

Richard opened the note Loren had left him and slid it across the table. With shaking hands, Duke picked it up and read it.

The tears just came. "No," Duke whispered.

"What happened?" Richard was trying desperately to hold his temper.

Duke looked up at him. "She left?"

"Looks that way. Cupcake is gone."

"I have to find her. I have to explain."

"What happened, Duke?" Richard raised his voice.

"I'm not sure. I don't know why she would leave. Julie attacked her yesterday, at least I think it was yesterday. How long have I been asleep?"

"What do you mean, Julie attacked her?"

"I saw Julie on the hill by Loren's watching us. So, we went to Teddy's place to talk to her, and she attacked Loren. She is fine, and Julie is in jail. Well, when we got back to Loren's, I went to feed the chickens and Loren took a shower. When I came back into the house, she made me leave. She just wanted to be alone, so I went to talk to Julie in jail, to get her to stop. I told her she could have all my money if she just left us alone. Then I came back and Loren and I talked. Then we went to bed, and while we were... well, it hit me that I was treating her like I treated Julie, and it freaked me out. I was confused about it all. She tried to talk to me. She asked me if I still had feelings for Julie, and I couldn't answer her. She ran away to the field, and I left to come here to figure out what the fuck is wrong with me. Dad, I didn't think she was going to leave."

"Did you figure out what is wrong with you?" Richard was

steaming mad. He was doing everything in his power not to throttle the shit out of his son.

Shaking his head, he said, "I love her. I love Loren. I want to marry her. Dad, do you know where she is?"

"No, and even if I did, I don't think I would tell you. Duke, that girl has been through hell in a hand basket. She gave herself to you, and you treated her wrongly. I want to get up and kick your ass right now, but you look like you are suffering enough. She is gone, and she isn't coming back. It's over."

Duke couldn't stop his stomach from rolling over. He turned and ran to the bathroom to throw up. He had lost her. She was gone. All because of him, all because he thought he wasn't worthy of her, because he couldn't get fucking Julie out of his Goddamn head. He deserved every ounce of pain he was going to feel. He didn't deserve to have one ounce of happiness, ever. When he finished, he sat on the floor and cried. He'd never felt this pain before, this gut-wrenching pain that was ripping him to shreds.

When Loren woke, she made her way to the stable to find John. He was in his office. "Loren? What are you doing here? Your mother is on her way up north."

She half smiled. "John, I need for you to not tell anyone that I am here. Not even Richard Reynolds. No one."

"Loren, are you all right?"

"No, John, I'm not. I just need some peace for a while. Can I count on you to not give out any information? I will contact Richard and my mother so they know I am all right, but please, if anyone is looking for me, you haven't seen me."

He smiled. "I will keep your secret for as long as you need me to."

"Thank you, John. I just want to be alone and to ride my horse."

John nodded. "I will keep you safe."

She smiled and went to get her stuff out of her truck and to unhitch her trailer. Once in the kitchen, she noticed that there wasn't much food. She made a list and then asked John if he would get her what she needed. There was no way she wanted to go anywhere near a town or people. As far as she was concerned, she was never leaving this ranch again.

After John left, she pulled out her phone and turned it on. There were twenty missed calls from Duke. She immediately blocked his number, erased all his messages, and then called Richard.

"Loren?" he said.

"Yes, it's me." Her voice was soft.

"Dear God, child. It's so good to hear your voice. Are you all right?"

"I'm alive, but I'm afraid that I'm far from all right. I just wanted to let you know that I'm alive, and I'm sorry for bringing such havoc to your family. Please forgive me." She felt the tears coming. "I'm sorry, Richard, but I need to go."

"Loren, don't hang up. Talk to me, you know you can."

She shook her head, trying to stop the tears, but it didn't help. "I can't," she whispered. "I need to go."

"Aww, darlin', tell me where you are and I'll come. We can talk."

She sniffled. "I can't. I'm sorry." She hung up and turned off her phone. Running to her room, she fell on her bed and cried herself asleep.

When she woke, it was dark out. She had slept the day away. Dragging herself down to the kitchen, she let Jaz out and then grabbed something to eat. She sat on the back porch and ate. When Jaz finished, she came and laid down next to Loren.

"Oh, Jaz, what did I do? I fell in love with a man who wasn't in love with me." Jaz whimpered. Loren felt the tears coming. "Why can't he love me?" she asked the dog. The tears came again. She dragged herself upstairs again and crawled into bed, crying herself to sleep again.

❧

DUKE FINALLY CAME DOWNSTAIRS. HE HAD BEEN UP THERE FOR FIVE days, just crying and drinking and hurting. He hadn't taken a shower or eaten in days.

"Loren called. She said she is alive," Richard said to him.

Duke's heart started beating again. He felt a bit of excitement. "Where is she? I need to change and go find her."

"She wouldn't tell me. She sounds pretty messed up, Duke."

"Dad, I've called her and texted her like a million times. She blocked my number. I need to find her. Maybe she went back to Texas."

"Already thought of that. I called John, the ranch manager, and he said he hasn't seen her."

"Do you think he would lie to you?" Duke asked.

"There would be no reason for him to lie to me. You are going to have to face the fact she is gone. It's been nearly a week, Duke. You need to snap out of this and bring yourself back to life."

"Dad, she is my life. I was so stupid."

Richard patted him on the back. "You'll recover."

He shook his head. "No, Dad, I won't. She is the love of my life. I can't do this without her."

"It'll get easier, son. I promise." Richard walked out the door.

Duke felt the pain rip through him, and he went back upstairs to sleep. It was the only time it didn't hurt. Loren was with him in his dreams, and that's where he wanted to be.

WEEKS AND WEEKS HAD PASSED. LOREN NEVER LEFT THE RANCH, AND Duke didn't talk to anyone. He stayed by himself, not leaving the ranch, not talking to his brothers. He just worked and then slept. She was with him in his dreams, and that was where he lived his life. Her mother had come to visit, and she called John, but there was still no sight of her.

Julie had not given up on Duke. She still tried and failed to get him back. Time and time again, she was arrested for coming to the ranch, and time and time again, she got out. In a way, Duke was glad Loren had left so she wouldn't have to deal with Julie. Each time Duke saw her, he felt like snapping her neck for doing what she did. He hated her, but he was so depressed he didn't have the strength.

September came, and it was time for the cattle to be rounded up and brought to the market. It took nearly two weeks to herd them in toward the ranch. Everyone was out. Derek, Joe, Alex, Richard, Duke, and Jose` and his crew. They had ten thousand cattle to herd. Duke kept to himself, and his brothers all worried about him, but Richard told them to just leave him be. Finally, they got them all to the coral. It was time to bring in the trucks and get them loaded to go to the market.

This was a big time of the year for the ranch. The trucks started coming, and one by one, they loaded the cattle in. Duke was in the middle of the herd when he heard a woman yelling his name. Turning in his saddle, he saw Julie on a four-wheeler waving at him.

Shaking his head, he turned back around. "What the fuck is she doing here?"

"That bitch is crazy. Why don't they do something about her?"

"Who the fuck knows." Duke said.

"Is she the reason Loren left?" Derek asked gently.

Duke froze. Looking at his brother, his eyes filled with tears. He turned his horse just as a shot rang through the air. The bullet tore through his chest. Derek sat there in shock as his brother fell off his horse and the cattle started to run, trampling him.

"NO!" Derek shouted.

The cattle headed toward Julie. Derek grabbed his walkie talkie. "Dad, fuck. Duke's been hurt. Call for help. Fuck." He was on the ground next to Duke. He felt for a pulse, but it was weak. He was bloody and broken. The cattle trampled him. Derek felt the ground rumble. Looking up, he saw his father and brothers riding up. Richard jumped off his horse, dropping to the ground next to Duke.

"What the hell happened?" he asked.

"Julie shot him, then he fell off his horse and cattle trampled him."

"What the fuck?" Turning, he screamed at Alex, "Go call for help! Get a helicopter out here. Hurry the fuck up."

Alex took off, and Richard turned to Duke. "Come on boy, hang on."

It took thirty minutes for the medivac to show up. While they waited, they found Julie. She had been trampled as well but didn't survive. "Call Charlie and let him know. Get him out here," Richard ordered.

When the medivac got there, they loaded Duke up and flew him to Bozeman. Derek went with him, while Richard, Alex, and Joe drove. Once there, they rushed him into surgery to remove the bullet and fix the damage done by the cattle.

They all sat in the waiting room waiting for the doctors to come and talk to them. Six hours later, Richard heard a man say, "Are you here for Duke Reynolds?"

Richard stood. "Yes, I'm his father, Richard. Is he alive?"

The doctor nodded. "We got the bullet out. It just missed his lung. He has a broken leg, a broken arm, we had to remove his spleen, and he has six broken ribs."

"Jesus, well, at least he will live," Richard said.

"Mr. Reynolds, Duke suffered a brain injury. It is operable, and our neurosurgeon can do it, but he recommends that we call in a specialist."

"Well, then, why aren't you calling him?" Alex yelled.

The doctor rubbed his head. "I'm not sure how to say this, but we have no idea where she is."

Alex looked at him, remembering what Duke had told him about Loren. She was a neurosurgeon. "Dad," he whispered. Richard turn to him. "What's he saying?"

Richard turned back to the doctor. "Excuse me, but what do you mean?"

"Well, she is the best in the country. But she is... she is unavailable."

"Make her available. Call her. Tell her this is my brother," Alex shouted.

"I'm sorry, Mr. Reynolds, but Dr. Mitchell doesn't practice anymore. She hasn't for two years."

No one in the room moved. No one breathed. They all turned to Richard. "Dad," Derek whispered. "Dad, is he talking about Loren?"

"Yes, Dr. Loren Mitchell," the doctor said.

Richard pulled out his phone and dialed her number. He hadn't talked to her in a few weeks. She was still as bad as Duke. He walked out the door and down the hall as the phone rang. It went to voicemail. "Loren. this is Richard. I need you to call me right away. It's an emergency."

He disconnected and dialed it again, and again it went to voicemail. He continued for the next ten minutes then went back to the waiting room.

"Well?" Derek asked.

"She didn't answer." Richard looked at the doctor. "How long does he have before the surgery won't save him?"

"We have no idea, but the longer we wait, the less chance he has. Time in our enemy here."

Richard turned to Derek. "I need you to get on a plane and head to Austin. I will have someone waiting for you with a helicopter. They will take you out to the ranch there. Get Loren and Jaz and bring them back here. Don't let her argue. Don't tell her that Duke needs this surgery. Just tell her what happened and that we need her." He reached into his pocket and pulled out his credit card. "Take a private plane. I will have everything ready for you when you get to the airport. If she isn't there, then she is on her way here."

"You knew where she was all this time?" Derek asked.

"Just go, and hurry."

Derek took the card and ran out of the room. Richard pulled out his phone and dialed Cathy.

"Hello, Richard, how are you?"

"Not good. Listen, Cathy, I need you to get to Bozeman General Hospital as fast as you can. Duke has been in a horrible accident, and Loren is the only one who can save him. I have my son, Derek, on his way to get her."

"Oh, Richard, I am so sorry. I don't think she can do it."

"Neither do I, but I need you here to help me convince her."

"We will be there as soon as we can."

"Thank you, Cathy."

"Richard, she will need a headset with a playlist of Mozart. It's the only way she can operate."

"Got it, it will be here. Hurry."

He hung up. Looking at Joe, he said, "I need you to find me one of those music players with headphones. It needs to be filled with every song Mozart ever wrote. Go."

Joe got up and left. He looked at the doctor. "You need to get clearance for Loren's dog to accompany her into the operating room. Loren suffers from PTSD, and Jaz comforts her."

"Mr. Reynolds, I don't think that is going to be possible."

"You need to make it possible."

The doctor nodded and turned to leave. Richard and Alex headed to Duke's room to wait. He tried Loren again and again, but there was still no answer. Time ticked on. Derek had called when he landed in Austin. Joe had returned with the music player. The doctor had managed to get clearance for Jaz to accompany Loren into the operating room, and Cathy and Liz were on their way.

THE HELICOPTER LANDED IN THE FIELD ON THE NORTH SIDE OF THE ranch. Loren came out to see what the hell was going on. John had come running up from the stables.

When Derek jumped out and started running toward her, she froze.

"Loren, you and Jaz need to come with me. There's been a terrible accident, and Duke has been hurt really bad. My dad sent me to get you. Why aren't you answering your phone?"

Her heart slamming in her chest, she nodded and took off toward the house. Derek followed her. She ran in and changed into a pair of jeans. Grabbing her boots, she ran back downstairs. "Let's go!" she yelled, and they ran out the door with Jaz behind them.

Three hours later, Loren was running into a hospital for the first time in two years. She mentally prepared herself on the trip here. Her heart was slamming in her chest, her hands were shaking, and Jaz was always touching her. No one said a word to them as they ran through the halls to the elevator. When they got off at the I.C.U., she froze when she saw her mother standing in the hall with Richard.

"No," she whispered. Richard and her mother turned to look at her. She saw the fear in Richard's eyes. Shaking her head, she whispered, "No," again. He was moving toward her. She backed up. "No, I can't." Loren knew why she was here. With her body trembling, she shook her head. Derek stood there and watched her fall apart. "No," she whispered again. Her body hit the wall, and Jaz leaned across her legs. As Richard approached her, Jaz growled. He stopped.

"Loren," Richard said.

She looked into his eyes, shaking her head. "No, I can't," she whispered.

"He is going to die. He needs you." The tears rolled down his face.

The world went black and Loren hit the floor. Jaz wouldn't let anyone near her. She kept pushing her nose in her face. A few minutes later, Loren's eyes fluttered. She wrapped her arms around Jaz. When she looked up, there were a bunch of people standing around looking at her. She sat up, leaning against the wall. Derek came over and sat by her.

"He's my big brother, and that man loves you. He has been a shell since you left."

Loren closed her eyes. "Who shot him?" she whispered.

"Julie, but she's dead. She got trampled by the cattle. Loren, I know we don't know each other very well." He chuckled. "Only in passing, really. But that man in there needs you. He needs to know you are here so he has something to fight for. No one is asking you to do anything but get up and go in that room. He needs to know you are here and that you love him."

She nodded. "Okay, I can do that."

Derek looked at his father and nodded. Richard moved everyone back away from her. Derek helped her up, and Loren and Jaz walked very slowly down the hall to his room. A nurse said, "You can't take that dog in there. It shouldn't be here."

Loren looked at her. "Tell her that."

The nurse looked at Loren and gasped when she saw her eyes, and then at Jaz who was baring her teeth and growling at her. Richard walked up to her and said, "We have special permission." The nurse nodded.

Loren walked up to the doorway and closed her eyes. Jaz stuck her nose in her hand and whimpered. Then she leaned on Loren's legs, pushing her forward into the room. Everyone in the hallway just stood still watching them. "I'm all right, girl." Moving slowly, she opened her eyes, and everything she had ever felt for him came rushing back. Such a strong man lay before her broken. Shaking her head, she felt her body lower to the floor. She sat on her knees and cried. Jaz leaned on her back while she sobbed. She wiped her face and stood up, moving to the bed. Her hands were shaking so bad as she reached to touch him, to hold his hand. "I love you," she whispered as she leaned in to kiss him. Her tears fell on his cheeks.

After a few minutes, she walked out into the hall and said to the nurse, "Where's his chart?"

"I can't let you read it," she snapped.

"My name is Dr. Loren Mitchell, give me the Goddamn chart," she yelled.

Duke's doctor came running up. "Dr. Mitchell?" Loren looked at him, and he gasped and stood there looking at her. "Dr. Branson." He reached out to shake her hand, but Loren just looked at him.

"I would like to see his chart please."

Dr. Branson looked at the nurse. "She has special privileges in this hospital. Give her anything she wants. Do not question her."

The nurse gave her a dirty look and handed her Duke's chart. Loren took it and walked back into Duke's room. Dragging the chair over to his bed, she sat down and pulled her legs under her. Reaching up, she took a hold of Duke's hand and started reading. Jaz laid down on the floor in front of her.

Richard, Derek, and her mom quietly looked in the room to see what she was doing. "I know you're there. Could you please leave me alone?"

They all backed off and went to the waiting room. Loren sat in Duke's room for hours going over his x-rays, his scans, and his chart. It was time to talk to Dr. Branson. She walked out to the nurse's desk. "Could you please page Dr. Branson for me? Thank you."

She went back into Duke's room and climbed in the bed with him, on the side that wasn't broken. Laying her head on his chest, she held him the best she could. It took about fifteen minutes for the doctor to come in.

Loren got up. "Is there somewhere we can talk?" He nodded and walked to a conference room at the end of the hall. "I've read his charts, but I'm going to need a few more scans of his brain now. How long has he been like this?"

"Fourteen hours total."

"We are losing our window of twenty-four. Has he woken up at all?"

"No, nothing."

"His pupils are responsive, and there seems to be brain activity. I need those scans as soon as you can."

"Everything is waiting. We can do them now."

"Then do it," she said and got up, going back to Duke's room. Jaz followed her.

She climbed back in the bed to whisper in his ear. "Duke, my love, I need you to hear me. I need for you to wake up, baby. I need to see your beautiful eyes." There was nothing. She knew he needed to know she was there. He needs a reason to live. Climbing off the bed, she leaned in and kissed him. "I love you," she whispered on his lips.

She heard people in the hall and walked out as the machine was being moved into his room. Jaz growled at one of the technicians. "No, Jaz," she said softly. Sitting on the floor outside his room, she waited.

A nurse walked up to her. "Dr. Mitchell, it's an honor to have you here with us. Is there anything I can get you?"

Loren smiled at her. "A bowl of water for my dog would be nice." Jaz picked her head up, laying it in her lap.

"Sure, I'll be right back." Loren watched her run down the hall. She came back a few minutes later with a plastic bowl for Jaz.

"Thank you," Loren said as she took the bowl from her.

"Is there something I can get for you?" she asked.

"No, thank you, I'm fine." Although she knew she wasn't fine. She was struggling with the thought that she was the only one who could save him. She wasn't sure she could do this. She put her head on her knees and tried to will him to wake up. *How can I do this? I haven't held a scalpel in my hand in over two years. Please don't let him need this.* Her stomach growled. She needed to eat something. She looked up at the nurse. "Excuse me, could you get me a cookie and some orange juice please?"

"Of course. I'll be right back."

Loren watched her go into a room and come out with a cookie and a glass of juice. "We have all kinds of stuff in there. Just let me know if you need anything else."

"Thank you." Loren took the cookie and juice. She inhaled it. As she was drinking the last of her juice, Dr. Branson came out.

"They are ready for you," he said to her. She could tell by the look on his face that Duke was getting worse.

She got up and went into his room. She stood for maybe twenty minutes comparing them. Dr. Branson stood by the door. She had no choice. She needed to operate, or he was going to die. Turning, she looked at him, tears filling her eyes. "Could you please excuse me for a few minutes? I would like to talk to him."

Dr. Branson nodded and walked out. Loren moved to the bed. Taking his hand in hers, putting it against her heart, she leaned down and whispered to him, "Don't you die on me. I have no choice but to try and save you. I'm so scared, Duke, so scared I'm going to make a mistake. Please wake up. Please, baby, I need to see your eyes. I need you to see me." She felt his fingers move. She moved her eyes to his.

"Come on, baby, open those beautiful eyes of yours. I need to see them. I need to see you. I love you."

Duke's lips moved, and his gentle smile came. She looked up to see him looking back at her. She bent to kiss him. "I'm here, baby, I love you."

He tried to squeeze her hand. Then he was gone again. *He knows I'm here. I have to do this.* Closing her eyes, she laid his hand on the bed and walked into the hallway.

"I am going to need an O.R. and a staff that can handle orders without question. Who is the in-house neurosurgeon? I am going to need him or her as well."

"We have everything you need ready."

"And Jaz?"

"She will be accommodated."

"I am going to talk to his family."

"I'll get everything ready, and then I will come and get you."

"Thank you." Loren turned and walked out of the I.C.U. and into the waiting room. Richard stood and headed toward her. Loren put her hand up to stop him.

"He needs surgery. I'm not sure I can do this, but I have no choice or he will die." She wasn't looking at anyone; she just stared at the wall. She needed to be cold. She couldn't let the gates of her emotions go or she wouldn't be able to do this. "They are getting him ready now. I don't know how long this will take or if he can survive it. But I will do what God put me here to do, and with a little luck, he will survive." Joe walked up to her, handing her an iPod and headphones. She looked at him. "Thank you," she whispered.

Just then, the door opened, and Dr. Branson came in. "Everything's ready, Dr. Mitchell."

Loren turned and walked out of the waiting room with Jaz following behind her. Dr. Branson led her to the O.R. where she changed into scrubs. Putting her earbuds in, she turned on her music and stood in the prep room leaning against the wall, letting Mozart flow into her mind and body.

She scrubbed in while they got Jaz decontaminated and dressed in makeshift scrubs. She even had on a mask. Loren chuckled when she came into the prep room. With her hands in the air, she said, "You ready, girl?" Jaz wagged her tail, and Loren pushed the door open, where nurses clothed her the rest of the way. Before they put her mask on, she said, "Wait." Walking over to Duke, she leaned in and kissed him. "I love you," she whispered.

The team just stood there looking at her. They knew who he was to her. She nodded and they finished dressing her. "Hello, everyone, my name is Dr. Loren Mitchell. I am going to need someone in here to work my iPod for me. I won't be able to hear any of you. This is how I do it. If there is a problem, simply touch my shoulder."

"I'll do your iPod," a nurse said.

"Thank you. This is Jaz. She won't be in anyone's way, but she will lay at my feet until we are done." Looking at Jaz, she said, "You stay." She laid her head down. "Now, let's get this started."

RICHARD PACED THE ROOM, CONSTANTLY LOOKING OUT THE DOOR. "SHE was so cold, so unfeeling. Is she going to be all right?" he said to the room.

"Dad, she wouldn't be doing this if she couldn't handle it. She is the best in the country," Derek said.

Cathy spoke. "Richard, I know my daughter. She wouldn't be in there if there was any other choice."

He nodded and continued to pace. Hours and hours passed and no word. The more time that passed, the more anxious Richard became. Duke was his first born. He had helped him through the loss of his wife at the age of eighteen. No child should have to do that.

The woman who he was meant to spend the rest of his life with was operating on his brain. *How fucked up is this?* She was still so broken, and Richard basically forced her to do this. He put his head back against the wall and closed his eyes. *God, if he fucking dies, Loren will be destroyed. I will be destroyed. She will never recover.*

Richard felt a hand on his knee. Opening his eyes, he saw Loren kneeling on the floor in front of him crying. "It's done," she whispered.

Richard reached out and grabbed her, pulling her into his embrace. Loren went willingly and burst into tears, sobbing almost to the point of hysteria. Richard held her tight. "Thank you," he whispered to her. She cried harder. Everyone in the room just sat there watching her crumble, watching her at one of her very weakest moments.

When she started to calm down, Richard lessened his hold on her, and her mother grabbed her hand. Loren looked up and climbed into her lap for comfort.

After a few minutes, Loren pulled away from her mom and wiped her face. "He came through the surgery fine. He woke up before I started, so he knew that I was there. I needed him to know that I love him. But it's done. Now, the next twenty-four hours will tell the tale of whether or not I did the right thing. I'll be in recovery with him." She turned to Derek. "Jaz has accepted you. Would you take her for a walk please and maybe get her something to eat? When you get back, she will find me."

"Anything at all. Can I get you something to eat?"

She nodded. "Whatever you can find. Thank you, Derek."

He stood. "I can never repay you for what you just did, so whatever you need, whenever you need it."

She reached up and touched his arm. Smiling, she said, "Just doing my job." She knelt down by Jaz. "Derek is going to take you out. I need to stay with Duke. Go with him, then come find us." She hugged her. "Thank you, Jaz." Jaz in turn licked her face.

She got up and looked at Derek. "She doesn't need a leash. If anyone gives you a problem, just tell them you are with me. Apparently, we have all kinds of special privileges."

"You're a rock star." He smiled at her.

Loren nodded and left to go sit with Duke. About an hour later, Jaz came walking in the room wagging her tail with a bag in her mouth. "What have you got there?" Loren smiled, reaching for the bag. Inside, she found a chicken sandwich and a note.

I'm at your service.

D

Loren laughed. "Thank you," she said to Jaz who laid at her feet. Loren ate her food and then curled up in the chair and took Duke's hand. She fell asleep almost instantly. It was the movement on her hand that woke her.

Slowly, Loren opened her eyes. She picked her head up to see his beautiful green eyes looking at her. "Hi," he whispered.

Smiling with tears in her eyes, she got up and kissed him. "Hi," she whispered in his mouth. "It's going to be rough talking, so save your breath. You are hurt pretty badly, but you will recover."

"I'm sorry for what I did. I love you. Please come home," he rasped out.

She cried, shaking her head. "Not now, Duke. You rest."

Just then, Jaz put her paws on the bed and pushed her nose against Duke's hand. He smiled. "Hey, girl," he whispered. Jaz wagged her tail and then got down. "You have a dog in the hospital?"

She giggled through her tears. "She was in the operating room with me, too. You rest. I'm going to tell your father that you are awake. They are going to take you down to I.C.U. while I'm gone."

He squeezed her hand. "You're not leaving, are you?"

She shook her head. "I'm not going anywhere." She knew it was a lie, but until he was out of the woods, she was staying. She kissed him again and left.

When she walked into the waiting room, Richard stood. "He's awake and talking. He isn't out of the woods yet, but they are taking him back to I.C.U. You should be able to see him in a little while. I will have someone come and get you when he is moved."

"Thank you, Loren," Richard said.

"When he is past the danger zone, than you can thank me. I'll be with him until he is out of danger."

She went to leave. "What do you mean? Loren, are you leaving again?" Derek asked.

She turned and looked at him, then his brothers and his father. "He doesn't love me like I love him. He told me that himself. He still thinks of Julie. I can't be with someone like that."

"But you love him."

"I do, but sometimes it's not enough. I can't make him love only me. I will stay until he is out of the woods. After that, I am going back to Texas." She looked at Richard. "How did you know where I was?"

"I've known all along."

"Why didn't you tell him?"

"Because it wasn't my place to tell him. This is between the two of you. Would it have made a difference if I had?"

Loren looked at him for a long time. "No, it wouldn't have. I'm sorry this happened to him. It is going to be a long road for him." She looked around the room. "I hope you all have it together. He is going to need you."

Joe spoke up. "Loren, he loves you. He hasn't left the ranch since you left. He doesn't want Julie. He wants you."

"Perhaps, but he still loves her. He was thinking about her..." She stopped. "It doesn't matter now. His life is his and mine is mine. As I said, I will stay until I know he is going to come out of this." She nodded and then left.

She made it about halfway down the hall before she passed out. Jaz started barking, and Derek was the one that found her. Picking her up, he sat on the floor with her in his arms. She was pale, cold, and clammy. A nurse came running up. "Oh my God, is she all right?"

"Could you get me a doctor? Maybe a cool rag?" Derek said to her.

She ran off, coming back a few minutes later with Dr. Branson and a cool rag. Derek put the rag on her forehead. "What happened?"

"I don't know. She came in and gave us an update on my brother and then she left. Jaz was barking, and when I came out, she was lying on the floor. This is the second time it's happened." Derek sounded panicked.

The nurse came back with a gurney, and they got Loren on it then wheeled her into a room. Looking at the nurse, he said, "Get me a blood panel." She nodded and ran out. A few minutes later, she came back and took a few vials of blood.

Just as the nurse was leaving, Loren woke up. Looking at Derek, she asked, "What happened?"

He chuckled. "I have no clue. I found you lying on the floor."

She looked at the doctor. "I have to get back to Duke. I'm fine. I think I'm just exhausted and overwhelmed."

He nodded. "Yes, I'm sure you are, but you need to get some sleep."

Loren sat up. She felt dizzy but didn't say anything. "I'll sleep when he is out of the woods." She got up and left the room, leaving Derek and the doctor standing there looking at each other.

Dr. Branson smiled. "Doctors make the worst patients."

Derek went back to the waiting room. "Loren passed out again. She is exhausted, so she is going to get some rest in Duke's room. He should be there in a few minutes. So, let's go see him and then get some rest ourselves."

Richard nodded. "I got us rooms across the street."

Derek nodded and sat down. Something wasn't right with Loren. Why wouldn't she stay here with him? He must have hurt her deeply for her to not want to come back. He was determined to get to the bottom of this, to fix this for his brother.

WHILE LOREN WAITED FOR DUKE, SHE VIEWED HIS POST-OP SCANS. THE damage had been repaired. Now to get him to a stable recovery stage. She knew she couldn't leave him for a few days. Lying to him was the only way to get him past this. She did love him. With all that she was, she loved him. But he didn't love her like that. She could still hear his words in her head. He couldn't stop his feelings for Julie.

She needed to get it all out of her head. The time to break would be when he was in the clear. She would go back to Texas, and his family would help him recover. She would arrange for the doctor here to take over once she was sure.

They wheeled Duke back into the room. She waited for everyone to do their thing, and then she checked him out. While writing in his chart, she asked a nurse to go get his family. She smiled and left.

Loren put his chart down and went to sit in the chair. Richard came in first. Loren smiled at him and got up. Taking his chart, she went to the nurse's station.

"Can you call Dr…" she looked at the chart, "Jones for me please?" she asked the nurse.

"Of course, Dr. Mitchell."

Loren smiled at her and went to sit on the floor outside Duke's room. Bringing her knees up, she laid her head down and closed her eyes.

RICHARD WAS TERRIFIED TO WALK INTO THE ROOM, BUT HE FORCED himself to. Loren smiled at him as she got up to leave. He took her seat next to the bed. Picking up Duke's hand, he squeezed it. "You're going to be fine," he said to him, not really believing it, but he trusted Loren.

Duke squeezed his hand. "Dad," he rasped out.

"Yeah, son. I'm here." The tears rolled down his cheeks.

"What happened?" Duke whispered.

"You were shot and then trampled. You have a broken arm, broken leg, and six broken ribs. They had to take out your spleen."

"Why is Loren in scrubs, Dad?"

"Duke, you had a brain injury. She operated on you. She saved your life."

Richard saw the tears slip down his face. "How did you find her?"

"Don't worry about that now. We will talk about it all later. She is here now, keeping watch over you. You rest. Your brothers are waiting to see you. They'll only let one of us in here at a time. I'll go send in Derek. Don't worry, we aren't going anywhere."

"The cattle, Dad."

Richard chuckled. "Don't worry about the cattle. Jose` and the guys are taking care of it. I'll be back."

Duke nodded slightly, closing his eyes. He let go of Richard's hand. A few minutes later, Derek walked in. "Fuck," he whispered.

Duke opened his eyes to see his brother crying, standing next to his bed. "Don't," Duke said.

"That fucking bitch got what she deserved. I am so sorry this happened to you."

Duke shook his head. "I'm fine."

Derek laughed. "Yeah, sure you are. Listen, the doc said only a few minutes. Apparently, you need rest. I love you, man."

"Love you, too," Duke said.

Joe and Alex both came and then they all went to check into the hotel to get some sleep. Loren came in a few minutes later to check him out. He moved his hand to her stomach while she checked his eyes. "I love you," he said. She smiled at him and took his hands in hers.

"Squeeze my hands." He did and she smiled at him. "Good." Then she walked to the foot of his bed and uncovered his feet. She took her pen out of her pocket and ran it up the center of each foot. She felt his reaction, which calmed her down. Picking up his chart, she wrote everything down with the time. Putting his chart down, she walked over to the chair and curled up. Holding his hand, she whispered, "Get some sleep. I'm not going anywhere. I've got you."

Duke squeezed her hand. Minutes later, she was sleeping with Jaz at her feet. She slept for two hours and then she was up, checking Duke again. Same routine. Hands, feet, eyes. He woke and smiled at her each time. She did this every two hours.

Richard came back and brought her food. She smiled, thanked him, and then left him alone with Duke. She shared her breakfast with Jaz while she waited for Derek to come. When he left Duke's room, she asked him to take Jaz out.

"Not a problem," he said. He looked at her, wanting to beg her not to leave Duke again. Loren smiled at him, not saying a word. She sat on the floor waiting for Joe and Alex to get done with their visits. Then she was up and checking Duke out.

Loren didn't talk to Duke. She was in doctor mode. He was her first priority, not their relationship or what everyone thought about her decision. It was his health. She needed for him to survive. She needed it like she needed her next breath.

Hours turned into days. The same thing every two hours. No one bothered her. They brought her food, a change of underwear, and they took Jaz out. Loren stayed in his room. Then, six days after the surgery, she was convinced that he would make a full recovery.

Smiling at him, she whispered, "You're going to be fine. I'm going to talk to your dad and brothers."

"Will you be back? We need to talk?"

"There will be plenty of time to talk. Your job is to get better, to make a full recovery. I need for you to survive this. I need for you to get better."

He nodded. Loren wiped the tear from his face. She bent down and kissed him one last time. Slowly, she trailed her tongue along his lips. Pulling back, Duke put his hand on her face. "I love you," he whispered.

Loren nodded, touching his face. She turned and walked out of his room. Leaning against the wall, she cried. She needed to walk away. She was still so in love with him, but he wasn't, not like she was. It didn't matter to her that Julie was dead; she was still in his heart. Pushing off the wall, she made her way to the waiting room. Richard saw her face and rushed to her. Pulling her into his arms, he whispered, "It'll be fine."

Loren hugged him and pulled back. "Duke is recovering nicely. They are going to move him out of the I.C.U. and into a private room. He is going to be fine. It's going to be a long road for him, but he is going to be fine."

"Thank you for all you have done," Derek said to her.

She nodded. "Dr. Jones will look after him now. If anything goes wrong, he will get in contact with me. I will call every day to check on him."

"Are you leaving?" Derek asked.

"I am." She turned to Richard. "Please don't tell him where I am. What he thinks he feels for me is not the same as I feel for him. It isn't going to be easy for him, but he will get over me. I love you, Richard. Thank you for everything."

Loren turned and walked out of the room, leaving them all standing there looking at her. She walked down the hall and pressed the button for the elevator. When the door closed, she saw them watching her. She just smiled.

～

"Dad, you can't let her go," Derek said.

"You don't know the whole story. She is justified in leaving. When you love someone the way she loves your brother, it's enough to destroy you when that person doesn't love you the same."

"What are you talking about? Duke loves her. You live with him; you can't tell me he doesn't."

Richard turned and looked at his sons. "You don't know the whole story. He has suffered by his own hand. Why do you think he gave up? Why do you think he hasn't turned this country upside down looking for her? He knows what he did to her."

"What did he do? Was it that bad?"

"It was the worst betrayal of the heart anyone could commit. Just leave it alone. Your brother needs us. She saved him because she loves him. She saved him because she wouldn't be able to live in this world if he wasn't in it. They both may be suffering, but it's between them. Your brother has a great deal to atone for. It's not our place to judge her for doing what is best for her. Trust me, when you love someone so completely and trust them with all that you are, and they betray that, there is no coming back. Your brother knows this."

"This is so fucked up," Derek said.

"You must keep her secret. You cannot tell him where she is. She gave us your brother back at a great expense to herself. You owe her."

They all nodded and waited for the nurse to come and tell them where Duke was. Then they filed into his room.

He was sitting up in his bed when they all came in. He smiled at his dad. "Where's Loren?"

Richard looked at his son. "She's gone. She did what she had to do, and that was saving your life."

He watched as the tears filled Duke's eyes. "She left?" Richard nodded. Then he held his son the best he could while he cried. No one said another word about her.

~

LOREN MADE HER WAY BACK TO TEXAS. SHE CALLED EVERY FEW hours to check on Duke. He was doing great. When she got home, she showered and crashed. Her dreams were filled with Duke. Waking up crying because her heart hurt again was not the way to start your day. She called the hospital to check on Duke and then went about her day. Day after day passed, and he was improving by leaps and bounds. Dr. Jones had mentioned that he was depressed, not talking to anyone, that his mental state could be better. But, physically, he was getting ready to be released.

Two weeks after the surgery, Duke was released. No more phone calls, no more progress reports. Her contact with him was finished. Now, it was time to heal, time to move on with her life. She threw herself into her projects for the house. Painting, redecorating, riding Cupcake.

A few days after Duke's release, her phone rang. It was a number she didn't know, but she answered it.

"Hello."

"Dr. Mitchell?"

"Yes, who is this?"

"This is Dr. Branson, from Bozeman General."

She swallowed. "Is Duke all right?" she whispered, fear running through her. *Did she leave too early? Did he relapse?*

"I'm sorry, yes, he is doing great actually."

"Then why are you calling me?" Loren's heart was slamming in her chest.

"Well, when you passed out, I had a blood panel run. The results just came across my desk. I don't know why or how they were misplaced."

"Please, Doctor, what is it?" She was really freaking out.

"Well, as it turns out, Dr. Mitchell, you're pregnant." The room started to spin. Loren grabbed the counter to stop herself from falling. "Dr. Mitchell, are you there? Are you all right?"

"Yes, no. That's impossible. It must be wrong."

"Dr. Mitchell, I'm sorry, but that's what the test says."

"Thank you, Dr. Branson." Loren hung up the phone and sat down on the floor. "This can't be true," she said to the room. Picking up her phone, she dialed a number she thought she'd forgot.

"Hello," the voice said.

"Hi, Jenny. It's Loren."

"Oh my God, Loren. How are you?"

Loren laughed. "Well, I'm not sure. Can you see me today?"

"See you as a friend or a patient."

"Both."

"Come on over now. I'll let Mary know that you are coming by."

Loren let out the breath she didn't know she was holding. Fighting back tears, she whispered, "Okay, thanks."

"Loren, honey, is everything all right?"

Loren shook her head. "No, not really. I'll see you in a bit."

"Okay, honey."

Loren nodded and hung up the phone as she burst into tears. *How in the world can this be possible?* She couldn't do this. She couldn't have his child and not tell him. He didn't love her like she loved him. Rocking back and forth while she cried, Jaz came over and laid her head on Loren's shoulder. "Oh, Jaz, what am I going to do?" She buried her head in her hands and cried. After a few minutes, she pulled herself together and looked at Jaz. "I'll tell you what I'm going to do. I'm going to get up, get dressed, and drive myself to Jenny's. Then I'm going to deal with whatever comes." She got up, went and changed, and drove herself to Jenny's.

When she walked in, Mary smiled at her. "Hi, Dr. Mitchell, come on back. Dr. Mellon is waiting for you."

"Thanks, Mary," she said as she and Jaz made their way to an examination room.

A few minutes later, Jenny came in. "Oh my God," she said as she hugged Loren. "You look good. How have you been?"

"Well, I've been a bad friend, that is for sure. You look great."

"Listen to me, if anyone understands what happened to you, it's me. You don't need to apologize to me. If ten years had passed, I would still be your friend. Now, tell me what's going on."

"Well, it seems I might be pregnant."

Jenny froze. "Loren, that's impossible."

Loren raised her eyebrows. "Yep, I know, but apparently some blood work I had in Montana says that I am."

Jenny sat there nodding her head. "Well, I'll have Mary get some blood. Then we can do an exam." She smiled. "I take it you're not a virgin anymore?"

Loren chuckled, shaking her head. "No."

"That's it, just no? We spent three years as roommates and have been friends for years, and no is all I get."

"It's over," was all she said.

Jenny nodded. "I'm here if you need to talk. Always. I'll send Mary in. Change into the gown and I'll be back." She put her hand on Loren's knee. "Anytime."

Loren smiled at her friend. "Thank you."

Jenny left, and Mary came in a few minutes after and drew her blood. She changed and got on the table. Looking at Jaz, she said, "Well, this is it. This is where we find out if miracles really do happen." Jaz wagged her tail.

A few minutes passed and Jenny came back in. "Well, it would seem to be true. Let's get an ultrasound."

"Jenny, how is this possible?"

"I'm not sure, I did the surgery myself. The damage to your uterus was tremendous. He severed one of your fallopian tubes, and the other was damaged severely." She wheeled the ultrasound machine over. Covering Loren's lower half with a sheet, she pulled up her gown and squirted gel on her stomach.

Loren laid there in shock. *This can't be happening. This can't be true.*

"You ready?" Jenny asked.

Loren looked at her and nodded.

She put the wand on her stomach and started moving it around. Loren heard the heartbeat and tears welled up in her eyes. She put her head back. It was true, but how? "How is this possible?" she whispered.

"Loren, you *are* pregnant. Look."

She picked up her head and looked at the machine. There it was, a baby. Duke's baby. She closed her eyes. "Oh my God," she said.

"Uh, Loren."

"What?" She picked her head up.

"It's twins. Look. Two sacks, two babies." Jenny looked at her. She had tears on her cheeks. "You are having twins."

"Jenny, how is this possible? I can't have any children."

"Well, apparently, God has other plans for you. Let me print you a few pictures and take some measurements for you, then we can do a pelvic."

Loren nodded and stared at the screen. *How is this possible? How am I going to do this? I have to tell him. Shit! Shit! Shit!* Her mind wouldn't shut off. She chuckled. "I guess it's time I put on my big girl panties."

Jenny laughed. "I would say so. It looks like you are around twelve weeks. Does that sound right to you?"

Loren remembered the last time she was with Duke. "Yes, that would be it."

"Do you want to talk about it?"

"Oh, God, Jenny, I am so in love with him. But he still has feelings for his ex. I left him nearly three months ago. I don't know what I am going to do."

"Well, I'm here if you need me. You know I miss you. But I understand."

"Thank you. I've been in Montana."

"Are you going back?"

"Looks like I have no choice. I can't do this alone, and his family would never forgive me if I kept them away."

Jenny proceeded to do the pelvic exam. When she finished, she said, "Loren, everything looks to be all right. I'm going to give you a prescription for pre-natal vitamins. I want you to get lots of folic acids. You know the drill. Please keep in touch. When you decide what you are going to do, let me know. Kate is up in Bozeman. Would that be anywhere near her?"

Loren nodded. "Thanks, Jenny, and I'm sorry I've been such a terrible friend."

Jenny hugged her. "Sweetie, you've been to hell and back again. I don't blame you, not at all. But I do miss my friend. I love you."

Loren started to cry. "I love you, too. I'll keep in touch this time. I promise."

Jenny left and Loren got dressed. She picked up her prescription on the way out and had it filled at the pharmacy. Making her way home, she had a great deal to think about. She knew she had to go back; she had to tell Duke. She knew she couldn't be with him, not like before, but these were his children and he deserved the right to help raise them. "Well, Jaz, looks like we are going back to Montana."

Jaz barked and jumped up and down. Loren went upstairs and packed her things. "No time like the present." Then she went out and had John hook up her trailer, and she loaded Cupcake in it. She told him goodbye and headed back to Montana.

DUKE HAD BEEN WITHDRAWN SINCE LOREN LEFT THE HOSPITAL. HE hated not being able to take care of himself. His father doted on him. He'd been home for a week now. Three more weeks and these casts would come off. His ribs were the worst. Coughing was hell. He needed a shower, desperately. He needed Loren. She saved his life. She came when he needed her. She loved him. She'd told him she loved him, or was she just saying that so he would survive? So many questions, so many feelings.

He needed to find her. If his father knew where she was, why didn't he tell him? Duke knew why; because he didn't deserve her. His feelings for Julie clouded his love for Loren. He fucked up big time. He destroyed her. He didn't deserve her.

LOREN STOPPED IN TOWN TO GET SOME FOOD AND THEN HEADED OUT TO her tiny house. It was cold. It hadn't started to snow yet, but her barn still wasn't finished. Hopefully, Cupcake would be all right in her little barn. Pulling up to her house brought back all the memories. She felt herself get sick at what took place there. When she pulled behind her tiny house, she was shocked to see that her barn was finished. "What the hell?" she said to Jaz.

Climbing out of her truck, she walked over to the new barn. Pulling open the doors, she was amazed. It was full of hay. There were two stalls and a small tack room. Smiling, she couldn't help but cry. "Who did this?" she said, even though she believed it was Duke.

She went and got Cupcake out of the trailer. "Hey, girl, look at your new home." She led her into the barn and her stall. She fed her and then went to unhook the trailer. Unloading her car, she carried her things to the house. Opening the door and walking in, she had a rush of memories flood her, knocking her to her knees. This place held the happiest of her memories and also the most devastating. Sitting on her knees with the door open, she realized how cold she was, so she got up and closed the door.

"It's freezing in here. How about some heat?" she said to Jaz, who ran up the stairs to her bed. "Traitor." She laughed.

Loren went about her tasks. She unpacked her clothes, put new sheets on her bed, cleaned the dust off of everything, and made herself something to eat. Then she went up and laid in her bed with her hand on her stomach. "Oh, God, babies. How are we going to do this? How am I going to face him?" Soon, she fell asleep.

When she woke up, she laid there wondering how she was going to do this. Finally, she decided she would just take her time and get comfortable with the idea that she was having a baby—well, two babies—before she called Richard. But she was pretty sure he already knew she was there.

Days went by and she still couldn't figure out how to tell them. She couldn't bring herself to go see Duke. He would want her back, and she would only hurt him by denying him. Days turned into weeks and she still couldn't do it. She just stayed by herself, riding Cupcake every day, just like she had when she first came here.

When the first snow came, it was huge. Loren had never seen snow before. She and Jaz went out and played in it like little children, laughing and running around. She was getting bigger as each day moved by. She had a little bump, but not enough to where someone would notice if she wore the right clothes. With it being winter, she was layered, and you couldn't tell.

DUKE WENT FOR HIS FINAL VISIT TO HAVE HIS CASTS REMOVED AND TO do a brain scan. Everything was perfect. His ribs were healed but still sore. His scans all came back positive. He had been cleared of any further medical treatment.

On the drive back to the ranch, he asked his father, "Where is she dad?"

"Where is who?"

Duke chuckled. "Loren. Dad, I need to find her. I need her to know how sorry I am."

Richard shook his head. "I don't know where she is."

"That's bullshit and you know it. I know you sent Derek to get her, to bring her to Bozeman. Why did she operate on me? Why would you force her to do that?"

"I didn't force her to do anything. She decided on her own."

"Dad, I love her."

"That may be so, Duke, but you crossed a line and promised her your love, but you didn't give yourself to her. You still had Julie in your heart. You know this. What you did to her destroyed her."

"She told me she loved me. That has to mean something."

"She does love you, but she is right. You don't love her the same way. You cheated on her in your heart. How is she supposed to come back from that? She operated on you because if she didn't you were going to die. No one else could have done that surgery and been successful. She couldn't live with herself if she let you die. You need to understand what you did to her. She stayed by your side until she knew you were going to pull through. I don't know where she went after or where she is now."

Duke sat there not saying a word. "I know you know. I will find her on my own."

"You might not like what you find when you do. She has changed yet again, son."

"What are you saying, Dad? Is she with someone else?"

Richard didn't say anything. Duke needed to suffer. His head was coming back to the here and now, and he needed to stop wallowing in his self-pity and man up about what he did to her. Richard knew where she was. He knew she was back in Montana. He just wasn't going to tell Duke.

LOREN WAS OUT FOR HER DAILY RIDE WHEN CUPCAKE STUMBLED AND Loren was thrown, hitting her head and knocking her out. Jaz was going crazy trying to wake her up. When she wouldn't wake, she took off. She ran through the snow all the way to the ranch. Running up the porch, she barked and barked and barked until Richard opened the door.

"What the hell?" he said.

"What, Dad? What's going on. I heard a dog barking," Duke said as he came down the stairs.

When he saw Jaz, his heart stopped. He knew Loren was here. But something was wrong; something was terribly wrong. Jaz was going crazy grabbing Richard's hand, pulling him out the door.

"What is it, girl?" Richard asked.

"Dad, something's wrong. She would never leave Loren." He

grabbed his coat, then after throwing on his boots, they both ran out the door. "You take the truck. I'll take Roxy. Go to her house. Call Doc and get him out there." Richard watched Duke run to the barn. He still had a bit of a limp. A few minutes later, he flew out of the barn and followed Jaz. Richard flew down the drive headed to Loren's.

He picked up the phone. "Derek, get Doc and get him out to Loren's place. Something has happened."

"She's back?"

"She has been for a few weeks now."

"Does Duke know?"

"He does now. Get moving. Hurry, son." Richard hung up the phone and threw his truck into four-wheel drive.

Jaz led Duke right to Loren, who lay in the snow with Cupcake standing next to her. He was in serious pain as he jumped off his horse and ran to her. He lifted her in his arms. "Oh, God, beautiful," he said. She was bleeding from her head. Looking at Jaz, he said, "Go to the house and get Dad. Bring him here. I can't get her on the horse."

Jaz barked and took off. Duke took off his coat and wrapped it around her, holding her in his lap off the cold ground. He could feel her warm breath on his cheek. He held her, rocking back and forth talking to her. "Come on, beautiful, open your eyes. I need to see those beautiful eyes." He was so scared, so terrified that he would never see them again. *Has she been here the whole time? Did they all know she was here?*

He heard the truck just then. Standing up took everything he had. He started walking with her. When Richard pulled up, he jumped out of the truck and took her from Duke. "Take the horses back to her house. I've got Doc coming." He put Loren in the truck with Jaz and took off.

Duke climbed on Roxy, then grabbing Cupcake's reins, he took off. When he rode up to her house, he came around the little barn to see the new barn. "What the hell?" He rode in and put the horses up. He didn't take the saddles off, just took off to the house.

Derek was standing on the porch when he rounded the corner. "Has she been here all along?"

"What?"

"Loren! Has she been here this whole time?"

"No, I didn't know she was here."

"Then who built that barn?"

Derek smiled. "Me and Dad. Why?"

"Why did you do that? Did you know she was coming back?" Duke was crazy.

"Listen, man, you need to calm the fuck down."

Duke pushed past Derek into the house. Loren was lying on the couch talking to Richard. She was wrapped in a bunch of blankets. Doc was on his knees next to her.

"You were out for a while; you should let me take you into town so we can get a work up on you."

"I'm fine. I have a headache, but I'm fine. Freezing but good," Loren said.

Her voice was music to Duke's ears. She was here. She came home. He stood there frozen. He wanted to go to her, to hold her. To explain everything to her. But he couldn't move.

"When did you get back here?" Richard asked her.

"A few weeks ago, just before the first snow. Who built the barn?" she asked.

Richard laughed. "Derek and I finished it for you."

"How did you know I would be back?"

Richard reached up and touched his head. "I got the sense."

When Loren laughed, Duke's knees buckled and he went down. It was the greatest sound he had ever heard. Richard turned to look at him then back to Loren. He saw the fear in her eyes. "I can stay," he said gently.

She shook her head. It was time for her to face him. To talk it out, to let him know they couldn't be together anymore. She came back here so he could be a father to his children, so Richard could be a part of his grandchildren's lives. This isn't where she wanted to be. Being this close to him hurt her deeply, but it was time for her to put her big girl panties on and be a grown up.

Doc told her to rest and take it easy. If she felt dizzy, she was to call him or come to the clinic. Loren promised she would, and she meant it. She had two babies growing inside of her. Her miracles. She wasn't going to do something to put them in harm's way. Doc got up and left. Richard squeezed her hand and kissed her on the forehead. "I'm glad you came home." Loren nodded, trying not to cry.

Richard got up, and she turned her head away from Duke. Jaz was lying on the couch with her, wrapped in the blankets as well. She heard the door close and she could feel Duke. He just sat there on his knees looking at her.

Her body was shaking; she wasn't sure if it was because she was so cold or that she was terrified she would give in to him. But she couldn't. He didn't love her completely.

"I'm so sorry," Duke whispered.

"There's no need to be sorry. The heart wants what the heart wants," she said softly.

"My heart belongs to you."

She shook her head. "Maybe a part of it does, but the other part belongs to Julie. It always will."

"What I did, Loren..." He stopped.

"What you did, Duke, was show me the truth. I was right that day in the yard. No man could ever love this."

"You are so wrong. I love you."

"Maybe you think you do, but I don't believe you. I will never believe you. You were having sex with me, thinking about her. You betrayed me, you used me, and then you ran from me." She sniffled. "I don't want to do this with you."

"No, baby, that's not what happened. You left before I could explain it to you."

She jerked her head to look at him. Sitting up, she screamed at him, "You didn't come for me! You just let me leave. You did it because I'm right. You know what you did. Now you sit here and try to justify it and blame me. Fuck you, Duke. Please, get out of my house. I don't want you here."

Her words hit him like punches to his gut. "Why did you come back here?"

"It's my house, my land. If I fucking want to live here, I am free to do so. Please, just get out. I need to take a bath to warm up. I don't want you here." God, her heart was ripping to shreds. She wanted him to hold her. She wanted to feel the warmth of his body next to hers.

Duke stood. He walked over and knelt in front of her. "I'll go, but I am coming back. I love you, and I am going to prove it to you."

"Don't waste your time. I'm not buying it this time." He brought his hand up to touch her face and she pulled away from him. "Don't. You don't have that right anymore." Closing her eyes, she whispered, as the tears fell, "Please, just go."

Duke got up and picked up his jacket. Looking at Loren one more time, he whispered, "I love you." Then he left, making his way to the barn. He took off Cupcake's saddle and put her winter coat on, gave her some food, and then headed back to the ranch on Roxy.

WHEN DUKE WALKED INTO HIS FATHER'S HOUSE, HE MADE A BEE LINE for him. "Has she been here all along?"

"Boy, you are some kind of angry."

"Dad, has she been here all along?"

Richard stood. "Don't think it's ever acceptable to talk to me like this."

Richard headed toward the door. Stopping, he turned to look at Duke. "No, she hasn't. I'm not sure when she got back here, but I've known for about a week."

"Why did she come back, Dad?"

"I don't know. I'm going over there. Doc said she needs to be woken up every couple of hours. I thought you would be staying."

"She's still pretty pissed at me."

"Well, you did shred her."

Duke hung his head. "How can I fix this?"

"Time, son, and a great deal of groveling." He smiled and walked out, headed to Loren's.

~

LOREN WAS TOO ANGRY TO HAVE A DECENT CONVERSATION WITH DUKE. She had a lot of hurtful things to say to him, to make him understand how much he hurt her. She wasn't sure she had it in her. She didn't get in the tub; hell, she didn't even move off the couch. About an hour after Duke left, there was a knock on the door. Taking one of the blankets with her, Loren went to open the door.

"Richard, what are you doing here?"

He came in, taking off his boots and coat. "Doc said you needed to be woken up every couple of hours, so here I am."

She smiled. "Thank you. I'm going to go up to bed then, if you don't mind."

"I'll just sit down here. I brought a book to read, so you go on."

Loren smiled at him and made her way up the stairs. Jaz followed her and crawled under the blankets with her. A few hours later, she heard Richard call her.

"Loren, you need to get up."

"I'm awake. Thank you, Richard."

"What's your name?"

She chuckled. "Loren Elizabeth Mitchell, born November fifteenth. I'll be twenty-seven years old. My Godfather's name is Richard, and he loves strawberry pie. Can I go back to sleep now?"

Richard laughed. "Yes," he said gently.

Loren was finally warm. She unrolled herself from all the blankets. Her hands slipped to her stomach. *Aww, babies. That was your daddy I was yelling at. I'm sorry for that. But we have some things to work through.* She had a mental conversation with her children. Jaz laid her head on her stomach. Loren petted her as she went back to sleep.

A few hours later, she heard Richard call her. "Loren, time to get up."

Opening her eyes, she chuckled. "I'm up."

"What's your name?" He chuckled.

She recited, "Loren Elizabeth Mitchell, born November fifteenth.

I'll be twenty-seven years old. My Godfather's name is Richard, and he loves strawberry pie. I'm going to get up now."

"Why don't you stay up there and sleep a bit more? I've got nothing to do."

Loren grabbed a sweatshirt that she had bought. "Because you've been here far too long. I need to feed you. And, besides, I'm hungry." She scooted to the stairs and then climbed down. Richard was sitting on the couch with a book in his hands. Smiling, she said, "You didn't have to stay here, you know."

"Yes, I did. I wanted to talk to you anyway. I was going to come by when you first got back, but I figured once you were comfortable you would have come over."

Loren sat down on the bottom step. "I don't think I would have come. Not with Duke there."

"I just want to go on the record here and say that boy has been miserable, and I mean miserable."

"Well, thank you. What can I get you?" She got up and went to the fridge. "I have eggs and bacon. I seem to have this thing for bacon," she said absentmindedly, taking the food out of the fridge. She began to cook and made coffee for Richard and poured herself a glass of orange juice.

While they sat and ate, he kept looking at her. She smiled. "Go ahead, say it."

"You going to forgive him?"

She shook her head. "I love him completely, Richard. There will be no other man. But he doesn't love me the same way. I know he loves me, but I want all of his heart. Is that asking too much?"

"No, it's not."

There was a knock on the door. Loren felt the gooseflesh run along her skin. She looked at Richard and got up. Duke was at the door with his hands full of grocery bags. "I went shopping for you. I know how much you like to cook." Shaking her head, she opened the door.

"Thank you, but this isn't going to do any good. I meant what I said. How much do I owe you?"

He chuckled. "I was just being nice. I know you meant what you said. Believe me, you said it loud enough. And you don't owe me a damn thing. Just doing the neighborly thing. You were injured and I am being helpful."

Loren turned to see Richard trying to hide a secret smile. "Thank you," she said and headed to the bathroom. She stayed in there listening to Richard and Duke talking.

"What are you doing, son?" Richard said.

"Just doing a good deed."

Richard chuckled. "I think you are pushing her."

"Dad, with all due respect, I love her. I want my life back with her. If I have to push, then I'll push. If I have to impose, then I am going to impose. We have a great deal to talk about. Granted, she seems to think we have more to yell about than we do talk, but I deserve that. I'm not going anywhere."

"Well, would it matter if I told you that you run the risk of pushing her further away?"

"If she runs, I will follow her. I'm not going to let her go this time. I know what I did, and I will do everything I can to make her understand how sorry I am."

Loren shook her head and walked out of the bathroom. She stood there with fire running through her veins. "Thank you, Duke, for getting me groceries." She was dismissing him.

He turned as he set the last bag on the counter. "It's not a problem." He smiled at her.

But she didn't smile back. She wanted to run into his arms and tell him he was going to be a father, but she just said, "Would you please go? I would like to be alone." She looked at Richard. "I'm fine. I will stay awake until bedtime."

Richard got up and hugged her. "I'll be back later to check on you." Loren nodded. "You coming," he said to Duke as he opened the door.

"I'm right behind you," Duke said, not moving from the kitchen.

Richard walked out, closing the door behind him. He wanted them to work this out, but he knew the pain she was feeling, the betrayal.

"You going to yell at me some more or can we talk?" Duke said softly.

"We have nothing to talk about." Loren snapped, moving to the couch. She pulled her knees up to her chest. *Pretty soon I won't be able to sit like this.*

"Oh, sweetheart, we have plenty to talk about." He walked over and pulled out a stool, sitting in front of her. "I need for you to hear what I have to say. You left before I could get my head straight."

She looked at him, her eyes full of anger. "Go to hell. You are the one who left."

"That night, I admit I crossed a line. But it wasn't because of some deep-seeded feelings you might think I had or have for Julie. What I was doing to you was not making love. You felt so good, so incredibly good, that I couldn't control myself. What I did to you... I had no regard for what you were feeling. It was so selfish of me. In mid-stride, I realized that, that is exactly how I felt about Julie. I never cared what she felt, only what I felt. I pulled away, Loren, not because she was in my heart, or in my head, but because I was taking from you the most beautiful thing I had ever shared with another person. I was taking your love and turning it into something dirty. I was sick at the way I was treating you in that moment. Not because I was thinking about her while I was with the woman I love, but because I was treating the woman I love with no respect, just the way I had treated her. I love you. I am so in love with you that every part of my soul died when my father slid this across the table to me." Loren looked down; in his hand was her ring. "I didn't come for you because I believed I wasn't worthy of your love anymore. How could I be, when I was so disrespectful of your trust? I didn't cheat on you in my heart. I treated you like some whore on the street. That's why I didn't come. I was so full of regret and shame that I couldn't see past that.

"But then I got hurt and you came. I didn't realize it was you that operated on me until after you left. You wouldn't have done that if you didn't love me. I know you love me. You saved my life." Loren wiped the tear from her cheek. Duke got off the chair and knelt in front of her. "Aww, beautiful, don't cry."

"I need for you to go," she whispered.

He nodded. "All right, but I'm coming back, and if you run, just know I'll be right behind you. You are my soulmate, Loren. I will spend the rest of my life trying to make you understand how sorry I am."

It took everything that he had not to grab her and kiss her perfect lips. But he got up and walked to the door. Turning to her, he whispered, "I love you."

Loren didn't look at him. She didn't say anything. Duke gently closed the door. He stood on the porch for a minute smiling. He wasn't giving up on her.

CHAPTER FIFTEEN

LOREN SAT on the couch and cried. Jaz climbed up and nestled next to her. "Oh, girl, what I am going to do? I love him so much. It's not fair that I am keeping the fact that I'm carrying his children from him." Laying down, she curled up in a ball and cried.

WHEN DUKE WALKED INTO HIS DAD'S HOUSE, HIS DAD WAS WAITING FOR him. He chuckled. "I see you're still breathing."

Duke smiled. "I love her, Dad. I'm not letting her go this time. I will explain it all and do it again and again until she believes me, until she understands that it wasn't Julie in my heart or my mind. It was me."

"Well, just be careful with her. Things have changed, Duke."

Duke stood there looking at his father. He hated when the man was cryptic like this. "What the hell does that mean?"

Richard laughed. "I've been around a lot longer than you have, son. You learn things as you grow old."

Duke chuckled and went to the kitchen. He sat at the table thinking about Loren. He wanted to hold her. He wanted to smell her, that vanilla and strawberry scent that was her. *What the hell am I doing here? This is not where I want to be. Too much time has passed. We need to settle this.* His mind racing, he got up and headed to the front door.

"Where you off to?" Richard said, knowing damn well where he was going.

"I'm going to get my girl back," Duke said confidently, and out the door he went. He smiled all the way to Loren's. He was determined to get her back. She was the love of his life and there was no way he was going to stop until she was back in his arms.

When he pulled up, he jumped out and knocked on her door. There was no answer. He walked around the house to see if her truck was there and it was. He saw her huddled in a blanket, sitting in the yard on a chair.

Walking up, he knelt in front of her. She was crying. "What are you doing here?"

"I can't stay away from you. Beautiful, please talk to me. Tell me how angry you are, tell me how you feel. Yell at me, hit me, scream at me. Do whatever it takes to let me know how you feel."

She shocked the hell out of him when she leaned forward and kissed him. His hand came up to touch her face. Fire blew through his fingers, all the way up his arm, straight to his heart.

"I love you," she said. "I am so mad at you, so hurt by what you did to me. So angry that you let me go, that we wasted all this time. I hate you for hurting me. But I love you more than all those feelings. I don't trust you, but I love you."

Duke smiled, leveling her with a kiss. "You are all I want in this life, Loren. I cannot say I am sorry enough. But if it helps, I have suffered so much by my own stupidity. Can you forgive me?"

"I don't know, Duke. I just don't know."

"Can I ask why you came back?"

"I had no choice," she whispered.

"You had a choice, Loren. You made that choice when you left. Why?"

Loren fought back the fear. She needed to tell him. He had a right to share this with her. With shaking hands, she took his hand in hers and pulled it to her. Opening his hand, she placed it on her stomach and waited for him to figure it out.

He sat there looking at her, terrified to move his hand. He wanted so desperately to touch her. She was letting him back in, but he knew he couldn't be selfish. This time, he would wait for her to make the first move. He would wait for her to come to him. He moved his hand to pull it away, shaking his head.

"No," Loren said as she put her hands back on his.

"Loren," he whispered, not understanding.

She moved his hand so he could feel the bump on her stomach. His eyes shifted down as she moved the blanket, opening it up so he could see her. Watching him come to the realization of what she was saying brought tears to her eyes. He moved his other hand to cradle her belly. When it hit him, his eyes shot up to hers.

"What? Really?" She nodded. "Oh my God. Your pregnant?" She nodded again. "When?"

She smiled. "Fourteen weeks."

"We are having a baby?" He sat down in the snow, shocked. His eyes moved to her stomach and then to her eyes. Her beautiful violet eyes.

She shook her head. "No, we're not having a baby?" His heart stopped. She wouldn't have been with someone else.

"We are having a baby?" She smiled and shook her head. "Loren, you're pregnant?" She nodded. "It's ours?" She smiled and nodded. "But you aren't having a baby?" She shook her head. He sat there confused, looking at her. His hands moved up to her stomach again. His mind was racing. Fourteen weeks... just over three months. She shouldn't be showing like this. "Uh," he looked at her. "Twins?" he breathed out.

Loren smiled and nodded. "Twins."

He grabbed her so fast, pulling her into his arms and hugging her. She didn't fight him. She didn't fight him when he kissed her. He was crying. "You came home for me?"

Loren pulled back. "I came home because they are your children, too, and you deserve to raise them as well. I didn't come back here to be with you. I came so you could be with your children." She pushed off of him. Picking up her blanket, she walked back into the house.

Duke just sat there staring at the chair. "Fuck!" he yelled. Standing, he walked to the door and opened it. "What do you mean?" he said in a very raised voice, a very angry voice.

Loren was in the kitchen. "Exactly what I said. I am not here to mend this fence or fix what you broke. I am here because you deserve to be a part of this. Richard deserves to be a part of this."

"Loren, you love me and I love you."

"I am not denying that I love you. If I didn't, I wouldn't be here." She raised her voice, nearly screaming at him. "I don't trust you." Her voice grew louder. "I gave you everything, all that I am, and you discarded me like I was a common whore. How dare you assume you can walk in here and look at me with those fucking green eyes of yours and expect me to crumble at your fucking feet. Trust me, Duke, it ain't gonna happen. Now, if you don't mind, get the fuck out of my house."

He stood there shocked, and then he smiled. "Come on, let it all out. Let it all go, so we can sit down and rationally talk about this."

He pissed her off. "I. AM. NOT. AN. OPTION. FOR. YOU. I will share these children with you because they are yours, too, but you don't get me in this deal. We are through. Move on with your life, Duke. I am not a part of it."

"How can you say that? You are the mother of the only children I will ever have. You are a packaged deal."

She picked up her keys, shoved him out of the way, and opened the door. "Jaz, come on." Duke reached for her, grabbing her arm. Out of nowhere, Jaz lunged at him, grabbing his arm. Duke immediately let go of Loren, and she and Jaz went out the door.

She drove to Richard's. When she pulled up, she was crying. Richard pulled her from the truck.

"It's all right," he said as he held her.

Loren pulled back. "I need to talk to you. I need to tell you some things."

He nodded. "Come on." He led them to the house. Loren sat on the couch and Richard in the chair.

"I'm pregnant," she said. Richard sat there in shock. This he did not know. Loren looked at him. "With twins."

He swallowed. "Have you told Duke?"

"He should be here in a minute. Jaz bit him pretty hard."

"What?"

"He grabbed me out of anger, and she bit him. It's not going to be pretty when he walks in the door, but he scared me, so I came here. I know this has to take place, but I didn't want to be alone with him."

"Aww, sweetheart, I'm so sorry he is an ass."

She chuckled. "He thinks, because I am having his children, that we should be together. I told him that the only reason I came back was so that he could be a part of it, and that I wasn't an option for him."

"Is that how you really feel?"

Duke walked in the door and looked at Richard.

"He hurt me, Richard. He tore me to shreds. I don't trust him. Without trust, there is no foundation. I am not going to wonder every time he makes love to me if he is thinking of her, or comparing me to her."

Shaking his head, he looked at Duke. "You're bleeding on my rug."

Loren turned to look at him. He dropped to his knees. "I am so sorry. Please, tell me what I can do."

"Just accept what I am offering. I don't want to leave. I want you to be a part of their lives."

"How can I do that and not be a part of yours?"

"I guess the same way I did it. Trust blindly. Yeah, probably not the smartest thing to do." She was getting angry again. "I gave you everything I had, Duke, and it wasn't enough for you."

He yelled at her, "It was more than enough! How many times do I have to tell you that?"

Jaz stood up and growled at him. "Jaz, no. Stay." She laid down. "Duke," she said very calmly. "When Bruce attacked me, when he plunged that knife into me here," she stood up and touched herself, "he severed my ovary. When he plunged it into me here," she touched the scar below her panties. "He severely damaged my uterus. Didn't you ever wonder why I didn't care if you wore a condom? Because I knew I would never get pregnant. I am not medically supposed to be able to have a child. Those times when you laid with your head on my stomach, I knew you were thinking about our child in here. I knew it would never happen. So, all of this," she threw her hands in a circle, "all of it is a fucking miracle. You were the one who convinced me that what happened to me was supposed to, so that we would meet. Then you betrayed me. You betrayed the love I have for you by thinking about or comparing me to fucking Julie. You are the one who deceived me, who lied to me, who cheated on me, who promised me, and who destroyed me. Not me. I gave you everything. I even gave you back your fucking life because I love you so fucking much. But you don't have my trust anymore. So, don't you see? It doesn't matter how we feel. We have no foundation. I am here to give you a chance to be a father, to be a daddy to the children growing inside of me. To the fucking miracles that are here." She lifted her shirt to show him her bump. "For whatever reason, they are in there. Please, stop thinking that I am coming back to you. I'm not."

Richard and Duke just sat there. Neither of them said a word. Loren turned to Richard. "I'm sorry. I need to go. I am so tired."

He stood. "Come on." He led her to his room. "Sleep in here. I will watch over you. Get the rest you need. Please."

She hugged him, and through her tears, she whispered, "Thank you."

Richard shut the door behind him, and Loren peeled out of everything except her t-shirt and panties and climbed in his bed. Jaz climbed up and snuggled behind her. Closing her eyes, Loren passed out and slept.

~

RICHARD WALKED BACK TO THE LIVING ROOM WHERE DUKE WAS NOW sitting on the couch with his jacket on the floor bleeding.

"I am only going to say this once. Stay away from her while she is here. You let her sleep. She is carrying twins, and trust me, I know she didn't sleep while you were in the hospital. You should get to Doc's and have him check that out."

"I love her so fucking much, Dad."

"Is what she said true?"

"Every fucking word of it."

"Go see the doc," he said and went to the kitchen.

Duke sat staring down the hall. He wanted to go lay with her, to hold her, but she was right. He did all those things to her, broke every fucking promise he made. Time was the only thing that would heal these wounds. He picked up his jacket and took himself to Doc's.

"What the hell happened to you?" Doc asked.

"I got bit."

"Did you report it to Charlie?"

"No, it was Loren's dog."

"She's back then. Congratulations."

Duke chuckled, shaking his head. "She wants nothing to do with me. Hence the dog bite."

Doc cleaned him up. "Yeah, she did a number on you. You're going to need some stitches."

Duke chuckled. "I had my coat on, too."

"Well, good thing you did. If you didn't, you might have lost an arm."

Thirty minutes and sixteen stitches later, Duke headed back home. When he walked in the door, his father was sitting at the dining room table.

"There's some dinner on the stove for you. What did Doc say?"

"Thanks. Sixteen stitches and a few shots. I'm going to eat and go to bed."

"Good choice."

"Is…" He stopped.

"Yep, and I meant what I said." Richard looked at him.

Nodding, Duke went into the kitchen and ate his dinner and then went to his room. Laying in his bed, he cried. *God, how can one person fuck up so badly? I fucking destroyed her. She is so strong, so beautiful. I need to be like her. I need to show her that I am grateful for the gift she is giving me. I am going to be a father. I need to respect her boundaries, her wishes. Can I be her friend?* He closed his eyes and fell asleep. Just knowing she was in the house was comfort enough.

When morning came, Duke rolled over and winced. "Fuck," he moaned. He got up, threw on some sweats, and made his way downstairs. Grabbing a cup of coffee, he went to the dining room. His father was at the table doing paperwork.

"How's the arm?" Richard asked him.

"Hurts like hell. Is…"

Richard looked up at him. "Yes, she hasn't gotten up yet."

"Is she all right?" Duke looked down the hall.

"I've been checking on her. She is fine. Sit down, son. We need to talk."

Duke sat in the chair. "Dad, I know what you are going to say."

Richard chuckled. "I don't think you do. I am going to suggest to Loren that she move her tiny house over here. She can put it out behind the big shed. If something happens to her while she is out there alone, she won't be able to call for help. I'm pretty sure she is going to say no, but if she agrees, you need to stay away from her. You need to respect her boundaries and stop harassing her. All the stress is not good for her or the babies."

"I know, I had this conversation with myself last night. I am grateful for what she is offering me, and I will accept her terms. If she is here, then I can be a part of it on her terms. I won't have to impose on her."

"Well, then I accept," Loren said from the hallway.

Duke turned to look at her. "Thank you. Thank you for coming home, for letting me do this with you. No more pressure, no more arguing. We are going to be parents. Our love will not go away, and our children will grow up in a loving environment."

"Thank you," she said. "Now, have you both eaten? Because we are starving. I didn't have dinner last night."

Richard laughed. "I have, but you help yourself to anything I have. I'm going to have the boys move your house over."

"Yeah, well, I am going to need to secure everything inside it first. Otherwise, it will be a mess when they get it here. How about we set it up for tomorrow?" she asked as she headed to the kitchen.

"You have a deal," Richard said. Looking at Duke, he said, "I need you to get the ground level. Let her pick the spot then you level it out."

Loren was in the kitchen making eggs when Duke walked in. "Do you want some?"

"If it's not too much trouble."

She laughed. "Pour us some orange juice and make the toast and I got the rest."

He nodded. It was very quiet while they ate. When Duke finished, he got up and put his dishes in the sink. As he was walking by, Loren stood up and stepped in front of him. "It doesn't need to be awkward. We are going to be parents, and we can be friends while we do it."

Duke just stood there looking at her. "I am going to do what you ask, because you deserve that from me. For everything I did, or didn't do, you deserve my respect. I will deal with my own shit when I am not near you or with you. But I love you. I can't stop that. I can't turn it off."

"Neither can I. Believe me, I tried, but you are in here." She touched her heart. "I will love no other," she said softly, turning away from him.

It took all that he had not to reach out and touch her, pull her into his chest and wrap his arms around her. "I will be here, right next to you, every step of the way. I will not fail you again," he whispered, fighting back his tears. "Anything you need, anytime, beautiful."

Loren felt him move closer, and then he moved away. He was going to give her exactly what she asked for.

～

RICHARD TOOK LOREN OUT TO THE SHED. THEY WALKED OUT IN THE field. "I like this spot," she said, turning around. "It needs to face north and south, so I have the sun all day."

"Duke is going to level the land, and I ordered some wood to build you a proper deck. I know you like to sit outside. Pretty soon, we are going to have too much snow for you to sit in the yard."

"Thank you, Richard. I'll go in and pay Mr. Jordon."

Richard laughed. "Listen to me. You may not be becoming my daughter in law, but you are the mother of my first-born grandchildren. You will never want for anything. Let me do this for you, for them."

She laughed. "Fine. I'm going to go get everything ready."

Loren and Jaz went back to her place to secure everything so they could move it. She went out and hooked up the trailer and then loaded Cupcake in. As she was carrying her saddle to the truck, Derek and Duke pulled up. Duke came running over. "What are you doing? You need to be careful."

Loren laughed. "I'm having a baby. I'm not crippled. I got this."

Duke took the saddle. "Who hooked up the trailer?"

She raised her eyebrows at him. "I did, why?"

He walked right up to her, stopping inches away from her. "Let me help you."

Laughing, she stepped back. "I'm a big girl."

Shaking his head, he walked away, heading to Derek who was backing the truck up to the house. Loren strolled up, telling them what to do and how to do it.

"So, I hear I'm going to be an uncle?" Derek smiled at her.

"Yep, twice," she said.

"What do you mean twice?" He looked at Duke.

Duke laughed. "Oh, I forgot to tell you. She is having twins."

"No shit?" Derek stepped forward to hug her, and she stepped back. "Sorry." Derek smiled at her.

"Okay, I think we've got this," Duke said.

Loren laughed. "You think? How about are you sure?"

He laughed. "I'm sure. Everything secure in there?"

"Yep, the panels are secure. I'm going to need someone to come and get my water tanks."

"Dad has Mr. Jordon coming in the morning with a truck with a crane on it to get them on the truck, so you are going to need to use the water from the house."

"I am staying in the house tonight. I won't have any electricity tonight, so no heat. It's all good. Your dad said we can sleep in his room again."

Duke smiled at her. He couldn't be happier. "Well, let's get this show on the road."

Loren nodded and Duke watched her and Jaz walk across the yard to her truck. Derek watched his brother. "No chance for the two of you?"

Duke chuckled. "Oh, there is a chance. I just need to earn it. I fucked up big time, brother. If she wasn't carrying those little miracles inside her, I would have lost her forever. But, for some reason, the cosmic universe is giving me another chance. If nothing comes of it, I will forever be grateful to her for letting me be their father."

Derek slapped him on the back. "Well, I'll be rooting for you."

Duke laughed as he walked to the truck. "Just be the best damn uncle you can be. That's all I need." They climbed in the truck. "If it takes me twenty years, I will get her back. She owns me."

"I'm waiting for it to happen to me."

"Yeah, well, learn from my mistakes."

Derek laughed. "I don't know what mistakes you made."

Duke shook his head as they pulled out onto the road with Loren behind them.

It didn't take long to get the tiny house in its spot and leveled out. Loren went about hooking everything up. She realized she had enough saved energy to stay there, so she did. Richard brought her up a few gallons of water.

"You going to all right out here?"

Loren laughed. "I will be fine. Thank you, Richard, for everything. Even all the stuff to come."

"You need anything at all, you call me. I've told Duke to back off and leave you alone for a while. If he gets to be too much, you let me know."

She laughed. "You don't need to do that. Jaz already let him know that he wasn't going to get away with anything. There is still a great deal more to be said. I'm sure you are going to hear us yelling at each other. But he needs to know and understand."

Richard laughed. "He knows, sweetheart. Trust me, he knows, but I'm not going to get in the middle. I love you both. But he knows."

Loren nodded as he walked out the door. Looking at Jaz, she said, "I'm hungry. How about you?" She barked at her. Loren laughed. She fed her, and then Jaz went up to the loft while Loren cooked herself something to eat. Then she walked over to the stables to check on Cupcake.

"Hey, girl. This is going to be your new home for the winter." Loren looked around. "Pretty nice digs. At least you're not alone. Look, Roxy's right over there." She nodded toward Duke's horse. "How about we go for a ride tomorrow?"

"Should you be riding?" Derek said from across the stable.

Loren jumped. She walked out of the stall. "There is no reason I shouldn't."

"You're pregnant."

"Yes, but I'm not broken. Is this what my life is going to be like? Everyone thinking they can tell me what I can and can't do?" she snapped at him.

Derek put his hands up. "I'm not your enemy."

"No, but I can hear it in your voice and see it in your eyes. You all think the same way, think the same thing, that it's acceptable to treat the women in your lives like cattle. Well, you know what, Derek? Go fuck yourself."

She spun around and stomped out of the stable. Derek came running out after her just as Duke and Richard walked out the front door.

"You got it all wrong," Derek shouted.

Loren spun around. "Do I? Do I really? Fuck you, Derek. No one runs me. No one tells me what I can and can't do. Both you and your brother can fuck off and go to hell."

Duke was off the porch and across the drive before she finished her first sentence. "Hey," he yelled at Derek. "What the fuck are you doing?" He looked at Loren, who was on the brink of tears.

"Oh, he thinks he can tell me what I can and can't do. No one, and I mean *no one* is going to dictate to me. So, if you feel the need to stick your two cents in where it concerns what I do, I don't suggest it."

Duke put his hands up. "I didn't do anything." He turned to Derek. "What the fuck did you do to her?"

He chuckled. "I just suggested she shouldn't ride a horse while she is pregnant. Just looking out for your children, man."

Loren spun around and walked right up to Derek, pushing him in the chest. "They are my fucking children. They are growing in my fucking body. Keep your thoughts to yourself. You have no say in what I do."

She stormed past Duke and headed to her house. Walking in, she slammed the door and burst into tears.

Richard walked up. "Derek, stay out of this. Stay away from her. It is perfectly acceptable for her to ride. Your mother did it nearly every day." Turning to Duke, he laughed. "That was the perfect example of raging hormones. Walk on eggshells. It doesn't get any better for at least a few months."

Derek looked at Duke. "I'm sorry, man."

"You should keep your ego in check, brother. That one bites."

Duke walked away toward Loren's. Derek said to Richard, "He's going into the lion's den?"

Richard laughed.

~

DUKE KNOCKED ON THE DOOR. LOREN RIPPED IT OPEN, TEARS RUNNING down her face. "What?" she yelled.

He stepped in and wrapped his arms around her, pulling her into his chest. She fought him, but he didn't let her go. Whispering in her ear, he said, "Let it go, beautiful. I've got you. I know you're angry. Let it go."

Loren relaxed in his embrace and cried. Duke kicked the door shut. Kicking off his boots, he carried her up the stairs to the loft and laid on the bed with her in his arms. She cried herself to sleep while he held her. It felt good to feel her in his arms again. She sacrificed so much of herself to love him, to save him, and to give him three of the greatest gifts any man could ask for—her love and two children—and she felt so alone. It was all his fault, because he was a selfish asshole. God, the things he was learning from her. His embrace didn't fail her. Even in sleep, he didn't let her go.

Loren woke slowly, still in Duke's arms. It felt like home. It was home. She needed him. She needed him like she needed air to breathe. Her hand moved on its own, resting on his stomach. She remembered his very defined muscles.

Duke woke to the heat blazing through his body. Her hand was on his stomach, slowly moving up his chest. Opening his eyes and breathing in, he smelled her vanilla and strawberry scent. This was home.

As her hand moved, she tilted her head up. Duke saw the blazing purple looking at him. *Oh, fuck.* He opened his mouth to say something, but Loren covered it with hers. Fire blew through his body. His hand coming up around her head, he rolled her over on her back and deepened the kiss.

Pulling back, he looked into her eyes. "What are you doing?" he whispered.

He watched as she drew her lip between her teeth. His heart slammed in his chest. God, what she did to him.

"I'm so scared, Duke. I've been so scared for so long."

"Aww, beautiful. I'm terrified. But you're here and we'll figure it out." He wiped the tear from the side of her face. "Don't cry anymore. It'll be all right."

She nodded. "Will you kiss me again. I missed..." She didn't finish. Duke covered her mouth with his, kissing her breathless.

He pulled back slowly, licking her lip. "We need to stop. We have a lot of things to work out. But I need you to know I love you, only you."

"I love you," she said.

"Come on, I'm sure we slept through the night, and I can just hear my dad now."

Loren laughed. "We are having babies. He can't possibly be angry."

Duke laughed as he scooted off the bed. "He told me in no uncertain words to stay away from you."

Loren laughed, falling back on the bed. "I am so glad I'm not you right now."

"Yeah, thanks," he said as he went to the bathroom.

Loren got up and changed into a pair of sweats and a t-shirt, making her way down the stairs just as Duke came out of the bathroom. "Well, I guess I'll go get my ass chewed out." He smiled at her. In a much softer voice, he said, "But let me say this, it was well worth it." He wrapped his hand around her neck. "You all right, beautiful?"

She looked into his eyes, his beautiful green eyes. Drawing her lip between her teeth, she nodded. Duke nodded to her. Letting her go, he walked out the door. He smiled all the way to the house. Even when he walked in the door prepared to get shit from his father, he smiled.

"Well, you look full of yourself. Everything all right?"

"It's getting there."

"Time and patience, son. Time and patience."

Duke nodded. "I'm going to change and eat something. Then I'm off to Loren's land to help Jordon with the tanks. She might be over later to shower."

"Duke," Richard said.

"She cried, Dad, for a long time. I held her and she fell asleep. It felt too good to have her in my arms again, so I slept with her."

Richard laughed. "Well, thanks for that, but I was going to say that you might want to have a conversation with your brother. He seems to think that Loren is playing you, and he isn't happy about it."

"Fuck Derek. I'll deal with him." He went upstairs to shower and then he ate. Driving over to Loren's land, he couldn't help but think how wonderful it felt to hold her. Pulling up, he saw Derek and Jordon strapping the first tank to the truck.

Climbing out of the truck, Derek laughed. "Well, from the smile on your face, I see you got some."

"Get off the truck, Derek."

Derek jumped down, and Duke punched him square in the face. "Don't ever think it is acceptable to handle a woman the way you did last night. If I even see you talking to her again, I'll do a hell of a lot more than that."

"Are you fucking kidding me? You broke my nose, you fucker. She is playing you, using those kids to get what she wants."

Duke grabbed him by the shirt and hit him again and again before dropping him on the ground. "I told you to shut your fucking mouth. You don't have a fucking clue what is going on or what I did to her. You are one of the most self-centered bastards I've ever known. Stay the fuck away from her and stay out of this."

"Come on, is that all you got?" Derek egged him on, spitting blood on the ground and getting up.

Duke shook his head and got in his Jeep and drove away. He was shaking. He just beat the shit out of his brother. He needed to blow off some of this steam. He hit the highway and drove. He wasn't going anywhere special, he just drove.

"This is so fucked up. I fucked it all up," he said to the air. He couldn't believe the anger she held for him. But thinking like that made him like Derek. It wasn't about him anymore; it should have never been about him. She was all that mattered. It should have always been that way. Pulling over, he put the Jeep in park and dropped his head into his hands and cried. *God, do all men act this way? Are we all such selfish pigs? Where did I learn this from?* "Fuck!" He dug his phone out of his pocket and dialed his dad.

"Where are you?" Richard said to him.

"Out on one ninety-one, just past Garneill. I need you. I need to talk. I just beat the shit out of Derek."

"You didn't hurt him, did you?"

"Broke his nose. Will you come?"

"He probably deserved that. Yep, I'll be there shortly." Richard hung up.

On his way out the door, Derek and Jordan came driving up. Richard waited until Derek got out of the truck. "You need to go home. Joe and Alex are on their way. I don't want to see you for a week. You are on vacation."

"Oh, why, because poor little Dukey is crying about his..."

He didn't have time to finish his sentence before Richard slammed his fist into his gut. "Get the fuck off this ranch." He climbed in his truck and drove away.

Duke was sitting on the side of the road with his head back against the headrest when Richard opened the door, scaring the shit out of him. He took one look at his son and his heart broke. "What's going on?" he asked.

"What's wrong with me?"

Richard laughed. "Why would you think something's wrong with you?"

"Dad, while I was beating the shit out of Derek, it hit me. I am always about me. I didn't consider Loren in any of this. Not really. It was always about me. I wanted to sleep with her so desperately that I asked her to marry me. Don't get me wrong, that woman will be my wife. But I didn't take into consideration anything. I didn't even think to use a condom because I was so selfish, and all I wanted was to feel her wrapped around me. She was, no, is so fragile, both mentally and emotionally, and I skated around it, thinking I could fix it all, when all I did was fuck her up even more. I mean, she fucking operated on me to save my life, and all I could do was feel sorry for myself because she left me. I wanted her to stay and take care of me. Why are men like this? Why do I think and feel the way I do? I sat in your house for months wallowing in my own self-pity. I want nothing more than to live my life with her and our children. I want... I say that all the time. I don't consider her feelings or her thoughts. I am just like Derek, only I'm defending my actions. How do I change, Dad? How do I not be this man?"

Richard just sat there. "Well, Duke, I think this is the first step. You are actually acknowledging that you do this, that you think this way. Son, any successful relationship is give and take. You have to decide what is more important to you, your happiness or hers. Loving someone is not as easy as people make it seem. When you love some-one, it's their happiness that matters, and with that comes yours. When you were together, how did she treat you?"

"She always made sure I was first, in everything."

"And how did you treat her?"

"Like she was the prize."

Richard nodded his head. "Do you see? Everything she said, Duke, is everything you just said to me. She gave you everything, and you took it, giving only what you needed to give to continue getting what you wanted. Even with what you did, the reason why she left, you knew it far too late. You can't change that. You can't change anything; you can only learn from it. She is here, living in our backyard, carrying your children, taking care of them. She came back here so you could be a father. She is giving and giving and giving. What are you doing?"

"Taking."

"Duke, you have to change because you want to. She can't be the reason. It has to be because that is what you want to do. She came back, and I know the love she has for you. It's the same your mother had for me. I nearly lost her, just like you and Loren. I was sidetracked by a pretty young woman and your mother left me. I never physically cheated on her, but like you, I cheated her out of my heart. It nearly ended her. I spent the next twenty years making sure she knew exactly how I felt about her, and to this day, there hasn't been another woman in my heart. Make your choice. Do what needs to be done if you love her like that. Don't put the pressure on her, just let it happen. Be what she needs, who she needs. These are your children, and you cannot walk away from them. She is giving you a miracle. I know her medical history, and what she said to you was the truth. These are all just words of advice. In the end, Duke, you are the one who needs to decide."

"Do you think she will ever forgive me?"

"Maybe when you start to forgive yourself and realize that it is not about you. It was Loren that was destroyed."

"See, I'm such a selfish bastard." He put his head back. "I don't know how she can stand me."

His father laughed. "Just take your time. Don't make her feel anything less than comfortable. You need to maintain a good relationship, whether it be intimate or not. You are going to be parents."

Duke turned his head, looking at his father. Tears rolled down his cheeks. "I love her so much, Dad. She is the greatest gift."

"That she is, son. I'm glad you finally figured this all out. Now, go home and tell her. Accept what she is giving you and be thankful she is letting you in."

Duke nodded. "Thank you, Dad."

Richard patted his son on the leg. "Anytime."

Duke watched his father get out of the Jeep, and he waited for him to turn around, then Duke followed him back to the ranch.

LOREN STOOD IN THE SNOW WITH HER FURRY BOOTS ON, WATCHING AS they lowered her second tank. When they finished, she went about hooking everything up. Duke stood watching her. She didn't need him to save her, to rescue her. She needed him to love her. Nothing more. He couldn't help but smile at her.

Jordan used the crane to lower the wood for her deck. Joe and Alex had already begun digging the holes for the supports. He walked over and started helping them. With the three of them, it didn't take long. Joe mixed the cement, and they set all the posts, covering them so the snow wouldn't get the cement wet. It would take a few days for it to harden.

Loren came out with a pitcher of hot chocolate. "I made dinner for everyone. I could use a few hands carrying it over to the house." She poured each of them a cup. "Looks good. Thank you, guys so much."

"So, we are going to be uncles?" Joe asked.

Loren giggled. "Twice."

Alex looked at her. "Twins? Holy shit. That is so awesome. Do you know if they are girls or boys?"

"Well, they are in separate sacks, so I would guess it could be one of each." She looked at Duke. He hadn't said anything to her, just watched her.

He smiled from ear to ear. "One of each. I like that idea."

They finished the hot chocolate, and she loaded them all up with food. Duke waited for her to come out with Jaz. She was carrying a pie. "You want me to take that?"

"No, I've got it." They walked in silence to the house.

Richard had set the table, and they all sat down. "Where's Derek?" Loren asked. "I owe him an apology."

"Yeah, you're not the only one," Duke said.

"I gave him a week off," Richard said.

Loren looked at Duke. "Why do you owe him an apology?"

"Well, I sort of beat the shit out of him today. Broke his nose."

"Care to elaborate?" She raised her eyebrow at him.

He chuckled. "No, not really. But in my defense, he had it coming to him."

"I have to agree with you," Richard said.

They finished their meal. "Well, I'm going to excuse myself. I'm tired." Loren scooted her seat back and got up.

Everyone said goodnight and thanked her. Duke stood. "I'll walk you home."

She smiled. "Thanks."

As they were walking, Loren said, "Why did you beat up your brother?"

"Because he's an asshole and had it coming. I didn't like the way he talked to you last night, and I certainly didn't appreciate what he said to me this morning."

She nodded. "You were gone most of the day. Is everything all right?"

"It's going to be."

"That's good to hear. You want to come in for some hot chocolate?" she asked as they reached her house.

"I'd like that very much." He put his hand on the small of her back while she stepped up the makeshift steps.

Duke took off his boots and his coat and sat on the couch while she warmed it up. Bringing him a cup she, climbed on the couch at the other end. "I wanted to thank you for holding me last night, and to apologize for kissing you."

He smiled as he brought the cup to his mouth. "You never need to apologize for kissing me, and anytime you need someone to hold you, just let me know."

She stared at him, looking into his beautiful green eyes. "My friend Jenny in Austin is an OB. She did the surgery to repair my uterus. Well, she told me that my friend Kate is in Bozeman. She is also an OB. I wanted to know if you wanted to go with me for my next visit?"

"Of course, I do. When is it?"

"A week from Tuesday. I'm getting another ultrasound. You can see the babies."

Duke's heart nearly jumped out of his chest. "Really?" he whispered. She nodded, smiling. "Will we get to see what they are?"

"I don't think so, not yet. But, eventually, we will. If you want to," she said shyly.

He set his cup on the floor. "I want to. I want to do everything. Can we talk?"

"I thought we were talking." She giggled.

He took her hand in his. "I know this is beating a dead horse, but I want to apologize to you. There is no excuse, no reason that I can give, except for I was a selfish bastard, and I am sorry for hurting you."

"Thank you. I accept your apology."

"Yeah?"

"Yeah. Did you want some more hot chocolate?"

He smiled. "No, I'm going to go and let you get some sleep." He got up, pulling her up with him. "May I kiss you good night?" She nodded, and he put his hands on her face and slowly kissed her. "I love you, beautiful. Sleep well."

Loren nodded. "Goodnight, Duke."

He put his boots on and his coat, then turning, he looked into her eyes. Leaning down, he kissed her again. "Goodnight, Loren." Turning, he left.

Loren touched her lips as she smiled. *Maybe he is sorry. Maybe...* "Stop it, Loren," she said to the room. She cleaned up and brushed her teeth and then went to bed. Sleep came easy for her now that it was all out in the open. Now that he knew how much he hurt her. Maybe now she could begin to forgive him.

Duke smiled all the way to the house. He had a long road ahead of him, and he was gladly taking one step at a time.

As he walked in the door, Richard looked at him. "Things working out?"

Duke laughed. "I apologized to her, and I didn't make it about me, and she accepted it. So, I would have to say it's a first step."

Richard nodded. "Walk carefully."

"One step at a time, Dad. One step at a time. I'm going to go over to Derek's in the morning. I think it's about time I filled my brother in on what took place and to apologize."

"Sounds like a plan."

Duke smiled and went to his room. He laid in bed and thought about how he would take his next step. He needed to accept her terms and build the friendship. He needed to come to terms with the fact that they may not get to the point that they were healed completely, but they were going to raise some babies together. He knew she loved him, and he most definitely loved her.

Morning came and went for Loren. She slept until nearly noon. Upon opening her eyes, she smiled at the fact that Duke wasn't beating her door down wondering why she was still in bed. She hoped he would accept her boundaries, even if she wasn't so sure she could keep them herself.

Duke had been up just before sunrise. Feeling refreshed, he showered, dressed, and headed to town. It'd been a long time since he felt this way. He stopped in at the diner to have some breakfast.

Millie smiled at him. "Good to see you Duke."

"Well, Millie, it's good to be seen. How have you been?"

"It's been busy around here. Why don't you grab a table and I'll get you some coffee? Are you alone?"

Duke chuckled. "Yeah, I've got some stuff to do today." He found a small table and sat down.

Millie followed him over and poured him some coffee. "I'll just have some eggs, over easy, with toast, bacon, and some hash browns."

Duke ate his breakfast with a little smile on his face. He couldn't stop thinking about Loren and that kiss they shared the night before. He was going to win her back with his respect for her. She deserved nothing less. Finishing up, Duke dropped forty dollars on the table, picked up his hat, and walked out the door.

Pulling up in front of Derek's house, he shook his head. "Time to eat shit," he said to himself. He didn't bother to knock, just opened the door and went in. The place was a mess. Shaking his head, Duke walked to his bedroom. Derek was lying in bed with two naked women. He chuckled and sat in the chair. *This ought to be interesting.*

Duke kicked the bed, and one of the girls rolled over. He couldn't help but notice that she had really nice tits. Not as nice as Loren's, but they were nice. He kicked the bed again. The same girl sat up and stretched. *Fuck, if I wasn't so in love, I would definitely fuck her.*

She opened her eyes and smiled at him. Getting on her hands and knees, she crawled to the end of the bed. "You are beautiful. Can I help you with anything?"

Duke chuckled. "No, thank you."

"Aww, come on, I'm pretty sure I could relieve you of some of that stress I see on your face," she purred.

"Really, I'm good," he said.

"Suit yourself," she said as she climbed off the bed. Duke watched her walk to the bathroom. She smiled at him as she closed the door.

Shaking his head, he kicked the bed again. Derek rolled over, wrapping his arm around the other woman in his bed. His hand moved down her body to her ass. Duke watched in amusement as his little brother's cock got hard. If he didn't stop this, he would soon be watching him fuck this chick, so he kicked the bed again.

Derek lifted his head and looked at him. "What the fuck do you want?"

The woman turned over, grabbed his cock, and whispered, "This."

Duke laughed. "Certainly not that." The woman continued to play with his brother's cock. The bathroom door opened and woman number one came out walking past Duke. She smiled as she climbed back on the bed, giving him a full view of her center. Shaking his head, Duke said, "Get up, little brother, we need to talk." He stood up.

The second woman looked at Duke. "Well, good morning. Why don't you shed some of the clothes and join us?" She started to get up.

Duke put up his hand. "No, thank you." Looking at Derek, he asked, "Living room?"

"I'm kind of busy here," Derek said as he cupped the second woman's breast. "I'm on vacation." His mouth engulfed her nipple.

"Now, Derek," Duke said and walked out of the room. He sat on the couch and waited. He could hear the women talking. Then the door opened and they both walked out naked, picking up their clothes.

The first woman said, "You really know how to kill a party. You seem a bit uptight."

The second woman said, as she bent down to pick up her panties, "We can relieve that stress for you."

"Again, ladies, thank you, but no thank you," Duke said.

Derek walked out and smacked one of them on the ass. "Thanks, girls, maybe we can get together later tonight and play some more."

They both kissed him, dressed, and left.

"What the fuck do you want, Duke? As you can see, I was enjoying my vacation."

"Sit down. We need to talk." Derek sat in the chair across from him. "First, I am sorry for what I did to your face. But you deserved it."

Derek laughed. "Why would I deserve this when I am stating the truth about Loren using her pregnancy to control you?"

"Because I was ashamed and embarrassed to tell you what really happened. Why she really left."

"Yeah, I got bits and pieces. You still had feelings for Julie. She got upset and took off."

Duke shook his head. "Not even close. I basically cheated on Loren. Without the physical part of cheating, I cheated. I used her for my own gratification. Loren was a virgin. I took that from her. Don't get me wrong, I am totally in love with her and I plan on marrying her. But I wanted her, and with no regard to her mental and emotional being, I did everything in my power to have her. She wasn't ready. Hell, I wasn't ready. I still had shit in my brain about Julie. I had no right to do what I did to Loren. I was just being a selfish, egotistical bastard.

"I don't know if you know what happened to her, but she was stabbed eleven times in the chest and stomach. The guy tried to slit her throat, and when she stopped fighting, he dropped her on the ground. She tried to get away and he sliced her open from the shoulder to her hip, nearly severing her spinal cord. She was in a medically induced coma for five months. Her father died of a heart attack when he saw her. It took her a year of therapy to come back from that. But she came back. She kept herself away from everything that life had to offer. She believed herself not worthy of love.

"She was a brilliant neurosurgeon, and she couldn't operate anymore. She became a recluse; she couldn't even go to the grocery store. Loren suffers from PTSD, and I bulldozed myself into her life, into her heart, and I destroyed every bit of confidence she had built back up.

"She let me in. She let me in, and I won her heart. Then I used her for my own self-gratification. I'm the bastard here, not her. When I finally admitted it to her, she had every right to run. I destroyed her completely when she was already so fragile. I was the bastard that ripped her trust to shreds. I wanted to find her, but I couldn't even face myself. I couldn't look in the mirror; I felt so disgusted with what I had done, with who I had become.

"Then, when Julie shot me, she did the one thing she hadn't been able to bring herself to do. She walked into a fucking operating room and she saved my fucking life. You know why? Because she loves me. She completely and totally loves me. But she will never get over what I did to her. How I used her, how I destroyed her.

"When she found out she was pregnant, which is something that is medically impossible for her to be, what did she do? She made her way back here. She has been here for almost a month, trying to figure out how to tell me. She isn't using me. She isn't trying to control me. She is giving me the opportunity to be a father, to share this miracle with her. And it is a miracle. She could have stayed in Texas, and I would have never known because I would not have gone after her. I couldn't. I am that ashamed of what I did, who I had become. All because I wanted what I wanted, and I gave no regard to how anyone else felt. I'm the one that is not worthy of her. I'm the one who did this, not her."

When Duke looked up, Derek was sitting there in shock. "I had no idea. I am so sorry. So very sorry."

"Thank you, but I just wanted you to know. I've apologized to her, and she has accepted. She is offering me her friendship and the opportunity to be a father." Duke looked at him with tears in his eyes. "I'm going to be a father, and I need my brother to help me be the best that I can be. I would appreciate it if you could stop being an asshole and be my brother."

Derek stood up and hugged him. "I'm sorry, brother. I'm here, man."

They stood there hugging each other and then Duke pulled away, slapping him on the back. "I need to get going. I'm going grocery shopping for Loren. She likes to bake and cook. It helps her stay calm."

Derek nodded. "You want some help? I need to apologize to her and to Dad. He threw me off the ranch."

Duke chuckled. "I would love some help."

Together, they went to the grocery store. When they finished, they filled Duke's Jeep and half of Derek's truck. "Jesus, man, I think we bought out the store," Derek said.

Laughing, Duke said, "Yeah, you might be right. See you back at the ranch."

LOREN ATE HER BREAKFAST WITH A SMILE ON HER FACE. SHE DRESSED and walked over to the house to see Richard. Secretly, she hoped to see Duke. Knocking, she pushed the door open. "Richard?" she called out as she walked in.

"In here," he said. Loren came around the corner after taking off her boots and jacket. "To what do I owe this pleasure," he asked as he got up to hug her.

"I just thought I'd come by and see if you needed anything. I'm going to run into town and get some groceries. I feel like baking and cooking."

Richard looked at her. "Loren, you don't need to feed me. I am capable of cooking."

"I know, but it helps me calm myself down. I like to do it. Will you let me cook for you?"

He chuckled. "Far be it for me to deny you anything."

The front door opened. "Hey, Dad. Oh, hey, Loren." It was Joe. "Alex and I are going to ride into Bozeman today. Is there anything you need?"

Richard looked at him. "Why don't you wait until the storm passes?"

"Dad, have you been outside? There isn't a cloud in the sky."

Loren looked at Richard. "He's right. It's a beautiful day."

Richard laughed. "You've lived here your whole life. Just because it's a clear sky doesn't mean anything. Give it a day or two. I know you're both grown men, but I would appreciate it if you would stick around town. We've had enough drama, and I don't need to be searching for my sons in a blizzard. Besides, Loren is going to do some cooking. I think we should have a family night."

Joe laughed. "All right, Dad, you always know when the storms are coming." Looking at Loren, he asked, "You ready for your first winter storm in Montana?"

She laughed. "Oh, I am." She stood. "If there is a storm coming, I better get going. I'll be back in a few hours." She grabbed her coat, put on her boots, and headed back to her house.

As she walked through the drive, Duke and Derek pulled up. He jumped out. "Hey, beautiful, I've got a surprise for you."

Loren smiled. "You do?"

He wiggled his eyebrows at her and opened the Jeep door. "We went shopping for you. There's a big storm coming, and I know that cooking calms your nerves so..."

Derek got out of his truck and walked up to Loren. She stepped back. "Listen, I really need to apologize for being such an asshole to you."

She smiled. "I'm the one who is sorry for ripping into you."

Derek laughed. "I deserved every word you said. So, we are okay?"

She nodded. "Yeah, we are."

"Good, now, open the door so I can haul all these groceries in."

"You have more in your truck?"

He laughed. "Yeah, we bought out the store."

Loren looked at Duke. "Yes, you have surprised me." She walked past them and opened the door. Jaz came out to greet them. She was still a bit unhappy with Duke, but she let him pass.

Loren went in and started unpacking everything. When Derek put his last bags down, he smiled at her. "I'm going over to talk to Dad. See you two later."

Duke nodded and headed out for more bags. When he finished, he took off his boots and coat and proceeded to help her put things away. It took a good twenty minutes. Loren started some spaghetti sauce and began making two apple pies while Duke sat on a stool and watched her.

"Can I help?" he asked.

"Well, you can wash all the apples. That would be helpful. Do you know how to skin them?"

Duke laughed. "Not a clue, but I'm willing to learn."

Loren watched as he rolled up his sleeves. "Oh my God, what happened to your arm?" She saw the bandage.

He looked at Jaz, who put her head down. "Jaz let me know, in no uncertain terms, not to ever lay a hand on you in anger."

Loren looked at Jaz. "You bit him?" Jaz crawled over to Loren. "No, Jaz. Not Duke. Say you're sorry."

Duke stood there watching her scold the dog. Jaz crawled over and laid her head on Duke's feet, whimpering. Duke squatted down. "It's all right, girl. I deserved it. You were just protecting her." He scratched her head.

Jaz wagged her tail, then picking her head up, looked at Loren. "Good girl," she said and smiled.

Duke stood and started washing the apples. Loren started to peel them. Duke noticed her shifting on her feet and went to get her a stool. She smiled at him. "Thank you," she said softly.

Duke reached up, putting her hair behind her ear. "Anything, anytime, anywhere."

They spent the afternoon peeling apples, making pies, and laughing. When it was time for dinner, they put on their boots and coats. Duke carried the pot of sauce over and came back for Loren and the pies. Walking into Richard's house, they were laughing.

Alex was sitting at the table. "Here let me get that." He stood up and took the pie from Loren. "What can I do to help?"

She shook her head. "I've got this, thanks." And off she went to the kitchen. Duke ran upstairs to take a shower and change his clothes. When he came down the back stairs into the kitchen, he stopped when he saw Loren with her hands on her stomach.

"Your daddy is going to meet you next week. I know he is going to love you as much as I do." She was smiling. Then she turned to stir the sauce.

Duke wiped his tears and cleared his throat. "You need any help?"

Loren turned and smiled at him. "Actually, I forgot the bread dough I made. It's in the fridge wrapped in clear plastic wrap. Would you go get them for me?"

"I'll be right back." He turned to leave.

Loren stood there watching him. She couldn't help but wonder what had changed about him. A few days before, he was desperate to have her, but now, he was respecting her boundaries.

WHEN DINNER WAS DONE AND ALL THE DISHES WERE CLEAN, LOREN said, "Well, I'm going to head home. I've got some cleaning up to do." She headed for the door.

Duke got up and followed her. "Can I walk you home?" he asked her shyly.

"I'd like that."

They walked to Loren's. Turning, she asked him, "Can we talk?"

"Of course."

Opening the door, they went in and took off their boots and coats. Loren reached over and took his hand. Duke didn't argue as he entwined their fingers. "You okay?" he asked.

"I know what I said to you about being friends, but I was wondering if you would hold me for a while?"

"Loren," he whispered. "Would that be a good idea?"

She let go of his hand. "Probably not. I'm sorry, it's just... it's just." She shook her head. "It's not important. I'm sorry. You don't need to stay. I'm just going to clean up and then go to bed. I'm pretty tired." She had her head down.

"All right. I will see you tomorrow?"

She nodded. "Sure." She didn't move while he put on his boots and jacket.

"Good night, beautiful," he said softly. It was killing him not to hold her. But he couldn't do it. He wanted her so desperately, but he needed to take his time.

Loren nodded, and he walked out the door. The tears fell from her eyes. She needed him so desperately. She needed him to hold her. She was so scared of what they had done to one another. She needed the physical connection to him. He almost died; he'd almost left her. She kneeled down as the sobs began. She was so lonely. After having him, after holding him, she needed him.

Duke made it halfway back to the house before he realized that she needed him. She wouldn't have asked him to hold her if she didn't want him to. "I am such a fucking idiot." He turned to look at her house. He couldn't see her in the window by the kitchen. His feet were moving. He was running back.

When he opened the door and saw her sobbing on the floor, he couldn't get his boots off fast enough. He pulled her into his arms. "Oh, God, baby. I am so sorry." She was heaving sobs into his chest. "I don't know what to do anymore." He tried to quiet her. "I miss you so Goddamned much it hurts."

"I'm... so... scared... so... alone," she sobbed out.

Duke picked her up and carried her upstairs to the loft. Gently, he laid her down and wrapped her in his arms. He held her while she cried. He held on to her like she was a life jacket on the open sea.

Loren let the flood gates open. "You... were... dying. I... didn't know." She sobbed a few more times. "I... didn't... know... if... I... could... save... you. I've... been... so... scared."

"I know. I've been so terrified that I destroyed you. That I would never get the chance to tell you how sorry I was. Loren, I'm so sorry, so sorry for everything."

She slowed down and caught her breath. "I don't want to do this alone. I want us to be a family. I want you to be a daddy. I had to come back. I love you so much. You hurt me so bad, Duke. You hurt me so bad."

He couldn't stop the tears. "I know, baby. I know. I was such a fool. I had you, I had everything I could ever want, and I fucked it all up. I was so stupid, so arrogant, thinking I could just take what I wanted. God, can you ever forgive me?"

"Please, Duke," she cried, pulling him closer to her. "I don't want to do this alone."

"You're not alone, beautiful. I'm right here."

"I love you," she whispered. "I love you."

"I love you, beautiful. So much."

Soon, Loren had cried herself to sleep in his arms. Duke laid there holding her. He was home. He'd fucked her up so bad. God, the guilt he felt, the pain of knowing she was so distraught, so hurt. She had been through hell, and then she gave herself to him, trusted him to love her, and he fucked it up. Closing his eyes, Duke fell asleep, wrapped around the only woman he would ever love.

Loren woke because she needed to use the bathroom. When she moved, Duke pulled her closer. Closing her eyes, she took a deep breath, his musky scent filling her nose. She smiled and tilted her head up. Her eyes swollen from crying, she touched his lips. Duke kissed them. "Hi, beautiful," he whispered.

Loren's heart jumped. She remembered all those times they woke up like this and he said that to her. "Hi, I need to go to the bathroom."

"But I don't want you to go," he pouted.

She giggled and pushed up, scooting to the end of the bed. She made her way to the bathroom. When she came out, Duke was sitting on the stairs. "Come here," he whispered to her. Walking up, Duke pulled her into his arms. "You all right?" He kissed her lightly.

"I'm better, thank you." She pulled back, her fingers touching his lips. "Duke," she breathed as she leaned in to kiss him.

His heart stopped. He wanted to kiss her; hell, he wanted to take her up in the loft and make love to her. But he couldn't. He needed to change. He needed to be worthy of this incredible love she had for him. When her lips touched his, it was gentle and sweet. She pulled back, and then opened her eyes, looking into his.

"Oh, God, beautiful," he whispered. He knew this look. He wanted her; he wanted her so bad he hurt. "Fuck," he said as he grabbed her neck and kissed her deeply. Loren crawled up his body and straddled him. He pulled back. "I made a promise to myself that I was going to earn your love. I want to take you back to bed and make love to you. But I'm not."

"No?" She smiled.

"No, beautiful, I'm not. It would just be my egotistical ass doing what I want, not what is right for either of us. I hurt you, and I need to make sure that I never do that again. I'm not going anywhere. We need to deal with everything, and we need to know one another, and we need to share life together. I won't make love to you until I am comfortable with how you feel about me. I'm going to go home. I will always be here to hold you. I'm so sorry I left earlier. I shouldn't have done that. I'm weak, and I am so in love with you. I'm terrified I am going to make love to you, and I am not ready to do that again. Do you understand?"

Loren smiled. "Yes, thank you. I love you so much. Thank you."

He put his forehead on hers. "But I am going on the record and saying that I have got the worst case of blue balls on the planet."

Loren smiled. "Me too."

He kissed her again and put on his shoes and coat. "Are you going to be all right?" She nodded. "Loren?"

"I am, I promise," she assured him.

"All right, we are going to start on the deck tomorrow. The cement should be set. I will see you then."

She walked up to him and put her hands on his chest. Standing on her tippy toes, she kissed him. He pulled her into his chest, hugging her. "I love you, beautiful."

"I love you, too."

Duke walked into a dark house. It must have been late. Making his way to the kitchen, he grabbed a drink and headed to his room. Stripping, he crawled into bed feeling better than he had in months. He did the right thing. Closing his eyes, he slept.

∼

THE DAYS ROLLED BY. THE GUYS FINISHED LOREN'S DECK SO SHE COULD now sit outside like she liked to. The storm came, and she couldn't have been more thrilled. She had never seen so much snow before.

Duke watched her from a distance playing with Jaz in the snow. They ran around, and she threw snow at her. He found himself laughing at them. Finally, she went in. Duke assumed it was to make herself some hot chocolate. Deciding he wanted to share some with her, he headed over to her house.

"Oh, hi," she said. "Come on in." They had become civil to one another. It wasn't awkward, but it was offsetting for Loren. She wanted to know what was going on in his head, why he suddenly pulled away from her.

"I saw you out playing in the snow with Jaz. You looked like you were having some fun," he said as he took off his boots and jacket.

"It would have been nice if I had someone to play with, but I guess in a few years I will." She put her hand on her belly. "I hope you didn't forget about Tuesday. I'm leaving around nine. My appointment is at eleven-thirty."

Smiling, he said, "I haven't forgotten. I'm really nervous about it." He hadn't touched her belly since that first day.

"I was just going to make some hot chocolate. Would you like to share a cup with me? I just need to change out of these clothes."

"I would love to."

Loren climbed the stairs to grab some sweats and a t-shirt. Coming down, she went in the bathroom and changed. She purposely grabbed a tight fitting shirt. She wanted him to see her bump. Walking out, she went straight to the kitchen and started making the hot chocolate. She could feel Duke watching her.

"You're doing it again," she said softly.

He chuckled. "I can't stop myself."

"And why is that?"

"Because you are so fucking beautiful." He was just inches from her neck.

Loren closed her eyes. It took everything she had not to lean back against him. "Thank you," she whispered.

She felt Duke's breath on her neck, then he inhaled. "Vanilla and strawberries," he moaned.

Loren swallowed. God, if he touched her, she was going to turn the burner off and jump him. She wanted him so bad. Her panties moistened as he breathed her in. "Duke?"

"Yes?" he said next to her ear.

She reached down and turned off the burner, resting her hands on the stove. He brushed his lips along the curve of her ear. The heat of his breath gently blew in her ear. "I am doing my damnedest to stay away from you, to respect your boundaries."

Her mouth went dry, her throat parched all of a sudden. Her panties were now soaked. "Why now?" It was barely a whisper as she licked her lips.

"I promised myself I wasn't going to be a selfish bastard. That I wasn't going to fuck this up," he moaned out as his lips skimmed her neck.

"I'm so wet, Duke," she whimpered.

"I know, baby." His lips closing around her earlobe. He moved behind her, putting his hands on the stove next to hers. He wasn't touching her, but she could feel the heat radiating off his body. Loren had her hair up in a ponytail. His mouth landed on the spot where her neck and shoulder met. She shuddered, goose flesh running down her spine. "I need to touch you," he said as he sucked her skin into his mouth.

Loren's head dropped down. "Please," she whispered.

He moved his hand off the stove, gently placing it on her stomach, on her bump. "These are our children, Loren. Conceived in love. Do you believe that?"

"Yes." Her eyes filled with tears as she watched his hand cover her bump. "Yes, with all my heart."

Duke brought his other hand up to cup her chin, tilting her head up and turning it so he could kiss her. He pulled her to his chest, his hand holding their children, his mouth making love to hers. The kiss ended, and Duke slowly let her go. Stepping back, he went to the couch and sat down, watching her.

It took Loren a few deep breaths to gain her composure. She turned the stove back on and continued to warm the hot chocolate. She could feel him watching her, a smile on her face.

Duke was hard, but he would suffer. He'd hurt her so badly, so he needed to suffer. Wanting her to know that he desired her, that he hadn't forgotten her, was his goal. Smiling, he knew he'd achieved it.

As Loren walked toward him, he could see her nipples sticking out of her shirt like hard little bullets. Groaning inwardly, he reached for the cup. "Thank you." He smiled at her.

Loren sat on the other end of the couch with her legs tucked under her. "Thank you."

"I just wanted to let you know that I am thinking about you." He stood and put his cup on the counter. Loren watched him with a smile on her face. She couldn't help but lick her lips. She wanted him.

She stood and set her cup next to his. He didn't move out of her way; she had to reach around him. Slowly, she tilted her head to look up at him. His hand reached up to curve around her head, and he trailed his thumb along her bottom lip. "You are so beautiful," he whispered as he kissed her. She couldn't stop the tears. She needed him to hold her, to make her feel his love. Pulling back, he saw her tears, so he pulled her to his chest and wrapped his arms around her. "Aww, baby. It hurts so much not being here with you," he whispered into her hair.

"Stay with me."

Against everything he vowed, he picked her up and carried her up the stairs. He laid her on the bed, kissing her deeply. She grabbed at him, desperate to feel him against her. Reluctantly, Duke covered her body with his. They kissed for a few minutes. He reached up and turned off her light then rolled onto his side, pulling her to his chest. He held her close until she fell asleep. Quietly, he got up, looking at her one more time before he left. He felt the pull. It took all that he had to leave her. He wanted nothing more than to strip off all their clothes so he could feel her next to him. "I love you, beautiful," he whispered as he made his way down the stairs and then home.

Walking in the door, Richard said, "She all right?"

Duke smiled. "Not really."

"Something I should know? She hasn't been around much."

"Dad, I need her. I want her, and I'm terrified I am going to fuck it all up again. I'm trying to do the right thing."

"What does Loren think?"

"She wanted me to accept her offer of friendship, and to raise these children with her. No expectations, just parents and friends. It's killing me, but I love her that much that I am going to abide by her request."

"I hope you know what you are doing."

"That's just it, Dad. I don't have a fucking clue. I am flying by the seat of my pants. It is taking me to edge of my sanity not being able to hold her."

Richard chuckled. "When you don't feel that way and you can accept all that you have done, then you will be able to love her fully, the way she loves you."

Duke shook his head. "That doesn't even make sense."

"You are reacting to her as you did before, not with your heart but with your body. Get it under control. Stop thinking in terms of sexual gratification. That's not how you love someone. That is just an extension of that love. Who is she? What's her favorite color? Her favorite flower? Her favorite food, book, movie? What makes her laugh? Do you know these things?"

Duke stood there like an idiot. Shaking his head, he replied, "No."

"So, the only thing you can think about is climbing into bed with her. Your own sexual gratification."

"Dad, am I ever going to get it right?"

Richard laughed. "I sure as hell hope so. You're going to be a father in five months, and I would really like to know that she is a member of this family when it happens. If you don't get it together and figure it out, that isn't going to happen. Now, I'm going to bed. See you in the morning." He walked down the hall to his room, leaving Duke standing in the front hall feeling even more like shit than he did when he walked in the door.

After dragging himself up the stairs, he dropped his clothes and then laid on his bed and thought about what his father said to him. He needed to not avoid her but to get to know her. To really know her. Smiling, he promised himself that he would do it. He needed her, and it was obvious to him that she needed him as well.

~

LOREN WOKE IN THE MIDDLE OF THE NIGHT TO USE THE BATHROOM. When she opened her eyes, she hoped that Duke would be there. Yes, she was disappointed when he wasn't, but she knew he wouldn't be. He was doing exactly what she wanted him to do. Shaking her head, she climbed down the stairs. She brushed her teeth and looked at the clock in the kitchen. It was just about midnight.

Smiling, she put on her boots and grabbed her coat. "Jaz, I'll be back. You stay here." Walking across the yard, she hoped the door was open and was relieved to find it was. She took off her boots and put her coat on the chair before making her way up to Duke's room.

When she opened the door, he was lying on his back, completely naked. Closing her eyes, she tried to move. *This is so wrong. This is what Julie did to him.* Chickening out, she turned, putting her hand on the doorknob. Taking a deep breath, she turned the knob and pulled the door open.

Duke wasn't asleep when she walked in his room. When she turned around, he got up. Placing his hand around her on her stomach, he leaned in. "What's the matter?" he whispered on her neck, his lips barely touching her.

"I'm sorry, I shouldn't be here." She closed her eyes and pulled the door open.

"Loren, why are you here?"

She swallowed, the minutes ticking by. Duke's breath was on her skin, buts his lips barely touched her neck and shoulders. "I don't know," she whispered. "I should go."

Duke slowly slid his hand across her stomach, across his children. Taking a step back, he let her open the door all the way. He watched as she opened the door and walked out, not turning around.

Loren made her way down the stairs, fighting the tears all the way to the yard. Like flood gates, they poured out of her. She made it halfway across the drive to her tiny house before she bent over sobbing. It hurt so much. *Why? Why am I doing this to myself? He is doing what I asked.* She felt so lost, so alone. Something she wanted months ago, something she worked so hard to achieve, and now, now she couldn't handle it. She couldn't take being alone. They should be happy. They should be sharing everything, and yet they did anything but. Casual conversations and deep kisses once in a while wasn't enough.

She brought her hand up to her mouth to cover her screams, her heart wrenching from the pain of not being with him. It was just like when she left. It was too much for her to handle. She went down on her knees. Burying her face in her hands, she bent so her head was nearly to the ground.

Duke dressed as fast as he could. He knew something was wrong. She was there alone, without Jaz. He ran out the door without his jacket. It was so dark out, and he took off across the drive. He nearly fell over her. He picked her up, pulling her to his chest.

"Oh, God, beautiful. What in the world is wrong?" He headed to her house.

Loren leaned into him, wrapping her arms around his neck. Duke got her in the house. Standing her up, he took off her coat. "Take your boots off." She did, and he picked her up and carried her to the loft. When he laid her down, he could see her pants were wet, so he gently pulled them off. Quickly, he went to cover her. As he pulled the blanket up, he saw her stomach for the first time. Sitting back on his heels, he couldn't take his eyes off of it. Loren moved her hands down, pulling her shirt up so he could see it all.

Duke was stunned; his children were in there. He looked at her, and she had tears streaming down her face. Then he looked back at her stomach. His whole world changed in that moment. It was as if a light bulb went off in his brain. The only thing that mattered was this woman and this incredible gift they were given.

"Oh my God," he whispered. "Oh my God, Loren."

She saw it happen. She saw him physically change. He raked his eyes up her body, locking them with hers. "Can you ever forgive me?" he whispered.

Loren sat up, climbing onto his lap and straddling him. "I need you. I'm so scared, Duke. I don't want to do this alone. I love you so much it is tearing me apart not being with you."

He closed his eyes. "Is that why you came over?"

Loren nodded. "I forgive you."

Duke kissed her, but it was a different kind of kiss. A kiss Loren had never had from him. A kiss that made everything else go away. It was gentle, loving, slow, perfect. Laying her down, he pulled away and took off his shirt and jeans, then he climbed under the covers with her in his arms. They laid on their sides looking at one another.

Loren closed her eyes. She was so tired. "Thank you."

Duke laid there looking at her beautiful face. His children were growing inside of her. She had dark circles under eyes from not sleeping. *She must be so scared.* The tears slipped from his eyes as he closed them, then fell asleep smelling his favorite scent, vanilla and strawberries.

Duke woke first with the light of the new day. A new day for him, a change within him. As he opened his eyes, he looked at the beautiful woman sleeping next to him. They had come full circle. He would not deny her anything anymore. Whatever she wanted, when she wanted it, whatever she needed. He smiled at the thought.

It took all that he had not to touch her. She needed to sleep. He quietly climbed out of the bed and grabbed his clothes then made his way downstairs. Jaz wanted to go out, so he opened the door and let her go. He made some coffee for himself and then proceed to make her breakfast. Bacon, eggs, and toast with a tall glass of orange juice.

After letting Jaz in, he made his way upstairs and set the tray on her little dresser. As he lay there next to her, looking at her, she opened her eyes.

"Good morning, beautiful," he whispered, moving the hair off her face.

"You're still here?"

He smiled. "I am, and I made you and our children some breakfast."

Her smile said it all for him. "You did?" Loren sat up and leaned her back against the wall.

Duke got up and got the tray. "I did." He set the tray on her lap.

"Mmm, bacon. I have this thing for bacon." She chomped on a piece.

"Is that because of the babies?" Duke picked up a piece.

"I think so. It's like, once I have some, that's all I want to eat."

"Loren, what's your favorite color?"

She smiled. "Yellow, what's yours?"

"Blue. What's your favorite flower?"

"I don't really have one. I love them all." He nodded and just sat there watching her feed his children, smiling. When Loren finished, he took the tray and set it on the floor before pulling her into his arms.

"I think it's time we had a very long, overdue talk." He smiled at her.

"I think you might be right."

"Okay then, let me start." Duke sat up, crossing his legs, and pulled Loren up to sit across from him. "Last night, you came over. Why?" She pulled her lip into her mouth. Duke reached up and gently pulled it out with his thumb. "We need to just put it out there, so we aren't dancing around this anymore," he said softly.

"I came over because I miss you. Because I'm scared, and I feel so alone it hurts. Why do you keep coming over here and kissing me, teasing me?"

He smiled. "Because I don't want you to think I don't want you. You were very clear on what you wanted from me. Has that changed?"

She nodded. "I think so. I mean, I am still struggling with trusting you. But I am so in love with you, and I am terrified you are going to shred me again."

"Fair enough. Well, I'm glad you are so in love with me, because I feel the same way. I, too, am terrified I am going to hurt you."

"Then why do you kiss me the way you do? Why do you tease me?"

Duke chuckled. "Because I'm a man, and I'm suffering from the worst case of blue balls any one man can suffer from."

Loren giggled. "You do know that's not a real thing?"

"I know. Why did you really come back here?"

"Because we are having babies, and I love you, and I want to do this with you."

"You said you wanted us to be a family?" She nodded. "Do you want us to live together while we are being a family?" She nodded, looking at him. "Loren," he whispered.

"Duke, you are the only person I feel completely comfortable with. I feel safe with you."

"Thank you, but that is not a reason to do this." He watched as tears filled her eyes.

"You don't want me?" she said so softly. Duke watched her shatter.

He shook his head. "Aww, beautiful, don't ever think that." He wiped her tears. "I want you so badly that it hurts. Please, don't ever think that. But I know what I did to you. I understand it all. I have been working on myself for a while now, trying to change so I can be the best father I can be. So I can be the best husband to you that I can be."

"You want to marry me?"

"With all that I am, yes, I do. You are the love of my life. There will never be anyone else. If I have to spend the rest of my life alone with a constant erection, then I will. No one will ever touch me again. Not after knowing the touch of your love. I was an idiot, an egotistical bastard. I can't apologize enough for the way I treated you. I can only work on myself so I make sure I never do it again. You are all that matters to me, you and these babies." He put his hands on her stomach. "Loren, I need to see you. I need for you to show me your body."

She got up on her knees and lifted her shirt to her chest. "I've been trying to wear tight shirts so you could see. I didn't know how to ask you to look at me. Our children are growing inside of me, Duke."

His eyes filled with tears. "So beautiful," he whispered as his hands held their children. He leaned forward and kissed her stomach, looking up at her. "I love you, beautiful."

Loren let go of her shirt and put her hands on his face, bending down so her hair surrounded them, and she kissed him as she climbed onto his lap. "I love you so much. I need you so much, Duke."

"Can we do this? Can we come back from what I did to you?"

She nodded. "I forgive you. I know you mean what you say to me. I know you won't hurt me again."

He wrapped his arms around her and laid her back on the bed, holding her. "I will never hurt you again. And if I am doing something stupid, you have my permission to smack me."

She laughed. "How about we do this? Instead of one of us leaving to think, we talk first. There isn't anything we can't say to each other. Deal?"

"Deal. Now, how about we go for a ride. I'm sure Cupcake could use a workout."

Duke laughed when her face lit up. "Really? You aren't going to police me?"

"No, beautiful, I'm not. Come on, put on some warm clothes. I'll run over to the house and put on my warm clothes, and I'll meet you in the stables."

She nodded.

DUKE WALKED OUT THE DOOR FEELING BETTER THAN HE HAD IN THE nearly five months since she left. He needed to take his time, and he knew it. Too much was at stake here. If she needed him, he would be there for her, even if his cock stayed hard for the next ten years. He was not about to cross that line again until he was sure that he could be the man she deserved.

He walked into the house, and Richard said, "So, you spent the night?" He wasn't happy, but he knew they needed to figure this out. "Sex is not the way to go, Duke."

Duke chuckled. "Dad, she needed me. She came here last night, and before I had a chance to talk to her, she ran out. I found her on the ground in the drive, crying so hard she could hardly breathe. I took her home and she asked me to stay. I did. Dad, while I took her soaking pants off and I was pulling up the blanket to cover her, it was the first time I saw her stomach. The first time I saw my children growing inside her. It changed me. We slept laying on our sides, not touching. When I woke up, I don't know, I felt different. Like the only thing that matters is them. This morning, we had a long talk. She needs me, and I am going to be there, no matter what she needs. We didn't discuss sex, but it isn't going to happen until I'm sure. I'm not sure yet, and I explained all that to her. She told me the same thing. So, there was no sex."

Richard smiled. "It makes me proud, Duke, that you are learning. Just stay strong for her as well as yourself."

"Thanks, Dad. Now, I need to change. We are going riding for a bit. Oh, and her favorite color is yellow, and she loves all flowers."

Richard laughed. "Good to know. Have fun."

Loren beat Duke to the stables and was getting Cupcake's saddle on when he walked in. "Okay, remember how I said I wasn't going to police you?" he said gently.

She turned and smiled at him. "Yes."

"Well, I lied. Let me do that for you, please. You shouldn't be lifting anything that heavy. Please, just humor me."

She giggled and handed him the saddle. "I am not going to argue with you. Besides, a girl could get used to this."

He dropped the saddle and grabbed her, pulling her to his mouth, kissing her deeply. "Good, because I plan on taking care of you for the rest of your life."

"You think?" she said with her smart mouth.

"No, baby, I know."

He let her go and saddled the horses. They didn't ride hard or long because the snow was deep. The horses got a good workout. Duke dropped Loren off at her house, and while she made hot chocolate and lunch, Duke put the horses up. When he finished, he knocked on her door.

She was smiling when she opened it. "You don't need to knock. In fact..." She turned and went to the drawer. When she turned around, she handed him a key. "So you don't have to knock anymore."

He stood there looking at the key. "You're giving me a key to your house?"

"No," she whispered.

Duke tilted his head to catch her eyes as she lowered her head. "Hey," he whispered to her, reaching up to turn her face. "Remember what we said upstairs? Talk to me, beautiful."

She wiped her tears and nodded. "You said you wanted to be a family."

He smiled a gentle smile. "You told me you wanted us to be a family. Loren, I do, too, more than anything, but I don't know that I can move in here with you yet."

She stepped back from him. Turning, she went up to the loft, buried her head in the pillow, and cried. Duke saw the pain in her eyes, the fear again. *God, am I ever going to get this right?* He turned and left. He needed to talk to his father.

"How was your ride?" Richard asked when he walked in the door.

"It was fine. Dad, I keep fucking this up. Why do I do that?"

Richard chuckled. "What did you do now?"

"Loren gave me a key to her house. I told her I didn't think I could move in with her yet. She ran up the stairs crying."

Richard looked at him long and hard. "And you're standing here talking to me?"

"Seriously, Dad, I don't want to rush this. I don't want to make the same mistakes again, not that I would ever make that mistake again. But I need to get myself in check."

Just then, Loren came rushing in the door. They both turned to look at her. "You want to talk? Well, I'm going to do some talking, Duke Reynolds, and you are going to shut the hell up and listen."

Richard smiled and Duke took a step back. She was pissed. "Leaving here made me so miserable that I cried for over a month. Then I had to come back here and save your ass, because the bitch who destroyed our relationship shot you and... well, I can't even tell you what that did to me. Then, two weeks after, when I was starting to get my balance again, I got a fucking phone call telling me I'm pregnant. Apparently, the cosmic universe has decided that we are bonded together. I came back here terrified to tell you that I am having a baby, our baby. And I'm terrified because I'm not so sure you want me like that. You never came for me. You just let me go.

"Then, yet again, the universe steps in and you discover me here and go all fucking caveman on me. I am finally at a place where I want to be with you, where I need you, where I want you with me, and you don't think it's the right fucking time.

"Well, let me tell you something." She lifted her shirt so he could see her stomach. "These are your children, too, and by being a jerk, you are missing everything. So, the way I see it, if you don't go up those stairs and pack your shit and move in with me, I'm leaving. You are missing it anyway, so what difference does it make if I am a hundred yards away or two thousand miles away?"

Richard chuckled. Duke just stood there looking at her. He opened his mouth a few times but nothing came out.

She raised her eyebrows. "Well?"

He nodded. He was speechless. He went upstairs and packed his stuff.

Richard smiled at her. "Sit down."

"Was that a bit brazen?"

He laughed. "Nope, it's exactly what he needed. A good swift kick in the ass. You all right?"

Loren put her head in her hands. "God, I don't know, Richard. I just know I can't do this like this anymore."

He put his hand on her head. "Aww, sweetheart, you two will be all right."

Raising her head, she whispered, "I hope so. I was so scared to say all that to him."

Richard busted out laughing as Duke came down the stairs.

"Can I say something?" Duke said.

Loren turned. "If it is any kind of rebuttal, then no."

Richard chuckled. "I'd be careful, boy."

Loren turned to Richard, smiling. "Oh, Richard, he is no boy."

Duke felt his face flush. "I'm standing right here."

"So, what did you need to say?" Loren turned to him.

"Nothing." He laughed. "You ready?"

Loren got up and kissed Richard on the cheek. "I'm making dinner tomorrow night, so tell the boys. We can have a nice meal as a family."

Richard nodded and watched them walk out of the house. Before they stepped off the porch, Duke grabbed her hand, turning her around. His other hand came up and wrapped around her head. He pulled her to his chest. "Did you enjoy yourself in there?" he whispered.

The heat of her breath spilled out on his lips. "Very much."

Duke kissed her. He kissed her deep and he kissed her hard. They walked hand in hand back to her house, back to their house.

CHAPTER SIXTEEN

DUKE AND LOREN HAD LUNCH, then he unpacked and went back to the house to get more stuff. He couldn't have been happier. This was what he wanted all along. He still wasn't sure it was the right thing to do yet, but she needed him and he needed her. After his third trip, Loren had set the table and they ate dinner.

She cleaned up while he unpacked and put everything away. Duke was still putting things away as she climbed the stairs. She pulled off her clothes, leaving just her t-shirt and panties on, and crawled into bed. When Loren closed her eyes, she fell asleep almost instantly.

When Duke finished, he left her to sleep. Going downstairs, he sat on the couch looking up at the loft. He was where he wanted to be; well, not really. He wanted to be naked lying next to her. But he knew she was exhausted. It seemed all she did lately was cry. All of this mess he made, he did this. She was right. He was missing everything because he used her for his own gratification. Shaking his head, he stood up and pulled off his shirt and jeans. He climbed the stairs and crawled into bed next to her.

Lying on his side, propped up on his elbow, he watched her breathing in and out. His hand moved on its own to touch her arm. Loren rolled over and tucked herself into his chest. Duke kissed her forehead and wrapped his arm around her. Laying his head down, he fell asleep.

LOREN WOKE UP TO THE FEEL OF WEIGHT ON HER SIDE, A HAND ON HER baby bump, and a smile on her face. She didn't want to move, but she needed to go to the bathroom. Gently, she slid out of his embrace and made her way down the stairs. When she came out of the bathroom, Duke was sitting on the stairs in his boxers. Loren just stood there looking at him.

Duke reached out, and she walked into his embrace. He pulled her to his chest. "I love you," he whispered in her ear, kissing her shoulder.

"Thank you," she said as she pulled back.

Duke smiled at her. "For what?"

"For staying with me. For not leaving in the middle of the night."

He chuckled. "You told me I had no choice."

She smiled. "You always have a choice. It was really hard for me to say those things to you. I wasn't sure you would come home with me."

"Aww, beautiful, there is no other place I want to be. I just don't want to hurt you again."

"Do you still think about her?" she asked.

"Loren, I never thought about her. What happened wasn't about her. It was about me, and taking from you what I wanted, and not caring about what you wanted."

"And now? Do you care about what I want now?"

He nodded, smiling, his hands leaving her waist and moving to her face. He kissed her. "I will not fail you again. You are my family; you are my life." He kissed her again. "And you will be my wife."

She giggled. "You are so sure of yourself, Mr. Reynolds."

"Oh, I am, indeed, Miss Mitchell."

"We need to eat and then get on the road. Today is the big day. You get to meet your children."

Duke looked into her eyes. They were deep purple and full of excitement. He knew this look; he wanted to take her back to bed and make love to her. But she was right. They had a big day ahead of them. He nodded and let her go. As she walked into the kitchen, he couldn't help but admire her perfect ass in her lace panties. Closing his eyes, he moaned. God, he wanted her.

"I'm going to jump in the shower."

"All right, I'll get breakfast going. Three eggs, right?"

He laughed. "Yes."

After they ate and Loren had showered, they were off—Duke, Loren, and Jaz. It was an uneventful drive. They talked and laughed all the way there.

Walking into the doctor's office, Loren said, "Hi, I'm Loren Mitchell. I'm here to see Dr. Miller."

The nurse smiled at her. "Oh, yes, Dr. Mitchell, please come on back."

Duke was shocked at how fast she was ushered into a room. She reached out and took his hand, pulling him along with her. They walked into a room. "Change into the gown and Dr. Miller will be in shortly," the nurse instructed.

Loren nodded and waited until she left, then started to take her clothes off. Duke stood leaning against the door watching her. When she was down to her bra and panties, he felt himself getting hard. Loren looked at him and giggled, whispering, "You should get that under control." She nodded to his erection.

He stepped forward. "I have no control over this." He pulled her closer, his hands reaching around her and landing on her ass. "I've had it since I met you." He watched as Loren blushed. He kissed her sweetly and then let her go, moving back to the door. Loren put on her gown and then removed her panties. Duke put his hand out for them. She smiled and handed them to him, watching as he put them to his nose and inhaled. His eyes never left hers. He watched as her pupils dilated and eyes turned purple. "Heaven," he whispered as he stuffed them in his pocket.

Loren swallowed and got on the table just as the doctor knocked on the door. Duke moved out of the way.

"Hi, I'm Dr. Kate Miller."

Duke looked at her. She was stunning. "Duke Reynolds, father." They shook hands. Loren watched, smiling.

Turning to Loren, she smiled. "Jenny called me. I can't believe you live up here, too. God, it's so good to see you. I've missed you. How are you?" Duke watched two women hug.

"I'm good, Kate. I didn't know you were here in Montana. When Jenny told me, I was so excited. I couldn't ask for a better doctor."

She laughed. Leaning in, Duke heard her say, "I followed a man up here. I loved it so much I stayed. It's so good to see you again. I heard about what happened to you. I am so sorry, but I'm glad you survived."

"Me too, so you've read my file?"

"I have, and I spoke to Jenny about it to great lengths. It's nothing short of a miracle, that is for sure. How about we get an ultrasound, and then I'll do a pelvic and we can have a chat in my office afterwards?"

"Sounds good to me," Loren said. She looked at Duke still standing by the door. "You ready to meet your children?"

Duke smiled as Loren reached for his hand. Stepping forward, he took it, entwining their fingers. He watched as the doctor put a paper sheet over her lower half and then lifted her gown. He couldn't help himself; he reached down to touch her stomach. His children were in there. When he looked back at Loren, his eyes were filled with unshed tears. She squeezed his hand.

Duke moved his hand and watched as the doctor squirted the gel on her stomach. "You ready?" Kate asked him.

He nodded. Then she put the wand on Loren's stomach. Duke could hear a thumping noise. "What's that?" he asked, looking at Loren.

"The baby's heartbeat." She smiled.

"Well, there you are," said the doctor.

Duke turned his head to look at the screen. It was a baby. "Oh my God," he whispered.

"And there is baby number two," she said.

Loren watched Duke, his eyes filling with more tears. He kept looking from her stomach to the screen.

"Do you want to know their sexes?"

His head snapped to Loren, and she nodded. "Yes, if you can," he whispered as the tears fell off his cheeks.

She was pushing buttons, taking measurements. "From the size of these two I would say that you are about eighteen weeks. Let's see. We are looking like perhaps your due date will be late March, early April." She paused, clicking more buttons. "Their hearts look good. Lungs seem to be developing." Duke's eyes never left the screen, and his grip on Loren's hand got tighter every time the doctor spoke. "Well, baby A looks to be a girl. And baby B…" She paused, moving the wand to the side of her belly. "Looks to be a boy." Loren laughed, and the babies moved. "Well, look at that," Kate said.

"What?" asked Loren.

"Laugh again."

Loren giggled and the babies responded. "Look at them. They like it when you laugh." She took the wand away and pushed a few more buttons. Pictures came out and she handed them to Duke. "Your children." Then he heard a click. Kate turned back to the machine. "A DVD of what we just saw." She looked at Loren. "I know this is an impossible pregnancy, and it will more than likely never happen again for you. So, I am going to need to see you every two weeks. You are a very tiny woman, and these babies are going to compromise your body, so any discomfort you feel, any strange pains, you call me. There is a helicopter here, so if I need to fly down, I will. Anytime, day or night, Loren. I mean it. Jenny would never let me live it down if we didn't do everything to give these miracles to you. Now, let's do the pelvic and we can get you dressed."

She moved the sheet over her stomach and put her legs in stirrups. Duke just stood there. He didn't want her to touch Loren down there. "I'm going to step out," he said. He couldn't handle watching it.

Ten minutes later, Dr. Miller walked out. "You can go back in now."

Duke nodded and walked back into the room. Loren leaned against the table. "I believe you have something that belongs to me, Mr. Reynolds."

He chuckled. "I don't know what you are talking about." He kissed her.

"Suit yourself," she said, pulling away from him and dropping her gown. She made sure her back was to him when she bent over to put on her pants. She felt his hands on her hips.

"Fucking beautiful," he whispered as he cupped her cheeks.

Loren laughed as she pulled up her jeans. Turning to face him, she said, "Would you mind handing me my shirt?"

When Duke looked down at her breasts, he closed his eyes and swallowed. "Fuck, Loren." He reached for her shirt and helped her put it on, not wanting her to cover herself.

After putting her boots on, she took his hand and smiled. "Come on, time to talk to Kate."

Like a little lost boy, he followed her out. After talking with Kate and setting up Loren's next appointment, they walked out hand in hand.

"How about we go get something to eat before we head back?"

"Sounds good to me, but are you sure you want men looking at my ass knowing I'm not wearing any panties," she said, giggling.

He pulled her up to him. "I'm all right with it, simply because," he grabbed her ass, "I know that this ass is going home with me."

Laughing, they got in the Jeep and headed to the restaurant where they saw each other for the first time. They had a lovely lunch and then headed home.

"I'm going to lie down. I'm a bit tired. Can you let Jaz in when she's done?" Loren said as she hung her coat up.

"Go on, I'll come up in a bit." He kissed her on the forehead then watched her climb the stairs. Duke waited for Jaz. Once he let her in, he went up to snuggle Loren. She was under the covers, so he took off his clothes and climbed in with her. Snuggling up behind her, he wrapped his arm around her and held his children. Closing his eyes, he fell asleep. When Loren opened her eyes, it was dark out. Looking at the clock, she saw it was nine at night. Giggling, she moved to get up, but Duke pulled her back.

"Don't leave," he whispered.

"I have to go to the bathroom. I'll be right back," she whispered.

Duke watched her crawl out of bed. She had put on another pair of panties, which made him chuckle to himself. When she came back, she crawled under the covers and snuggled up next to Duke. "I'm cold and tired."

"I'm tired," Duke whispered. "I haven't really slept since you left. This feels good." His hand moved slowly up and down her arm.

"I know, me neither. Thank you for today, for going with me."

"Aww, beautiful, thank you for giving me no choice. Loren, again, you managed to take my breath away. Seeing those babies inside you like that was like nothing I have ever known. Such a miracle to be able to do that." His hand slid across her belly. "I love you."

"I love you. Now, can we go back to sleep?" She moaned.

Pulling her close, he kissed her forehead. "Yes."

Duke woke first. He scooted out of bed to use the bathroom. Looking at the clock, he saw it was just coming up on six in the morning. They had slept nearly eighteen hours. He let Jaz out and then decided to make breakfast. She had to be hungry; he knew he was. Fifteen minutes later, he was climbing the stairs with a tray full of food. After setting it on the dresser, he climbed back in bed.

Loren snuggled up to him. "Mmm, is that bacon I smell?"

Duke laughed. "Yes, I made you breakfast."

Her head popped up. "Breakfast? We didn't have dinner yet. What time is it?" She turned her head. "Oh my God, we slept like eighteen hours."

"I guess you were tired."

She turned and looked at him. Smiling, she nodded. Duke sat up and grabbed the tray. Together, they sat on the bed eating, just looking at each other and smiling. When the last piece of bacon was gone, Loren laid on her back with her hands on her belly. "That was so good. I'm so full." She turned her head. "I thank you, and these babies thank you."

Duke laid on his side next to her. "May I?" He asked to touch her.

She nodded and moved her hands. Duke put his hand on her belly. Sliding down the bed, he kissed it. "Our children are in there," he whispered, moving around so he could put his head on her. "God, Loren, yesterday was so beautiful, seeing them. Do you have names picked out for them yet?"

Her hands were in his hair. "No, I thought we could do that together. Duke?" she whispered in her sexy voice.

He turned his head up. *Fuck,* he thought when he saw her eyes. "Yeah, beautiful?" She started to sit up. Duke pushed himself off of her belly and sat back on his heels. He watched as she lifted her shirt off. "Loren," he whispered, swallowing hard. "So fucking beautiful."

She got up on her knees and knelt in front of him. His eyes trailed down her body then back up it. Her breasts looked a bit bigger. Licking his lips, his eyes met hers. She had her lip in between her teeth. Loren moved her hands, placing them on his chest. Duke closed his eyes as fire moved through his body. Slowly, she moved them up to his neck, pulling him forward.

"Loren," he whispered as he kissed her.

"Duke," she whispered, looking into his deep green eyes. Her hands moving from his neck down his chest, she outlined each of his muscles. His cock was aching to be touched by her. When her hands reached the waistband of his boxers, she slipped them behind him. Her fingers glided under the band, and she slowly pulled them down. Duke raised up on his knees a little so she could pull them over his ass. As she moved around, she pulled the waistband over his erection. Duke watched her as she licked her lips. Pulling them to his knees, her tiny hands wrapped around him.

"Aww, fuck, Loren," he cried out, his body jerking from the sensation.

"Take them off, Duke," she said softly as she let go of him. He let her take control. He let her do this at her own pace. His boxers landed on the floor next to the bed. "You are so beautiful," she said as he knelt in front of her. Her hands started at his chest again, moving down his body to his hips, then onto his thighs. She pushed them apart, moving up to his balls. Gently, she cupped them. "So big," she moaned as she bent down to lick the bead of cum off his head. Not giving him time to assimilate, she covered his head with her lips, sucking him into her mouth. Not pausing, she continued to inhale him, further and further into her mouth. She pushed down with her head, taking him down her throat.

"Fuck," he whispered. His mind filled with the sensation of this beautiful woman and her love for him. When her nose touched his stomach, she swallowed and he let go. "Oh, God, Loren. Aww, fuck," he cried out, tears filling his eyes. Having this woman suck him was a religious experience. He pulsed and pulsed, filling her mouth time and time again, and she swallowed each and every drop of him. When she finished, she sat back on her heels and watched him quake.

As he lifted his head to look at her, she saw the tears on his face. Pushing herself up, she reached for his face, wiping his tears. "I love you," she whispered as she kissed him.

Duke managed to push himself up and wrap his arms around her, pulling her to his chest. They both moaned as they came in contact with each other. Wrapping his arm around her, he leaned her back on the bed. "You, beautiful crazy girl," he whispered as he moved down her body. His hands having a mind of their own, he cupped her rather full breasts. As his mouth moved in to suckle her nipple, he whispered, "So beautiful. Our children are going to feed off of these." He licked one then drew it in his mouth. "So hard," he moaned as his tongue wrapped around her huge nipple.

Loren moaned as her core heated. "Ah, Duke," she whispered, her hands moving to his hair. He moved on to the next one. He spent a long time sucking, nipping, and licking her nipples, squeezing and massaging her ample breasts. His mouth and body moved down hers to her stomach. Duke kissed her and held her belly.

Positioning himself between her legs, he slowly pulled her panties off. "Oh, God, baby, you are so wet."

"I want you," she moaned as his finger brushed through her hair.

"You have me. You've always had me." He groaned as he found her bud. "Aww, baby, look at you." He licked his lips as he bent down to take what she was giving him. "So good," he whispered as he drank her up.

He couldn't take it anymore. His tongue darted out, pulling her essence into his mouth, and he wrapped his lips around her. He felt her body jump off the bed as her orgasm ripped through her. He moved up her body while she shook and pushed so slowly inside of her. He didn't pause; he wanted to feel her pulse around him. When he reached her end, he stopped. "I love you, beautiful. Will you be my wife?"

"Yes," she moaned as he kissed her. "Yes, Duke."

Slowly, he made love to her. He didn't stop; even after he came, he was still hard. It was never ending, the two of them holding on, kissing softly, making love for such a long time. When she took him over the edge of reason the second time, he burst into tears. Loren held him.

"I can't believe I nearly lost you," he sobbed.

She shook her head. "You never lost me. I've always been yours. Always."

He kissed her deeply. "I'm so sorry, beautiful."

"I know, me too. Let's put it behind us. We have so much more to look forward to."

He nodded. Reaching for his jeans, he pulled her ring out of his pocket. He picked up her hand and slipped it back on. "I will never give you cause to take this off again. I want to marry you now. Today."

Loren kissed him. "Okay."

He laughed and kissed her again. When they finally separated, he reached for his t-shirt and cleaned her up. "I'm going to take a shower," she said with a smile.

Duke watched her get up and climb down the stairs. Laying there, he couldn't help but be happy. He followed her to the bathroom, and when he moved the shower curtain, he was instantly hard.

"You are so beautiful," he said as he stepped in.

Laughing, they tumbled out of the bathroom just as someone knocked on the door. "Who is it?" Loren called out.

"It's me, Richard."

Loren looked at Duke and busted out laughing, running toward the stairs. He grabbed her, kissing her. "Traitor," he whispered, letting her go. She threw down his jeans. "Hold on a sec, Dad," he yelled at the door. Loren laughed as she started to get dressed.

Duke opened the door. "Did I catch you at a bad time?" Richard asked, chuckling.

"Yeah, something like that." Duke turned to go up and get a shirt. Loren headed down and handed him one.

"Hi, Richard." She smiled at him.

"I haven't seen you two in a day or two, and I just wanted to make sure you were still breathing." He was looking at Duke.

Loren laughed. "Yes, he is still alive. Hey, we had a doctor's appointment yesterday. Would you like to see your grandchildren?"

Richard's eyes opened wide. "Really?"

Duke laughed. "I had the same reaction." He walked over to the counter and picked up the pictures. "This is your granddaughter, and this is your grandson."

Richard's eyes filled with tears. He looked up at Loren. "The greatest gift."

She smiled and hugged him. "I was wondering if you had a problem with the name I was thinking of for her."

"What name is that?"

"Well, I was thinking of Alison Catherine Reynolds."

Richard looked at her. "Really?" She nodded, looking at Duke who was fighting back tears. "That would be wonderful. What about the boy's name?"

Looking at Duke, she said, "William Richard Reynolds. So, she would be after your mother, and he would be after my father."

Duke nodded. "Our parents' names. I couldn't be happier."

"Nor I. I will tell you, though, I wasn't expecting this when I came over." Richard picked up Loren's hand.

"Well, I love him. Richard, we want to do it as soon as possible. Can we do it at your house, like as soon as my mom can get here?"

He pulled her into a hug. "Of course, you can. You sure you want to join this family?"

She laughed. "It's the only family that would have me. I need to call my mom." She grabbed her phone and went up to the loft. "Mom, I need you to come to Montana as soon as you can. Like tomorrow."

"What's wrong, sweetheart? You're back in Montana?"

Loren laughed. "It's really important, Mom. So, can you come?"

"Aren't you going to tell me what's going on?"

"No, so can you?"

"Of course, darling. We will be there in a few days."

"Great, let me know when. I love you, Mom."

"I love you, too, darling."

Loren smiled and hung up. "Duke," she called out as she was coming down the stairs. "We need to get a license. Can we go now?"

Duke laughed. "Yep."

Richard smiled. "What can I do?"

"Don't tell my mom I'm pregnant or that I'm getting married." She smiled at him.

"Not my story to tell," he said, laughing. "Well, I'm going to go. Come by for dinner. I'll have Derek bring pizza," he said as he walked out the door.

Duke looked at her. "You really want to do this now?"

Loren smiled. "Do you?"

He grabbed her up in his arms. "Fucking right I do." He smacked her on the ass. "Let's go."

They went to the town hall and got their license. If they wanted to, they could have gotten married right then and there.

"I can't do this without my mom," Loren said.

Nodding his head, Duke agreed. "I think my dad would kill us both."

They laughed and then went to find the judge. He agreed to come out to the ranch on Saturday to marry them. On their way back to the car, Loren said, "Can you give me a few minutes? I need to make a phone call."

Duke smiled at her, kissing her on the forehead, and got in the Jeep. Loren walked away and dialed her phone.

"Jenny, hi, it's Loren."

"Well, hi, I talked to Kate. She said you're doing fine and that your baby daddy is gorgeous."

Loren laughed. "Yeah, he is pretty special. Listen, I was wondering what you were doing this weekend."

"The same as every weekend. Spending it at home, watching chick flicks and eating ice cream. Why? What's up?"

"Well, I was wondering if you would be interested in being my maid of honor on Saturday."

"Oh my God. Seriously? I would love it. Oh, God, I can cancel my appointments on Friday. Shit, I don't have anything to wear. Crap, I need to go shopping. Okay, I'll cancel tomorrow as well. Where do you want me?"

Loren was laughing. "Calm down. I'm in Bozeman, Montana. You let me know what time and I will pick you up. You can wear whatever you want, but I was wondering if you wouldn't mind stopping by the ranch and picking up the dress."

"Oh my God, Loren, you still have that dress?"

"I do. I was going to have John send it up, but I realized that I don't have any friends up here. You are my oldest friend, and I don't have anyone else I can ask."

"Oh, shut up. Even if you had a million friends, I know you would ask me anyway. Hey, one question though. Does this guy have any brothers?"

Loren busted out laughing. Duke watched her with a smile on his face. "Um, yeah, he does. Three of them actually."

"No way. All right, for sure I am getting a new dress. Okay the dress is in your closet, same bag I'm guessing."

"Yes, so call me with the time. I love you. See you in a few days."

"I love you, too. Call John. I don't want to get shot."

Laughing, Loren said. "Next call I make. By, Jenny."

Loren hung up and called John to make sure Jenny could get in the house. When she got in the Jeep, Duke looked at her. "Everything all right?"

She leaned over, kissed him, and said, "It will be, come Saturday afternoon."

"So, you're not going to tell me anything?"

"Nope," she said and smiled. "Oh, wait, I need to go into Bozeman on Friday, but I am going to go alone. I'll take Jaz with me." He just smiled.

When they got back to the ranch, they went to see Richard. "Your mom and Aunt Liz will be here on Friday, in the evening. I'll go up and get them."

"Thanks, because we are having a wedding on Saturday. I'm going to go home and cook so we have food to eat, and you," she turned to Duke, "can pack some more of your things."

"Well, before you do that," Richard said, "I would like it if the two of you would take a ride with me."

Loren and Duke looked at him. "Sure."

They went out and headed toward Loren's land that Richard had given her. When they pulled up, Loren looked at Richard. "What is going on? I don't understand. I thought you gave this land to me."

Richard smiled. "I did. I wanted to give you a wedding present."

"Richard, this looks like the foundation for a house."

"It is. I don't think you are going to be able to raise two children in your tiny house. So, I wanted to do something for you both. It's just a foundation. I have an architect who is waiting for you to design a home that is perfect for the both of you."

Duke and Loren just stood there looking at each other and then at Richard. "Dad, you can't afford to build us a house."

Richard laughed. "You think you're the only one who invested their money?" He laughed. "Don't tell your brothers, but I have a hell of a lot more than you do, son." Duke just stood there looking at him. "So, what do you think? I'll make an appointment with Jim for Monday, and you can see his design and change it, or give him your own. This is my gift to you both."

Loren threw her arms around his neck. "Thank you," she whispered into his neck.

"Anytime. Come on, let's go. They boys should be over soon."

~

WHEN THEY GOT BACK TO THE HOUSE, LOREN SAID, "RICHARD, WILL YOU excuse us for a little bit?"

"Everything all right?"

She nodded. Taking Duke's hand, she led him back to her tiny house. When he closed the door, she turned around with tears running down her face. "What's wrong?"

"I don't want him to build us a house. I like my tiny house. I was miserable in my house in Austin. I was miserable on the ranch. I don't want a house, Duke. We can bring the babies home to this house."

"Aww, baby. We don't need to build a house."

"But he has everything laid out for a house. The only reason he hasn't poured the foundation is because it's too cold. Duke, I don't want to hurt his feelings. He is doing this because I'm pregnant. I don't want it."

He pulled her into his arms. "Loren, calm down. We don't need to accept this from him."

She wrapped her arms around him. "Will you talk to him? Will you tell him? I can't bear to see the hurt in his eyes."

Duke chuckled. "He will not be hurt. Come on, go wash your face and we will go talk to him." She nodded and went into the bathroom.

"You sure you want to marry a crazy woman?" she asked from the bathroom.

"With all that I am."

They walked back to the ranch house. "Dad, can we talk to you?"

Richard stood, and they all went into the kitchen. Loren started. "Richard, I just want to say thank you for the offer to build us a house. But I can't accept it. I don't want to accept it."

Duke stepped in. "Dad, we want to bring the babies home to the tiny house. We want to be a family there."

"To be honest, Richard," she squeezed Duke's hand, "I don't want a traditional house. I like that I can move my house whenever I want. I can," she looked at Duke, "we can go anywhere we want. We will manage with the babies, but we want to leave the offer on the table, just in case."

Richard smiled. "The offer stands. I just thought you might want something more permanent." He chuckled. "It's not a worry. Come on, let's get something to eat. Then we can talk about Saturday."

Duke squeezed her hand and they went back into the dining room. Dinner was a success, laughing, talking, and being a family. They discussed how the house would be set up, who would come, and the fact that Duke would, in fact, stay at the ranch house the night before. The boys all said goodnight, and then Duke and Loren headed back to their house.

Duke used the bathroom first while Loren let Jaz out. Then she went in. After she made her way up the stairs, Duke propped up on his elbow and watched her as she undressed. When she reached for her sleeping pants and t-shirt, he gently said, "Come to bed like that. I will keep you warm."

She smiled at him, crawling into the bed. "Why, Mr. Reynolds, are you planning on having your way with me?"

Kissing her, he whispered in her mouth, "You are so fucking beautiful." With her hair surrounding their faces, his hands moving up to cup her breasts.

"Duke," she moaned.

He laid her down, pulling her next to him, his hand resting on her belly. "I just want to hold the woman I love. Nothing more. In fact, I think we should wait until our wedding night to make love again."

Loren snuggled into him. "Mmm, okay. I love you."

He kissed her forehead. "I love you too, beautiful."

Loren's phone ringing woke Duke. Looking at the clock, he saw it was around midnight. He kissed her on the head. "Hey, beautiful, your phone is going crazy. Where is it?" he whispered.

"Mmm, on the counter. Just leave it," she whispered as she moved in closer to him.

Duke chuckled. "It rang twice. I'm going to go get it. What if it's important?"

"Hurry back." She moaned as her hand trailed down his chest. She watched him as he pulled the covers off his naked body. As he crawled to the stairs, she moaned. Duke turned to look at her. "You are so fucking beautiful," she whispered. "Hurry back."

He chuckled and went down and grabbed her phone then tossed it to her. "I'm going to use the bathroom."

She smiled at him as she turned her phone on. "What are you calling so late for?" she said as she saw the caller I.D. and dialed the phone.

"Oh my God, I looked up your groom. Are you fucking kidding me? I would have given my virginity to him," Jenny said.

Loren busted out laughing. "You do know it's like one in the morning, right?"

"Yeah, sorry, I think I had a bit too much to drink. I got the dress and one for me. So, do his brothers look like him?"

Loren giggled. "Similar, but no, he is one of a kind."

"Shit, I am so excited. Hey, is Kate coming? We could fix her up with one of them, too."

Giggling, Loren said, "Well, the two younger ones might be too young. Not sure how old they are."

"Doesn't matter, I have first dibs."

"You are so funny."

"I know, right. Okay, listen, I get in at like one in the afternoon. I am taking the earliest flight I can get."

"Great, I will see you there."

"Goodnight."

"Goodnight."

Duke was on his way up. He had heard her laughing and giggling while he was in the bathroom. "Should I worry about mysterious phone calls in the middle of the night? And the fact that my soon to be bride is lying in bed giggling."

Loren dropped her phone on the floor and got up on her knees, kissing him. Duke sat back on his heels. "No, baby, my heart belongs to you," she said as she kissed him. Her hands trailed along his shoulder, down his chest to his cock. "So hard," she whispered as her mouth moved to his neck. Her hand pushed his legs apart so she could touch his balls. "So soft," she whispered as her tongue swirled his belly button.

Lower, she moved her head. Duke moved her hair off her face so he could watch her. Wrapping her hand around him, she pumped him a few times.

"Oh, God, baby," he moaned.

"You like that?" she asked in her fucking sexy voice. Duke felt himself get harder.

"Yesssss…" he hissed out as she wrapped her mouth around him. Her hand slid up his stomach, pressing gently. He knew what she wanted. He put his hands back on the mattress.

Loren pulled back. "Look at you," she whispered. "So fucking beautiful, Duke."

He looked at her, with her lip pulled into her mouth. Her deep purple eyes. He knew what she wanted. Pushing off the bed, he wrapped his arms around her, pulling her onto his lap. Their kiss was deep and long. Duke wrapped his hands around her thighs, lifting her up, pulling her core to his chest. Loren's hair fell around his face as he lowered her onto him. "Fuck, beautiful," he moaned as she sheathed him. "So wet." When he was balls deep inside of her, she started to rock back and forth. "Oh, God, beautiful, take me with you."

She kissed him and he held her close to him. While she worked her hips on him, he could feel her bud rubbing on him. She was getting herself off, and he was loving every second of it.

"Duke," she cried out as she fell over the edge.

He wanted to go with her, but he held out, watching her come undone in his arms with her head back, her skin full of goose pimples. "You are so fucking beautiful," he whispered as he covered her mouth with his, pushing up into her as he did. Slowly, he made love to her like this. Lying her back on the bed, they made love for a long time. Loren tightened around him again. "That's it, beautiful, take me with you." Tighter and tighter she got, and he felt her push her stomach into his as she soaked him. Crying out his name, she came apart. "Aww, fuck," he yelled as he came undone.

Pulse after pulse, she hung onto him. "I've got you," she moaned.

She felt his body shudder. "Hey," she whispered, pushing up on his shoulders. "Duke?" He shook his head. "Hey." She put her hands on his face, pushing it up so she could look at him. "Baby, what's the matter?" He shook his head again. "Talk to me." She kissed his tears away.

"I can't believe I nearly lost you."

She smiled at him. "You never nearly lost me. I will always be yours. You just hurt me, but we're okay now. I will never be anyone else's, only yours. Forever yours."

He kissed her sweetly, deeply, lovingly. "Forever yours," he whispered into her mouth. Slowly pulling out of her, he wrapped her in his arms and held her close. Sleep took them both from exhaustion.

CHAPTER SEVENTEEN

WHEN DUKE WOKE at first light, he smiled. In two days, she was going to be his wife. They were going to have a wonderful life together. Just the four of them and Jaz. Loren stirred in his arms, her lips wrapping around his nipple. Chuckling, he whispered, "You are insatiable."

"It's the hormones. I just want you inside me all the time."

Duke pulled her on top of him. "Is that right?"

She nodded as she sat up. "It is."

"God, Loren, you are fucking beautiful," he said as his hands held her stomach then moved up to cup her breasts. "They are getting bigger. I'm not sure I like that."

She busted out laughing. "Most men like huge boobs."

"I love yours. They fit perfectly in my hands. Just enough, but now they don't fit." He pouted.

She giggled. "Well, then in a month or two you are going to hate them. Because they are going to get huge. But they will go back to normal."

His hands moved back to her stomach. "Our children will feed off of them. So beautiful."

Loren felt him getting harder as he touched her body. "Duke," she whispered, drawing her lip into her mouth. She leaned down to kiss him, sliding herself along his erection to the tip. She pushed back taking him in her.

"Aww, fuck," he moaned.

She pushed herself up, taking him deep inside of her. "Oh my God, Duke. You are so deep like this." Her hips rocked back and forth.

He forced his eyes to stay open so he could watch her. His eyes raked over her body as she rolled her hips. So tiny, her belly growing, her breasts so full. He couldn't stop himself. It shocked him how quickly he came.

"I feel you," she moaned. "I feel the heat of you. Oh, God, Duke, I'm coming, too."

Duke sat up, wrapping his arms around her, kissing her. "I love you, beautiful."

"I love you."

They kissed for some time until Duke pulled back. "Why don't you go take a shower and I'll change the sheets and make us something to eat."

"We are both a mess. Why don't you join me?"

He smiled. "You don't have to ask me twice."

When they got out, they both went upstairs to get dressed. Then they stripped the bed. "You're sleeping at your dad's tonight."

"What if I don't want to?"

She giggled. "You'll be fine." She kissed his lip.

"Come on, beautiful, let me make you breakfast."

They gathered the sheets and Duke carried them downstairs. Loren got them in the washer while Duke started cooking. They were falling into a simple routine. She would walk past him, touching him lightly. He would do the same. After they ate, they cleaned up and then went up to make the bed. As they finished, Duke pulled her into his arms, and they fell onto the bed. "I don't want to sleep at my dad's," he whispered into her mouth as he kissed her.

"When you leave here in a few minutes, you won't see me again like this until tomorrow night. You will be fine."

Shaking his head, he said, "No, I won't." He pulled her close.

She giggled. "I have to go. I am bringing food over later tonight, so you will see me then."

"Yes, but I won't be able to do this." He slipped his hand down her jeans.

"Mmm, Duke," she whispered. "If you don't stop, I'm going to be late." She gently and reluctantly pulled his hand out of her pants. "I love you," she said as she kissed him. Then she crawled out of the bed and headed down the stairs.

After putting on her boots and coat, Loren grabbed her keys, wallet, gun, and phone off the counter. "I'm going. I love you."

"Be careful. Call me when you get there," Duke yelled down.

"I will. Bye."

DUKE GOT UP AND HEADED OVER TO THE RANCH HOUSE. "HEY, DAD, PUT me to work."

He laughed. "Where's Loren?"

"She is on some secret mission. She wouldn't tell me what was going on."

Richard laughed. "Well, your brothers will be here soon, then we can start moving the furniture out of here. I thought we could hang some of those Christmas lights around the room. Jordon is bringing some chairs out. I've got to head into Bozeman around four to get Cathy and Liz."

His brothers showed up and they got to work.

LOREN PULLED UP IN FRONT OF THE AIRPORT TO SEE JENNY WALKING out carrying her dress. She jumped out of the truck. Jenny squealed and they hugged like teenagers. After they loaded everything in the truck, they headed to Kate's office.

"God, I can't believe you are getting married."

Laughing, Loren said, "I can't believe I'm pregnant and getting married."

When they pulled up in front of Kate's office, Jenny ran in and got her. The girls laughed and talked about old times.

"So, you met this mysterious Duke Reynolds?" Jenny said to Kate.

"Oh my God. He is gorgeous. I might be jealous if he didn't look at her the way he does."

"And just exactly how does he look at me?" Loren asked, laughing.

"Like you are lunch."

They laughed all the way back to the ranch. As they pulled in, Loren noticed all the trucks parked about. "Looks like all the boys are here."

Jenny sat up in her seat. "Well, tell me where to go."

They laughed. "Let's get everything in the house first. Then we can carry over all the food I made, and I can introduce you to everyone. My mom should be here tonight. Richard is going to pick her up at the airport."

She pulled up to her tiny house. "Oh my God, I love it," Kate said.

They all climbed out and made their way into the house. Loren hung the dress in the back of the kitchen by the washer and then showed them her place. "We can all sleep up there in the loft."

"Is it big enough?" Jenny said as she headed up the stairs.

"It better be. Wait until you meet Duke. The man is huge." Kate laughed.

"Oh my God, get up here, Kate. Check this out. It's freaking huge. I can kind of stand up."

Loren laughed while they checked stuff out. She took everything out of the fridge and freezer and set it on the counter. She picked up her phone to text Duke.

~Hi, baby, I'm home. Can you and Derek come over and help me carry some stuff?~

A few minutes later, the door opened just as Kate and Jenny were coming down the stairs. Duke walked in and then Derek. Loren heard Jenny say 'fuck me' when she got a good look at him. Duke smiled at her. He had heard her as well.

"Jenny, Kate, this is my soon to be husband, Duke, and his brother, Derek."

Duke looked at Loren and smiled. "The Jenny who operated on you?"

"The one and the same," Jenny said as she stuck her hand out to shake his. But when Derek stepped out from behind Duke, she stopped breathing.

Loren was looking at Derek, and the look on his face was the same one Duke had on the first time they met. Jenny forgot to let go of Duke's hand while she stood there speechless.

"I'm Derek," he said to her.

She just nodded.

"Well, I'm Kate, her doctor and college roommate."

"All of you went to Harvard?" Derek asked.

"We did, all of us top in our field. But Loren is by far the smartest. She left us in just three years. We've stayed friends until the... Well."

"Okay, there will be time for all of this later." She didn't want Derek to have too much information. "Can you guys take some of this food?" She handed a huge baking pan to Derek, and then one to Duke.

"I'll come back for more," Duke said to Loren. He reached up and wrapped his fingers around her neck, pulling her to him. "I missed you," he whispered on her lips, kissing her.

She felt her face flush. He watched her eyes turn purple. Smiling, he turned and walked out the door following Derek.

"Are you fucking kidding me right now?" Jenny blurted out. "Holy shit."

Loren and Kate busted out laughing. "I told you," Kate said.

Shaking her head, Loren said, "We will have plenty of time to talk about this. Right now, we need to get this food over there. But wait until you see the other two brothers. The genes are strong in this family."

"I need to move up here," Jenny said, turning to Kate. "You got any openings where you work?"

"Just a receptionist position."

They all laughed. A few minutes later, the door opened. "Ladies," Duke said.

Loren handed him another pot. "We're right behind you."

"I'll wait. We can walk over together."

The girls got their coats and boots on, each taking a giant bowl. Duke held on to Loren as they trekked across the drive to the ranch house. Kate and Jenny giggled like school girls.

"Wait until you see what we did," Duke said.

"No, I don't want to see. I want to be surprised. I'm going to close my eyes. Will you lead me to the kitchen?"

Duke laughed. "Of course. I'll have the boys hang sheets up so we can at least sit in the dining room."

"Sounds good to me."

"So, the girls were a surprise."

Loren laughed. "We've been friends for years. But when... well, we kind of lost contact. Now, Kate is in Bozeman, and well, Jenny, she is a free spirit."

"Yeah, I would keep an eye on her. Derek is drooling."

Loren busted out laughing. Kate and Jenny stopped walking and turned around. "What's so funny?" Jenny asked.

Still laughing, Loren said, "Oh, you'll see."

They turned and kept walking. Loren leaned in and whispered to Duke, "I think you should keep an eye on Derek. I know Jenny, and she is going to chew him up and spit him out."

Now, Duke busted out laughing as they walked up the steps. He opened the door for them, and Kate and Jenny went in first. Loren closed her eyes and Duke guided her in. She stood still as he took her bowl, setting it on the table. He came back and took off her boots and coat and then picked her up. As he was walking toward the kitchen, he said, "Joe, Alex, can you get some sheets to hang up? Loren doesn't want to see anything until tomorrow."

"You got it," they both said.

He carried her into the kitchen and sat her down. "You can open your eyes now," he said in his sexy voice only for her. Kate and Jenny stood there and watched them. Loren opened her eyes to see his perfect green ones looking at her. His hand moved up to run along her cheek. Duke watched her eyes dilate, his heart slamming into his chest when they turned deep purple. He couldn't stand it anymore, so he kissed her. "I can't wait to make you my wife," he whispered to her.

"I can't wait to be your wife," she whispered back.

Richard cleared his throat, and they smiled. Loren turned to see Kate and Jenny wipe their eyes. "Oh my God, I'll have one please," Jenny said.

Loren giggled, moving toward her. "Sorry, but I told you he was one of a kind."

They all laughed. Loren hugged Richard and proceeded to tell him what she had made and how to cook it all. "But my mom will be here, so she will know."

"Speaking of which, I'm going to have to go pretty soon to pick them up."

"Can you drop them off at our house first? I'll walk them over."

"Not a worry," Richard said.

"Oh, and tomorrow night, do you think Jenny and Kate can stay here?"

"Don't worry about tomorrow. Everything will work itself out. Now, I have to get going, but I should be back around six."

Loren hugged him. "Thank you, Richard."

He chuckled. "Nonsense. Now, have some food and I will see you tomorrow."

"Hey, I haven't had time to ask you, but will you give me away?"

Richard smiled. "I would be honored. But I'm not giving you away. I am welcoming you to this family."

She smiled and nodded. When he walked out of the room, Duke came up behind her, leaning down to kiss her neck. "Sometimes, I think he loves you more than he does me."

"Don't be silly, he just loves me differently."

"I suppose."

"God, can you two be any cuter?" Jenny said, smiling at Loren. "I am so happy for you."

Loren stepped from Duke's arms into Jenny's, then Kate joined in.

"I love you guys, and I am so sorry I became a nut job and let our friendship fall away."

"Don't be silly," Kate said. "Shit happens."

They all laughed. Duke moved out of the room as they hugged.

Derek was sitting at the dining room table. "What's the long face for?" Duke asked him.

"Nothing," Derek answered.

"Dad told him that Loren's friends were off limits." Alex chuckled.

Duke laughed as he bent down and whispered in Derek's ear, "I know for a fact that she wants you. Just don't fuck with her. She is one of Loren's oldest friends, and the woman is the reason I am going to be a father. She isn't the fuck em' and leave em' kind. She's the keepin' kind."

Derek chuckled. "I need to talk to you."

The kitchen door swung open, and Duke patted him on the shoulder. "Later." Derek nodded as the girls walked in.

"So, who's hungry?" Loren asked. The guys just looked at her and laughed.

Derek spoke up. "Dad had me grab a bunch of food from town. He said you shouldn't have to cook the night before your own wedding." He stood. "I got a little bit of everything from Millie's. It in the oven on warm."

Loren smiled. "Thank you, Derek." Looking at Duke, she said, "It's a good thing because these babies are starving."

Jenny put her arm through Loren's, and Kate did the same. "Come on, kids, let's feed your mama," Jenny said, and they headed back to the kitchen.

All in all, they had a great time. Duke walked them back to the tiny house. At the door, Kate and Jenny went inside.

Duke pulled Loren into his arms. "I won't survive tonight. I'm not going to be able to sleep without you."

Loren giggled softly. "You'll be fine. I love you, Mr. Reynolds. I will see you at four o'clock."

He kissed her. "I'll be waiting, Dr. Mitchell. I'll be the one in the suit."

"Mmm, can't wait to see how well you clean up."

Duke laughed. "Goodnight, beautiful." He kissed her deeply.

"Don't drink too much." She smiled.

"Never again. The last time I got drunk, you left me."

She put her hand on his face. "It's in the past. We've only the future to look forward to. I love you." She pulled away from him.

He didn't want to let her go. He never wanted to let her go. "Goodnight, beautiful."

She looked up at him with blazing purple eyes. "Goodnight, Duke." Turning, she walked into the house and closed the door.

DUKE WALKED BACK TO THE HOUSE. DEREK SAT AT THE DINING ROOM table. "Where are the boys?" Duke asked him.

"They took off. It's just us. Can we talk?"

Duke chuckled as he headed to the kitchen to grab a few beers. Derek followed him and sat at the table. "I think I know how you felt when you saw Loren for the first time. Duke, that woman is fucking beautiful."

"To be clear, we are talking about Jenny, right?"

Derek chuckled. "Oh, yeah." He took the beer from Duke. "How the hell do you talk to someone that beautiful?"

"Well, if you want my advice, I suggest you put all your bullshit pickup lines away and grow a pair. She is so far out of your league. She is an obstetrician, top of her field. She is the reason Loren is pregnant. Apparently, Kate is the same. Jenny is a surgeon, though, and I'm not sure if Kate is. But the girl is wicked smart."

Derek sat there staring at the bottle in his hands. "I haven't had a conversation with a woman in a long time. It's all been about sex. How the hell do you do it?"

"Just let it happen. That is what happened with Loren. I forgot that she was the person I loved. I made it about sex, about having the virgin, about getting off. I nearly lost her. She is a person with feelings and thoughts. Thoughts that matter to me. If you just want sex with Jenny, then make sure she knows that is all it is. What do you want?"

Derek laughed. "I want the sex. Hell, who wouldn't? But, I don't know, there was something in that girl's eyes. Something a bit deeper than just sex. I'm fucking nervous."

Duke chuckled. "Yeah, I know that feeling. Listen, just let it happen. I know she was stunned into silence when she met you. Maybe she might want to chat. Just be careful, man. I don't want you to fuck up and use Loren's oldest friend. I know you two are adults, but you know sort of what Loren went through. Just be kind."

"So, you're getting married tomorrow?"

"I am, and I couldn't be fucking happier. I saw the babies in her belly the other day. It was fucking incredible. Just knowing they are inside her, growing, becoming babies. We aren't ever going to get another chance to do this. She shouldn't be pregnant. I guess Jenny is better than anyone knows."

"Either that or Mom's looking out for you."

"We are naming our daughter Alison Catherine and our son William Richard, after Mom and Loren's dad."

Derek nodded. "So, one of each?" Duke nodded. "Dad wants to build you a house."

"Yeah, but we turned him down. For now, we are going to bring them home to the tiny house."

"Is that place big enough?"

Duke laughed. "It would shock the shit out of you if you knew what's in that place."

"Not that I want to know, but what's it like in that loft. Do you even have any head room?"

Duke laughed. "Oh, God, yeah, she has a dresser up there. Storage in the floor on either side. I can kneel without hitting my head. The place is so spacious."

They heard the door open. "Anyone here?" Richard yelled.

"Yeah, Dad, we're in here," Derek yelled.

"Come help me with these bags." They both got up and walked out.

"I dropped Cathy and Liz off over at your place. Take them up to Alex and Joe's rooms."

"We left some food for you in the oven," Duke said as he grabbed a suitcase.

"Thanks." Richard smiled and headed to the kitchen.

LOREN WAS IN THE BATHROOM WHEN THE KNOCK ON THE DOOR CAME. She heard Jenny squeal when she saw her mom. Kate, too. Loren walked out and her mother turned to look at her.

"Hi, Mom."

Cathy's eyes nearly popped out of her head, "Oh my God. Sweetheart, how?"

Loren giggled. "Mom, really, you don't know how to get pregnant?"

Her mother pulled her into her arms. "I know, silly, but how are you?"

Jenny answered, "We aren't sure. But we aren't going to argue the point."

"Mom?" Loren pulled away. "I wanted you to come because I am going to marry Duke tomorrow. We are going to have twins."

Her mother's eyes filled with tears, tears of happiness for her daughter who had been on death's door. "Your father would be so happy."

"I know." Loren wiped her tears.

They visited, and then Loren walked them back to the house. She stayed for a few minutes. "I will be over in the morning to help you get ready," her mother said.

Loren smiled and hugged her.

Duke grabbed Loren's hand. "Come on, beautiful, I'll walk you home."

Hand in hand, they made their way back to their house. "I can't wait to be your wife."

"I can't wait to be your husband."

They kissed goodnight at the door and Loren went in. "I'm tired, you guys."

"Me too, I was up late," Jenny said and laughed.

"Yes, I know. Come on then. I think our bed is beyond big enough for us all." She climbed the stairs first. "Can I use the bathroom first? I really need to pee." She grabbed her shorts and t-shirt.

"Go for it, Mom," Kate said as she dug through her bag.

CHAPTER EIGHTEEN

LOREN WOKE to the sounds of whispers downstairs. Giggling, she got up and sat on the stairs. Jenny and Kate were whispering and having coffee.

"What's a girl got to do to get some coffee around here?"

They both looked up at her. "It's your wedding day." Jenny smiled at her.

Climbing the rest of the way down, she said giddily, "I know." Making her way to the kitchen, she made herself a cup of decaf. "Okay, who is hitting the shower first?"

They both looked at her. "You have the most hair and it will take the longest to dry, so you go," Kate said.

"I won't argue that, but I'm just going to blow dry it. So, feel free. I kind of just want to sit here for a bit. It's the last day I am going to be single."

Kate went first, then Jenny. Loren went last. Her mom came over with her Aunt Liz, and they all wanted to make her up, but she put her foot down. "I don't need make-up, or my hair done. Duke likes me just the way I am. Besides, that's not me. I will put on some mascara and lip gloss, but that's it."

"What about your hair, honey?" her mom asked.

"I'm just going to blow dry it and leave it down."

"And a dress. Did you get a dress?" Loren and Jenny looked at each other and laughed. "Not the dress from home?" her mother said.

"Yep, the dress."

"Oh, honey, is that appropriate? It's been in that closet since you left for Harvard."

"Mom, I saved my money all summer to buy that dress. It's the dress I wanted to wear when I married the man of my dreams. He is the man of my dreams. I am so wearing the dress."

Shaking her head, Cathy said, "Sweetheart, it's not a proper wedding dress."

"Mom, I'm nearly five months pregnant. There is nothing proper about today, except for the fact that I am going to marry a man who is totally and utterly in love with me, as I am with him."

"I suppose."

When three-thirty came, and it came fast with all the chattering and remembering, Loren took her dress and went into the bathroom. As she opened the cloth bag, her eyes filled with tears. She remembered standing in front of the store looking at the dress. Every day, she went to look at it. Every job she did, she would put her money away. Three hundred dollars was a lot of money for a fourteen-year-old. But she wanted it, and she worked all summer doing whatever she could to get the money to buy it.

Taking it off the hanger, she admired the beadwork on it. Each crystal bead was hand sewn so delicately on the white lace. She only ever put it on once, and that was the day she bought it. She had to try it on, making sure she got it a size bigger than she wore because she knew she would grow into it.

Closing her eyes, she stepped into it and slid it up her body, praying her boobs weren't too big for it as she brought the straps around her neck to fasten the little buttons. When she opened her eyes, she smiled. It fit perfectly. You couldn't even see her little bump, but her boobs looked spectacular in it. Turning, she looked at the back; it was open to the top of her butt. The white lace panties she had on were just enough. She could see the dimples at the top of her butt.

"Oh my," she whispered to herself. Then she giggled. "He is going to lose his mind." The train on the dress was just long enough that she wouldn't kill herself walking. Reaching in the bag, she pulled out the white ballet slippers she bought to go with it. They had the same crystals sewn onto them.

Taking a deep breath, she walked out of the bathroom. Everyone stopped talking and looked at her. "My God, you are stunning," Kate whispered.

"He is going to lose his mind when he sees you." Jenny walked up to her and hugged her. "Fucking gorgeous," she whispered.

"Okay, Mom, you guys go over and let them know we are ready."

"Oh, darling, you look beautiful."

"Thank you." Loren kissed her.

When her mother left, Loren looked at Jenny. "Did you bring it?"

She giggled. "You know I did. I can't believe you are going to do this."

"I don't want him to see my dress until it's time for him to see it, or anyone for that matter."

Jenny pulled a long black cape out of her bag, wrapping it around Loren. It went to the floor. "Okay, are we ready?"

Loren nodded. "I need to put on Duke's boots so my shoes don't get dirty. You guys are going to have to help me." Just as she said it, there was a knock on the door. Loren yelled out, "Who is it?"

"Derek. Duke wanted me to come and carry you over to the house. Something about not getting your dress dirty."

"Oh my God, that's so sweet," Jenny said as she opened the door.

Jenny pulled the cape around Loren so he couldn't see her dress. "Thank you, Derek, but I think we've got this."

"Come on, Loren, you know how he is."

She shook her head. "It doesn't matter. I've got this. Just go and make sure everything is ready. The minute you are in the house, we are coming over."

"He isn't going to be happy."

Jenny laughed. Leaning in, she whispered, "You want to bet on that?"

Derek smiled at her. "I might." He chuckled and walked out the door.

"Damn, he looks just as good walking away." She looked at Loren. "I am seriously going to have a difficult time not sleeping with him."

Loren laughed. "Just wait until I'm gone. I don't want to see it."

They all laughed. "Okay, he went around the corner. You ready?"

Loren gathered up her dress and slipped on Duke's boots. "Ready. Come on, Jaz."

The four of them made their way to the house. On the porch, Loren took off Duke's boots. "Go in and make sure the sheets are closed."

Kate went in, coming right back out. "They are. Now, come on. Richard is waiting for you."

Loren took a deep breath and walked through the door, turning her back to the sheets while Kate and Jenny went in. Looking up at Richard, she smiled. "You ready?"

He chuckled. "Are you?"

"Yes, I need to walk in like this. When we get past the sheets, I need for you to turn and remove my cape."

"Got it. Oh, Duke got these for you."

Richard handed her a bouquet of wildflowers. "Oh my God, where did he get these?"

"Don't know. You ready? He is waiting for you."

She nodded and they turned. She put her head down and they walked through the sheets. Richard stopped and did what Loren asked him to do. She heard the oohs as he dropped the cape on the floor. When Loren turned, Duke was standing ten feet from her. "Fucking beautiful," he said.

She smiled, shaking her head. He had on a black suit with a white shirt and a black tie. Richard walked her up to him. Loren didn't see anyone but him. She didn't realize that there were at least thirty people sitting in chairs. She didn't hear the gasps as she passed the people. She didn't notice the hundreds of twinkling lights that lit up the room. She didn't see anything but him. When she reached him, his hands came to her face, his thumbs wiping her tears, and he kissed her. "Fucking beautiful," he whispered on her lips.

"Right back at you," she whispered back.

The judge cleared his throat. "Loren and Duke have decided to forgo the traditional ceremony and want to speak from their hearts."

Loren looked into his eyes. "After everything that happened to me, I never believed that I was good enough to be loved. I had resigned myself to the fact that it would be just me and Jaz. But then one day, sitting in a restaurant, I looked up, something I hadn't done in a long time. But, that day, I looked up and my life changed. It was these beautiful eyes," she reached up to touch his eye, "that saw me. You showed me in every possible way that I am worth something. That I am worthy of love, and you gave it to me with no restraint. You saw me for me, not the marred woman I am. Now, I stand here before you, pledging my love to you for the rest of my life. You are the first man I have ever loved. You are the first man I have known. I am yours. You own my heart, my mind, my body, and I give you my soul today, bonding us forever. I love you, Duke Reynolds, and I wed thee." She reached up and wiped the tears from his cheeks, gently kissing him.

Duke took a deep, shuddering breath. "That day in the restaurant, that was the day I knew my life was going to change. I thought I knew what love was." He chuckled. "Boy, did I have it all wrong. I nearly lost you. I did lose you for months, but you came and you saved my life. You stayed with me, loving me. I've never known a love like this. I never want a day without it. You blow my mind every day with your strength. I've never known someone so strong, so fierce, so independent, so beautiful, and so perfect. You are right; I see past everything, past the scars, because there is nothing to see but you. You are incredible, and I feel honored and privileged to be loved by you. You are worth everything to me. You are the air I need to breathe. You are the sun on a cloudy day. It is my honor to take you as my wife, to love you beyond this life. I am yours. You own my heart, my mind, my body, and I give you my soul today, bonding us forever. I love you, Loren Mitchell, and I wed thee." He reached up and wiped her tears, kissing her gently on the lips.

The judge wiped his eyes. "Do you have rings?"

Duke smiled and put his hand out. Derek dropped two rings in his hand. He handed one to Loren. Taking her hand, he slipped the wedding band on her finger. "I love you."

She took the ring he gave her and slipped it on his finger. "I love you."

"By the power vested in me by the state of Montana, I declare you husband and wife. Duke…"

He didn't finish; Duke pulled her into his arms and kissed her. Everyone wiped their eyes and cheered. Smiling, he pulled back a bit. "You look fucking gorgeous," he whispered.

Before she could say anything, they were surrounded by people, hugging them, congratulating them. Loren hadn't realized that all these people were here. She looked around at what a fantastic job they all did. Duke stood and watched her. As everyone started to move into the dining room, Loren turned to Duke.

"You did this?" she whispered.

"It was Dad's idea, but yeah, we did this."

"Duke, it's beautiful."

His hand came up and touched her face. "Nothing compares to you. Until you walked in the room, it was just a room. Now, it's more beautiful than ever. And this dress… Fuck, Loren." Leaning in, he whispered, "I was so hard last night. I finally got myself under control and you walked in. Just so you know, I got married with a raging hard-on."

Loren busted out laughing as Duke pulled her closer, kissing her temple. She got up on her tippy toes and whispered in his ear, "My panties are soaked." She nibbled his earlobe.

"You are killing me slowly. You know that, right?" His hands on her hips, he slowly trailed them up her spine. "Loren," he whispered, covering her mouth with his. When he pulled back, looking into her eyes, they were deep purple. "Fuck," he moaned.

Loren pulled her lip into her mouth. Leaning into him, she smiled and whispered, "Yes, please."

Duke chuckled, closing his eyes. It was Richard who interrupted their little tease. "Come on, don't hog the bride. There are some people who would like to congratulate the both of you."

Loren busted out laughing, knowing damn well Duke had a raging hard-on. She turned in his arms, standing directly in front of him. Her hands went to rest on his thighs. Smiling, she said, "Could you give us a minute, please?"

Nodding his head, he gave Duke a strange look and walked away.

Duke leaned down and kissed her neck. "Thank you."

She just giggled. "You need to get this," her hand slipped behind her, grabbing his cock, "under control. We have a room full of people we need to entertain."

Duke chuckled. "Well, if you don't get your hand off of me, we'll be doing it with a huge wet spot on my pants."

Loren giggled and stepped forward, releasing him. She gave him a minute, and he adjusted himself. Touching her on the shoulder, he whispered, "Okay, I think I've got this."

"I love you, Duke Reynolds."

"I love you, Loren Reynolds."

Together, they walked out into the dining room. The evening was wonderful. They ate, they laughed, and they shared their day with the people who mattered to them. Loren wandered into the living room to find Joe sitting by himself. She sat down next to him.

"You are stunning in your dress." He smiled at her.

"Thank you, and can I ask why you are here alone?"

He chuckled. "Didn't have a date."

Loren looked around, making sure they weren't overheard. "Why is that?"

Joe smiled. "Not sure what you mean."

"Why isn't Steven here with you?"

Joe looked at her, terrified of what she'd just said. "I don't under-stand." He needed to play dumb. Coming out at his brother's wedding is not what he wanted.

"I've seen the two of you together. I ride this ranch. Well, I rode this ranch every day for three months. Two people with that much passion should be together."

Joe felt his face turn red; he was in shock. "You haven't told them, have you?"

She shook her head. "No, but Joe, you should. They love you. It'll be all right."

He whispered, "You've seen us?"

She smiled. "More than I should have. I'll admit that I sat and watched you two. I've never seen love like that. It was so beautiful. How long have you been together?"

"Three years. They wouldn't understand. In case you hadn't noticed, we are a very traditional family."

"Does his family know about you?"

He shook his head. "No, no one does."

She bumped his shoulder. "I do."

"Well, thank you for not outing me."

"It's not my place. It's yours. But, can I just say that I'm pretty sure your father already knows. He has a way about him." She giggled. "I think today is a good day to share this great love with your family. Call him, tell him to come. I'll stay and be your support."

Joe just sat there looking at her. "I can't," he whispered, terrified at what his brothers would think of him.

"Yes, you can. It's not fair that he isn't here to share your family with you. How about as a wedding present to me? I am, after all, your new big sister."

He laughed. "So I should expect to be bossed around?"

She laughed. "Yes. Now, call him."

Duke stood watching the two of them, wondering what they were going on about. Joe got up and smiled at him, then headed out to the porch to make a phone call. Duke walked up to sit with Loren.

"Everything all right?" He kissed her forehead.

"It will be."

"You look tired. Should we go?"

She shook her head. "I am tired, but no, not yet." She laid her head on his shoulder. "I love you," she whispered.

"Come on, beautiful, let's go say goodnight."

"We can't yet."

He chuckled. "Well everyone has left, except the family. So, I think they will excuse us."

When Joe came back into the room, Loren looked up at him and he nodded. Taking Duke's hand, she said, "Come on." Standing, she pulled him up with her.

"Where we going?"

She just chuckled and walked into the dining room. "Could everyone find a seat, please?" They all sat down. "I just wanted to say thank you for all that you have done to make this day so special for us. We love each of you in our own way. Richard, you have gone above and beyond the role of godfather. Thank you. Mom, you and Dad made the best choice when you chose him to watch out for me. I love you. Aunt Liz, you take care of her. Jenny, without your brilliant mind, I wouldn't be standing here holding two miracles inside of me. Kate, without your friendship, I don't know where Jenny and I would be. I love you both. Derek, at first, we had a clashing of the heads, but in the end, I have come to depend on you. Thank you for loving this man beyond words. Alex, you are such a sweetheart, and I hope one day your life is bigger than you. Joe, you know how I feel." She turned and looked at Duke. "You are the only man who has ever captured my heart. I give it to you freely and without restraint. I love you." Duke nodded to her. "Joe?" She put her hand out to him. He walked over and took it, giving it a squeeze.

"Loren brought it to my attention this evening that I am here without a date." He smiled at her. "Little did I know that she has seen me and knows my partner." He looked at his brothers and his father who had a peculiar smile on his face. Taking a deep breath, he continued. "We've been together for three years. I must admit that I have been worried," he chuckled, "well, scared to tell you." There was knock on the door. "But Loren made me realize that you all love me and that today is a day for sharing love." He watched Loren walk to the door and open it. No one could see who came in. "So, I would like for you all to meet the person I love." He turned as Loren and Steven walked in. "This is Steven Cummings."

Steven smiled. "Hi," he said softly.

Joe turned to look at his family, at his father who just sat there looking at him. Richard stood up and Joe swallowed. He was prepared to defend Steven, to defend his choice. Richard walked over and pulled Joe into a hug. "It's about time you told me," he whispered. Joe hugged his father back. Then Richard turned to Steven. "Welcome," he said, putting his hand out.

Steven shook his hand. "Thank you, Mr. Reynolds."

"I'm Richard, grab something to eat."

Loren stood back with a huge smile on her face, Duke watching her the whole time. He couldn't have been prouder of her. Steven met everyone, and everyone seemed totally all right with the fact that Joe was gay. As long as he was happy, that's all that mattered. Duke watched Loren walk up and touch Joe's arm. He turned to her and hugged her.

"Thank you," he whispered.

"I told you," she said back. When they separated, her eyes locked with Duke's. "Well, I am going to take my husband home with me now. Jenny, Kate, you guys are going to sleep here tonight. The guys will get you settled. I love you both. See you in the morning." She put her hand out for Duke.

Pushing himself off the wall, he walked up to her and pulled her into his arms. "You are fucking incredible." He grabbed her cape, wrapping it around her, and lifted her into his arms.

They all cheered and hooted them as they walked out the door, with Jaz following behind. Duke carried her into their tiny house, setting her down. He locked the door and proceeded to undress, throwing his clothes on the couch. When he had nothing, but his boxers left, he turned to Loren.

"You look incredible in this dress. You take my breath away. But, right now, I would love to take it off you."

Loren took a deep breath and nodded. He moved closer to her. His hands moved up her sides, to her neck, where he unbuttoned it. Slowly, he lowered it down her body, lowering himself as he went. He helped her step out of it, removing her slippers. He stood and put the dress on top of his clothes on the couch, his eyes never leaving hers.

His hand came up to touch her face. "I love you, wife, and I would very much love to make love to you."

Breathless, Loren whispered, "I love you, husband, and I would love to make love to you."

Duke gently lifted her off the floor and carried her up to the loft. Laying her down on her back, he sat back on his heels to look at her. His eyes moved slowly down her body, stopping to admire her full breasts. "So beautiful," he whispered. Slowly, he glanced down at her stomach. His hands moved to gently hold their children. "So fucking beautiful."

Looking at her white lace panties, he licked his lips. His hands moved down to Loren's thighs. He knew she was wet, so he bent down to inhale her scent. While pressing a kiss on her mound, his hands moving to her ass. He slowly rolled her over. Duke's breath caught in his throat as he admired her ass dressed in white lace. Trailing his fingertips along the edges of her panties, he watched as the goose flesh rose on her skin. Planting his lips on her skin, he slowly and lovingly kissed and licked every inch of her body.

Loren lifted her hips off the bed as Duke pulled her panties off, tossing them aside. She pulled herself up on her knees, spreading her legs. Duke had to concentrate or he was going to explode. He was so wanton of her, he couldn't stop himself. Slowly, he pushed deep inside of her.

"Ahhhh," Loren moaned, and he moved in and out.

He was going to lose it, so he pulled out, sitting back on his heels to look at her dripping for him. Loren got up and turned to face him. Placing her hand on his chest, she pushed him back. "Let me," she whispered. Closing his eyes, he leaned back. Loren didn't wait. She bent down and took him all the way down her throat. When the head of his cock passed the ring in her throat, he couldn't stop it. He came, and he came long and hard, pulsing as she worked him out. She took every drop of him. Duke felt like a kid. He had no control when it came to Loren. She did this to him. She was the only one who could do this to him.

Her mouth continued up his body, flicking his nipples as she went.

Duke was getting hard again. When she straddled him, he pushed, up wrapping his arms around her as she kissed him. There was nothing rushed; it was a deep, sensual kiss, not like before. This kiss was different; this kiss was between a husband and a wife. This kiss brought Duke to a full erection minutes after he came like a teenager. Loren continued to move up his thighs until her core encased him. She moved up and down him, rubbing herself on him, getting herself off.

Pushing up a little more, she pushed him inside of her. Slowly, without stopping, she took all of him deep. "You are so beautiful," he whispered in her mouth. She moved up and down on him a few times, and Duke felt her tighten around him. "That's it, beautiful. I feel you. Let it go."

It was all she needed. Her head fell back as she exploded around him. "Oh, God, Duke," she moaned, lifting her head, looking him in the eyes. He was amazed at how purple they were.

Pushing up, he laid her on her back, making love to her for a few minutes. Then he pulled out and worked his way down her body to his prize. When he reached her core, he couldn't control himself. He had to have her. He needed to taste her sweet, sweet nectar. Closing his mouth over her, he got his wish. Loren's body began to convulse as she went over the edge of reason, and Duke drank her up. When she calmed down, he moved back up her body and slid deep inside of her.

They made love for a very long time, their mouths never leaving each other's. When Duke felt her growing tighter, he pulled back. "Take me with you, beautiful," he whispered as he watched her come undone in his arms. Together, they exploded. Together, they loved each other.

EPILOGUE

As the winter months passed, Jenny had taken the job at the local clinic. Doc staying on to help her with the transition. Kate had moved down and was practicing with her. Loren had agreed to partake in the practice once the babies were bigger. Duke had made it a mission to build some sort of hospital for them, converting one of the huge old houses into a state of the art hospital. Kate had met Charlie at the wedding, and they have been dating regularly.

Jenny and Derek had become an item. He was getting ready to propose to her. Duke went with him to Bozeman to buy a ring.

"You sure about this?" Duke asked him.

Derek laughed. "Oh, I am, brother. She is a spectacular woman. Since your wedding, I haven't even wanted another woman. I finally get what you feel about Loren."

Duke laughed. "I should harass you like you did me, but I won't. I am happy for you. I told you one day it would hit you like a ton of bricks falling from the sky."

"It did."

"You think she will say yes?"

"Well, we've been living together for, what, three months now. I think she'll say yes. I love her. I didn't ever think I would be the brother who wanted only one woman. But I do."

Duke smiled. His heart couldn't be any fuller. "Now, don't buy her some huge ring. After getting to know her better, she isn't that kind of girl."

"I'll know the ring when I see it. Don't worry. Besides, I couldn't afford a huge ring anyway."

As it turned out, he bought her a lovely ring, one carat round cut. Derek was so happy. Now, all he had to do was figure out a way to ask her.

AS WINTER LEFT THE PLAINS OF MONTANA AND SPRING CREPT CLOSER, Loren grew bigger and bigger. She couldn't tie her own shoes, and Duke had to help her dress.

"I don't know if they are ever coming out," she moaned one day while she lay on the couch with her feet up.

Duke laughed. "They have to come out one day. Besides, Kate said the longer they are in there, the better it will be."

"Yeah, well, Kate doesn't have a huge balloon inside of her either."

Duke got down on the floor next to her, kissing her sweetly. "You know, we could do as she says and hurry them along."

Loren laughed. "My poor husband, is he wanton of his big fat wife?"

Duke laughed. "Every fucking minute of every fucking day. You haven't looked more beautiful than you do right now."

Loren rolled off the couch into his arms. "Duke," she whispered in her sex-laden voice. He knew that look in her eyes. She pulled her shirt off. He couldn't get over how huge her breasts were.

"You are so beautiful," he whispered. Turning her around, he unhooked her bra, sliding it down her arms. His hands cupped her breasts. "They are so big," he said into her neck as he rolled her nipples. His hands moved over her belly, pausing to hold his children, then moved into her shorts. "So wet," he moaned as he slipped a finger into her.

"Ahh, Duke. Please," she moaned.

Smiling, he said, "Please what, beautiful?"

"Please, I need you."

He didn't need anything more than that. Slipping his finger out of her, he pulled her shorts off then undressed. Loren backed up a little, so her belly wasn't laying on the couch, and Duke slid into her from behind.

"Ahh, fuck, Loren."

"Fuck me," she cried out.

He hadn't fucked her since that one night, when he lost his mind and she left him. "Loren," he said wrapping, his arms around her.

"Please, Duke." She turned her head to kiss him.

Pushing up, he put his hands on her hips and slammed into her. "Ahhh," she yelled. "More."

He didn't disappoint her. She kept encouraging him and he kept going, fucking her long and hard. He was getting ready to blow when she screamed. Out of nowhere, they were soaked. He froze. "What the hell?" He was freaking out.

Loren chuckled. "I think my water just broke."

"Oh my God, I hurt you. Never again, Loren." He was in full blown panic mode. "Oh my God, honey." He helped her sit up. "Oh my God." Loren giggled. "This is not funny. I did this. It's not time yet. You have another three weeks. Holy shit."

She was laughing now. "Duke, help me get dressed." She couldn't stop laughing. He was dripping her amniotic fluid all over the place as he flung his body around trying to figure out what to do. "My shorts and panties, honey," she giggled out. He bent and grabbed them, helping her put them on. He put them on backwards. "Duke?" She put her hands on his face and leaned in to kiss him. "Calm down, baby. I am fine." He went to open his mouth, and she kissed him again. His hands came around her and he pulled her to him.

"God, Loren," he whispered in her mouth, kissing her deeply.

"Ahhh," she moaned, pulling back.

"What the fuck," he freaked out.

She started breathing in and out, in and out, until the pain left. "Shorts, I'm in labor." She looked at the clock. It was one-thirty.

"Stand up," Duke said. She put her hands on his shoulders and he helped her stand. Pulling up her shorts, he grabbed her shirt. Loren pulled it on. Duke hurried and put his jeans and shirt on.

"Grab my bag," she said nodding to the loft. Picking up her phone, she dialed Kate. "My water broke. I had my first contraction four minutes ago. We are leaving now."

"I'll call Jenny and see you at the hospital."

Loren hung up and dialed Richard. "It's time, and you need to drive. I don't think Duke can do it." Just then, she heard him fall down the stairs. Laughing, she said, "Oh my God. Hurry up before he kills himself."

Hanging up, she waddled over to help Duke up. "Oh my God, your head is bleeding. Jesus, honey, calm down." She went to the bathroom and got a washcloth and wet it. When she came back out, he had put his boots on. Picking Loren up, he made his way out the door while she wiped the blood off his head.

"Come on, Jaz," he yelled. Jaz came running out, and Loren managed to close the door. When Duke hit the ground, Richard pulled up. He jumped out and opened the door for Duke to put Loren in. "What are you doing here?"

"Driving. Now get in."

Duke laughed and put Loren in the front, and he and Jaz climbed in the back.

When they walked into the hospital, which was actually an old house that Duke had renovated for Jenny, Kate, and Loren, everyone was there. Derek, Joe, his partner Steven, and Alex.

Kate came out to get her. "You ready?"

Loren nodded. "My contractions are about seven minutes apart and are lasting about a minute and a half."

Duke looked at her. "I am so sorry."

"I'll come and get you when I get her in a bed and check her out," Kate said to him.

Duke grabbed Loren's face and kissed her. "I love you, beautiful, and I am so sorry."

Giggling, she said, "I love you, too."

As Kate helped her get out of her clothes, she asked, "What is he so sorry for?"

As casual as can be, Loren said, "Well we were fucking and my water broke. He thinks he did it."

Kate busted out laughing. "You could use that."

Jenny walked in. "What's so funny?"

They helped Loren on the bed. "Oh, we were getting pretty wild and a bit hard, and Duke thinks he broke my water."

"Unless he is some kind of god, I don't think so." Jenny chuckled.

Loren laughed so loud, everyone in the waiting room heard her. "He so is."

~

AFTER KATE GOT HER ALL CHECKED OUT AND ON FETAL MONITORS, SHE went out to get Duke, letting the family know how she was doing. "She is dilated to four, and her contractions are coming fast, so this shouldn't take too much longer. Duke, you can come with me."

Everyone nodded and Duke followed Kate. She handed him some scrubs to put on. "Here, you can change into these." He took them, looking at her. He didn't have any boxers on. "What's the matter?"

He felt his face flush. "Um, I'm not wearing anything under my jeans."

"Oh," she said, grabbing another pair and handing them to him.

Duke nodded and stepped into the bathroom to change. Then Kate took him to Loren. He grabbed her hand. "God, baby, I am so sorry," he whispered as he kissed her forehead.

"You didn't do anything wrong. It was time, that's all." She smiled at him, then a contraction came, and she started to squeeze his hand.

Duke's eyes got bigger as she squeezed harder. She didn't yell; she didn't wince. "What's the matter?" he said, freaking out.

"Con... trac... tion," Loren puffed out.

Then she gradually released her grip. She was going to enjoy this. There wouldn't be another time that she would give birth.

"Okay," Kate said. "They are coming fast. Let me check you. I don't think we are going to have much longer to wait for these two." Duke watched as Kate sat in the chair at the foot of the bed. She lifted the sheet. "Take a deep breath and release it slowly," she said to Loren. Duke looked at her and watched her face become uncomfortable as Kate did whatever she was doing. "You're going fast. You're dilated to eight now. I'm going to get Jenny in here."

Loren nodded, and her grip on Duke strengthened again. "Breathe, Loren," he whispered. "Oh my God, baby, I am so sorry." She tried not to laugh, but she couldn't help it. "Kate knows what we were doing." That caused her to laugh harder.

"I know, I told her," she whispered.

"I forgot to put on my underwear." He blushed.

Loren just started giggling. Then Duke started to laugh. They both had tears running down their cheeks when Kate and Jenny came back in the room.

"What's so funny?"

They both shook their heads. "You had two more contractions while I was gone?"

"Y...es," Loren hissed out as her grip on Duke tightened.

"She's having one now," he groaned.

Kate sat down, putting on her rubber gloves. "Shit,"

"What?" Duke was in full blown panic mode.

"We're having some babies. You ready, Loren?" She nodded. "Duke, you want to watch your children being born?"

He looked at Loren and she nodded. Trying not to let go of her hand, he stepped over and looked under the sheet. "Oh my God," he whispered. "I can see a head." His grip grew tighter.

"Push, Loren, one big one."

Loren pushed and hard.

"Oh, God, it's coming. Shit." Duke looked at Loren. He was crying. "God, baby." His eyes went back just as the baby's shoulders cleared and out it came.

"Well, hello there, William," Kate said as she cleaned out his mouth. He was screaming. "You want to cut the cord?" Duke nodded. Letting go of Loren's hand, he cut where Kate told him to. She turned and handed him to Jenny. "Okay, you ready for baby number two? Come on, one more big push."

Loren squeezed Duke's hand and pushed. She felt the baby move.

"Oh, God, there she is." He looked at Loren. "Our daughter is coming."

"One more push," Kate said. Loren pushed again. She felt the baby's shoulders pass through. "There she is. Hello, Alison." She cleaned out her nose and mouth, but she didn't cry.

"Kate, is she all right? She's not crying." Loren was panicked.

"She's fine."

Duke couldn't take his eyes off of them. "God, Loren, they're beautiful." He turned to see her crying. He pulled her to him. "Oh, beautiful, don't cry."

"I want to see them," she whispered.

Jenny and Kate brought them over to her. She smiled and kissed them on the head. "I love you," she whispered and then closed her eyes.

The alarms started going off. "Shit," Kate yelled. "Duke, get out." Turning, she laid the baby in the warmer. "Go get Doc in here."

Jenny was moving. It all happened so fast. They pushed Duke into the hall, and he was in shock. Jenny was yelling for Doc. He heard Kate yell, "Clear!" Then he heard her shock Loren. She did it three times before Duke heard the beep, beep, beep of the machine. He slid down the wall crying.

Jenny came running down the hall with blood and disappeared into the room. Duke was looking in the room, and the floor was covered in blood. He sat there in shock. He couldn't move. Richard came running in and saw the look on his son's face.

"No," he whispered. "Oh, God, no." Dropping to his knees, he pulled his son into his arms and held him while he cried. They sat there together for what seemed hours. No one came out of the room to talk to them.

Duke couldn't stand it anymore. He needed to know what was going on. He stood up, just as Kate and Doc came out holding the babies.

"What is going on?" Duke was so scared. "Where's Loren?"

Kate looked at him and then at Richard, her eyes damp. "I'm sorry, Duke. We did everything we could, but we..."

He shouted, "NO! No. Where is she. Where is my wife?" He pushed past her, pushing open the door. There was blood everywhere.

Jenny was standing next to Loren, rubbing her head and crying, whispering, "I'm so sorry." Duke just stood there frozen. Jenny turned to him. "Duke, I'm so sorry. I tried so hard."

"Get out!" he yelled. "Get the fuck out." He moved toward Loren. Jenny moved away. His tears wouldn't stop. "Oh, my beautiful girl," he whispered when he saw her pale, lifeless body. He started to sob as he pulled her into his arms, kissing her forehead. "My beautiful girl." He was heaving breaths, rocking her back and forth. He didn't know what he was going to do without her. How could he go on? His mind went numb. He couldn't comprehend any of it. How could she be gone? "I love you, Loren. Please, I love you." He stood there bent over her bed, holding her for such a long time, saying I love you over and over again.

How was he going to do this? How could he live in this world without her? Everything they had been through was for nothing. "Loren," he sobbed. "Oh, God, baby. I love you so much. Please."

His mind was playing tricks on him. He thought he heard her say, "I love you." He cried even harder. Her voice would live inside his mind, inside his heart forever. "Duke." He heard her voice. For sure, he thought he was losing his mind. It wasn't until he felt her cold hand on his arm that he stopped breathing. Pulling back, he looked at her face. Her eyes opened. "I'm sorry," she whispered.

Her beautiful violet eyes were looking at him. With a shaky hand, he touched her face. Her eyes closed again. "No," he said. She opened them. "You're here?"

"I'm here," she whispered with a faint smile.

"I love you," he whispered on her lips. I'm so sorry." He cried, kissing her gently.

He felt a hand on his back. "Duke," Richard said. "Duke, you have to let them move her out of this room. You have to let them help her.

"No, I won't leave her." His eyes never left her face.

"Go," she whispered.

He shook his head. "No, I won't leave you. You didn't leave me. I am not leaving you."

"Duke." It was Kate. "You can come with, just let us get her out of here." He nodded and laid her back on the bed. Still holding her hand, he let them work on her. He let them move her to a different room. He never took his eyes off of her. He sat next to her bed for hours and hours just looking at her face. His eyes grew heavier and heavier. Finally, he laid his head down. He couldn't keep them open any longer.

Not sure how long he slept but he was awakened by a hand in his hair. Turning his head, her hand slid across his mouth. He reached for it, pressing it against his lips. When he picked his head up, he was greeted with bright eyes. He couldn't stop the smile.

"You scared the fucking shit out of me," he whispered as he stood to kiss her.

"Does this mean you are going to fuck me again?" she whispered on his lips.

He chuckled. "God, I was so scared. I love you."

"I was, too," she said weakly. "Duke, where are the babies?"

He gently climbed in the bed with her, holding her properly. "I don't know, baby. I couldn't leave you."

She snuggled into his chest. "Mmm,"

Duke closed his eyes and they fell asleep. Kate woke him, "Duke, you shouldn't be in bed with her. She had major surgery.

"I'm fine," Loren whispered. "Where are the babies?"

"Well, they are in our makeshift nursery with your family. None of them have left this building. Your mom is even here," Kate said. "Would you like to see them?"

Loren smiled. "Mmm, in a minute. Kate, can you leave us alone?"

Kate chuckled and left the room, closing the door behind her.

Loren's hand moved down Duke's body. "You didn't get to finish," she whispered, kissing his neck as her hand wrapped around him. "So hard," she moaned as she stroked him.

Duke moved her hand away. "I am fine, beautiful." He chuckled as he turned on his side. "You don't need to worry about me."

She smiled. "You sure?"

He laughed. "I'm sure, beautiful. God, Loren, I was so scared. I thought you died. I didn't know what to do. I yelled at everyone."

"I know, Jenny and Kate told me while you were sleeping. Jenny had to remove my uterus. I can't have any more children."

"Oh, God, baby, I am so sorry."

She smiled. "Don't be sorry, we shouldn't have the babies we have, but we do. Are you all right with that?"

"I don't care as long as I have you. William and Alison are more than enough." He kissed her.

There was a knock on the door. When it opened, Kate and Jenny came in holding the babies. "There's some little people here who would like to meet their mom and dad." Jenny pushed the button on the bed and it raised up. She laid Alison in Loren's arms, and Kate laid William in Duke's.

"Oh my God," Duke whispered. "They are so beautiful. They look like you."

Alison opened her eyes, looking first at Loren and then at Duke. His breath caught and his heart slammed in his chest. Loren smiled at her. "Hi, beautiful, I'm your mommy." Alison's eyes moved back to Loren's.

"Her eyes," Duke whispered. "They're violet, like yours." He bent down and kissed Alison on the forehead. "Hi, beautiful, I'm your daddy."

William started moving. Duke looked at him. "Hey, buddy, I'm your daddy." He opened his eyes, looking right into Duke's, stealing his heart. Then William looked at Loren.

She smiled at him. "Hi, beautiful. I'm your mommy." Duke lifted him so she could kiss him.

"Loren," he whispered. "You're my hero. I love you more today than yesterday." He kissed her softly. They laid in bed holding their children. Duke couldn't have asked for a better life.

More Books by Cin Medley

Broken
Is this Life
Six Months
Winter Harbor
Beautiful Liar
Secrets
Lines Crossed
Lyssa's Journey
Everything She Thought
Justice
Within The Ashes
Echoed Heartbeats
High Country
Ice

ALSO BY C. J. MEDLEY: FOR YOUNG
ADULTS

Whispering Wind Series

The Legend

The Mist

The Awakening

The Tomes

Printed in Great Britain
by Amazon